"The Embrace. That's what it's called,"
said the guard a little louder, and this time
his voice carried around the room.

"Those who come back."

Rees wasn't really paying attention, but he nodded along.

"That's right. The embrace, whatever that means."

"The Embrace will bring you peace. It is glorious." As the guard spoke he pushed himself away from the wall. His eyes burned with an intense passion, bordering on the zealous.

At the same time Balfruss stood up, keeping his axe ready to strike, just in case. Tammy glanced at him and quickly scrambled back from her chair, drawing Maligne. The unusual blade glimmered in the flickering torches, catching the light or perhaps reacting to something in the air.

The room began to empty as the priests sensed imminent violence and ran to get out of the way as quickly as possible. Rees and the other guards drew their swords, forming a ring of steel around the peculiar man.

"No, no, no," said Rees. "Sornan. Not you."

"What's happening?" asked Tammy.

"They got to him," said Rees. "He's one of them."

By Stephen Aryan

Battlemage
Bloodmage
Chaosmage

CHAOS
MAGE

STEPHEN
ARYAN

www.orbitbooks.net

Copyright © 2016 by Stephen Aryan
Excerpt from *The Summon Stone* copyright © 2016 by Ian Irvine

Cover design by Nico Taylor—LBBG
Cover illustration by Steve Stone
Cover copyright © 2016 by Hachette Book Group, Inc.

Orbit
Hachette Book Group
1290 Avenue of the Americas
New York, NY 10104
www.orbitbooks.net

Simultaneously published in Great Britain and in the U.S. by Orbit in 2016
First U.S. Edition: October 2016

Orbit is an imprint of Hachette Book Group.
The Orbit name and logo are trademarks of Little, Brown Book Group Limited.

The publisher is not responsible for websites (or their content) that are not owned by the publisher.

The Hachette Speakers Bureau provides a wide range of authors for speaking events. To find out more, go to www.hachettespeakersbureau.com or call (866) 376-6591.

Library of Congress Control Number: 2016941491

ISBNs: 978-0-316-29834-6 (trade paperback), 978-0-316-29835-3 (ebook)

Printed in the United States of America

LSC-H

10 9 8 7 6 5 4 3 2 1

For Chris

CHAPTER 1

By the time Zannah had climbed the twenty-seven steps to her post, the dead man was waiting for her in the street below.

"Come down, Zannah!"

It was two hours before midnight and the pitch-black sky seemed to bear down on her with an oppressive weight. Far away in the east a scattering of stars offered little relief from the otherwise featureless void above.

Voechenka, once a city renowned for its music, art and beauty, had been reduced to a desolate landscape. It stretched out before her in all directions, wrapped in grim silence. The bleakness of the shattered buildings and broken streets was mostly hidden from view, but a few tallow candles burned here and there in empty windows. Thick shadows, clinging to the skeletal frames of once-grand structures, hid a multitude of sins.

Torches burned at several points around the city, their flames dancing in a faint breeze coming in from across the lake. They did little to chase away the terrors that lurked in the city at night, but it was all they had. Two similar torches were set in the rampart below Zannah, one on either side of the lop-sided gate. A stout wagon loaded with heavy rocks blocked the entrance to their shelter. It was another illusion, designed to give the idea of safety and keep the fear at bay. After seeing some of their friends torn apart, Zannah wondered if any of the children still believed they were safe.

She didn't stare at the torches for long. Keeping her eyes away from the light protected her night vision. As a Morrin she could see in the dark almost as well as in daylight. Before coming to Shael, before coming to this city and the terrors that were hidden from most, Zannah had considered her sight a blessing. Now, being able to see the horrors was part of her penance. Another weight to bear stoically and never complain. She would never tell anyone about everything that she saw at her post during the long hours of the night. The ghosts, the Forsaken, and the tall woman who always stood in the shadows.

Zannah just choked it all down like another meal in this cursed city. While food served to nourish her body, the nightmares kept her alert and on edge. They served a purpose. They also reminded Zannah of her role in bringing the people of Shael to the brink of destruction.

"Come down, Zannah!" shouted Roake in a harsh rasp.

"Is he there again?" said Alyssa, wearily plodding up the stairs. She leaned against the battlements and peered down into the street. "Doesn't he ever get tired?"

"No. Never."

As Alyssa stared out over the city of her birth Zannah studied her profile. Tufts of yellow hair stuck out from a skull crisscrossed with fading bruises and old purple scars. Once, her blonde hair had been long and the envy of many, but not for years. Her golden skin had lost much of its lustre and, despite her being as thin as a broom, the hollow cheeks didn't distract from a beautiful face and striking green eyes.

"You're staring again."

"Sorry," said Zannah, turning away. "Were you a poet?"

Alyssa's rich laugh was at odds with her skeletal frame. "No, but your guess is closer than the others."

It was a game they played every night. Alyssa allowed Zannah one guess about what she had done before the war. Four years ago her life had been very different. One lived in comfort where she'd wanted for nothing. Then an army of Vorga and Morrin had marched into Shael and the widespread slaughter of her people began. Alyssa had spent the duration of the war in a torture camp being starved, beaten and abused, while all around her men, women and children were butchered. When the war finally ended she, and many others in Shael, were left to fend for themselves. The Queen was dead. The country was in ruins, but some of the enemy hadn't gone anywhere. Those survivors with any strength fought to reclaim their homeland. The last invaders were eventually driven out by an alliance between the Queens of Seveldrom and Yerskania. Finally, the slow process of rebuilding the country began.

Aid came to Shael, but being so far from the capital, Voechenka was always among the last on the list. Two years ago the situation had changed from desperate into something much worse.

At first no one noticed that some thing had taken root in the shadows. During the first year after the war the people in Voechenka were focused on rebuilding their homes and planting crops to get them through the winter. In the spring when a few faces were missing people put it down to the severe weather and not enough food. But once the ice had melted they found the bodies. The terror etched into their faces had nothing to do with hunger.

"Here," said Alyssa, offering Zannah a small cloth bag. Her

sensitive nose picked up a mix of sour bread, salted fish and wild garlic.

"I'm not hungry."

"Liar. I can hear your stomach growling from here."

Zannah took the bag with a grateful smile and pulled out the slightly burned trencher. It was the size of her fist and the hollow was stuffed with fish, tangy root vegetables and wild garlic.

Zannah frowned at the fish. "You shouldn't have risked the lake. It's too dangerous."

"I didn't. Someone else went out on the water."

"And he just gave it to you?"

Alyssa shrugged.

Zannah wanted to ask what she had given the fisherman in trade but knew that Alyssa wouldn't answer. Instead Zannah took a bite and turned her gaze back to the empty streets. Roake wandered up and down, calling out to her periodically, and she did her best to ignore him. Part of her wanted to feather his body with arrows, but she'd tried that before and it hadn't worked. He'd just come back the next night. Arrows were a rare commodity and she couldn't waste them on Roake. Even so, she was tempted to put one in his throat, just to stop him shouting for the rest of the night.

"Did you get much sleep?" asked Alyssa.

"Some."

"Did anyone speak to you?"

"No, but they didn't try to kill me in my sleep last night, so it's progress," said Zannah. Alyssa grimaced and flushed with embarrassment. "It's all right."

"No, it's not," insisted Alyssa, gritting her teeth.

A strained silence fell on them, broken sporadically by Roake. Zannah couldn't blame the others in their shelter for how they treated her. After all it was her people, the Morrin, who had invaded Shael with the Vorga. It was her people who had slaughtered them, burned down their cities and herded them into camps to be starved, beaten and experimented upon. It was her people who made them fight each other for food, and sometimes, just for sport. It was her people who had abandoned them to die at the end of the war, leaving them to the mercy of the savage Vorga.

If the weight of their hatred rested only with her people, Zannah could forgive herself, but during the war she had been among the invaders.

She had followed her orders like a good soldier and killed prisoners, never hesitating or worrying about her actions or the cost. The people in Shael weren't Morrin, so why did it matter how many of them died?

Towards the end of the war, when the cities had been razed and the mass graves were so big as to be mistaken for hills, something changed inside her. Even here in distant Voechenka, word reached them about a rift in the Council that was threatening to tear Morrinow apart. Her country, her whole world, was in danger. Not from another army, but from an enemy within.

The order came through and Morrin warriors started to return home. Zannah's unit was among the last to leave. On the final day she was ordered to command squad leaders to kill all remaining prisoners and burn Voechenka to the ground. After that they would sail north to deal with the troubles at home.

Zannah could still clearly see the look of surprise in the eyes of her Commander as he died with her sword buried in his throat. He tried to choke out accusations, or perhaps another order, but only managed a faint gurgling sound. She burned the document, gave the order to free all prisoners and told her people to sail home. Most went willingly with the fleet but a few refused, abandoning their posts or feigning illness to stay behind. They had grown used to indulging and were not willing to return to the orderly life of a soldier.

Once the fleet had left port, Zannah searched the city and surrounding countryside for her people. Then she stalked and hunted them down, one by one. They cursed her as they died, each and every one, telling her she was forsaken by the Blessed Mother. Zannah didn't need to hear it from them. She already knew she was damned. Only one of the rogue soldiers had evaded her and now it was too late to deal with him.

Hated by her own people for betraying them. Loathed by the people of Shael for her crimes during the war. She could never go home and, until yesterday, those she sought to protect had tried to kill her on a daily basis. For some reason, Alyssa didn't hate her. Zannah had no idea why.

A disturbance in the street drew Zannah's attention.

"I'll be back," promised Roake before scuttling off, disappearing down a side street. He could certainly move quickly for a dead man when he needed to.

"Here they come," said Zannah. "Get the others."

Alyssa ran down the stairs and started shouting for help. Almost immediately people poured out of the main building in the courtyard. They collected their weapons in a hurry before joining Zannah on the wall. The defenders carried a mix of edged weapons, swords, axes, pole-arms and even a few spears. Each weapon had been honed to razor sharpness. The invaders hadn't left much behind but there was no shortage of steel.

Alyssa flexed her longbow with ease and strung it in one practised move. There was a deep core strength in her body that belied her slender frame.

Looking into the street Zannah saw only a dozen bodies tonight. Normally they came in much larger groups than this. She didn't recognise most of the people in the street, but unfortunately Jannek was among them. Yesterday he'd been screaming in terror as they pulled him off the wall, begging for death rather than being taken alive. Tonight he looked healthier and happy. His once sallow and dull skin shone like burnished gold and the hollows in his cheeks had been filled. It was amazing. It was a miracle. He had to be destroyed.

Seeing the dead come back to life, like Roake, was one thing. This was something else. They'd taken to calling them Forsaken, although in this city that applied to everyone.

Further along the wall Liselle, Jannek's sister, sobbed then raised her bow with steely determination.

"Hold," warned Zannah, knowing that the Forsaken were still out of range. This would only be the first wave. It had to be. But why only a dozen? It wasn't enough to overpower their defences.

Alyssa was watching them keenly, waiting until they came closer before raising her bow. Ignoring Zannah the others took their lead from her and readied to fire. "Now," she whispered.

"Fire at will," said Alyssa and six bows hummed in unison.

Moving with extraordinary grace, Alyssa carefully fitted an arrow to the string then fired at another of the Forsaken. Perhaps she'd been a dancer. If they lived through the night it was a good guess for tomorrow.

Alyssa's arrow hit one of the Forsaken in the right eye. It punched the woman off her feet and she appeared to be dead. For now at least.

Most of the other Forsaken had arrows sticking out of them. None of the wounds stopped them, only slowed them down.

Jannek and the other Forsaken scrambled up two rudimentary ladders and tried to claw their way onto the top of the wall. The defenders dropped their bows and switched to swords, spears and axes, driving the Forsaken back by sheer numbers rather than skill. The defenders were all malnourished and until last year few of them had ever held a weapon before. It wasn't a good combination, even in a fight for their lives.

As a man climbed over the wall Zannah stabbed him in the back with her short sword, severing his spine. Wasting no time she yanked it free and kicked him over the wall. He struck two more Forsaken on his way down. She stormed along the wall, severing limbs, and beheading people where she could, if only to save time later. With a short sword in either hand the Morrin cut a bloody path through the Forsaken. Others followed in her wake, prodding and stabbing, fighting with less energy and ferocity, but gradually getting the job done. Most Forsaken were knocked off the wall, falling into the street below, and only a few made it to the top of the ladders.

At the far end of the wall a knot of four was clustered together, forcing Zannah's momentum to slow down.

She dodged a crude swing, took off the offending arm above the elbow and kicked the injured man over the wall. Two more Forsaken died before she finally made it to Jannek. Liselle was squashed against the wall, curled up in a tight ball, screaming in terror. Her axe lay within reach but all thoughts of it were forgotten. Jannek was beseeching her to come with him. He put down his sword to show his goodwill and reached out with an empty hand towards his sister. It would almost have been better received had there been a blade in his hand. Liselle's terrified wail increased in volume, making Zannah wince.

Jannek was starting to turn around when Zannah stabbed him through the neck. No more words. No more lies. No more promises of freedom and something better. They'd heard it all before.

Jannek's blood splashed over his sister's face and her cry became one of anguish. In his last few seconds he stared at his sister, trying to depart a final message. Finally he slumped forward off Zannah's sword and fell into Liselle's lap. She hugged the corpse of her brother and began to sob.

The wall was clear. They were safe for now and none of the Forsaken had escaped to carry someone away. Working methodically Zannah tipped the bodies over the wall, throwing stray limbs as well, although she was less worried about those. The other defenders withdrew to the courtyard. They didn't want to see what happened next and liked to pretend it didn't happen.

"Bring the rope," said Zannah, and Alyssa nodded. She went down into the courtyard and came back with a long knotted rope that was attached to the laden cart. Alyssa threw it over the wall then returned to keep watch as Zannah approached Liselle.

"Stay away from him," screamed Liselle, pulling the bloody corpse to her chest. "Haven't you done enough? Haven't you killed enough of my people?"

Zannah said nothing. There was nothing she could say. Jannek was already dead and had been for some time, long before she'd stabbed him in the neck. Whenever someone was taken by the Forsaken they always came back different. They walked and talked the same. They had the same face and voice, but they were changed. Something had been cut away, or scooped out.

Monella, a stout woman with one rheumy eye, came up the stairs. She pointedly didn't look at Zannah and went straight to Liselle, who fell into her arms. After a few minutes Monella was able to pull the younger woman to her feet and guide her away down the stairs. Zannah waited until they were out of sight before throwing Jannek's body over the wall.

Working hand over hand on the rope, she went down into

the street. The long shadows hid from view most of what she was doing, but not the sounds. The others pretended not to hear those too.

Zannah beheaded every corpse, including Jannek's, before making sure the bodies rested a good distance away from the heads. It was the only way to make sure they didn't come back, again and again.

Next was actually the most difficult part of the evening. Zannah grabbed the rope and started the slow climb back to the top of the wall. One night she would be climbing up and the rope would snap. Someone inside would have disarmed or distracted Alyssa and cut the rope.

A fall from the top wouldn't kill her, but it might break an arm or leg. Then she'd be trapped on the street for the rest of the night with the Forsaken. The others desperately wanted to see her torn apart and butchered. Maybe some wanted to see her carried away only to return the following night. Some nights Zannah wanted it too. Not because she believed she'd earned anything beyond her current situation. She just wanted to know where people were taken and how they were being changed.

Zannah reached the top of the wall and heaved herself over, landing amid the blood. She sat for a minute, catching her breath, staring at the endless dark above.

"You should have more faith," said Alyssa, offering a hand and pulling Zannah to her feet. She chose not to comment, not wanting to cause offence.

They stood in silence for a time, watching the street.

"Do you think they'll come again tonight?"

"At least one more time."

"How long do you think we can keep doing this?" asked Alyssa.

It was a question Zannah had asked herself many times. Any defence in the city was gradually being eroded and the Forsaken were growing in number. Once, dozens of torches had burned in the night, driving back the darkness. Now there were maybe six shelters left.

Zannah didn't answer Alyssa as they both knew the truth. They were running out of time.

CHAPTER 2

Overnight a thin layer of snow had dusted the streets of Charas like a fine layer of sugar. Talandra and the rest of Seveldrom were used to harsh winters, but so far the weather had been unseasonably mild.

Staring down at the streets of the capital city from the palace, the Queen noted a few changes. Even from this height she could see all of the shops had left the awnings tied up and there were no seats outside for eating or drinking. It was a new trend from the west that had steadily crept in over the last four years which she had encouraged.

The streets looked a little bare without the tables and brightly coloured canopies, but no one was fooled by the mild reprieve. They all knew the snow would come soon enough, thick and heavy, and no one wanted an awning full of snow falling on their customers.

Trade continued to flourish between Seveldrom and the west, and she was doing all that she could to keep goods flowing both ways. Valuable information came in through the city gates with every wagon train, and fresh orders went out the next day for the return trip. Her spy network in the west was much larger than before the war. The more she knew the easier it would be to defuse situations before they could escalate.

Talandra closed the window, shutting out the chill and moved back to her desk. The sea of papers scattered across it never seemed to dwindle. There was always a host of fresh reports, official requests and invitations. It was rare that she received any papers that weren't a demand on her time. The days and weeks were being gobbled up and the years seemed to be growing shorter. Talandra knew the truth of it. She was forever busy and the list of responsibilities that came with the throne had not decreased. She also had difficulty delegating. The excuse about not being able to find good people wasn't fooling those closest to her, but it was so hard to let go.

As ever when she thought about time, Talandra's mind turned to the future. She ran a hand across her swelling stomach and although she didn't mind, as long as the child was healthy, she hoped for a girl this time. His tiny lordship was currently being entertained elsewhere, giving her a few hours of peace to get some work done. But so far all she'd achieved this morning was staring out the window and thinking about the future.

A frantic knocking disturbed her thoughts. Before Talandra had a chance to respond Alexis threw open the door to admit a flustered-looking Shani. Her head of intelligence looked scared, which terrified Talandra. Shani was always in control of her emotions.

"By the Maker, what's happened?" asked Talandra, guiding Shani to a chair. In the corridor outside she heard the rattle of many feet. "What's going on out there?"

"We're tripling the guard," said Alexis. "No one will get anywhere near you. We're sending more to protect the Prince." With that she pulled the doors shut. There hadn't been an assassination attempt in nearly three years, not since Shani had taken matters into her own hands.

"It's not assassins," said Shani in a raspy voice. Despite being well before midday, Talandra poured a generous splash of whisky into a glass. She pressed it into Shani's trembling hands and helped her take a sip. After the third gulp her shaking faded and she pushed the glass away.

Talandra pulled up a chair beside Shani, doing her best to quell the flutter of fear in her stomach that threatened to blossom into something else.

"From the beginning. Tell me what's happened," she said gently, holding one of Shani's hands in both of hers.

"I was in the Black Library. I was filing some new information," said Shani, shaking her head to dismiss the question before it was asked. The specifics would have to wait and clearly weren't relevant. Talandra bit her lip and gestured for Shani to continue. "I was just about to leave when I noticed it was missing."

A cold prickle ran down Talandra's spine. "What? What was missing?"

Shani stared into the distance. "I see it all the time. It's become just another relic from the past. I'd forgotten what it really was."

Talandra's mind went through all the possibilities that would rattle Shani so thoroughly. The Black Library was mostly full of notebooks, floor to ceiling, but there were also a few other objects. Items that she didn't want stored in the royal vault. Items that shouldn't exist. Items that no one knew about, except for a handful of people. All of the objects were dangerous in their own way, but as she ran through the list in her mind there was only one that made her heart skip a beat. Talandra stared at Shani, a question on her lips, and the Morrin just nodded.

Alexis came back into the room, clanking in her armour, Hyram a step behind. Although neither of her bodyguards had drawn their swords, both had a hand resting on their weapon. They were still alert but some of the tension had eased from their shoulders.

"Tell everyone to stand down," said Talandra. "We're not in any immediate danger." Whether they heard the tremble in her voice, or perhaps it was just her expression, neither of her bodyguards looked convinced. Talandra wasn't sure she really believed it either, but there was nothing anyone could do.

"What's going on?" asked Hyram. "What aren't you telling us?"

"Alexis, please tell the others to stand down. Then come in and close the door."

The big blonde did as she was asked, but there was a sour twist to her mouth. Spending so much time together every day for years meant there were few secrets between them. There were aspects of her position that Talandra didn't share with Alexis or even her brother, Hyram. The full extent of the work carried out by her spy network at home and abroad wasn't something they needed to know. They may not have liked it but they accepted it.

"There's a secret vault in the palace, we call it the Black Library," said Talandra. From the furrows between her eyebrows Alexis thought the Black Library was something Talandra should have told her about. She ignored her bodyguard for now and turned towards Hyram. "Father showed me where it was hidden when I turned thirteen."

Hyram's eyes became distant. "One summer you became very withdrawn and quiet."

"Yes, it was that year."

"Me and Thias thought you were starting your cycle," said

Hyram with a grin, but Alexis's grim expression didn't change. Despite their apparent differences they normally shared a coarse sense of humour. It seemed as if today all humour had been drained from her body.

"What's in the vault?" asked Alexis.

"Secrets," said Talandra, staring at her bodyguard. "A vault of secrets. Enough to change the world, or destroy it, in the hands of the wrong people. By the time Father showed me the room I already knew about his spy network. That day he told me the rest and it was a heavy burden to carry for a child."

"What else was in the vault?" asked Alexis.

"This isn't about you," said Talandra, hearing the accusation in her tone.

"It seems to me, your Majesty, that it's about trust," said Alexis. The only time she used Talandra's title in private was when she was annoyed.

Talandra ignored the jibe, focusing her attention on Hyram again. "As well as secrets, I also stored a few sensitive items in there."

"I thought that's what the royal vault was for," said Hyram.

"These items don't exist," said Shani, finding her voice again. Some of the colour had returned to her face but she was still visibly rattled. "There's no written record of them anywhere. Only a handful of people know about them, and only three have access to the Black Library."

"Someone stole something from the vault," surmised Alexis.

"We are two of the keyholders," said Talandra, gesturing at herself and Shani.

"Then it was the other keyholder," said Alexis.

"No, he's not in the country," said Talandra, thinking of her husband.

"What was stolen?" asked Hyram.

"A sword called *Maligne*. It's the only one of its kind, crafted from star metal."

Talandra watched as realisation dawned on her brother's face. Hyram swore and started to pace around the room, trying to work off some of the adrenaline that had built up.

"I don't understand," said Alexis.

Talandra spoke carefully, choosing her words precisely. "It was forged by one of the Battlemages during the war. Finn Smith."

"I thought he died," said Alexis.

"He did."

"Then if it wasn't one of your people, who does that leave? Who else knew about the sword?"

"Only one person who's still alive," said Talandra, sharing a look with Shani. "And no one has seen him for years. Most people won't even say his name out loud. He changed the course of the war, he killed the Warlock and we rewarded him with exile."

"It can't be," whispered Alexis, a hint of fear creeping into her voice. "I thought he was dead."

Talandra shook her head. Suddenly she wanted a drink of whisky as well, maybe a whole bottle, but she couldn't touch a drop.

Somehow he'd found out that she still had the sword. Then he'd walked into the palace, completely unnoticed by any guard or servant, found his way into the most secret vault and walked out again with a sword. And not once had he used a key, broken a lock or been seen by anyone. The only reason they knew he'd even been there was the sword's absence.

Talandra knew he'd been a powerful magic user during the war, but where had he been and what had he become in the interim? She also wondered why someone like him would need a sword, and who it would be turned against.

Instinctively she wrapped her arms around her stomach, a thin shield against all of the terrors in the world, but it was all she could offer her unborn child. Talandra had to say his name aloud, if only to become used to hearing it again without it being used to scare people.

"Balfruss has returned."

CHAPTER 3

The hallways of Unity Hall rang with the sound of Tammy's boots as she marched towards the Old Man's office. Other Guardians of the Peace smiled or nodded, a brief sign of respect between equals. There were no ranks here, no ladders to climb.

Long before Tammy became a Guardian she had worked for one of the crime Families of Perizzi, rulers of the underworld. Each Family was led by one or two Dons or Doñas, and arrayed beneath them were tiers of followers, from lowly Paper jackals right up to the most trusted Silver and Gold.

The faded scars on her body and the sunken knuckles on her hands spoke of her old life. One where strength, cunning and brutality were cherished traits. Where compassion was a weakness that would get you killed. Or worse, it would cause the death of those closest to you. That was why they were called jackals. Like their namesake they would turn on the weakest of the pack to further their own ambition.

But all of that was a long time ago. Part of another life that she'd left behind. Now the law was her shield and her mind the best weapon in her arsenal. Tammy wasn't stupid. She still carried a sword and practised with it every day. She still trained hard and kept her body in good condition. But a strong arm wasn't always enough and it had taken her years to realise that.

And while she now embraced compassion, the shadow of her old life still haunted the dark recesses of her mind. It also gave her a unique perspective and framed her view of crimes in a way that was different to other Guardians. Only a few people knew what she'd done before, the Khevassar, and one or two others, but they didn't talk about it. Everyone had secrets they'd rather stayed buried.

The Old Man's fussy secretary was busy scribbling a note when Tammy stepped into the outer office. Two novices were sat waiting for their first interviews with the head of the Guardians. Both looked very young and naïve. The girl was sweating profusely and the young man beside her couldn't sit still. His left leg bobbed up and down, tapping out an endless rhythm on the wooden floor. Tammy remembered her first interview with the Old Man. They were right to feel nervous. He had a mind like a butcher's blade that could cut through fat and gristle right down to the bone. You couldn't lie or hide something from him. He could see to the heart of any matter. It seemed like a blessing and a curse.

Rummpoe had noticed her arrival but he carefully blotted the page and cleaned his nib before looking up at her. He had to crane his neck a long way. She towered over most people in Yerskania, thanks to her father who'd come from Seveldrom.

"He'll be a couple of minutes," said the secretary, glancing at the seats before returning to his notes. Tammy ignored the chairs, instead opting to peruse the notebooks on shelves that stretched from floor to ceiling. They were the Khevassar's history of the city stretching back decades. Every murder, every assault, every theft and wrongdoing, every crime severe enough that it came across the Old Man's desk. Here was the real history of Perizzi, written in blood for all to see. Tammy knew that somewhere, buried within these pages, was the list of her old crimes.

The Khevassar's office door opened and a flustered novice hurried past, his face blotchy and close to tears. The words spoken in the office had been for his ears only and would not be repeated or shared with anyone. They would wound him deeply, but should not have come as a surprise. If they did it meant he had never looked inside, never questioned what he did or the reasons why. It meant he wasn't suitable for a job in the Guardians. It wasn't the only requirement, but it mattered a great deal. Either the boy would take the blow on the chin and keep moving forward, or he'd stay where he was in the Watch. There was a world of difference between being a Guardian of the Peace and being a member of the Watch.

Rummpoe stepped into the Old Man's office and emerged a minute later. He gestured for Tammy to go inside ahead of the waiting novices.

For once the Khevassar wasn't sat behind his desk attending to the mountain of paperwork that never seemed to decrease in size. He stood reading from one of the journals taken off his shelves, his brow furrowed and eyes distant. Tammy closed the door, took a seat and waited for the Old Man to finish. With a sigh, the Khevassar carefully replaced the journal and then sat down.

As she saw his face clearly for the first time Tammy struggled to hide her shock. He looked frail. Ever since she'd joined the Guardians he'd been old, but like the mountains he simply became more craggy over the years. He never lost any of his vitality or energy. Staring into his icy blue eyes Tammy thought he looked diminished, as if something had been taken from him. His weathered skin seemed thin and the knuckles on his hands impossibly large. It made her rub her own hands, tracing the scars and hard tissue.

She tried several times to ask about his health but couldn't find the words. Tammy wondered if he was ill, or perhaps time had finally caught up with him.

"I'm not done yet, Baker," he said, showing her a full set of white teeth.

"Sorry, Sir."

He waved it away and his expression turned serious. "Are you happy?"

The question stumped Tammy. It wasn't one she'd expected him to ask. She couldn't remember the last time anyone had asked her that question. "Sir?"

"Let me try an easier question. Do you feel as if you're being challenged in your role as a Guardian in Perizzi?"

"Sometimes."

"Ah."

"Why do you ask?"

Instead of answering the Old Man rummaged around in his desk drawers for a minute before producing a document with an unfamiliar wax seal. It bore a strange symbol Tammy didn't know, perhaps from a foreign King or Queen.

"Do you know what that is?" he asked, barely waiting for the shake of her head. "It's a request from Drassia. There are a number of unusual murders in one of their cities. Something they've never seen before. Some kind of ritualistic serial killer. They would like the Guardians to investigate."

"Is it genuine?"

"Oh yes. The Guardians of the Peace are unique. We're the only group that sometimes works outside our own borders. What do you know about Shael?"

"That the country is a mess," replied Tammy, absently rubbing her knuckles.

"Be more specific."

"It was invaded and shattered during the war when they refused to join the Mad King's alliance. Now it's being rebuilt, piece by piece."

"And?" pressed the Old Man.

"And despite the best efforts of Queen Olivia and her Regent, large portions of the country remain a lawless waste-land. Criminals have taken over whole towns and cities, running them like their own fiefs. Some areas have been completely abandoned."

"The cities along main trade routes have been reclaimed and cleansed," said the Khevassar, putting the letter away and taking another from the pile on his desk. Although she didn't recognise the crest, Tammy could guess where it was from by the way the Old Man gripped it. His fingertips turned white from the pressure. "But it will be a long time before the country can sustain itself. It may never be what it once was."

"I've heard other stories about Shael. The kind people tell only in whispers."

The Khevassar released the letter and sat back in his chair. He looked off to one side, staring in the distance, and for a minute he was elsewhere. Tammy thought his sparse white hair looked thinner and there were more liver spots on his hands than the last time she'd see him.

"I have many regrets," he murmured, almost to himself. "But the worst are those where I didn't tell someone the whole truth."

"Sir?"

His attention returned to the present and the Khevassar's piercing eyes focused on Tammy. "The stories you've heard, the ones whispered in dark corners. Most likely they're true. Guardian Fray recently returned from Shael, after visiting a city called Voechenka. It's surrounded by mountains on two sides and utterly secluded. It used to be a place of quiet reflection. A haven for artists. Now it's a ruin, overrun with crime. It had been forgotten until stories started to emerge."

Part of her didn't want to know, but Tammy had to ask. "What kind of stories?"

"Stories where people come back from the dead. Stories where strange lights are seen over the lake at night. Stories where mutilated bodies turn up with unrecognisable teeth marks."

"Was it a desperate plea for help or genuine?" she asked, gesturing at the letter in his hands.

"That's what I sent Fray to find out. I had my suspicions, but I didn't tell him everything. The doctors tell me he will recover in time, but it's going to be a long road."

A heavy silence settled on the room. The Old Man seemed to be waiting for something.

"Are you asking me to travel to Voechenka?"

"Knowing what I've just told you, would you want to go?"

"Maybe. But why did you send Fray? He's not been a Guardian for very long."

"Don't play games," said the Old Man. "You know why."

"Because you suspected that magic was involved, and he inherited his father's gift."

The Khevassar grunted. "It was a mistake to send him. I thought he would be the ideal choice, given the situation, but the opposite was true. The city is saturated with the lingering dead. I'm told he'd barely crossed the threshold into the city limits before he was overwhelmed. Amid his ravings, Fray spoke about something else flooding his magical senses. Something was lurking. He barely escaped with his sanity intact."

"Then why me? Why not someone else?"

"Because you've no sensitivity to magic. Because you're not being challenged here, and because I think you can get to the bottom of the mystery. You're good at what you do and I need someone I can trust."

Tammy folded her arms. "Now who's playing games?"

The Old Man flashed his teeth in a wolfish grin. "All right. Voechenka has turned into a cesspit of despair, murder and chaos. Parts of it are being controlled and run by criminal gangs and you know how to navigate those channels better than most."

"Is that it?" asked Tammy, feeling disappointed. "That's the only reason?"

"We all have a history that we leave behind when we become a Guardian. I don't care who you were or what you did, but in this case it might keep you alive longer than most. Because if you do go to Voechenka, it won't be as a Guardian."

"Then what will I be?"

The Old Man leaned forward across his desk. "There's no law there. No courts, no jail. Whatever the threat is, someone is responsible. They're doing this for a reason, however twisted. I need you to investigate and find out what that reason is. I need you to find whoever is behind it and kill them."

The words echoed around the room and when they settled Tammy felt a surge of fear but also excitement.

"I'm asking you because I think you have the best chance of surviving." The Khevassar wasn't holding anything back, and from his pained expression it wasn't something he did very often.

"What about the magic?"

The Old Man waved it away as if unimportant. "It was presumptuous of me to think Fray could handle it. The Red Tower is sending someone more qualified. They'll be on hand to offer you magic support, if it's needed. You would run the investigation and they'll help. That's the deal."

"Do I have to decide now?"

"No, but I'll expect your answer in the morning."

Tammy left without another word, barely seeing the cowering novices or the uniform corridors of Unity Hall. She only came back to the present when she found herself down at the docks. She had the rest of the day to make up her mind, but in truth the decision had already been made.

The endless sounds of the sea called to her. A rhythm as familiar as the beating of her own heart. Most of the time she didn't realise the waves were even there, lurking in the background. Shael would seem very quiet by comparison.

CHAPTER 4

No one paid much attention to the bearded man sat outside the Hog's Head tavern, eating his lunch on the street. It was a popular place in the heart of Perizzi, which meant they were used to dealing with people from all over the world.

From a distance the man looked fairly nondescript. Middle aged with grey in his beard and a close-shaven head. His height and build spoke of a Seve heritage, but Eloise thought that, unlike his countrymen, there was an unusual stillness to him.

His clothes weren't expensive and she guessed they were chosen for comfort rather than style. He wore no jewellery and there were no other signs of wealth. The vicious axe on his belt looked as if it had seen a lot of use and he sat with an air of confidence. Unusually he wore a sword on his back as well. Weapons weren't uncommon, but two seemed a little excessive. Perhaps he'd just come from a war zone or was on his way to another. The sword seemed familiar, but Eloise couldn't think why.

A few others were eating nearby and a low murmur of conversation hung over the tables. All talk ceased when she walked up to the bearded man and sat down opposite. It was then that Eloise noticed the scar, a faded but thick white line running vertically down his right cheek, disappearing under his jaw. A second and faint third line ran in parallel. Old claw marks from something big and dangerous. She noticed other changes about him too. An unusual and intricate black tattoo around his left wrist. There was also new pain showing behind his eyes. The lines between his eyebrows were deeper than she remembered, from worry and time spent frowning.

He continued eating as if he were still alone, slowly chewing his food, but his dark eyes studied her. She knew what he was seeing. The hood, the dark bulky robe and the gold mask. When nothing unusual happened the other people went back to their food and conversation, but Eloise knew they were listening. They feigned disinterest but she could feel their eyes resting on her from time to time, a small but persistent pressure.

Finally he finished eating his food and sat back. "I'd heard stories that someone had taken up residence in the Red Tower. And I'm glad to see that Seekers are abroad again, but why the masks?"

"To protect us from violence. The war made people even more afraid of magic. They're scared of what they don't understand."

"Despite all of the sacrifices made by the Battlemages?" he said, frowning at the street as if the people walking by were to blame. "How quickly they forget."

Eloise shrugged. "It's safer. This way they can see us coming and we can move freely and live among them without the mask."

"I can see the wisdom in that."

"Can we speak in private?" she said, glancing at the people sat behind him. "Perhaps we could go inside?"

He raised one hand and made a series of quick twisting gestures. Eloise felt a brief surge of power, a loud pulse as the Source echoed between them, and then nothing. Everything seemed as it was before, except when she looked over his shoulder there was a peculiar heat haze floating in the air. The other patrons were still talking, but their words stretched on and on, making them barely understandable.

"I've never seen anything like that before," she said, carefully studying the weave. It was incredibly delicate work, thin as a spider's web, and she sensed it would break very easily if she touched it.

"Who are you?" he asked.

"Don't you recognise me?" asked Eloise, heart thumping loudly in her chest. He cocked his head to one side in a peculiar manner, studying her with one eye partly closed. "I'm your wife, Beloved."

Balfruss sat forward quickly, reaching one hand towards hers and then quickly pulling back as if afraid she were an illusion.

They were not, in truth, husband and wife, but some would have expected them to marry. According to the tradition of her late husband's country, Balfruss had not only inherited the man's estate, but the right to marry the widow. He'd also seen her die during the war.

"How?"

It was still difficult to speak about what had happened, but if anyone deserved to know it was him.

"As I lay dying, overwhelmed with pain from my burns, time stretched on. The moment between one heartbeat and the next felt like hours." Eloise still had nightmares where she was a prisoner in her own flesh, unable to move or cry out. She would wake up in a cold sweat, clawing at the sheets.

Balfruss gripped one of her hands, his eyes filling with tears. "If only I knew then what I know now, I could have helped."

Eloise pushed away the memories and focused on the present. "But you did help me. While I floated in the dark, wrestling with the agony of my body, I felt something. It washed over me like a cool wave, soothing my pain. And for the first time I was able to think clearly again. I became aware of the room, the bed, and you, focusing your power on me for hours."

"The Source," said Balfruss.

Eloise smiled even though he couldn't see it behind the mask. "After you'd gone the pain returned, but I had hope. I don't know how long it took, hours, maybe days, but eventually I blocked the pain long enough to embrace the Source. The pain diminished again and I held on to it tightly, for hours at a time. Then I started to experiment. Time lost all meaning. The world consisted only of the Source and my next breath. I started with my lungs, as breathing was difficult, but by holding my breath I tried to heal a tiny portion."

"We thought you were dying. I came and said goodbye."

"I know. I heard every word," said Eloise, squeezing Balfruss's hands.

"After my battle with the Warlock I thought you were dead."

"So did everyone else. The hospital was busy, and they all expected me to die. I suspect when they found an empty bed they assumed someone else had dealt with my body. I walked out dressed in rags. Over the course of many months I healed myself."

"You've done more than that," said Balfruss, gesturing at the Seeker's mask and robe. "It was you. You reopened the Red Tower."

Even across the Dead Sea, stories must have reached him about the rebirth of the Red Tower. For years he had probably wondered who had done what he could not. It was something they had hoped would happen, but with so few magic users abroad it had seemed impossible, but she had done it.

"If the war taught me anything, it's that people need magic. They need our help, just as they did when the Warlock threatened our homeland. One day, a new threat will rise up, and the scale of it could rival the war if it is not opposed. When that day comes I intend the Red Tower to be ready to answer the call."

"You've changed," said Balfruss. "You were never so fierce."

Eloise shrugged. She wouldn't apologise for what she'd done.

"I had no choice. But what about you? After the war, where did you go?"

Balfruss sat back and stared off into the distance with a sad smile. "For a time I stayed with the First People, just as Ecko predicted. After that I travelled across the Dead Sea to live among his ancestors with the tribes in the emerald jungle."

"What did you see?"

A child-like smile touched his face, one that spoke of awe and amazement. "Wonders. Wonders and terrors like you cannot begin to imagine," said Balfruss, his eyes drifting away. "I watched a drammu give birth to a calf the size of ten horses. I heard music so beautiful it stilled the wind and made the stones weep. I journeyed for years and travelled thousands of miles, but when I woke up, only one day had passed. My mind was opened to the Source in ways like never before. I fell in love, I had a wife, and for a time I was happy." A shadow passed across Balfruss's face and for a moment there was terrible pain in his eyes, but then it was gone.

"And now?"

"Now, my path lies elsewhere," he said. There was much he wasn't saying but the pain in his bearing spoke of terrible loss. Eloise didn't push. They both carried a lot of secrets and he didn't owe her an explanation. "You sought me out for a reason. Why?"

"The Warlock."

"The Warlock is dead," he said with confidence. "I know this because I killed him."

"Did you know before the war he spent some time in Shael?"

"No."

"Did you also know that two years ago a madman called a Flesh Mage tried to open a rift here in Perizzi?"

"I've been hearing stories."

"He also spent time in Shael."

Balfruss frowned. "Just before the end, the Warlock tore open a rift. I don't know what he was going to do but I didn't give him a chance."

"In the past other Flesh Mages came here to Perizzi. All of them displayed dangerous Talents beyond anything we've seen before. And all of them came from Shael."

"Where?" asked Balfruss.

"A source told me they passed through a remote city called Voechenka. Whoever is behind this has remained hidden for almost a dozen years, training pupils and sending them out into the world, armed with dangerous and destructive magic."

Eloise saw the muscles in Balfruss's jaw tighten. It was a glimmer of the same fury she'd also felt at the discovery. This shadowy puppeteer was a dark reflection of the teachings of the Red Tower. As pupils she and Balfruss had been taught to use their magic to help others and promote peace. Their ability to touch the Source made them more powerful than a hundred warriors, but they were never to use their strength to force others to their will.

Discoveries deemed too dangerous by the Red Tower were buried so that others with fewer scruples didn't use them for selfish ends. Whoever had taught the Warlock, the Flesh Mages and probably others they'd not yet discovered, was partially responsible for countless deaths. Until recently Eloise had heaped all of the blame for the war on the Warlock. Now she knew that, in his own way, he'd been nothing more than someone else's puppet.

"There's more," she said, breaking the heavy silence. "The Red Tower has been commissioned to investigate another matter in the city. One that involves talk of people coming back from the dead."

Balfruss shook his head slowly. She knew that, like her, he was thinking about the Splinters and how they had been dead and alive at the same time. They had been changed, hollowed out by the Warlock's dark magic and turned into mindless tools created for war.

"Such a thing is not a coincidence," he said.

"No. Perhaps other dark powers are being drawn to the city in Shael. Whatever the reason, the Queens of Yerskania and Seveldrom have commissioned the Red Tower to send someone to resolve this."

"And you thought of me?"

"No, I sought out the strongest echo of the Source in the city and it led me to you. I need someone powerful and experienced, because whatever is festering in Voechenka is even more dangerous than the Warlock."

Eloise reached up to scratch her face and then cursed as her fingers touched metal. She wore the mask so often she sometimes forgot it was even there.

"Let me see your face," said Balfruss.

"They're watching," she said, gesturing at the people behind him.

Balfruss raised his hand again and she felt a brief surge of power. The air around them remained undisturbed, but beyond their table everything was blurred, as if looking into an old murky mirror. It seemed there was much he had learned during his travels in the last few years.

With nervous fingers Eloise lowered her hood and carefully removed the golden mask. The bright winter sun was a balm against her skin and a gentle breeze blew loose strands of hair across her face. A big smile stretched across Balfruss's face and yet she could see his eyes remained sad. Her thoughts turned to the last time the two of them had sat together like this, face to face. It was just before she and the others were consumed by fire on the walls of Charas.

"You look exactly the same," said Balfruss, his eyes lingering on her face. He was searching for any trace of burned flesh or scar tissue, but there was none. It had taken her years, working every night to heal her whole body, inside and out. Even now Eloise felt as if her understanding of healing was rudimentary, and she continued to make new discoveries all the time.

"I could heal those," she said, gesturing at the claw-like marks on his face.

"Thank you, but no. I have acquired some healing talent as well, but the scars serve as an important reminder." He offered another of those smiles, full of sadness and remembrance. "Were you going to ask me something else?"

It had been on her mind since the moment she'd seen him. Now, after hearing a little about his time abroad and seeing some of his abilities, all remaining doubts fled.

"I want you to join the Grey Council and help me run the Red Tower."

Once the Grey Council had comprised the respected leaders of the Tower, until they had abandoned their posts because of a ridiculous prophecy. Without them the Red Tower fell into disarray and across the world children began to suffer. Magic became wild and unpredictable and soon people began to fear it and those who wielded it. She hoped to change that but it would not be easy and it would not happen overnight.

For the second time since sitting down Eloise had genuinely surprised him. "I wasn't expecting that," murmured Balfruss. "Ask me again if I return from Voechenka."

"Are you sure?"

"Yes. Even now the Warlock laughs at me from beyond the grave." Balfruss shook his head. "If not me, then who else?"

Eloise shrugged. "If I didn't find anyone in time, I would have gone."

"The Red Tower needs you. The children need you. If you don't return, what would happen?" he asked.

Finding children born with any magical ability was no longer an issue, thanks to the monthly testing that had been agreed in Seveldrom and Yerskania. In time she expected other nations to follow a similar path. Her network of Seekers also continued to grow every year.

Now parents brought their children from the remote villages to the towns and cities for testing. Setting up the network had been difficult, but the hardest challenge remained clothing, feeding and training the children once they came to the Red Tower. Money was constantly in short supply and commissions from rulers helped enormously. But all of it needed to be managed and Eloise feared that, without her, it would fall apart again. She had others to help, but all of them continued to look to her for guidance.

"I don't know what would happen if I didn't return," she finally admitted.

"It should be me. No one knows I'm here and if I don't return, I won't be missed."

"I would miss you," said Eloise, and this time Balfruss's smile reached his eyes.

"When does the ship leave?" he asked.

"In two days."

"Then we still have some time to catch up."

Some of the weight that Eloise had been carrying on her shoulders eased a little. "I'd like that. Tell me, why does that look familiar?" she asked, pointing at his sword, and Balfruss began to laugh.

CHAPTER 5

Another long night of fighting the Forsaken ended in yet another stack of dismembered corpses littering the street outside their shelter.

Alyssa and the others had done their best, mostly slowing them down with arrows and occasionally getting lucky and stopping one in its tracks. Once the invaders breached the defences, as they did most nights, she and the others hacked and chopped, shoved and tipped them over the wall. Anything to slow them down and stop them dragging people away.

She and the other defenders had no weapons training and any fighting skill they did display was crude, learned through surviving over the last three years. Any attempt at formal training from Zannah had been instantly rejected, despite the fact that it could save their lives. Alyssa had tried to argue but it had been pointless. Their hatred, while understandable, blinded them to the obvious truth. Without the Morrin they would all have died months ago. Or worse. They might have been taken.

Zannah was the deciding factor every night. It was her ferocity, her strength and her skill with a blade that turned the tide, over and over again.

Everyone desperately wanted the Morrin to leave, but without her they would die. Equally her guilt, for what she and her people had done to Shael, kept her with them as if she were their prisoner. They were all trapped here together, marking time.

Part of Alyssa was angry at the quarantine put around the city, but most of the time she understood the reason. The risk was just too great. If the Forsaken were to spread beyond Voechenka it would be impossible to contain them. There would be no way to know who had been taken and the madness and distrust would spread. Fear and terror worse than what had happened during the war would tear the world apart. Even so, part of her was furious at being abandoned, but she smothered it because it would not help the others. There was already enough bitterness and anger to go around.

Alyssa watched as Zannah, the corded muscles jumping in her arms and shoulders, climbed down the rope into the street to perform her final grisly task of the night. Others turned their faces away, hiding indoors where they pretended not to hear the squelching sounds, but Alyssa always stayed on the wall. Someone had to offer a final prayer to the Blessed Mother for their souls in the hope of granting them eternal rest. Once, some of them had been good people, before they were taken, before they changed inside and out. Alyssa believed a tiny spark of humanity still existed within them and that it could be redeemed. After all, Jannek had come back in an attempt to save his sister. She knew Zannah had other ideas but kept them to herself.

The rope creaked as Zannah started her climb back up the wall. A few people lurked in the courtyard, alternately staring up at Alyssa and then at the rope attached to the laden cart. She knew what they were thinking. They'd told her their plan to cut the rope on a number of occasions and each time she'd managed to dissuade them. Most had come to understand their new world and Zannah's place in it. They didn't fully accept it though, and every day many still had murderous thoughts towards the Morrin, causing them to stare at the rope and ponder.

With a grunt Zannah slid over the top of the wall and slumped down on the other side. There was blood on her face and clothes, and a long red streak down her right arm.

"Is that yours?" asked Alyssa.

"I don't know," said Zannah, noticing it for the first time. Alyssa wiped off the blood and found a deep gash as long as her index finger. "It's not too bad."

"It looks nasty."

"I heal very quickly. It will be gone by morning."

"Don't move," said Alyssa, going down the stairs and returning a minute later with a skin of water and a small sewing kit. She passed Zannah the water and quickly threaded a curved needle. They had little in the way of herbs or salves to prevent infection, but at least there was no shortage of needles and thread. Perhaps tomorrow she could take a walk into the hills and see if she could find any wild herbs. She'd found a patch of wild garlic a few days ago that had flavoured their food for a while.

Once, the city had produced the finest silk carpets in the west. Some were masterpieces that took years to complete. Now all of the remaining carpets and looms in the city had been burned for fuel, the shops stripped bare of anything that could be resold or reused, and all the artisans were either dead or had escaped. Thread was cheap and useless to most so Alyssa found plenty of it lying around during her scavenger hunts.

Using small neat stitches Alyssa pulled the wound closed as Zannah sipped the water. The Morrin didn't even flinch as the puckered flesh was pulled tight. It wasn't the first wound Alyssa had sewn up in the last few months and she knew it wouldn't be the last. Zannah always did the most damage to the Forsaken, but by throwing herself into the densest pockets of fighting she also bore the brunt of the attacks. Alyssa knew why she did it, but in her mind Zannah had nothing to prove to them. The Morrin and everyone else thought different.

Dawn had broken unannounced, the sun creeping across the buildings as silent as a shadow. With the approach of winter it offered little real warmth, but at least it took some of the chill from her skin. The Forsaken always vanished with the arrival of dawn. She didn't know why but was determined to find out.

"Time to get some sleep," said Alyssa, offering Zannah a hand.

The Morrin regarded her with slow blinking yellow eyes for a minute. Her impenetrable stare bothered some but it held no fear for Alyssa. The Morrin didn't look like any other race. That scared many and made them think the Morrin were demons or evil spirits clothed in borrowed flesh. For Alyssa it was another example of the glorious variety found in nature created by the Blessed Mother. There were hundreds of varieties of flowers, and many that would look alien and unnatural to her. No one thought they were demon-spawn.

Zannah grunted and allowed herself to be pulled upright. "Were you a dancer?" she asked.

"No, but you already asked me that."

Zannah scrubbed a hand across her tired eyes and shook her head. "Sorry."

They walked into the main building, where Zannah collapsed on her bed fully clothed. Alyssa pulled a blanket over her and waited until the Morrin's breathing was slow and even before she slipped out and gently closed the door.

Monella sat on a low stool in the corridor outside, two wooden needles clacking together in an endless and soothing rhythm. She and a couple of others were turning out socks, scarves and gloves as fast as they could manage. Winter was not far away and the nights and early mornings were getting colder. One morning in the next few weeks they'd wake up to find frost on the ground. After that their wood supply and anything else flammable would become priceless.

"Will you keep an eye on her?" asked Alyssa. Monella didn't respond and her needles didn't stop moving until Alyssa put a hand on them. "She's not to blame."

"So you keep saying," said Monella. "And yet I remember her standing by and doing nothing as our people were slaughtered and tortured for fun."

Alyssa sighed, knowing there was no way to win this argument. She'd had it so many times, with Monella and others. It hurt Alyssa most to hear such words coming from Monella, who was so different from the person she'd been before. As one of the Faithful, a priest of the Blessed Mother, it should have been Monella that sought to preserve all life, but her faith had been shattered by the last few years. All that remained was a bitter and hollow shell. There was no love and not even a sliver of forgiveness inside her.

"Does your lack of faith allow you to stand idly by while someone else is murdered?" asked Alyssa.

Monella hissed between her clenched teeth and her hands shook, threatening to knock her knitting to the floor. Alyssa gripped her hands tightly, forcing the other woman to look her in the eye.

"I'm sorry, that was callous. I'm tired, but it's no excuse."

Slowly Monella regained control and Alyssa released her hands. "I'll make sure she's not disturbed," said the older woman. "But I can promise nothing else."

"Thank you."

Monella returned to her knitting as Alyssa went out into the courtyard. A few children were playing a game against one of the walls, throwing a ball and taking turns to try and dodge it. Their innocence and high-pitched laughter made Alyssa smile, chasing away some of her fear. A couple of adults were keeping watch on the children from the wall above, but most of the others were inside trying to catch a few hours' sleep.

Alyssa joined the two women keeping watch on the wall, each armed with a sword and a bow within arm's reach.

"You shouldn't go out there alone," said one of the women, a newcomer whose name she hadn't learned yet. The tall redhead had joined them when their last shelter had been overrun. She'd come from one of the other communities and claimed to be a former mercenary, although that was likely a story to make others keep their distance.

"I'll be fine," said Alyssa, uncoiling the knotted rope and throwing it over the wall. The other sentry, a slight woman from Yerskania, scanned the street carefully.

"It seems quiet. Even so, be careful."

"Always," said Alyssa, making sure the bag on her back was secure before gripping the rope. The second her feet touched the ground Alyssa drew her dagger. Once a dog had rushed her before she'd taken half a dozen steps. It had kept biting even after being peppered with arrows and stabbed. Its hunger had been so great that it hadn't felt its injuries until the very end. There were no dogs any more. They'd all run away or most likely been eaten. There were no pets anywhere in the city and no rats, although she thought the latter was because of the Forsaken.

A gentle breeze from the east tugged at her clothes, bringing with it the smell of the lake. Other smells sought to dominate. Ash from the torches that burned throughout the night. Decay from the rotting corpses left behind. The Forsaken would not come for them until dark and Alyssa did her best not to stare at the faces in case she recognised them. She'd stopped counting the number of friends and acquaintances she'd lost over the last few years.

Alyssa stepped out of the shadows and set off down the middle of the street, never straying too close to buildings on either side. Some were whole, apart from broken windows. Others were nothing more than shells where the roof and insides had been removed as if scooped out by a giant's hand. A few were marked with soot where they'd been put to the torch. There were deep shadows in many of them and all sorts of nasty surprises could be lurking within.

Alyssa stayed alert, kept moving forward and scanned both sides of the street for any movement as she went. Sticking to the widest roads she travelled west, away from the lake towards the craggy hills that sheltered the city from high winds. When she reached Debrussi square, where they used to have a weekly fruit market, Alyssa hesitated. She thought about taking a longer route out of the city, but was already tired from another difficult night, so instead opted for the most direct. It was no less dangerous than the other route, but it was more unpleasant in other ways.

"There she is!" called one of the mercenaries from the roof of an old bank. The stocky building had been reinforced with boards across all of the ground-floor windows in addition to the metal bars. The bank had been built with security against theft in mind, not what lurked in the city. Now the money inside was worthless and the building housed a mix of mercenaries and criminals.

Even in a city dominated by artists there was always a demand for somewhere to enjoy a quiet drink and maybe a hand of cards. And where there was gambling and money to be made, a variety of other criminals and time-wasters followed. Some were unlucky to have been caught here when the Forsaken had first appeared. Despite warnings about the quarantine, others had travelled here shortly after to exploit those left behind. Once the first person to be snatched had come back to life the mercenaries quickly realised their mistake. But it was too late by then and there was no way out. Mountains cradled the city on two sides, but they were impassable with no routes across. That had not stopped many people trying, but either they froze to death or starved. The sea offered a possible escape, but with tools only sufficient to make handmade rafts, every single person who attempted it had drowned. It didn't help that huge waves had been plaguing the coast for a while now, as if the sea were angry.

The only road in and out of the city was patrolled by soldiers from Shael and they shot anyone on sight. It was up to those left behind to sort out the problem and find a way to survive in the meantime.

"Have you got a present for me today? Maybe you want to show me something?" shouted the gangly mercenary and his friends laughed. They'd had the same conversation many times and apparently it never stopped being amusing for them. Alyssa decided to try a different approach.

"All right. I'll show you something, maybe everything," she said, running a hand over her stomach and across her chest. Once she had been curvy, now all of that had been lost, together with her luscious hair.

"Oh really?" said the mercenary. A couple of the others whooped and whistled as she continued to touch herself.

"Yes, but I'm shy. So why don't you come down here?" asked Alyssa.

The mercenary considered it. "No, ah, I'm fine up here," he said, nervously glancing around the street.

"You have a big mouth. In my experience that means you're

very small somewhere else," commented Alyssa, pointing at her groin and wiggling her little finger. The mercenaries cackled at that, mocking their friend who was turning red.

Alyssa moved on before he had time to think of a witty comeback. Once the bank and the mercenaries had faded behind her, the hollow silence of the city enveloped her like a thick blanket. Every street used to ring with sounds of creativity, from composing musicians to serenading poets to the clack, tap and rattle of artisans shaping cloth, metal and glass into objects taken directly from their imagination. This pregnant silence felt more out of place than anything. It hummed in Alyssa's ears, making her heart beat faster as fresh sweat broke out across her brow.

She kept walking, dagger held ready, eyes constantly moving. The streets curved one way and then the other around large homes, making it difficult to see what lay ahead. This was the most dangerous part, but the west gate lay just beyond what used to be the grand homes of rich patrons, often the most blessed citizens of Voechenka.

The road straightened and the gate came into sight. Alyssa slowed her pace but never stopped. The tall buildings had many alcoves and peculiar-shaped walls, turrets and towers. Even now, just after dawn, inky black shadows clung to some walls like fungus, as if not even sunlight could burn them away.

She heard something moving on her right. A faint scuffing sound. The patter of flesh against stone shuffling forward and then it was gone. Alyssa didn't wait to see if anything emerged. She muttered a prayer and kept going.

After passing through the open gates unmolested she didn't relax until the city was just out of sight behind a low hill. Only then did she take a moment to rest and slow her frantic breathing.

After twenty minutes of climbing up a dusty trail she came

to the edge of an old wood. Beneath the gently swaying trees, surrounded by greenery on all sides, Alyssa could pretend the horrors behind her didn't exist. Birds flittered above in the canopy, insects buzzed and small creatures shuffled about in the undergrowth. The area was teeming with life. It was a stark contrast to the unnatural stillness and silence of the city. If she didn't look up at the mountains boxing her in, Alyssa could pretend that even this quiet space wasn't a prison.

After an hour of foraging she'd collected several handfuls of blackberries, some wild onions, a few clumps of herbs to flavour their food and even some truffles. Sticky red juice clung to her hands and mouth from where she'd eaten a few berries, and she washed it off in a small stream that trickled down from the ice-capped peaks.

Alyssa filled her water-skin and drank deeply before looking for fish in the deep pools. She'd visited them before and been lucky, but today all she saw were tiny slivers of silver in the water. Thankfully her traps weren't empty and she picked up four fat rabbits. The area was riddled with warrens and what had once been an amusing and cute distraction was now an important source of food. Alyssa gave thanks to the Blessed Mother for the bounty, reset the traps and then headed back down the hill.

As she passed through the city gate she felt as if she were being watched. A cold prickle ran across her neck and shoulders. Alyssa quickened her pace but so far all she had was an uneasy feeling. She refused to run, even though her instincts were telling her to flee. When she came abreast of the mercenaries' bank the initial wave of catcalls and jeers died as the weighty presence of whatever pursued her fell over the mercenaries. They felt it almost immediately and began to scan the street for trouble.

"Get out of here, girl," one of them called down, all humour draining from his face. "It's not safe."

Alyssa kept to a fast walk until she heard something scrabbling in the shell of a building on her right. Her instincts told her to move but instead of running she threw herself to the ground. A shadow passed across her as something flew overhead, sailing close enough for her to smell it. It crashed into the building on the opposite side of the street, going through the stone wall as if it were made of paper. She had a brief glimpse of dark purple skin, corded muscle and unnaturally long arms.

"Run, girl! Run!" shouted the mercenaries, who started screaming and creating a racket to distract whatever was behind her.

Alyssa scrambled to her feet and ran. The weight of the food dragged at her, slowing her down, but fear gave her a burst of speed. They needed it and she couldn't afford to leave it behind. Their supplies were always dangerously low and few dared go outside to scavenge.

She heard the creature stirring in the rubble but didn't look back. Perhaps it would decide to go after the mercenaries, or perhaps it had ignored them and was coming after her. Alyssa felt the weight of the creature's stare against her back and she heard its huffing breath. The din of the mercenaries faded as she sprinted for her life, heart pounding in her ears, her breathing so loud that she couldn't hear anything else.

Debrussi square went by in a blur and she turned sharply at the last second. There was a rush of air and something heavy crashed into the building behind her, shattering the front. She heard a howl of frustration and a beastly snarl as mortar shifted and huge stones tumbled down.

"Blessed Mother protect me," she murmured over and over as a litany and rhythm for her feet. It also gave her something to focus on other than the sound of the creature's breathing, which seemed to be getting louder and louder.

Finally the shelter came into view at the end of a long wide street. She thought about ducking into different buildings, but given the creature's apparent weight and power, there seemed little point. Pushing herself to the limit, her feet pounding on the uneven ground, Alyssa sprinted for home.

The prickle down her spine became a constant pressure. On the wall of the winery she saw the sentries pointing in her direction and shouting. Her heart felt ready to explode and her sides began to ache with every breath. As she glanced down to avoid tripping, Alyssa saw her shadow overlaid by something massive that was right behind her. With a scream of terror she dove to the ground. The air whooshed behind her and an unholy bellow ripped into her eardrums, making her head swim. It smashed into another building and disappeared from view. When her vision cleared she could hear the sentries screaming at her to get up.

With unsteady legs she scrambled upright and hobbled forward, never daring to turn her head to see how close it was. She bumped into the wall of the winery and grabbed onto the knotted rope.

"Hold on!" shouted a voice and she gripped the rope with both hands. It immediately started to move upwards and she was dragged up the wall.

"Fire!" shouted Zannah and the hum of bowstrings filled the air around Alyssa. That dizzying scream came again from somewhere below her. Something silver flashed by her face and the scream changed in pitch. Alyssa bumped against the wall and several pairs of hands pulled her the last few feet to safety.

By the time she could breathe normally everything had fallen silent. The others shuffled away, but the sentries on either side of her were focused on the street. They remained perfectly still and didn't look at her. Alyssa offered Zannah the bag. She looked inside and shook her head.

"Don't say it," gasped Alyssa. "It's worth the risk."

"I was going to say you should've let me come with you."

"You do enough for us, and besides, normally it's quiet out there in the day."

Zannah looked as if she wanted to say something more but she just bit her lip. When Alyssa felt as if she could stand without her knees shaking she looked over the wall into the street. There was no sign of the creature apart from a splash of dark purple blood, the broken haft of a spear and several broken arrows.

"Did we kill it?"

"I don't know," said Zannah.

"Do you know what it was?"

"I've never seen anything like it before."

"You should go back to bed. Get some sleep," said Alyssa.

Zannah laughed. "I don't know if I can sleep after that."

"You should try, because we'll need you on the wall tonight."

That thought sobered them both. Zannah nodded grimly and went back down the stairs. Alyssa stared out at the drying patch of blood and was tempted to ask the sentries what it had looked like. In the end she changed her mind. Sometimes it was better not to know.

CHAPTER 6

Tammy took a deep breath and then knocked on the door. She heard the light patter of feet inside and then the door opened a fraction. A small blonde girl of perhaps six years peered out, craning her neck to stare up at Tammy.

"Who are you?" she asked.

"Laurie, what have I told you? Don't answer the door without me," said a familiar voice from inside. A moment later Mary-Beth appeared behind the girl. She stared at Tammy for a few seconds, noting the Guardian uniform, and then forced a smile.

"Come in," she said, shooing the girl to one side and opening the door wide. As soon as the door was closed Mary embraced her in a tight hug. She was one of the few people tall enough to hug Tammy without standing on a box. Mary looked exactly the same as the last time they'd seen one another, chubby and content. There was a touch more grey in her hair, but it suited her and she looked quite distinguished.

They sat down at the kitchen table and looked at each other in silence for a long while, noting the growing differences and remaining similarities. The lingering smells in the kitchen spoke to Tammy of good food and warm bread. Battered pans and drying herbs hung from a metal rack above her head, a heady aroma tickling her nose. It reminded Tammy so much of their mother's kitchen.

"You look just like my mummy," said Laurie, staring at Tammy and then back to her mother. The last time she'd visited, the girl had been very small.

"This is your aunt, Tammy. She's my twin sister," said Mary.

"Where's your husband?" asked Tammy, shooing Laurie away from touching her sword. Instead the girl ran her small hands over the red and black leather of her distinctive Guardian jacket.

"At work. Would you like some tea?"

Bored by their conversation Laurie wandered off into another part of the house.

Mary set the kettle to boil on the huge black metal stove which she stoked up with some more wood. A double stack of chopped rounds ran up to the mantelpiece of the wide stone chimney. A tidy row of carefully labelled jars sat on a shelf behind Mary's head. Several pairs of children's shoes were lined up by the back door.

Everything in the kitchen was neatly ordered and arranged. Everything had its rightful place. The need for order inside the house in opposition to the chaos of the world outside was a trait they shared. It was one of only a handful that remained.

"I'd hoped the next time I saw you it would be without those," said Mary, gesturing at Tammy's uniform and sword.

"I'm not ready. I'm not sure that I ever will be."

Mary smiled and nodded, doing her best to hide her disappointment, but Tammy could see it in her eyes. "I'd hoped that given time, you'd make peace with losing your husband."

"He's not lost, Mary. He didn't wander into a forest and go missing. He's dead. He was murdered, for no reason."

"Just because we don't know why, doesn't mean there wasn't a reason. Only the Maker knows the plan for each of us."

Tammy gritted her teeth to stop herself offending her sister's beliefs. They'd had this conversation many times over the years and her sister's attitude still annoyed her. She was one of the few people who could get under her skin so easily. The reverse was also true, and Mary's normally calm face was screwed up in frustration at Tammy's lack of faith. Despite having not seen each other for a few years it seemed as if very little had actually changed.

The heavy and awkward silence between them was broken by the shrill whistle of the kettle as it started to boil. Mary set a pot of tea on the table between them to brew and busied herself around the kitchen doing odd jobs for a few minutes, tidying and polishing, bringing order to the mess generated by her children.

"Where is he?" asked Tammy.

"Upstairs, playing with the others," said Mary, without looking around.

"How is he doing at school?"

Mary finally sat back down and the familiar placid expression was back in place. "His teachers tell me that he's doing well. He's taller than most of the other boys in his class now, and he likes reading. He sometimes helps Korrain at the shop, but I don't know what his true passion will be."

"Is he happy?" asked Tammy.

Mary laughed briefly, but it held no mirth. She poured the tea, her eyes focused on the task, but in truth Tammy knew she was doing it to buy herself some time to find the right words.

"He's healthy and well fed. He has a safe home, a family, and as much love as we can give him." Mary glanced at the open door and lowered her voice to a whisper. "What he doesn't have is his mother."

Tammy frowned. "I don't know how to be one of those. You

were always better at it than me, even when we played with dolls."

"You can learn," insisted Mary. "Just as I did."

Tammy shook her head. "No. It's better this way."

"For him? Or for you?"

Tammy ignored the questions and the barbs attached. Instead she put a heavy money pouch on the table. "I'm leaving Perizzi for a while and I wanted to make sure you had enough money for him."

"You don't need to keep giving us money."

Tammy left the pouch on the table. "Thank you for caring for him. I'm not sure when I'll be back, but I'll send money on my return."

"What aren't you telling me?" asked Mary, staring at her intently. A few seconds later realisation dawned on her face. "You're not sure if you're coming back. That's it, isn't it?"

"I've made arrangements, just in case," said Tammy, getting to her feet.

"Don't you want to see him before you leave?" asked Mary, putting out a hand to stop her running out the door. Part of Tammy wanted to walk out, forget about all of this and never come back. Every time she came here it only made things more difficult and each visit left her feeling torn and distracted. It was one of the reasons she didn't come very often. The other reason was that every time she saw him he looked a little more like his father, and that hurt worse than anything else.

"Hello," said a familiar voice from the door. He'd taken the decision out of her hands. Corran towered over little Laurie even though he was only a few years older than her. She clung to one of his hands with both of hers.

"Corran, do you remember your aunt?" asked Mary, trying to smile but failing.

Tammy struggled to keep her emotions under control as he studied her. He had the same dark hair and brown eyes as his father. The nose and height came from her, as did the unwavering stare.

"You came to visit a couple of years ago," said Corran.

"I just came to see if you and your sisters were well," said Tammy, glancing at Laurie.

"I had a bad cough a while back, but it went away," said Corran, shrugging his shoulders. "I'm tough, just like my dad."

"You'll grow up to be very tall and strong," said Tammy, resting a hand lightly on his shoulder. "I'm sure of it. It was good to see you."

"Are you staying for lunch?" asked Laurie. "Mummy makes really tasty soup. You should have some."

"Maybe next time. I have to go," said Tammy, getting to her feet. She turned her face away and wiped at her eyes before embracing her sister.

"Be careful," whispered Mary. "I know you don't believe, but I'll say a prayer to the Maker for your safe return."

"Thank you, for everything," said Tammy. Sensing there was something going on Laurie began to cry and she hugged Tammy's leg, sobbing into her trousers. Mary gently extracted the girl, gathering her up in her arms while Corran just watched. Tammy ruffled his hair affectionately and quickly went out the door, before anyone could say anything else.

The *Snow Leopard* was a sleek merchant vessel that usually transported goods up and down the west coast. Today it had been commissioned by several people with influence and power to take them east to Shael. The last of the supplies were being lowered into the cargo hold and the dozen priests and priestesses joining them on the voyage were just crossing the gangplank.

Tammy noted they wore white robes, and all but one was decorated with a single candle, the symbol of the Lady of Light. The last priest was different from the rest and his grey robe was marked with the symbol of an open eye. He was one of the new plague priests she'd seen around Perizzi in the last couple of years.

"They volunteered," said a voice from Tammy's left. The stocky bald man had a bearing of authority and the weather-beaten face of a sailor. He shook his head in dismay and tied a red bandanna to protect his head from the elements. "Despite knowing where we're going."

"Captain Parrick?"

"Aye," he said, glancing out at the sea and sniffing the air. "Tide's changing. We're leaving in less than an hour, so get your stuff stowed on board as soon as you can. We're just waiting for one more."

The last priest shuffled onto deck and then they milled around not sure where to go or what to do. The sailors went about their business, ignoring the passengers.

"Nethun give me strength," said Parrick, crossing the gang-plank in two quick hops. He started ushering the priests below while bellowing at his sailors to get ready to leave.

It was strange to be out of uniform after wearing it every day for so many years. Tammy felt a little peculiar without its familiar weight and smell, but she'd made suitable substitutions to help her feel safe. The worn leather breastplate was old but tough, and had been made to fit her. Bracers covered her forearms, a pair of steel-trimmed leather gloves were hooked through her belt and a steel-rimmed wooden shield sat by her feet with her belongings. The sword at her waist was the same one she'd used for the last eight years as a Guardian and she hadn't considered replacing it.

"Are you Guardian Baker?"

She turned to find a tall Seve man with serious eyes regarding her. He carried an axe at his waist and a sword on his back and yet she didn't think he was a warrior. He didn't hold himself in the same way as most warriors she'd met. His clothes were made for hard travel, much like the worn pack at his feet. His face was scarred on one side and the tidy beard and receding black hair were run through with lots of grey.

"Yes. You're from the Red Tower?"

"Not what you were expecting," he said with a grin, offering her a callused hand, which she shook.

"No. I thought you'd be more mysterious and maybe wearing a mask," she admitted, and he laughed.

"I'm not a Seeker. I'm a Sorcerer," he said proudly.

"What's that? Is it different from a Battlemage?"

"That is an excellent question," he said, picking up his pack. "We've a long voyage ahead, so I'm sure there will be plenty of time for me to answer."

"I didn't catch your name," said Tammy, moving to one side to obstruct the gangplank. She expected him to get angry but instead he put down his pack and regarded her calmly. His eyes sparkled with intelligence and a smile tugged at the corners of his mouth, but she also sensed a deep sorrow in him. It was all too familiar, and Tammy looked away first, not wanting him to see her pain reflected there.

"Once I tell you my name it may change how you see me. If we're to work together in Shael, then you deserve to know, but I'd rather everyone else on board didn't. It will make the voyage less awkward for everyone."

"That's fair," said Tammy, as a prickle of anxiety ran through her. She knew of only a handful of names that would affect people so quickly, and only one with connections to the Red

Tower. This had to be Balfruss, the Battlemage who defeated the Warlock and ended the war.

"Ah, I see you've worked it out," he said. "I have a gift for you."

Moving slowly he reached over his shoulder and with something approaching reverence held out the long sword towards her in both hands.

"I already have a sword. One that I'm used to," she said.

"I'm sure your superiors have told you what we're facing in Voechenka. Magic is most likely involved. Plain steel may not have any effect, but," he said, hefting the blade. "This will even things out."

"Is it dangerous?"

"To you? No. To anyone or anything that tries to use magic against you?" Balfruss offered her a wry smile. "They'll be in for an unpleasant surprise. This is just a loan." He offered her the blade again and Tammy slowly took it from his hands. As she touched the plain leather scabbard she expected something to happen. There was no flash of light or burst of energy through her fingers. It was just a sword.

She drew the blade and saw colours swirling in the steel, but otherwise it was an ordinary blade, slender and well balanced, without any gaudy decoration or embellishment.

"Her name is *Maligne*," said Balfruss, staring at the naked blade with a troubled expression.

"It's beautiful," said Tammy. She sheathed the sword and heard Balfruss sigh in what she thought sounded like relief.

"Shall we go on board?" he asked and she led the way onto the main deck of the *Snow Leopard*. Tammy stowed her belongings in one of the cabins and made it back on deck in time to see the sailors casting off. Balfruss was stood at the rail staring back at the city and she leaned against it beside him.

Perizzi was the source of some of her best and worst memories. She'd spent so long walking its winding streets she expected to feel more of a lurch as it started to recede, but all she felt was a sense of relief. There were so many emotions tied to the city that it was liberating to be cut free from the weight of them. Everything would still be waiting for her when she came back, if she came back, but for now all of her thoughts turned to Voechenka and the mystery that lurked within its desolate streets.

CHAPTER 7

Balfruss sat quietly off to one side with the priests while Tammy dealt with the officers at the Shael garrison. As far as they knew he was there to assist her, nothing more. They'd agreed to keep his identity secret from as many people as possible to avoid making a delicate situation even more uncomfortable.

Since returning to Seveldrom Balfruss had slowly come to realise the fear that his name inspired. The irony was not lost on him. No one spoke about the Warlock or the terrible things he'd done during the war. In hushed voices they told stories about the man who'd beaten him. The Battlemage who should never be named. It was worse than being forgotten by history. It also pained Balfruss to admit it, but the Warlock had been right. Just as he'd predicted, Balfruss had been exiled by his own people and now he was a bogeyman of almost mythic status.

At present they were waiting for the Captain of the Shael garrison to return from patrolling before they could press on to Voechenka. His men were incredibly nervous. Every warrior sat or stood with a hand resting on their sword and all were armoured and ready for battle. It would take only a small push to send them over the edge, so Balfruss avoided eye contact and kept his mouth shut.

The guards were also unwilling to make any decisions without their Captain's authorisation, even one that wouldn't put them in any danger. Despite Tammy being in receipt of a letter from the Queen of Shael explaining their purpose, the guards still refused.

It showed a level of fear and paranoia Balfruss had not been anticipating. So he waited patiently and conserved his energy, while Tammy chatted idly with the guards, subtly gathering information as she went. They probably didn't even realise she was doing it.

The voyage to Shael had been fairly uneventful, but over its course he'd come to respect the tall Guardian. She had pale white skin from Yerskania but the height and build of someone from Seveldrom. Her position in the Guardians indicated she had a methodical mind and he'd been delighted to find her intelligent and possessing a dry wit.

With little to do at sea, Tammy spent her time getting used to *Maligne* by practising on deck for a couple of hours each day, while he dozed in the sun or read one of the books in the Captain's limited library. Parrick was an unusual man with eclectic tastes, and amid the journals of famous voyages and studies of western history, Balfruss found books of poetry and even a guide to eastern culture. He was tempted to correct the mistakes but didn't think the Captain would appreciate him writing all over his book.

Balfruss spent a portion of each day by himself while Tammy spoke with the sailors. Her position as a Guardian earned their respect and she seemed at ease in their company. A few years ago he would have sat with them, laughing and drinking, swapping stories and jokes, but not any more. Not after the war. Not after what he'd seen in the jungles of the north. Balfruss traced the intricate pattern of the marriage tattoo on his left wrist with the fingers of his right, his mind swimming with memories. He spent a lot of time wandering the corridors of the recent past, listening to the voices of old friends, and inevitably his thoughts kept returning to her.

After a couple of days at sea Balfruss took off his boots and walked barefoot around the ship. The sailors noticed the thick calluses on his feet, but they knew from the way he walked and lack of nautical knowledge, they'd not been earned at sea. Even then the sailors didn't ask, but he'd seen them looking at him speculatively from time to time.

With so little to do each day, as Parrick's sailors were competent men and women, even Balfruss felt the need for company. During the voyage he and Tammy would sometimes sit in companionable silence or chat while watching the waves. She would tell him a little about herself and he would share what he felt comfortable with about the last few years since the end of the war. She didn't press him for more details, which he liked about her. But he also knew she was smart enough to fill in some of what he'd left out. Likewise, when she'd said there was no one waiting for her back home in Perizzi he'd spotted the lie. They both had parts of their life they wished to remain private.

Balfruss tried talking to the priests, but he found them to be a pious group who made him uncomfortable. It wasn't long before any conversation returned to their religion and way of thinking. After his travels in the north and all that he'd witnessed before the war, the established faiths no longer seemed to intimidate or impress him as they once did.

The priests' devotion to the Lady of Light was very different from what he remembered seeing a few years ago. Now the Lord of Light was rarely mentioned and his companion had become dominant in the church. Tammy had told him that those priests from the church of the Holy Light who were more interested in getting rich and doing little real work, had all but disappeared. Now those who followed the Lady of Light could be found in some of the worst places in every city, offering comfort to the poor, the diseased and the dying. The churches had become refuges where every coin donated was spent on helping clothe, feed and support people, not lining the coffers. The priests on board ship had not completed the Iron Challenge or taken the Long Walk, but nevertheless they'd endured a crucible of the soul, as each had haunted eyes as if they carried the weight of many. As someone who had enough demons of his own, Balfruss did his best to avoid long conversations with them. Nevertheless he could respect their dedication, even if he didn't want to spend too much time with them.

The only exception was the lone plague priest, a blond-haired man called Kai. He had a dark sense of humour and sarcastic tongue, which meant he also spent much of the voyage alone. Balfruss thought himself a decent student of history, but he'd never heard of Akharga. Kai assured him that it was a very old religion, with its roots in some of the earliest records, but with no way to check, Balfruss had to take him at his word.

The sound of raised voices brought Balfruss's thoughts back to his surroundings in the garrison, where the Shael guards were drawing their weapons. He looked across the room at Tammy and raised an eyebrow, but she shook her head and gestured for him to stay put while she investigated. A few minutes later she returned with a haggard Shael warrior he'd not seen before. The relief in the room was palpable and Balfruss saw the guards relax at the newcomer, who had to be their Captain.

Every Shael warrior in the garrison was lean with a gaunt face, but the Captain made them all look fat by comparison. His grey hair was cut close to his scalp and the white stubble on his face did nothing to hide the deep hollows of his cheeks. His deep purple eyes sparkled with so much vitality they looked out of place in such a weathered face.

"I'm Captain Rees," he said, sitting down with a grunt of relief. "I know that you've come a long way, but before you decide to venture into Voechenka, I think you should know what awaits you."

"Any information would be appreciated," said Tammy, declining the offer of a drink. One of the guards brought a modest plate of food for the Captain, who started to eat with vigour. His armour was still covered with dust as he'd come straight from the saddle to see them. He smelled of horse, leather and stale sweat, but there was no pageantry out here on the edge of the world.

"There's no law in the city any more," said Rees around a mouthful of beans. "It wasn't always that way, but you're not interested in history. The only rule in the city is that of survival. The strongest, cruellest and most cunning survive. All others are grist for the mill. The meek and the pious were among the first to die. The rest enslave themselves in different ways in return for protection." Rees tore off a chunk of bread and dipped it into the gravy on his plate. He chewed slowly as if thinking, but Balfruss could see he was savouring every mouthful. "If you go into Voechenka and get into trouble, no one will come in to help. My orders are to wait three weeks and if you don't emerge by then, you'll be declared dead. Word will be sent back to your families."

Rees looked up from his plate for the first time to gauge their reaction. Tammy watched him with a calm expression, unperturbed by the news. He glanced around the room, passing over the priests before pausing briefly on the axe at Balfruss's waist. Rees narrowed his eyes and looked Balfruss up and down, his gaze lingering on his hands, the axe again and finally his face. Balfruss saw Tammy tense, but thankfully Rees didn't seem to recognise him and returned to his food.

"My information is weeks out of date, but what I can tell you will still be of some use. Once fear took hold in the city, people started banding together to protect themselves. There were eight camps, five were controlled by criminal gangs, two were independent and we had a garrison. There will be fewer camps now, but your best chance of surviving the first night is to try and get into one of the independent bases, if they'll have you."

"Who's killing them?" asked Tammy.

Rees took a deep breath and shook his head. "It changes. Friends sometimes, enemies on other nights. Sometimes the dead come back to steal away the living."

It sounded like the ravings of a madman or a story meant to scare children, but no one was laughing. Rees spoke so matter-of-factly it was unnerving. The haunted look in the Captain's eyes told Balfruss he'd been in the city and seen these terrors for himself. Normally people would be quick to shy away from such an unsettling figure, but the guards were drawn to Rees because he'd faced the darkness and survived to tell them the story.

"What happened to your garrison in the city?" asked Tammy.

"We were overrun in the night," said Rees. "The guards on duty didn't cry out because they saw familiar faces in the crowd. Friends who'd gone missing that we thought were dead or had fled the city. Our relief soon turned to surprise and horror when they tried to kill us."

Tammy was puzzled, but kept driving forward with questions. "Why? Why kill you?"

"They offered us a choice first." The tone of Rees's voice told Balfruss it wasn't much of a choice. "To come with them and be reborn. They kept talking about the 'joining' or the 'blending'.

Something like that. When we refused they said it would happen anyway."

"Did you ever capture one of them alive?" asked Balfruss, drawing every eye in the room.

"No."

"Was it some kind of disease? Did they have any marks or strange bruises on their skin?" Balfruss wasn't sure if magic was involved or not, but he needed to eliminate the obvious. There were blood parasites that could drive a person insane and make them want to drink blood to spread the disease. Others affected the brain, creating visions that slowly affected the victim until they couldn't tell the real world from illusion. The First People and the tribes in the endless jungle had encountered and cured many unusual diseases which they'd taught him about. So far the symptoms didn't sound familiar, but he'd need to see one of those affected to be sure.

Rees shook his head. "They seemed normal. Healthy, in fact. They were just different," he said, tapping the side of his head. "We killed friends and strangers and in the morning all of the bodies were gone. The next night many of those we killed came back again. It happened the same way on the second night and on the third we were outnumbered. We fled the city and didn't stop running until we reached this garrison. I went into Voechenka with a hundred men and came back with six. After receiving my report the Queen ordered the city quarantined. Now we do all we can to keep everyone inside. My orders are to shoot anyone on sight, no questions asked, in case they've been changed. I'd like to believe you can help those who are left, but I don't see how."

Balfruss thought that telling the story might have made Rees lose his appetite, but he persisted and was clearly determined to eat every scrap on his plate.

"How do we find the independent camps?" asked Tammy, breaking the heavy silence that had settled on the room.

"I can draw you a map of the city and the last known locations of all the camps. All of them are guarded during the day, but you'll soon know which are run by mercenaries and which by local people."

One of Rees's men went to fetch some paper and ink while he finished eating. As they waited Tammy asked him more questions about the layout of the city and landmarks to help them navigate. Balfruss listened with one ear, but the rest of his focus was resting on a single soldier. His armour was dusty and Balfruss hadn't seen him earlier, which meant he'd come in with the Captain. At first glance he seemed like all of the other guards, a tall golden-skinned man in battered armour, but there was something amiss. He seemed lost in thought and his right hand twitched uncontrollably.

"The supplies will be useful currency," said Rees. "But they'll also make you a target. No one has escaped the city in weeks, so they'll be desperate and will try to kill you for the food you're carrying."

"Who will?" asked Tammy.

"Everyone," said Rees with a feral grin.

Balfruss noticed the distracted guard wasn't following the conversation. So far all he'd done was stare at the floor, but adrenaline began to flood Balfruss's body, amplifying his senses.

"Can we borrow a couple of horses to transport the supplies?" asked Tammy.

Rees shook his head. "They would be slaughtered for meat the minute you set foot inside the city. There are no animals anywhere in Voechenka. No cats or dogs, no birds, not even a rat. You'll have to carry the supplies."

"The Embrace will not be denied," muttered the guard, but

no one except Balfruss noticed. Moving slowly so as not to cause any alarm, Balfruss released the axe at his belt, gripping it tightly in one hand. The guard remained unaware, muttering to himself and shaking his head. Like every other guard his gold-tinted skin was pale, but as Balfruss watched, it regained some of its natural sheen. The gauntness of his features began to fade and the heavy shadows beneath his eyes completely disappeared. The transformation took only a few seconds and when it was over the guard looked healthy and well rested.

"The Embrace. That's what it's called," said the guard a little louder, and this time his voice carried around the room. "Those who come back."

Rees wasn't really paying attention, but he nodded along. "That's right. The embrace, whatever that means."

"The Embrace will bring you peace. It is glorious." As the guard spoke he pushed himself away from the wall. His eyes burned with an intense passion, bordering on the zealous.

At the same time Balfruss stood up, keeping his axe ready to strike, just in case. Tammy glanced at him and quickly scrambled back from her chair, drawing *Maligne*. The unusual blade glimmered in the flickering torches, catching the light or perhaps reacting to something in the air.

The room began to empty as the priests sensed imminent violence and ran to get out of the way as quickly as possible. Rees and the other guards drew their swords, forming a ring of steel around the peculiar man.

"No, no, no," said Rees. "Sornan. Not you."

"What's happening?" asked Tammy.

"They got to him," said Rees. "He's one of them."

"It's far easier if you surrender," said Sornan, beseeching his friends with a smile. By comparison their faces were tight with tension. Their discipline kept them from acting, but Balfruss knew all of them wanted to kill Sornan who, until moments ago, had been their friend. "Stand with me and together we will accomplish feats that seem beyond our reach. But now, as my eyes begin to open, I see what can be done."

"What do we do, Sir?" asked one of the men. Rees seemed torn with indecision as a range of different emotions ran across his face.

"I've become more than I ever was," said Sornan, reaching for one of his friends, who batted his hand away with the flat of his sword. "The pathways open to me now are vast and the truth is within ourselves. Don't turn away from this. The Embrace is the way to splendour and a future brighter than any we've seen before."

"Shut up!" someone shouted, but the words had no effect on Sornan. His words, rhythmic and almost poetic, had the seemingly familiar ring of ritual or a religious sermon. Although none of the words was unusual, each fitted together in a way that made the skin crawl on Balfruss's scalp with their strange promises.

"Look now, brothers and sisters, the dawn of—"

Sornan stopped talking suddenly, then stared down at the sword sticking out of his chest. Rees was breathing hard, his hands trembling on the hilt, but with a sharp movement he yanked the blade free.

Nothing happened but Balfruss still reached for the Source, expecting to need his magic. Then something flickered behind Sornan's eyes. This was something that didn't belong. He sensed what felt like an inhalation of breath and an echo of something far away experiencing a moment of surprise. The feeling quickly faded and now the light had faded from Sornan's eyes. Blood, slow and dark, trickled from the wound, and he slumped backwards and died.

"Behead the body immediately," said Rees, pointing at one of his guards. "You three, build up a pyre and burn it the moment the flames are hot enough."

"What was that?" asked Tammy as the guards got to work.

Rees wiped his blade clean and then sat down, far more weary than when he'd stepped into the room only minutes before. One of the guards returned with a cloak, which they draped around his shoulders. Rees clutched it to him, suddenly cold and shivering as the adrenaline faded and shock took hold.

For a time the Captain said nothing, his eyes staring into the past, regret heavy upon him as if the cloak were made of lead instead of wool.

Finally, with eyes clouded by grief, he stared at Tammy and then Balfruss.

"If nothing is done, that will happen to us all. You must stop this madness before it's too late."

CHAPTER 8

Kai's boots echoed loudly on the stone floor of the empty banqueting hall. Walking down the length of the vast table towards his seat, his attention was drawn to the Maker's chair. It towered over everything in the room. A huge edifice that was a constant, and seemingly eternal, reminder of the first and oldest of them.

No one had seen the Maker in a long time and yet his presence was still keenly felt around the world. Despite his absence time had not diminished people's belief in him or his power. There were a few theories to explain his absence, such as he'd grown despondent with the mortals and gone off into seclusion. Another claimed that he'd been driven mad. Yet another that he was actually still alive, living among the mortals as one of them. Kai wasn't sure what to believe, but throughout the many long years of his life he'd never seen the Maker in person.

With some trepidation Kai approached the chair, extending one hand towards it. At the last second he pulled back. Even he didn't dare touch it.

"I came as soon as I could," said a familiar voice. Kai turned to see Vargus striding towards him with purpose. He always walked like that and didn't even know he was doing it.

Somewhere in the back of Vargus's mind there was always a specific goal that he was working towards. His purpose might change with the years, but he was eternally driven and never drifted on the waves of fate. Vargus created his own path. He traversed the whims of mankind, but always kept moving forward. It was something that Kai was attempting to learn after nearly being unmade a few years ago by the idiot Lantern boy. A sneer twisted Kai's handsome features as he looked at the boy's empty chair and thought of his fate.

Every day more and more of the boy's followers turned away from him, choosing to follow the newly pious Lady of Light instead. His power would be waning as hers grew. If he returned at all he would be a shadow of his former self. Kai was looking forward to that day very much indeed. Then he and the boy would have words.

Vargus stopped behind his own chair but didn't sit down. "You said there was news."

"You were right. There's something festering in Voechenka."

Vargus grunted and moved to stand beside the far wall, holding his hands out towards something. In his version of this place it was probably a fireplace. For Kai the four walls were long windows, the glass tinted a sickly green. Beyond the glass were a myriad stars and brightly coloured planets extending in all directions as far as the eye could see.

"What have you found?" asked Nethun, his voice booming around the hall. As ever the old sailor was dressed simply in loose trousers and a plain red shirt with the sleeves rolled up to the elbows. His bare feet left damp impressions on the floor and as he drew closer Kai felt an enormous weight press against him from Nethun's presence. Nearly as eternal as the Maker, he warranted extreme caution and a great amount of respect. Kai did his best to smother his surprise at seeing Nethun by looking around expectantly. "No one else is coming. It's just the three of us," said the old sailor.

"Nethun brought this to my attention," said Vargus by way of explanation. "What did you see?"

"Something is infecting the remaining people in Voechenka."

"Is it something from beyond the Veil?" asked Nethun.

Kai shrugged. "Probably. They killed the infected man and burned the body before I had a chance to examine it. We're lucky that the city is remote, otherwise it would have spread much further and more quickly."

"Do we need to take steps to keep it contained?" asked Nethun.

"I think it would be wise. There's only one route into the city. No one is allowed in or out, and guards patrol the surrounding countryside. A few have tried to escape over the mountains or via the sea, but none of them made it. Despite all of that one of the guards on patrol was infected." Kai shook his head in alarm. "His Captain said he was only alone for a few minutes. Now they're working in pairs at all times. It will help, but only for a short time."

"If the population of Voechenka is small in number, it sounds like whatever is infecting people has become desperate," said Vargus.

"Either that, or it's just very hungry," suggested Kai. As ever the others thought in very narrow human terms. They saw mortals as groups and families, not food. To them mortals were special and important, but to something from beyond the Veil every creature might simply be a different type of meat to consume. They had no way of knowing how it thought, what it wanted or even what it was doing by infecting people.

"Where are you now?" asked Nethun.

"At a garrison a few miles outside the city. Tomorrow morning we're going into Voechenka and then we'll be completely cut off." The itch of worry blossomed into a frown on Kai's face.

"What is it?" asked Vargus.

"I can feel something lurking in the city," said Kai, hating how vague he sounded. "Even at this distance. It's shrouded somehow, but it's there, like an itch in the back of my mind."

Nethun grunted. "Makes sense. It's kept itself concealed from us for some time now."

"There's something else," said Kai, taking a deep breath. "At the moment of the guard's death, I saw something in his eyes."

Sensing his unease, Vargus came to stand beside him, resting a reassuring hand on Kai's shoulder. "What was it?"

Kai studied Vargus carefully for signs of deception or guilt. He needed to know if his old friend had sent him into this knowing more than he said, or if he was truly unaware. Kai saw no trace of a lie. As ever Vargus was being completely straight with him.

"As the life faded from the guard, I saw something lurking behind his eyes." Nethun came up on Kai's right side, a deep frown creasing his weather-beaten face. "Something was watching me."

Vargus was on the verge of cursing, but he glanced at the Maker's chair and bit his tongue instead. Nethun turned away and stood with both palms resting on the table, his eyes deep in thought.

"I think Balfruss saw it too," said Kai. "He's changed since he was in Charas."

"Elwei says he's *become*," said Vargus. "He's a Sorcerer, in the old sense of the word."

That was a word that had not been used about a human in a long time. Kai contemplated what it meant and a shiver of anticipation ran down his spine. Some of the old ways had not died off, as some of the others around this very table had predicted. The Red Tower was being rebuilt and more old magic was being rediscovered all the time.

"He's definitely more aware. I'll have to be careful he doesn't see through my mask," said Kai, gesturing at the youthful body of the man he wore. "They have three weeks to resolve this, after that they'll be declared dead. I suspect this is a last resort. If it fails the next step will be something more drastic."

"They'll raze the city to the ground," said Nethun, coming out of his stupor. "It's what I would do."

Kai shrugged. "They've not said as much, but that would be my guess too."

"Could it not be rebuilt?" asked Vargus.

"So much has already been lost. There's not much left," Nethun pointed out. "Large parts of the city were destroyed during the occupation, and more has been damaged in the last few years."

"What about the people still living there?" asked Vargus.

"After the war most refused to stay. They sailed abroad to start new lives away from the city and so many bad memories. My sailors took them all over the world," explained Nethun. "Sadly it's a common story all across Shael."

Kai knew that Vargus was finding it difficult to contemplate the idea of turning away from one's city, or one's country. After seeing the devastation in Shael, he could understand the need for a fresh start.

"I've been speaking to the guards about Voechenka. Anyone still in the city was too stubborn, or too stupid, to leave. When word spread about most of the city being abandoned it attracted a lot of people used to working in the shadows. Now there are several groups of mercenaries trapped inside."

A foreboding silence settled on the hall as the others became lost in thought. Coming so close to oblivion had made Kai more cautious and even hungrier for power. When Vargus had told him about a city, full of the desperate and the dying, it had sounded wonderfully delicious. A ripe feeding ground for horrendous diseases that often festered in such isolated places. At one time Kai's power would have rivalled Nethun's. To be brought so low and to become so little was humbling, but with the possibility of real power in sight once more his need outweighed the potential risk.

"I'll have a few of my people keep watch on the guards. Make sure no more of them are infected," said Nethun. "But I can't order them into Shael without it seeming like another invasion." Most of his followers were sailors and the Vorga. The people of Shael had only just driven the latter out of their country and would not welcome their return, regardless of the reason. "Vargus, can you help?"

"I can call in some favours to keep it contained. It won't get out," promised Vargus. Although Kai felt reassured that the shadowy presence in the city would not escape, it still left him with the responsibility of seeing that it was destroyed. He said nothing of his anxiety though, just gave them both a wolfish smile and vanished from the banqueting hall.

Something was waiting in the shadows of Voechenka and he was keen to meet it. Whatever it was, he knew it had never seen his like before and was in for a big surprise.

CHAPTER 9

With ash still swirling in the air from the dead guard's pyre, they marched away from the garrison towards Voechenka. In addition to her armour and sword, Tammy carried a heavy pack laden with food and medicine. Each of the twelve priests also carried a large pack, but she and Balfruss bore the heaviest items.

The priests would carry any weight stoically, never once complaining, right up to the moment they collapsed. It was the way with priests of the Lady of Light. They looked after everyone but themselves. The plague priest, Kai, had cursed at the weight, earning him disapproving looks from the others, but in some ways his grumbling had been reassuring. It showed he was more than just a priest and that as well as caring for others he cared about himself.

Despite travelling with the priests for days Tammy couldn't name them all and she knew very little about them as individuals. Not because they were secretive, but whenever she asked a question they always found a way to turn it back to their faith. They were devout to the point of having no real personalities of their own, which was slightly worrying.

They marched in silence wrapped up in their own thoughts

and weighed down as much by what had happened last night as by their backpacks. She knew something bizarre was happening in Voechenka, but had thought some of it exaggerated to bring attention to the city's plight.

Both she and Balfruss would have liked to inspect the guard's body, but they were so paranoid about what might happen if they didn't burn it immediately, she didn't ask. Captain Rees had asked again if she really wanted to go to the city and to his obvious disappointment Tammy had said she must. He gave her a tragic smile, as if she were already dead, before offering a half-hearted blessing.

It seemed that out here most had abandoned their religious beliefs. But in the face of such desperation Tammy couldn't think of much to be grateful for. It was a much shorter journey for her since she didn't believe in any of the gods.

At midday they stopped for a brief meal and a rest, but quickly got back on the road. Darkness came early at this time of the year and they needed to be inside the city and behind a secure wall before it was fully dark. It was also getting close to winter and it would be freezing if they were caught out in the open.

Captain Rees had been insistent about them finding shelter with one of the groups. No one had ever survived a night in the city outside one of the camps. He'd heard the screams but never found the bodies and when they came back the following night it was as if a stranger had taken up residence inside their skin.

Finally, after several hours of trudging along in silence, across a rotting, almost volcanic landscape of broken slate, grey rocks and gnarled trees, she spotted the city gates. The gates themselves were missing, presumably burned for fuel months ago. The surrounding decorative wall was six foot high in some places and as low as half a foot in others.

Art that had once been brightly coloured adorned the wall, depicting landscapes that made no sense, with trees growing from a sky with two suns and three moons. Animals that were predators and prey danced together with children, while nearby a crowd of people enjoyed a feast of roasted meat in the sun. Now, slogans of despair and warnings had been scrawled over the top, telling visitors to turn back and that the city was cursed.

Balfruss briefly glanced at the art and then at the sky. The afternoon was further along than they would have liked. It wasn't dark yet but Tammy guessed they had a couple of hours at best before long shadows started to form. Their pace had been slow due to the packs and the priests not being used to such long walks, but there had been no choice.

As they stepped beneath the stone arch and entered the city proper Tammy drew her sword. It was mostly for show, as fighting with the bulky pack would be nearly impossible. If the worst should happen though, and a fight became inevitable, she could cut the shoulder straps and be ready in a few seconds. Balfruss didn't draw the axe from his belt, but she saw him loosen his neck and carefully study their surroundings.

On board the ship he'd explained the necessity of being discreet. Not only with his identity but also his magic. Until they knew who, or what, they were facing and the nature of the threat, he wanted to keep knowledge of his abilities to a minimum. Throwing around a large amount of power would create a sound that anyone else with sensitivity to magic would be able to hear. It could even tell another mage exactly where he was in the city. That might draw unwarranted attention and at the moment they knew very little about what was waiting for them.

Tammy appreciated his caution. However, she wasn't sure that they could protect all of the priests in a fight without his magic. One thing she had learned on the voyage was that none of the priests were armed and violence was abhorrent to them. They would rather die than take up a weapon to protect themselves.

As they passed along a main street she glanced at the surrounding buildings. It looked as if an earthquake had struck the city or it had been under a lengthy siege. Every structure bore some kind of damage. Some had been reduced to rubble, others had gaping broken windows and roofs, collapsed walls and black smears of soot.

Looking at the buildings Tammy had never seen the like before in a city. Every one was slightly different from its neighbour. Tall thin buildings stood alongside what had once been magnificent domed structures, large enough to be cathedrals. Beside them was a row of squat single-storey buildings that couldn't have housed more than four or five people. Each looked identical but a closer inspection revealed slight differences. Stacked up outside each on the pavement she saw the remnants of dozens of metal chairs. The wire frame of several awnings hung limply from the front of many buildings, but the material was long gone. Tammy guessed they had been a row of taverns where customers had sat outside on the street.

Staring in every direction all she could see was desolation and more rubble. The broken fragments of once-grand buildings reached towards the sky like beseeching fingers.

"Do you hear it?" said Balfruss, cocking his head to one side.

Tammy listened and at first didn't know what he meant. After a few seconds she understood. There was nothing to hear. Nothing at all. No birds, not even the buzz of a fly, just the endless rustling of grit and gravel being stirred by the wind.

"Keep moving," she said, realising that they'd come to a complete stop.

Working from the landmarks Captain Rees had told her about, she led them to what should have been the first of the independent shelters. A large hole in the ground was all that remained. There were a few blackened stones, a faint whiff of smoke in the air and nothing else. No bodies, no bones, not even a stray weapon to tell her what had happened. There were footprints in the surrounding earth but too many to tell her anything useful.

She didn't need to say it. The others just looked at the hole and kept walking.

Balfruss stared at the crater and she saw a muscle twitch in his jaw.

"What is it?"

"This whole place, it's saturated with echoes," he whispered, so that the others didn't hear.

"Echoes of what?"

"Pain, mostly. Ever since we crossed into the city I've been feeling them, but they're getting stronger. The whole area is criss-crossed with layer upon layer of suffering and memories of torment. There are also threads of magic all over as well."

"Will you be all right?" she asked, concerned that they'd barely been in the city for an hour and already he was showing signs of strain.

"I can shield myself," he said, heaving a long deep breath. Nothing visibly changed except that the tension eased from Balfruss's jaw and his shoulders settled from being hunched up. Tammy wondered if this was what had affected Fray when he'd been sent to Voechenka before them. He'd not been trained at the Red Tower and didn't have the same experience as Balfruss. After another minute of walking he offered a brief smile and dropped back to guard the rear.

At the next possible shelter, this one belonging to a group of

mercenaries, they found more than a crater but not much. Two
of the outer walls still remained, but the rest had been toppled,
seemingly from the inside out, and then ground into fist-sized
chunks of stone. Where the front door should have been was a
massive hole that extended to one of the windows. It looked as
if something the size of several barrels had broken through the
thick stone wall like it was paper and then rampaged around
inside. It had thrown its weight around so much it had brought
the whole building down. There were large heavy prints on
the ground in some places, but they didn't belong to any beast
she recognised. Balfruss shook his head but also made a little
gesture with one hand, moving his fingers up and down. She
grunted but said nothing. More magic.

"It must be disappointing," said a voice from off to her left.
Tammy raised her sword and span around, one hand on the
straps of her pack. She could drop it and draw her dagger or
pull her shield from her back, depending on how many they
were facing. A lean man dressed in battered mail armour sat on
a small pile of rubble not far away. He was armed with a short
sword and dagger but currently was focused on eating a slightly
withered apple.

Tammy scanned the area around them but couldn't see anyone
else. Even so, there were plenty of places to hide. Behind walls,
inside the hollow remnants of buildings or behind piles of rocks.

"What's that?" she asked.

"To have travelled so far, and instead of finding shelter there's
just that," he said, jerking his head at the rubble. He grinned,
showing her an even set of white teeth, then went back to his
apple, taking a few last bites before swallowing the core and
throwing away the stalk.

"Do you know where I can find one of the independent shelters?" asked Tammy.

"Oh they're no fun," said the man, who she guessed was a mercenary. He had a certain swagger and she noticed small patches of rust on his mail shirt. No soldier, even an ex-soldier, would let their equipment get in that bad a state. "They're all pious and serious. You should come and stay with us. We're a lot more entertaining."

"I don't think so."

"You might like it," he said, waggling his eyebrows before looking her up and down in a way she was very familiar with.

"You're starting to try my patience," said Tammy, playing for time. Balfruss was slowly herding the priests together into a tight group while he took up a position on the far side of them. It wouldn't offer the priests much in the way of protection, but it was better than nothing.

"Ooh, then maybe I should be punished."

"Come closer and I'll be happy to oblige you," said Tammy, slipping her pack to the ground. She thought about drawing her dagger, but opted for a two-handed grip on *Maligne* instead. Mercenaries didn't have the discipline of a trained warrior, but they knew how to fight. It was better not to underestimate them.

"I think you should drop your weapons and be nice to me, then maybe I'll be nice back."

Tammy raised an eyebrow. "Nice?"

"I'll let you keep half of whatever you've got in those packs," said the mercenary, jerking his head.

"And if I'm not nice?"

The mercenary shook his head, before putting two fingers to his lips and whistling. Seven men rose up from the surrounding rubble, armed with swords and axes. All of them were hard-looking mercenaries dressed in mismatched armour of leather and chain.

"Is that it?" said Tammy. "Eight of you."

The mercenary was baffled. "I don't need more. There are only two of you carrying weapons."

Tammy turned in a slow circle to get a better look at the men surrounding her. Balfruss met her eyes and inclined his head ever so slightly.

She turned back to the mercenary. "I have an alternative suggestion. One you might find personally satisfying."

"You're a whole lot of woman," said the mercenary, "and normally I'd love to go somewhere private to negotiate, but this isn't a discussion. Time is short, so leave half of everything and go." All traces of good humour had now evaporated from his expression. Tammy noticed he kept glancing at the sky. He knew time was marching on and obviously wanted to be indoors behind a wall before it was fully dark.

"Stop playing games, Del," said one of the mercenaries. "Let's take it all."

"Last chance," said Tammy.

Del shook his shaggy head. "You brought this on yourself." He flicked one hand towards the others and stood up. "Take them."

As he was the most immediate threat, Tammy focused on Del. She rushed towards him, blocked a crude swing from his short sword and riposted with a slice that caught him across his other arm. Del hissed in pain and fell back, dropping his dagger. The screams of the priests turned to yells of surprise, and then came a peculiar silence followed by the sound of retching. Del's eyes widened and his attention drifted, giving Tammy enough time to move closer and slug him in the jaw. As he dropped to the ground she kicked away his sword and put her blade against his throat.

"Everything under control?" she shouted over one shoulder.

"It's all fine here," came Balfruss's reply followed by the sound of more vomit hitting the ground.

"Now, Del, is it?" she asked and his frantic eyes found hers. "You've one chance to be useful to me. Where would I find the independent shelters?"

"There's only one left," said Del, staring up the length of her sword. Tammy pressed the point of her blade harder against the base of his throat. "I swear. The other was taken a few weeks ago. We're down to six in total now. The rest are all gone."

"Where is it?"

Del gave her directions, gesturing with one hand. "It's not very far. You can get there in half an hour. Maybe less."

"Are you trying to get rid of me, Del?" asked Tammy. "A minute ago you were interested in something else."

Del started to say something but then changed his mind. He glanced at the sky again and a hint of fear crept into his eyes.

"Last question," said Tammy, easing the pressure slightly on his throat. "Did you destroy the other independent camp?"

The question caught Del by surprise but he quickly recovered. "No."

"Then who did?"

"The Forsaken," he said in a whisper, as if afraid they might hear him.

Tammy stepped back a little and glanced behind her towards Balfruss and the priests.

The seven mercenaries were hanging upside down in the air by one ankle. Each was held in place by nothing she could see, but a quick look at Balfruss showed her what had happened. He had one hand raised towards the nearest mercenary and as he made a slight twisting motion the man rotated horizontally on the spot. The others spun at exactly the same speed and in the same direction, as if they were partners in a peculiar synchronous dance.

"No, stop, please," gasped one man and then he vomited

again, spewing bile on the ground beneath him. One or two others puked as well and she heard Balfruss chuckle at their discomfort. Most of them were red faced from being held upside down, but there was nothing they could do to prevent it.

Tammy checked the priests and found they were a little shaken but otherwise unhurt. She got them all moving towards the shelter and Balfruss followed at the rear.

The seven men continued to spin on invisible hooks. "Hey. Hey!" yelled Del as they walked away. "How do I get them down?"

Balfruss didn't answer but once they were a few streets away Tammy dropped back to speak to him.

"How does he get them down?"

Balfruss's grin was a little vicious. "Oh, they'll come down in a few minutes."

"We need to hurry," said Tammy, moving towards the front of the line again. The sky was changing colour and hints of red were starting to creep in around the edges of the blue. Night was fast approaching.

CHAPTER 10

King Bowyn, husband to Queen Talandra of Seveldrom, had made the long and boring journey into the west and then southwards to Shael. By himself he could have covered the distance in half the time, but as King there were formalities that had to be observed. Plus he was required to travel with a certain number of guards for his protection, and then an assortment of people to look after him as if he were a child. On top of that were the hundreds of Seve warriors following on foot a day behind his party.

At times like these he missed the old days when he could just look after himself.

On the journey to Shael he'd been required to stop off in the capital of Yerskania and pay his respects to Queen Morganse. While there he'd also passed along a few letters from his wife, who had become good friends with the Queen.

Further south a contingent from Drassia met them on the border and as King it would have been rude to ride straight past them without stopping. What followed was several hours of conversation about trade and the price of silk from the far east. Eventually Bowyn managed to extricate himself before he was forced to set up camp for the night.

At least the journey was finally over. Now he had a few hours to spare and explore Oshoa, the capital of Shael, before the first of many tedious meetings.

One of the reasons for this trip was to bring fresh warriors from Seveldrom to Shael. The war had not only damaged the entire structure of the country, it had also decimated the population. In other countries the war had left scars, but it was always spoken about in the past. Only three years had passed, but here in Shael it was as if the war had ended yesterday.

As they were being driven out of Shael, the Vorga had burned and destroyed everything in their path. When Bowyn's party had crossed over the border it was as apparent as if someone had drawn a line on the ground with chalk. One moment the hills were green and the trees healthy. The next minute the earth was a blackened husk and the trees were nothing more than charred skeletons.

As he walked through the streets of Oshoa, Bowyn finally recognised something familiar from what he knew about Shael. It had been a country renowned for its architecture, art and creativity, and thankfully the capital had only been damaged a little during the conflict.

Impossibly tall twisted buildings stood alongside glass-domed houses that shone in the sun like monstrous gemstones. Riding through the streets Bowyn had seen numerous spires rising up above the homes and businesses. From pointed spires belonging to ancient churches, to narrow stone towers of learning, to blocky towers attached to schools of philosophy. The gaudy stood shoulder to shoulder with remarkable feats of ingenuity that didn't seem possible. It was a city of dreams where radical ideas were embraced and allowed to flourish in such rich creative soil.

Bowyn doubted anyone here was expected to follow in their

father's footsteps and take over the family business. Thankfully that was a long time ago and he'd managed to step off the path that had been set out for him.

At almost every crossroads there were fountains adorned with mythical beings so wondrous they must have stepped out of someone's imagination. Statues of famous poets, playwrights, architects and philosophers were scattered throughout the city. After such a long journey, even a short walk through the streets of Oshoa was refreshing. The shadow that had fallen across the rest of the country had been driven away here. The people were more wary and less welcoming than their reputation for hospitality suggested, but after all that they had endured he couldn't blame them. He also noticed the armed guards patrolling the streets gave the local people some comfort.

The wall surrounding the city looked new and more warriors kept watch at all hours of the day and night. The city was maintaining the illusion of being a place dedicated to higher thought and art, but he knew more troops were being trained nearby by warriors from Seveldrom and veterans from Shael. The country would not be caught again without a more sturdy defence.

Bowyn wandered into a large park at the heart of the city. For a time he was able to pretend that he was alone and not shadowed by four royal guards. There were still a few brightly coloured flowers on display but most of the beds were just patches of black earth. A light breeze stirred the trees and the branches rustled overhead as he walked along curving stone pathways.

At the centre of the park he found a small pond surrounded by benches. A few ducks pottered about on the water and a small boy was feeding them peas as his mother watched with an indulgent smile. It made Bowyn think of his own little boy back at home. Out of habit he reached for his tobacco pouch, but then scowled as he remembered it was long gone.

"Majesty," said one of his guards and, looking around, Bowyn saw a squad of six royal guards from Shael spread out around the pond. A moment later a tall burly Seve man strode towards him. Although they'd only met once before, Bowyn recognised him immediately.

His moment of peace was over. With a small sigh Bowyn stood up to shake hands with his brother-in-law, Thias, the Regent of Shael.

"Bowyn," said Thias, his grizzled face showing something bordering on mild disdain.

"Thias," replied Bowyn, not taking offence as he was used to it. He knew his brother-in-law didn't think he was good enough for his sister. It was the same with her other brother, Hyram. No one would ever be good enough for her. They had both made that abundantly clear to him on his wedding day, which should have been a wonderful and happy occasion. Instead he'd been threatened by each of them, at different times during the day, and told in explicit detail what would happen to him if he hurt their sister. Being told he would be buried where no one would ever find his body had made for an even more uncomfortable and tense day than he'd anticipated. Bowyn hadn't mentioned it to his new bride, mostly to keep the peace, but also because she could take care of herself and would've been angry at her brothers.

"Would you care to sit?" asked Bowyn, trying to be civil.

"I prefer to stand," said Thias, turning sideways to stare out over the pond.

"As you wish," said Bowyn, sitting down again and lounging on the bench as if he were still alone. Formality required that he stand as well, but Thias had practically turned his back, which was equally impolite. Tired of all the ridiculous rules Bowyn closed his eyes and listened to the faint quacking of the ducks and the small boy's delight as they huddled around him for more treats.

"How is my sister?" Thias finally asked.

"I left a stack of letters from her at your office," said Bowyn, not bothering to open his eyes. Perhaps if he stayed here long enough everyone would just go away and leave him in peace.

"I know. I was asking you."

Bowyn cracked one eye open and found Thias glaring at him. It was a struggle not to grin and he was only partially successful. "She's well, pregnant again and she thinks it will be a girl this time. I don't mind, as long as the child is healthy."

"On that we agree," said Thias, leaving out the unspoken part, but Bowyn heard it nonetheless. It was the only thing they would ever agree on.

Closing his eyes again Bowyn remembered a time during the war when he'd sat like this, pretending the western army wasn't out there ready to besiege the city of Charas. It had been a much simpler time, more terrifying, but most days he still missed the camaraderie and his old friends. Many of them had died during the war, and he'd not seen the others for years, but he still thought about them often.

"And how is your lovely young wife?" said Bowyn, watching as a nerve twitched in Thias's jaw. "Any news?"

He knew it was petty to try and get under his brother-in-law's skin, but he couldn't help it. Despite Bowyn's heritage and upbringing Thias thought he was nothing more than a common farmer's son. He had yet to meet the Queen of Shael but Bowyn had been told she was young, pretty and, after a few years of marriage, still not pregnant. There were a number of rumours swirling, that one or both were infertile, or that Thias preferred the company of men. Whatever the reason, the people of Shael were still without an heir, and now more than ever they needed some hope for the future.

Bowyn knew the truth from his wife, which was a very mundane reason about it not being the right time yet, but he enjoyed getting under Thias's skin.

"Maybe I could give you a few tips?" he suggested with a wink.

"Listen to me, you little shit," hissed Thias, looming over Bowyn, who just grinned at him. He knew Thias would never hit him as etiquette forbade it, plus they were both being watched by guards who would intervene. But just for once Bowyn wished Thias would do it. Ignore all of the chains of office and get into a proper brawl. He'd not drawn a blade on anyone in years and hadn't been blind drunk since the war.

Thias cut off suddenly and his expression changed, melting to neutrality and then something bordering on a smile.

"Good morning," said a warm and pleasant voice.

Bowyn saw a tall young woman with golden skin, brown hair and glittering green eyes. Her features were elegant and she moved lightly on her feet like a dancer. Even without seeing the additional royal guards he knew who she was.

Thias stepped back as Bowyn stood up and bowed deeply to the Queen.

"Your Highness," said Bowyn. "It's an absolute pleasure to finally meet you. Your husband and I were just getting to know each other a little better."

Queen Olivia glanced at her husband and simply raised one eyebrow. Thias cleared his throat and moved to her side.

"I'm sure we'll have plenty of time to talk later in an official capacity," said the Queen, "but I wanted to thank you personally for bringing more warriors to Shael."

"You're most welcome, your Majesty," said Bowyn, bowing again. "My wife and I take our debts and obligations very seriously."

Thias frowned, thinking it was a jibe at him, and Bowyn said nothing to dissuade him. Let him stew on that.

"I know it must have been a long and tiring journey," said Olivia, approaching Bowyn, who tensed as much as the royal guards around him. But all she did was embrace him. After a couple of startled seconds he put his arms lightly around her. He didn't know if protocol forbade it but right now he didn't care. Bowyn was half the size of the guards looming all around, but even to him the Queen felt small and fragile in his arms. The country was barely holding on and this slender reed of a girl, and her thick-headed husband, were all that stood in the way of chaos. "I'm so glad you came," said the Queen. "Our family is very small and it's so nice to meet another member."

It was a sweet thing to say and Bowyn had to bite his tongue and repress his first instinct to make a dirty joke. Before he could think of anything nice to say in return she gave him a kiss on the cheek and moved away.

Thias frowned at him and then followed his wife, leaving Bowyn alone with his bodyguards and the ducks. The boy and his mother had wandered away and now a comfortable silence settled on the pond. Bowyn stayed for a while, staring at the water and contemplating the road that had brought him to this moment. He'd often dreamed about his future, but not once had he seen this as a possibility. Shaking his head before one of his melancholy spells fell over him Bowyn set off for the palace.

This time, with his thoughts turned inwards, he barely saw the remarkable sights of the city. The next few days would be taken up with meetings that would soon run into one another.

After that there would be a formal banquet or two, although he'd been told not to expect great extravagance. There was little enough food to spare and the Queen was not about to waste it on a grand gesture. Perhaps it would be a simple meal with just a few guests. That would suit him and make it slightly easier to pretend he was somewhere else.

As he went through the front gates of the palace, his body-guards finally peeled off, leaving him alone to wander the halls. He passed some enormous paintings and curious glass sculptures, but right now he wasn't in the mood to study them. All Bowyn wanted was some time alone to be himself before his role required him to be that other person. There were times when he struggled to remember who he'd been before he'd put on the crown.

He unlocked the door to his room, went inside and locked it again out of habit. No one would come into his room without permission, but Bowyn had spent too many nights in places where you always locked the door and put a chair against the handle. You also slept with one eye open and a weapon within arm's reach.

"Hello, brother," said a familiar voice. Bowyn spun around, reaching for a sword that wasn't there. No one was allowed to carry weapons in the palace except the royal guards. Even if he'd had a blade it wouldn't have helped much.

The man sat at his table drinking whisky was dead. They'd watched him fall to his death from the walls of Charas during the war. "It's been a long time, Black Tom. Or should I call you Bowyn?"

Vargus looked exactly the same as the last time he'd seen him three years ago. It was impossible. It had to be a trick.

"You're dead," said Tom. "We saw you go over the battlements with two Vorga. I went to your funeral."

Vargus shrugged. "And yet, here I am. I see you've stopped chewing tarr," he said, pointing at Tom's teeth.

"The wife said it was a disgusting habit," he muttered, still reeling with shock. He'd not chewed any tarr in years and gradually the black staining of his teeth had faded.

"Sit down before you fall down," said Vargus, kicking out a chair. "Join me for a drink."

Vargus poured a second generous helping of whisky and topped up his own glass. Tom sat down and picked up the glass, but then hesitated.

"How? How are you here?" he asked. Vargus sighed and glanced away. "We searched for your body. For days Hargo and me waded through mounds of rotting bodies, but couldn't find you." Despite the early hour Tom gulped down a large mouthful of whisky. He felt it burn and then settle in his stomach but he couldn't stop staring at his dead friend.

"It's a long story."

"How did you even get in here?" asked Tom, glancing at the door. It had been locked when he came in and the corridors of the palace were always busy with people. Surely someone would have seen him. Then there was the solid ring of guards around the outside of the palace. It didn't make any sense. Tom took another mouthful of whisky but didn't feel it. For a while Vargus said nothing and just sipped his drink.

"I came here because I need your help," he said eventually. "Isn't that what we agreed in the Brotherhood? To help each other when we were in trouble."

Tom scoffed. "If you can come back from the dead, I'm not sure what help I can offer."

"There's something very dangerous nearby. I need your help to stop it spreading," said Vargus, putting his drink aside. Tom stared at him, trying to find some detail that would tell him it wasn't his old friend, but everything was just the same. From the greying stubble on his shaven head to the steel tooth. It was him and yet it was impossible. Vargus touched him on the shoulder, startling him, but it also proved he was real and not a spirit. "Are you listening, Tom?"

"Barely," he admitted. No one called him Tom any more. It was his middle name. He'd gone into the army using it so that he could remain anonymous and be treated the same as the next warrior waiting in line to sign up. It had served him well for years, but when he'd been called to the palace to meet his future bride everyone had called him Bowyn.

"Tom," said Vargus, drawing him back to the present. "Do you know what's happening in Voechenka?"

"A little. There's some sort of plague."

"It's worse than that. There's something ancient and powerful lurking in the shadows. And there's a chance that it might escape. Shael has a small garrison of guards patrolling the area, but it's not enough. They have a lot of ground to cover. Something might slip through the net."

Tom frowned. "What do you want me to do about it?"

"Send some warriors from Seveldrom to support the garrison."

Tom laughed. "I'm not sure who you think I am, but I don't have that kind of power."

"I thought you were the King of Seveldrom," said Vargus with a frown. "I thought you'd led warriors here to protect Shael."

"I did."

"If this thing spreads it will destroy the entire country. It will kill everybody and then spread from there across the west." Vargus was deadly serious and all of the familiar good humour was missing from his expression. The last time Tom had seen him like this was on the final day of the war, when the Vorga had swept over the battlements.

"I have some friends inside Voechenka," he was saying, "but if they fail to stop it, the responsibility will fall to you and your warriors to contain it."

Tom shook his head. "How would I even explain why the warriors were out there?"

"I'm sure you'll come up with a story," said Vargus, draining his glass and standing up.

"Wait," said Tom, moving to block the doorway. "You can't just show up after all this time, ask for a favour, and then leave again. Where have you been? How did you survive? Who are you?"

Staring at Vargus he saw a sparkle of the familiar warmth and good humour return. It danced in his eyes but then it drained away and behind the smile Tom caught a glimmer of a very old and incredibly powerful being. Tom tried to pull his gaze away but found he was locked into a staring match and in Vargus's eyes he saw the passage of time.

He saw history unfold and no matter what he saw, Vargus was always the constant. Years flitted past like seconds. Decades became nothing more than a heartbeat until centuries of time had passed before his eyes. He watched empires rise and then inevitably fall and in the background Vargus was there, watching and waiting. Vast mountain ranges rose up from the land, were weathered by time and the elements until they fell apart and became tumbled stones, and still Vargus was there. The weight of it all began to press down on Tom until he felt his mind buckling under the strain of what he was seeing.

As a scream started to rise up in his throat Vargus closed his eyes and the spell was broken. Tom collapsed to the floor, tears running down his face, his heart hammering in his chest and cold sweat covering his skin. Vargus patted him on the shoulder and then unlocked the door.

"What are you?" gasped Tom as he tried to swallow the huge lump in his throat.

"I'm your friend, Tom, and right now I need the Brotherhood to act."

Vargus opened the door but stood waiting for Tom to speak. "I'll do what I can," he managed to gasp.

Vargus's smile seemed to contain genuine warmth. "As I knew you would, old friend."

"Will I ever see you again?" asked Tom.

"Maybe, one day," said Vargus before walking out. Tom stared at the open door and didn't know if that was a good thing or not.

CHAPTER 11

"There's someone in the street," yelled Alyssa from the top of the wall.

Zannah thought it might be Roake again. Perhaps today she would put an arrow in his throat to shut him up.

"Who is it?" asked Zannah. Alyssa didn't reply or stop looking into the road. The grey sky was starting to turn black and the sun was rapidly sinking behind the horizon. It would be fully dark in less than an hour. Already huge shadows clung to the corners of the surrounding buildings like massive black spiders, eagerly waiting for prey to wander past. Although Zannah hadn't seen such creatures yet, it wasn't impossible, especially after what she had seen lurking in dark corners.

"Is it Roake?" asked Zannah, stomping up the stairs and drawing her sword.

"See for yourself," said Alyssa.

About a dozen strangers were walking towards them in a single line. A tall pale-skinned woman led the group and a bearded warrior followed at the rear. The rest were all dressed as priests and each of them carried a heavy pack. Zannah didn't recognise any of them but that wasn't unusual. Occasionally individuals or small groups of people were forced out of other shelters and came here seeking refuge. Sometimes it was because they were no longer useful to the mercenaries. At other times, because they'd run out of money, which had previously kept them in favour. Every now and then the mercenaries just got bored and kicked a person out to see what would happen. The newcomers were always desperate, hungry, and willing to do anything to get inside before dark. But Zannah suspected these strangers were something else entirely.

"Praise the Blessed Mother," said one person on the wall. "We're saved." Zannah frowned but didn't voice her disagreement. A dozen people, however holy, wouldn't change their fate. Besides, in this city of lies and despair, nothing good was ever given freely. If something looked too good to be true, it was.

The strangers waited until they were close enough to talk without shouting but they didn't approach the gate. Zannah gestured for the archers on the wall to string their bows, which they did, but only after Alyssa asked them.

"My name is Tammy Baker," said the tall woman at the front. "I was sent by the Queen of Yerskania to help you."

"You've travelled a long way," said Alyssa. "Who are your friends?"

"Priests, come to offer comfort and prayer. We've also brought food and medicine."

Tammy slid off her pack, reached inside and threw something up to Alyssa. She caught the object and turned to show the others. It was an apple. Normally it wouldn't be an extraordinary sight, but they'd seen little fresh fruit in months. Occasionally Alyssa found a few berries, but these had been fewer in number as winter approached.

"Careful," warned Zannah. "There will be a high price for such generosity."

Alyssa frowned at her but didn't disagree. They'd brought

people inside before who had turned out to be duplicitous. Three strangers had arrived separately over the course of a week and each had seemed kind and generous. They'd performed every task they were given without complaint, defended the wall at night and been polite to everyone. It hadn't stopped them killing four people one morning and trying to open the gates to a group of mercenaries.

The pale scar on Zannah's left thigh was a reminder of the true nature of people. No one was capable of real change, no matter how much they wanted it. Even a place like this didn't change a person at their core. If anything such conditions crystallised a person into something more pure. She'd always been a soldier, but in the past killing had been only a small part of that. Now she had become nothing more than a weapon to be used over and over again until it broke against the relentless tide of the Forsaken.

"That's generous," Alyssa was saying to Tammy. "What do you want in return for your gifts?"

"Shelter," said Tammy. Zannah watched as the tall woman glanced at the sky. They hadn't been here long but already they knew enough to be worried. "I have papers signed by the Queen of Yerskania and the Queen of Shael, but I doubt they'll convince you of our identity."

"You're right," said Alyssa. "Out here it's just fuel for the fire."

"I don't understand what you've been facing here, but you should know word has spread of your plight. Captain Rees told me a little, but I think you know more about what's been happening."

Zannah knew the name. Rees had been one of the fools from Shael who'd tried to set up a garrison in the city almost half a year ago. They'd come in with smart uniforms, gleaming weapons and good intentions only to be dragged down into the mud like the rest of them. Zannah knew that their camp had been overrun and was surprised to hear any of them had made it out of the city.

"We want to help," Tammy was saying, "but if we can't come inside then we'll have to try our chances with one of the other shelters. I'd rather not, given what I've heard they're like, but we both know I've no time to debate this with you."

"Are the other packs like yours?" asked Alyssa.

"Yes. They're all full."

They desperately needed the food and the medicine. Even so it was a big risk. The twelve men and women dressed in robes might look like docile priests but they could be killers. They could be anyone.

Alyssa looked towards Zannah for her opinion and she firmly shook her head. Other people on the wall made suggestions but ultimately it came down to Alyssa. The others had informally chosen her as their leader and they trusted Alyssa to look after them.

"One night for half of everything," said Alyssa. "If we don't like the rest of your story you'll leave in the morning."

Zannah expected Tammy to argue but she didn't.

"They'll have to climb up the rope," said Zannah. "We don't have time before nightfall to move the cart."

Zannah had been adding more stones to the cart, making it even heavier and more immobile. The wooden gates themselves were not very thick and wouldn't stand up to much damage, but the mountain of rubble made them immovable.

"Climb up," said Alyssa as the knotted rope was thrown down.

"It's been a long journey. I don't think some of my friends are up to it," said Tammy, gesturing at the weary priests.

The bearded warrior from the back of the line approached the gates and peered through one of the cracks. He whispered something to Tammy, who agreed and stepped back so they could see her more clearly.

"If there's anyone near the cart, can you ask them to step back?"

Zannah felt a cold prickle run down her spine but before she could speak she heard the cart begin to move. Magic.

The bearded Battlemage had one hand pressed to the gate while, inside, the cart began to lift up into the air. She'd been adding to the weight for ten days now and there must have been at least three tons of stone. He lifted it six inches off the ground as if it were weightless, moved it to one side and slowly resettled it with a grinding of stone. The wooden bars blocking the gate on the inside gently rose up, lifted by invisible hands, and were neatly stacked to one side.

The Battlemage pushed the gates open with both hands and stepped inside. Zannah rushed down the stairs in time to see the dozen priests come in ahead of Tammy. Zannah drew her sword, expecting the priests to pull weapons of their own from under their robes, but they just milled around looking tired. Only one of them seemed alert, and he was scanning in all directions and sniffing the air like a dog.

Tammy strode forward towards Zannah as Alyssa came down the stairs with the serenity of a queen descending to meet her subjects. A sea of surprised faces stared at the Battlemage with a mix of awe and fear. On the wall above, a few people still held their bows ready, but they didn't lift them. There wasn't any point. He could have blown open the gate at any time or toppled the walls, but had chosen not to.

"Welcome," said Alyssa, covering her surprise and shock better than the others.

"We meant what we said," said Tammy, talking to Alyssa but also including Zannah. "We're here to help."

The tall woman had the bearing of a soldier, but there was something else too. A keenness to her eyes. Zannah could see her studying the people, the building and its defences, taking note of it all at once. The Battlemage replaced the wooden bars by hand and then moved the cart back with his magic to secure the gate.

No Morrin child had ever been born with sensitivity to magic, but Zannah had seen a few people with magical talent in her lifetime. Using magic was like anything else. It required skill and discipline, and it cost the person a certain amount of energy. The more difficult the task the greater the strain. Yet when he approached Alyssa the Battlemage wasn't out of breath and there wasn't even a layer of sweat on his forehead. He was stronger than any she'd ever seen before.

"Who are you?" asked Zannah and the man offered her a toothy grin.

"My name is Balfruss," he said and a ripple ran through the crowd of spectators. Even the docile priests looked startled and one or two took a step backwards in surprise. Everyone knew that name. Before the war had ended, even here in this distant corner of Shael, she'd heard it whispered among the guards. He had changed the course of the war. He had slain the Warlock and stood alone against an entire army, which had withdrawn from the battlefield. A few people fell to their knees, praying and crying out in fear. One woman fainted and another wobbled on her feet.

Balfruss was trying to reassure everyone that they were here to help but Zannah had already stopped listening. It didn't matter who he was or even what he had done before coming to Voechenka. The only thing that mattered here was power. If he could do even half of what the stories claimed she had a glimmer of hope that they'd make it through the night.

While Monella and Liselle took stock of the supplies and medicine, the priests spread out around the building, tending to the sick, offering comfort and prayers to the rest. Despite Alyssa's friendly demeanour her experience had taught her to be suspicious of their motives. She wanted to trust the newcomers but couldn't, not yet anyway.

Zannah had urged her to place armed guards beside each priest but she'd felt that was excessive. Instead several people were keeping a discreet eye on them. Each watcher carried a pair of daggers but kept these out of sight. At the first sign of trouble, or any peculiar talk similar to what they'd heard in the past from the Forsaken, her people wouldn't hesitate to kill them.

Alyssa made her way to the top of the wall where Zannah stood with Tammy and Balfruss. They were both looking out at the city and squinting up at the sky. She noticed the Battlemage kept glancing at Zannah and a slight frown pulled at the corners of his mouth. He was probably wondering why a Morrin was fighting to protect local people.

"How many attack each night?" asked Tammy, studying their defences and the street in front. It was obvious just from the way she stood that Tammy had some professional military training. Zannah would be glad to have another strategic mind to work with on their defence. Then again they also had on their side the most famous and feared Battlemage in the world.

"It varies," said Zannah, resting one hand on the hilt of her sword. "Sometimes two dozen, sometimes more. They always come in waves to wear us down and they're always gone before dawn."

"Why dawn? Are they scared of sunlight?"

Zannah shook her head. "We thought so at first, but once someone has been turned into one of the Forsaken, they change and become nocturnal. They thrive in the dark and seem to prefer it."

Alyssa noticed Zannah hadn't told them the full story. How

she'd captured one of the Forsaken alive and staked the woman out in the street. When the sun rose they'd expected something dramatic, for the woman's skin to burn or for her to transform in some way. All she'd done was keep screaming and cursing them until Zannah cut off her head.

"How many defenders do you have?" asked Tammy.

"Surely our number don't matter any more," said Alyssa, gesturing at Balfruss. "Can't you just wave your hands and stop them all?"

"It's not that simple," he said. "Using a lot of magic is like lighting a bonfire at night on the horizon. Anyone in the city with magic would feel it. At the moment they don't know I'm here or what I can do. I can channel small amounts of energy and remain unnoticed, but I'd rather not alert them to my presence just yet."

"They? Who are they?" asked Zannah.

"You know that something in this city is twisting and tainting people," said Tammy. "We believe the cause might be magical in nature. I'm here to find out what or who is responsible for the Forsaken and where they are in the city. Balfruss is here to deal with the threat if it is magic."

"When the time is right, I will use the full weight of my power," said Balfruss. Alyssa smiled in an attempt to pretend she felt reassured. Instead an icy finger of fear traced its way down her spine.

Alyssa could understand their reasoning, but a part of her was disappointed. She'd hoped their arrival marked the end of their nightly imprisonment in this makeshift shelter and that life in the city could return to some semblance of normality. Despite everything that had happened to her over the last few years Alyssa was amazed that she still had the capacity for hope in her heart. She murmured a silent prayer of thanks to the Blessed

Mother for her continuing strength and knew that she would and could endure life as it was for just a little while longer.

"Tell me more about what we can expect tonight," Tammy was saying, but Alyssa's attention had drifted. As Zannah lay out what normally happened she felt as if they were being watched. Peering down into the courtyard she saw that people had started to creep out of doorways and were staring up at the strangers. She drifted down the stairs and a cluster of children surrounded her, their tiny faces full of hope.

"Is he really a wizard?"

"Is he going to save us?"

"Is that woman a giant?"

The questions were endless and Alyssa found herself smiling down at the children. Whether the arrival of the priests and the Battlemage marked the beginning of the end, or merely another chapter, they had already made a difference. Some of the children didn't remember anything except poverty and desolation, but now for the first time in their lives their eyes showed a sense of wonder. The possibilility now existed that they wouldn't always have to live like half-starved prisoners. Balfruss and the others had given them a glimmer of hope.

"Yes, he's really a wizard," said Alyssa. "He's the most powerful Battlemage in the world. She is a giant and together they're going to save us."

It might prove to be a terrible lie but seeing the unbridled joy on their faces was worth it. If the worst should happen, and the Forsaken did overrun their shelter, she'd make sure the children were taken care of. It would be quick and painless, which was far better a fate than what might await them if they were taken alive.

CHAPTER 12

Zannah wiped the blood from her sword and noticed a few more nicks on the edges. She'd need to sort those out during the day before the Forsaken returned.

Dawn was a few hours away but there was still work to be done before she could rest. The attack had been moderate in comparison to some in the past. Almost two dozen Forsaken had attempted to breach the walls. The tall Seve woman, Tammy, had proven to be exceptionally skilled with a blade and possessing a huge amount of stamina. Throughout the fight she had remained calm and perfectly balanced, severing grasping arms and taking heads off with efficient strokes that wasted no energy. Her sword looked like Seve steel but the surface had an odd sheen as unusual colours swirled across it. Whatever it was made from didn't really matter. Any weapon was only as good as the person who held it. The sword became a deadly blur in Tammy's hands and she proved to be a stalwart ally on the wall.

While Zannah had expected Tammy to be adept, it was Balfruss who had really surprised her. She understood Battlemages wielded magic and could summon the elements, but they were not known for being warriors. And yet someone had trained

Balfruss to fight with the wicked axe he always carried on his belt. It became an extension of his arm that he used with brutal efficiency, lopping off arms and splitting skulls like overripe fruit.

Tammy's abilities spoke of precision and skill learned over countless hours of practice. Balfruss's ability was less well defined but equally devastating. Normally Zannah had to kill almost every Forsaken who made it to the top of the wall, while the other defenders just kept them busy. With the three of them working together they made short work of those who scaled the ladders, while archers under Alyssa's guidance took care of the others in the street below. No one even came close to being taken and the Forsaken quickly retreated before they were all killed.

When the last of the dead bodies and bits of limbs had been thrown over the wall the others retreated into the main building. They never wanted to see what happened. Balfruss and Tammy stayed on the wall, their blood-spattered faces set in an almost identical grimace.

Alyssa went below and returned with the knotted rope that Zannah had attached to the laden cart blocking the gate. With a casual flick of her wrist, Alyssa threw it over the wall then took up her post with a bow.

Tammy and Balfruss followed Zannah over the wall into the street to inspect the dead and dying Forsaken. Balfruss squatted down beside one decapitated woman before shaking his head and quickly moving on to the next. A man with his left arm ending at the shoulder and the right at the elbow was writhing in the street. His neck was bent at an awkward angle, one leg was folded beneath his body and his spine was probably broken. The fall from the wall wasn't lethal but it was high enough to break bones. Zannah raised her sword but Balfruss waved her away.

"Why not?"

"Give me a moment," said the Battlemage, holding one hand just above the man's heaving chest. Balfruss closed his eyes and a strange prickle ran up Zannah's arms, making the fine hairs stand on end. Magic.

An itch started at the bottom of her spine and worked its way to the top before settling on her scalp. She opened her mouth to ask a question, but Tammy shook her head. Whatever Balfruss was doing he needed to remain undisturbed.

Balfruss lowered his hand and then sat back on his heels, staring at the man with a thoughtful expression.

"What is it?" asked Tammy.

"It's not what I was expecting," muttered Balfruss. "The Warlock used magic to enslave people by hollowing out their minds. They walked and followed commands, but they weren't really alive. This is different," he said, gesturing at the man, who was trying to get up despite his broken bones and missing arms.

"I think I recognise him," said Zannah. "I killed him a few days ago, but they took his body away before I could take his head."

Balfruss pursed his lips. "And once you decapitate them, they never come back?"

"Never."

"Something is keeping him alive," said Balfruss. "If it's magic I can't feel it, but there's something tethering him. There's an echo of something I've never felt before."

"I don't understand," said Tammy, and Zannah felt equally confused.

"Something out there is connected to him," said Balfruss, gesturing vaguely at the wider city. "I can feel something, but it's barely there. It's like trying to grasp a single strand of a cobweb blowing in the wind. I can feel it against my face, but I can't see it."

"Can you sense which direction it's coming from?" asked Tammy.

Balfruss shook his head, visibly agitated at not knowing.

"We can't stay in the street too long," said Zannah, scanning the nearest buildings. With the torches at her back the gloomy street was as clear as day, but the situation could change at any second. Another attack in one night was not uncommon.

Zannah moved up beside the injured man and, with a practised manoeuvre, she nudged him forward with one foot until his head was hanging forward towards his knees. Before the Forsaken could topple to one side she sliced through his neck, severing the man's head from his body. It slumped to one side and his shuffling feet instantly stopped moving. There was no delay, no final gasp or burst of activity like a headless chicken. The man died just like any other.

Balfruss knelt down beside the man and held his hand over the silent corpse for a few seconds.

"There's nothing there now," he said. "Whatever was connected to him is gone."

As Zannah moved towards the next twitching corpse Tammy touched her lightly on the arm. "We'll help," she said, meeting Zannah's gaze. "You don't have to do this alone any more."

Zannah didn't say anything but she pointed towards the next flailing figure. They took turns dispatching the Forsaken until the road was silent except for the sound of their breathing and the sputtering of the torches above the gate.

Tammy and Balfruss went up the rope first while Zannah kept an eye on the street. For once, when Zannah climbed, she had no fear of it snapping when she was halfway up. Alyssa was there as always, a sad look on her face as she stared down at the headless corpses. Her lips moved in an almost inaudible prayer as she gave each of them a final blessing. Before a sneer could twist her lips Zannah turned away and went down the steps to her room to catch a few hours of sleep.

When Balfruss woke up the next morning his lower back and shoulders were aching from carrying the heavy pack and fighting on the wall. After dealing with the dying Forsaken on the street he'd been shown to a small cell-like room where he could sleep. Zannah had explained that the attacks were sometimes hours apart and he would be woken at the first sign of trouble. The golden light filtering in around the edges of his door indicated it was a few hours after dawn. It seemed as if the Forsaken had only attacked the base once last night.

Taking a deep breath he sat up and slowly began to ease the tension from his muscles with a series of stretching exercises. He moved from one position to another, his mind focused on his breathing, but on the periphery of his vision he knew someone was watching him. When he came to the last stretch, reaching towards the ceiling with his hands before lowering his arms, he glanced at the door, which was now slightly ajar. A small boy of maybe seven was staring at him with a mixture of fear and awe. When he noticed Balfruss watching he squeaked and hurried away.

Balfruss scrubbed the sweat from his body and then pulled on a fresh shirt before picking up his father's axe. He knew it was strange to still think of the weapon as his father's, but he couldn't help it. He'd only been carrying it for a year and was still getting used to it.

As he stepped into the corridor Balfruss saw a few other people moving about. Almost all were local people from Shael with golden skin. Every face was thin from lack of food and their skin looked dull and lifeless. Nevertheless they seemed reassured by his presence. It was a refreshing change compared to how he'd been treated during the war.

On his way to the stairs Balfruss passed several doors through which he saw rooms identical to his. Each narrow chamber had been converted into a bedroom, but most were empty of people. He could smell baking bread and hear a rhythmic sound he'd become familiar with in the northern jungle. Someone was grinding wheat or something similar to turn it into flour. Further down the corridor he heard the murmur of conversation and the rattle of needles as people continued knitting an endless supply of gloves and hats.

Balfruss ascended two short flights of stairs and emerged into the courtyard of their shelter. He took a moment to study the buildings around him in daylight. When they'd arrived at the gates yesterday the light had already been fading and he'd not seen much beyond the gloomy corridors and the top of the wall. Now he could see the four short towers around him with their connecting wall. There was only one way in and out of the shelter, through the main gate, and each tower was only two storeys high. A set of stairs on each wall zigzagged up to the walkway, which was protected by a waist-high parapet. Several people were keeping watch on the wall, including Zannah.

Balfruss felt a chill and rubbed the skin on his arms through his shirt. It was a lot colder here than in the north and winter felt much closer. He should have worn his coat.

He glanced around for Tammy and Alyssa but there was no sign of them.

"They've gone out on a supply run," said Zannah, coming down the stairs towards him.

"Did the Forsaken return last night? Did I sleep through it?"

Zannah's yellow eyes were troubled. "No, they didn't come back."

Having spent time among the Morrin he was comfortable with her slightly wedge-shaped face and pointed ears, but he'd noticed everyone else here stared at her with open hostility. Given what the Morrin had done during the occupation of Shael he certainly hadn't expected to find one defending the camp. Zannah was aware how much they loathed her and did her best to hide it, but Balfruss could see the continuous tension in the set of her jaw and shoulders. She expected them to attack her at any second, to stab her in the back or maybe smother her while she lay sleeping. He wondered how many times they'd tried and failed.

"Can you show me around?" asked Balfruss. "I'd like to see the rest of this place."

"Follow me," said Zannah, leading him back down the stairs and along the corridor.

"What did this building used to be?" said Balfruss, staring at the identical doors. "I can't work it out."

A brief smile touched Zannah's face. "You'll see."

They went down another flight of stairs and Balfruss found an identical corridor to the one above. There were more people down here, sewing, grinding wheat, talking and just spending time together. A few children ran around but even here, underground and behind a high wall, the parents kept an eye on them. Not every face was local and despite the danger outside they were nervous of strangers. Here and there he saw groups of people who were obviously family but others had banded together regardless of their nationality.

Zannah led him down three more sets of stairs with identical corridors before they finally reached something different. The air was much cooler here and a short corridor opened onto a long and broad brick-lined chamber. Running down both sides of the room from floor to ceiling were racks filled with hundreds of wooden barrels.

A network of glass tubes and heating pans connected several barrels, distilling the contents into something more flammable to burn for fuel.

Long tables with marble surfaces lined the centre of the room where a dozen people were kneading dough. They didn't stop their work but a heavy silence fell until he and Zannah had stepped into the next room.

"This is the city's only remaining winery," said Zannah, leading him through a network of small chambers which had been converted into bakeries, storage rooms for food and bathing rooms. They passed six stone-topped wells beside which several men and women were drawing up water. "There used to be a dozen in the city, but they were all destroyed. I'm told the wine in each barrel is priceless. Now we mostly distil it to fuel our fires and keep the dark at bay."

"And to cure the sick," said a familiar voice that was slightly slurred.

Kai was leaning against a nearby wall with a bottle of wine in one hand and a slightly puzzled expression. His eyes were glazed and he seemed unable to stand up by himself.

"Have you been drinking, priest?" asked Zannah.

"No," said Kai, shaking his head a little too emphatically before taking a swig from the bottle. "Well, maybe a little."

"I need to check on the wall," said Zannah, turning her back on Kai.

"Thank you, Zannah," said Balfruss. The Morrin nodded, frowned in Kai's direction and marched away.

"I don't think she likes me very much," said Kai, gulping down some more wine. He frowned at the label and then turned it around to show Balfruss. "Do you know anything about wine?"

"No, not really."

"Pah. It's wasted on all of you," slurred the priest. "Take my word for it. This stuff is like silk on the tongue and they just leave it sitting around."

"I thought you'd be too busy curing the sick to get drunk," said Balfruss.

"I'll show you. Come on," he insisted, wobbling from side to side. They walked along a winding corridor before coming to another brick chamber lined with racks for barrels. Half of the chamber had been cleared and a temporary hospital set up with beds fashioned from the wooden racks. Several white-clad priests moved around the room tending to the people lying in beds. Another pair of priests sat and prayed with the patients. The atmosphere in the room was not what Balfruss had expected. He'd spent time in several hospitals over the years, as a patient but also visiting friends. Each had the same atmosphere. One that spoke of sorrow. This hospital seemed lively by comparison.

All of the patients were painfully thin, but there were no obvious wounds or any missing limbs.

"Everyone here is tired and hungry," said Kai. "They're scared and not getting enough sleep. They need food, plenty of exercise and sunlight, but most of them are too frightened to go up to the courtyard, never mind set foot on the wall. Some of them only take up arms at night because Alyssa asks them to. If it wasn't for her they'd all hide down here, waiting to be slaughtered."

"What are you saying?"

"They're broken people," said Kai, shaking his head. "Their spirits have been shattered. We brought food and medicine, but that won't help them."

"Then it's a good thing we brought priests," said Balfruss.

Kai raised one eyebrow. "Why's that?"

Balfruss stared at him. "Because faith might help restore them."

"Of course," said Kai, laughing and then gesturing at the wine bottle by way of an excuse. "Of course."

Kai tottered off before Balfruss could ask him anything further. He noticed one or two of the other priests glanced at Kai, or more particularly his wine, but they said nothing.

A strange feeling prickled the edges of Balfruss's perception. Closing his eyes he reached out with his senses until they passed through the walls into the ground. Sinking deeper he tried to trace the peculiarity but it wasn't until he'd been searching for a few minutes that he realised what was wrong. This deep underground, the earth should have been teeming with life, even if it was just small insects, but beyond the brick chamber the earth beneath his feet was dead. There was nothing at all. Not even the faintest whisper or pulse of life. Something had drained every drop, leaving behind barren and infertile soil.

Balfruss made his way back to the surface and then up the stairs onto the wall. He stood beside Zannah and reached out across the city with his senses. There was only more of the same. A total absence of life in all directions. Not one rat or insect crawled through the rubble. He could sense the other camps, but in his mind's eye they appeared as tiny oases in a lifeless desert.

As he came back to himself, Balfruss sensed something unusual about the Morrin beside him. There was a peculiar imbalance compared to everyone else in the camp, even the sick and injured. He briefly touched her with his magic, then quickly withdrew in surprise.

"What's wrong?" she asked, scanning the street for trouble. He explained what he'd found in the earth, mostly to buy time as he double-checked what he'd discovered about her.

"It's whatever has poisoned the people in this city," said Zannah. "First it twisted them and they became Forsaken, then it continued feeding, taking everything from the land. Alyssa tells me there are birds, fish and insects outside the city walls, but there is nothing here. Not one stray dog or a rat. Not even a cockroach."

"I discovered something else by accident," said Balfruss, choosing his words carefully. The few people on the wall had moved some distance away from the Morrin, but nevertheless he lowered his voice. "Something about you."

Zannah stared at him for a long time before replying. "What do you know?"

There were so many layers to her question. He wondered how much she blamed herself for what had happened to the people in Voechenka and Shael. Her question suggested she was carrying many secrets around.

"I meant about your people and magic," said Balfruss. Zannah's whole posture changed again. Her right hand dropped to her sword and he saw her balance shift until she was poised to attack. "I know why there's never been a Morrin mage and why no Morrin child has ever come to the Red Tower."

"How?" she asked.

Balfruss shrugged. It was a long story and she didn't need to know all of the details. "You're a Vessel, aren't you?"

Zannah took a few deep breaths before slowly easing her hand away from her sword. "No one outside my people knows what that means, let alone truly understands it. If any Morrin heard you say it, they would try to kill you, just for knowing such a thing."

"But not you," said Balfruss, hoping that she wasn't about to attack him.

"There would be little point in trying. I believe you could easily stop me with your magic," said Zannah. "Besides, even if you told someone, it wouldn't matter. No one is getting out of here alive. It makes little difference that you know."

"Will you answer a question about being a Vessel?"

"Ask," said Zannah.

"How old are you?"

Zannah grunted and turned away to stare out across the city. "Sixty-three years old."

"Your people can live to be four hundred. How much time do you have left?"

Zannah didn't hesitate. "Two months, maybe three."

No Morrin child ever developed the ability to sense the Source because all Morrin were inherently connected to it. Almost every other race developed the ability during childhood to channel a small portion of the Source. The Morrins' connection meant they naturally healed faster and lived up to four times longer than everyone else. They were continually being sustained by its infinite power. However, there were a few Morrin who not only understood the principle, but were able to manipulate it. Known as Vessels, these Morrin could heal themselves from what would normally be fatal wounds, but in return it cost them years of their life. Borrowing time from their own future to sustain them in the present.

It was just as he had feared. Judging by how little energy was left within her, Balfruss guessed Zannah had been continually borrowing from her reserve to save the lives of others.

"How many times have you nearly died for these people?" he asked.

"Twenty-seven," said Zannah.

"Is it enough?"

Zannah shook her head. "It will never be enough."

"If you want, I can try to restore you," said Balfruss. Zannah's eyes widened and she stared at him in amazement. "If it works you won't be tired and sluggish any more. You fought well last night, but even I could see your fatigue. When was the last time you had a real night's sleep?"

"I don't remember," said Zannah. "I'm up all night, sleep for a few hours after dawn and then come back to the wall."

She had been pushing herself harder and longer than anyone else to protect people who would see her dead. They cared nothing for her and yet without Zannah to look after them they would all have died weeks, perhaps months ago. She had been sacrificing herself for them over and over and they didn't even know it.

"They must never know," said Zannah as he took her left hand in both of his.

Reaching out Balfruss embraced the Source and then sank into it while maintaining his link to Zannah. He felt her tremble only once and then she held perfectly still. The muscles in her hands and arms tensed up and he could hear her breathing getting louder and louder. Her pulse began to race but it was already nearly over. Acting as nothing more than a conduit for the Source, a river of power flowed through him into the Morrin. It was so simple, like pouring water into an empty cup, and required little effort on his part. It made Balfruss wonder about healing in general and if such a technique would work on anyone besides a Morrin.

After a few seconds it was over.

Balfruss opened his eyes and stared at Zannah. He gently let go of her hand and immediately noticed a few visible changes. Her shoulders and back were straight instead of being permanently slumped. The dark purple smudges beneath her eyes were gone, but for some reason her hair still remained mostly white with a few black streaks. The skin on her arms was tight and the muscles beneath firm and lean. Her whole body had regained its youth and now Zannah had many years ahead of her again.

She took a deep breath, opened her eyes and smiled. It was a remarkable thing, beautiful and rare for the Morrin, especially in this place. All too quickly it faded as Zannah turned back towards the city and her terrible burden.

CHAPTER 13

After the first night in the camp Tammy managed a few hours' sleep, but kept waking up, which left her tired and grumpy in the morning. The first time she woke it was still dark and the rest of the building was completely silent. It took her a few seconds to work out where she was before she let go of her sword and started to breathe more easily. When she woke for the sixth time the first hints of light told her dawn wasn't far away.

Zannah was still on the wall keeping watch but everyone else had gone to get some sleep. She and the Morrin watched the sunrise together in silence, each lost in their own thoughts. Yerskania and her life as a Guardian seemed as if it belonged to another person.

An hour later Alyssa emerged, juggling three bowls of porridge sprinkled with nuts. She passed them out and Tammy noticed the surprised look on Zannah's face after her first mouthful.

"Honey?" she asked.

"We brought a few jars," said Tammy. "Does this mean we can stay?" she asked, gesturing at the bowl.

"It does," said Alyssa. "I think you genuinely want to help."

"We've travelled a long way to turn back now."

"I'm going on a supply run," said Alyssa as she finished off the last of her porridge, scraping the bowl with her spoon.

"I'd like to come with you," said Tammy.

"If I said I didn't need your protection, would it make a difference?"

"I'm not going to protect you. I need a guide."

"Let me get my pack and we'll go," said Alyssa, collecting up the empty bowls. When Alyssa had disappeared inside Zannah turned towards Tammy.

"Keep an eye on her. She trusts people too easily, and always tries to see the good in them."

"What about you?" asked Tammy.

Zannah's smile held no warmth and showed off her slightly pointed teeth. "I see the world as it is, not as it should be. In this place, all of the good has been scrubbed away. All that remains are base needs. People want what others have and they will do anything to get it. One day, someone will use Alyssa's heart against her."

Alyssa brought up the knotted rope attached to the cart and threw it over the wall.

"Were you a painter?" asked Zannah.

Alyssa shook her head. "No, but I did work with a few."

The Morrin grunted and braced the rope with both arms to stop it swaying. Alyssa scampered down with ease, leaving Tammy with no time to reconsider leaving her armour behind. Using both arms and legs she clambered down to the street.

"Tell me about Voechenka," said Tammy as they set off from the shelter.

"What would you like to know?" said Alyssa. Tammy could see she was pretending that being outside the shelter didn't bother her, but Alyssa's eyes continually scanned the streets.

Tammy did the same, looking for any trouble while also taking in the layout of the city.

"When did you notice people were going missing?"

"A few months after the war ended. That first winter was agonising. We'd survived the camps only for many of my people to starve to death because food was scarce. That was when we started burning anything we could find to stay warm. When people disappeared we assumed they'd died from starvation or frozen to death. But then they started to come back at night."

They walked down a narrow street and then across a broad square framed by once-grand buildings. One of them had been shattered, as if something had collided with the front wall. Tammy noticed Alyssa gave that building a wide berth. Looking at the sky and the position of the sun she noticed they were travelling west.

"Was there any pattern to who was taken or when?"

"No. People were vanishing from all over the city."

Tammy glanced to the east, but there was nothing to see, just shattered buildings and the remnants of a once-great city.

"What's in the east of the city?"

Alyssa scrambled over a large pile of rubble and hopped down the other side before answering. "Nothing, just more of the same, and then the lake."

"Is the water clean?"

"Yes, but few people risk trying to fish," said Alyssa. "Something in the water has been attacking boats."

Tammy stopped dead in the street and Alyssa slowed ahead of her. "What do you mean?"

Alyssa shook her head and kept her back facing Tammy. "In the other camps the mercenaries make people earn their place or they throw them out. Sometimes they send them out to fish.

A few make it back but some won't risk the water so they come to us for shelter. One or two go out onto the water and are never seen again."

Tammy made a mental note to look into that area of the city first.

They walked in silence for a few minutes before Alyssa slowed again.

"Up ahead is one of the mercenary camps," she explained. "They're crude and loud, but harmless."

Tammy raised an eyebrow but said nothing. It sounded like Alyssa was defending them, which seemed peculiar given what she'd just said about them forcing people to fish. Zannah was right. Alyssa's worst enemy was herself.

A few minutes later they came to a wide street with fewer buildings remaining intact compared to what they'd seen so far. A hint of smoke and ash tickled her nose and the dust in the street had been churned by many feet. As they came abreast of what she guessed was the mercenary camp, Tammy noticed signs of recent damage. The front door had been dented in several places and it looked slightly askew in its frame. Barred windows on the ground floor had been broken and she could see ash around all of them. The smell of old smoke was much thicker here and there were splashes of dried blood on the street. A battered wooden sign hung outside, its surface black and charred, but Tammy could just make out the word 'Bank' on one side.

"Hello?" called Alyssa. "Anyone there?"

Two scruffy and soot-daubed faces appeared near the roof, peering down into the street. "What are you doing here, girl?" said one of them, a bearded man dressed in a mail shirt.

"What happened?" asked Alyssa, gesturing at the building.

The mercenary sniffed and ran a hand across his beard,

smearing the ash. "They tried to break down the door, and when that failed they tried to smoke us out. They lit fires downstairs before we noticed."

"Did they get inside?" asked Alyssa.

"No, but they took a few people," said the mercenary.

"Less mouths to feed," said the other man, trying to make light of it but failing. His friend didn't look amused and his eyes kept wandering to the stains on the street.

"Be careful, girl," said the mercenary. "Something has got them fired up. I've never seen them so determined."

"Blessed Mother watch over you," said Alyssa. Tammy expected the mercenary to jeer or mock her blessing, but he just nodded and stared grimly at the street.

As they walked away from the camp heading steadily west Tammy rested a hand on her dagger. She felt as if they were being watched but with so many gaping doorways there was a multitude of hiding places. All she could do was keep moving, scan the street and hold herself in readiness.

"Do you know where the other camps are?"

"Yes."

"Can you give me directions?" asked Tammy.

"Yes, but why do you want to visit them?"

"I need to find out what they know. You said there wasn't a pattern when people went missing, but maybe there was."

"How will that help?" snapped Alyssa. An angry retort was on Tammy's tongue but she took a deep breath to calm herself down. Alyssa was under an enormous amount of pressure and had been living in horrific conditions for months. The fact that her humanity, and her faith, remained intact despite everything she'd experienced was miraculous. A short temper now and again could be easily forgiven.

"The Forsaken. Why are they taking people? What do they

need them for? Why do they take away the dead bodies? We know that once they're decapitated they can't be brought back, so why take them?"

"I don't know," admitted Alyssa.

"Someone or something is doing this for a reason. It has a goal and it needs people, we just don't know why. The other camps may know something. They can also tell me how often they're being attacked and when. It's all pieces of a larger puzzle."

Alyssa smiled and some of her good humour returned. "Even without a uniform, it's easy to tell that you're a Guardian."

At the end of the street was a stone archway that they passed through without any trouble. A short walk took them into the hills and Tammy felt as if an enormous weight had been lifted off her shoulders. She breathed more easily and the permanent itch between her shoulder blades disappeared. No one was watching them here. At a leisurely pace they checked traps and wandered beneath the trees or sat beside the brook.

Tammy heard something peculiar and it took her a few seconds to identify the source. A small yellow and blue bird flitted between the branches above their heads. Its song was mellifluous and like none she'd heard before. It was also the first animal she'd seen since entering Voechenka. The air seemed alive with noise from the sighing of tree branches to the babbling of the brook over stones. A dozen other sounds all around her spoke of life. It was so different from inside the shattered city, where there was only silence. Despite the looming presence of the cliffs in the distance Tammy felt incredibly relaxed in the woods.

"It's difficult every time I go back," said Alyssa. "Getting used to the silence again."

"Why did you stay in Voechenka after the war?" asked Tammy.

Alyssa's answer was simple and yet all too familiar. "It's my home."

It was one of the reasons Tammy had stayed in Perizzi after her husband was killed. It was all she knew. She had family there but barely saw them, and each time she did it only caused her terrible heartache for weeks. Being a Guardian was the driving force of her life. She needed to make sense of things and find answers in a world rife with chaos and disorder.

"You could go anywhere. Start afresh," said Tammy, not sure if she was trying to convince Alyssa or herself.

"I can't abandon my people when they need me the most," said Alyssa. "I'll see this through to the end, one way or another."

CHAPTER 14

A couple of hours past midday, once he'd regained his strength from helping Zannah, Balfruss set off to explore Voechenka. He chose a direction at random, opened his senses to the surrounding city, and let his intuition guide him.

There was a heavy undercurrent of dark and unpleasant memories running through the city, staining every building and brick like black paint. It stretched as far as his senses would go in every direction, on the surface and right down into the bedrock beneath his feet. Older memories were faint, and these were more familiar compared to those found in other cities. Voechenka vaguely remembered a time before the war with a mix of good emotions and bad. Overlaying all of those were recent memories from people who had lived here during the occupation.

Balfruss could sense the hatred, cruelty and echoes of the many vicious deaths that had befallen the population. A host of horrors existed just out of reach, flickering at the periphery of his senses, but Balfruss made sure he kept them at a distance. In addition to memories, a sea of restless spirits lurked on almost every street corner. He did his best not to focus on any of them in case they noticed his awareness of their presence.

He was amazed anyone still lived in the city. Even without being sensitive to the presence of so many shades and so much raw emotion, it would be affecting everyone. They wouldn't know why it was happening, or perhaps wouldn't even notice because it was so gradual a process, but tempers would become frayed and emotions brought closer to the surface. Arguments would become more common until the cycle of violence that had spawned such a reaction came full circle and there was more bloodshed.

Taking a deep breath Balfruss shielded himself mentally from all of the horrors that surrounded him, weaving a fine net of magic to keep the worst at bay. He could still feel the emotions and sense the spirits, but he no longer felt hemmed in on all sides as if walking through a crowded street.

After another hour or so of wandering, seemingly at random, Balfruss came to an open area that might have been a market at one time. Compared to what he had seen so far the amount of destruction seemed very mild, with only half of the surrounding buildings turned to rubble. There were a few scattered pottery remnants and shards of coloured glass, but no wood anywhere in sight.

"It used to be a market," said a voice off to his left. Balfruss turned his head and saw an older man idly sat on a pile of rubble. He wasn't surprised to see the stranger, who seemed equally at ease in his presence. The whole city was covered with traces of new and old magic and Balfruss had known that eventually whoever was responsible would find him.

The man was surveying the square with a whimsical expression. Somewhere in his fifties, with a grey beard, scraggly long hair and deep-set brown eyes, he didn't look very dangerous. Despite being dressed in only a grey cotton robe and carrying no visible weapons, he seemed at ease in such a dangerous place.

"What sort of market?" asked Balfruss.

"They sold pottery, little glass sculptures and wooden figures for children," said the man, staring into the distance. "All sorts of things. Very little remains," he continued, making a peculiarly elegant gesture towards the few pieces of broken pottery and glass.

"My name is Balfruss."

"Ah," said the man. "That explains a few things. My students call me Master, but you may call me Kaine."

"Have you had many students over the years?"

Kaine raised one shoulder slightly. "A few. Only one or two ever became anything worth mentioning."

"Was the Warlock one of them?" asked Balfruss, scanning the market square for the presence of others.

"Ah yes, little Torval," said Kaine, chuckling to himself. "Such a grand title for someone so young, and in many ways, so weak. He was desperate for approval and when I didn't have time to shower him with affection he was angry and ran away."

"Do you know what he did? How many lives were lost in the war?"

Kaine shrugged. "They're just flies, crawling on a carcass."

"I can see where his arrogance came from."

Kaine's expression briefly soured before he shook it off with another shrug. "The boy had problems long before he met me. All I did was help him in his quest for power."

Balfruss shook his head as he slowly summoned his will. "You taught dangerous and destructive magic to someone who was unstable. You're partly responsible for every death during the war."

"And yet the world didn't come to an end," said Kaine in a bored voice. "Every day more squalling babies are being born. In a few years' time, who will even notice the difference?"

Balfruss couldn't comprehend his apathy towards the war and its lasting effects. Kaine was totally indifferent about the thousands of people who had died in the conflict.

"Look around you, there's your difference," said Balfruss. Kaine glanced idly about the square but seemed unmoved. "And the Flesh Mages? Were they pupils as well?"

Kaine laughed in delight and slapped his thigh, but it made no sound and his mirth didn't echo around the empty market. "Another extravagant title for my students. The Talent is called skinwalking, not that it matters. It's difficult, takes years of practice, but the strong always survive."

Balfruss had the impression Kaine didn't care about those who had failed and died during their training. Transforming yourself to take on another person's shape would require a remarkable level of concentration and skill. Getting it even slightly wrong would result in something horrific and deadly.

"Then you are the one I seek," said Balfruss, readying his magic.

"Have you come to kill me? Are you going to punish me for my crimes?" said Kaine with a smirk that quickly slid off his face. "Do your worst. I've beaten stronger and better wizards than you, boy."

This time it was Balfruss's turn to smile. "I'm ready."

Kaine shook his head and laughed. "We're not back in the dormitories of the Red Tower duelling to test our strength. This is a game of Stones and my pieces are already moving across the board."

Balfruss said nothing. Instead he reached out towards Kaine with one hand, and making a sharp twisting motion, he severed the connection shattering the illusion.

Kaine had been projecting an image of himself and was currently elsewhere in the city. He claimed to be the Master and yet hadn't risked coming to speak in person. It was the same trick that the Warlock had used during the war.

The arrogant inner voice, which sounded remarkably like his father, told Balfruss it was because Kaine was afraid. The cautious voice of Thule told him otherwise. Kaine had recognised his name, which meant he was aware of what Balfruss had done during the war and, perhaps, elsewhere. Stories of his deeds spread from place to place of their own volition and any attempts to squash them had failed. Instead Balfruss ignored them and laughed in private when the mundane was twisted into a tale of heroic majesty with only a grain of truth at its core.

Kaine didn't know truth from fiction. He was being cautious and what would follow would be Balfruss's first test, to gauge his strength and abilities.

Four figures came into view from the four corners of the square. Balfruss had sensed them approaching for some time and now he stood in readiness. They were each dressed in a pale blue robe with a deep hood, making them anonymous. Extending his senses Balfruss tried to gain a measure of their strength and was surprised at how weak they were in comparison to himself. They were not what he'd been expecting.

With every passing second he gathered more information. All four were young, eager and desperate to please. If this were a game of Stones then these four represented Kaine's weakest pieces, meant to test his defences. They were also his opponent's most numerous pieces on the board. Even so, if you were not careful sometimes a pawn could kill a king and the game was lost.

When one of the pawns moved Balfruss lashed out immediately, forging his will into a solid block of force the size of two clenched fists. With a burst of power he threw it towards the mage who had started summoning fire in his outstretched hands. The block slammed into the man's chest and Balfruss heard a crack of bone. The first pawn fell out of sight.

The second mage had already hurled something towards him, a tight cloud of icy spears, forged by drawing moisture from the already cool air. Instead of attempting a shield Balfruss simply rolled to one side, added some of his own will behind the ice cloud's momentum and let it fly. The third pawn across the square squawked in dismay and was only partially successful in blocking the attack. Several ice spikes tore into its robe and Balfruss heard a woman's scream of pain. She stumbled backwards and then fell to one knee, taking her out of the fight.

Sketching a shield with his feet, a trick he'd learned from Ecko, Balfruss drew power into his right hand, creating an icy ball the size of his fist.

The fourth pawn's attack, a nasty net of swirling energy, rebounded off his shield and he retaliated by throwing the icy ball into the air in a high arc towards the second pawn.

The young man watched the trajectory of the ice ball while weaving a hard shield above his head in a panic. Meanwhile the fourth mage switched tactics and tried to bring a hammer of pure will down on Balfruss. Expecting something drastic and clever from the ice ball the young man wove layer after layer of shielding above his head, creating a dense net in a half-dome.

Using both hands Balfruss blocked the hammer with ease, and then pretended to struggle to hold it at bay. Instead of attempting something else the fourth pawn tried to apply more power behind the hammer and squash him. While focusing some of his will on these efforts, Balfruss drew the axe from his waist and threw it towards the young man. He was so intent on shielding himself from the ice ball, that he'd left himself exposed to regular weapons. Balfruss's axe slammed into his chest, flinging the young mage backwards and killing him instantly. Dropping the farce Balfruss applied more force to the battle of wills, reversing the hammer's course until it came down on top of the mage. There was a sickening crunch and then silence.

Only one pawn remained and she had several ice shards buried in her leg and arm. Balfruss made sure the others were dead before retrieving his axe and moving to stand over the woman. She threw back her hood, on her second attempt, and stared up at him with defiance.

He'd expected her to be young, but she was somewhere in her thirties with white Yerskani skin and jet-black hair cut in a bob. Blood dripped from the corner of her mouth and she had to spit several times before she could talk.

"You will never defeat the Master," she said in a thick voice. One of the icy spikes had pierced her leg, severing an artery, and he could see a pool of thick blood beneath her. More had soaked into her robe and her pale skin had taken on a waxy sheen.

Balfruss said nothing. He made no threat, asked no questions and offered no blessing. The woman's strength started to ebb and she flopped down onto her back. The anger faded from her expression until all that remained was loneliness and fear of the unknown. Her hand flopped out, desperately seeking something, and Balfruss took it in both of his. He squeezed her hand and a faint smile touched her lips at the human contact.

"I can't see," she whispered. "Why can't I see?"

"Rest," said Balfruss, and her head turned towards the sound of his voice.

"Daddy?" she asked. Her chest rose one more time and then it stopped. A final sigh escaped her lips and her eyes stopped blinking, staring on forever until he closed them.

Balfruss gazed at the woman for a moment before finally

releasing her cooling hand. He cleaned his axe, scanned the area for remaining traces of magic but found none.

Kaine must have known they couldn't beat him and yet he had thrown away their lives as part of a test. Balfruss hadn't been sure if Kaine's pupils were being threatened, controlled or just coerced into doing what he told them, but the woman's words had told him a great deal. They were true believers and it seemed they had free will. They were not mindless slaves like the Splinters.

It didn't matter now. There would be more where these four had come from. This was just the beginning. It was going to get much worse before it was over.

Chapter 15

When darkness fell Alyssa lit the two torches above the gate. She stared out across the city, waiting for the brief flares of light to spring up from the other bases. There was nothing else to see at night and the faint glimmers in the dark were reassuring. It told her that their camp was not alone.

Before the destruction of Voechenka she wouldn't have been able to see so clearly because the city was always awake. It was full of sounds from festivals, theatres, musicals, and artisans working late into the night. The city had throbbed with a pulse of its own making, forged from a thousand creative minds, each intent on turning their imagination into a physical reality.

Now, light was expensive and the darkness ruled. The streets were silent, the forges cold and the theatres empty. There were no more songs. Nothing was created and very little joy remained. Alyssa closed her eyes and murmured a silent prayer to the Blessed Mother to give her strength so that she might help others fight the darkness within and without.

"Come down, Zannah!"

Roake shuffled into view on the street below. The dead man looked even more dishevelled than the last time Alyssa had seen him. His clothes had never been clean to begin with, but now they were ragged with holes. There were dark stains on his chest and more down the front of his trousers. His golden skin was almost yellow and his legs wobbled as if they were stiff from lack of use. He wasn't like the other Forsaken. They never saw him with them and yet he had died and risen again.

"Is he down there again?" asked Zannah, coming up the stairs followed closely by Balfruss and Tammy. They were rubbing their hands together and she noticed their breath smoking in the air. Alyssa had grown so used to the cold in the last few years she barely noticed it any more. Part of her worried about what that meant and whether she was becoming numb to the world around her.

Zannah seemed different from this morning. Alyssa couldn't put her finger on what had changed, but she'd noticed the Morrin was more alert. Someone who didn't know Zannah might think her spirits were lifted by the new arrivals. It was a small mystery to unravel another time.

"He's just arrived," said Alyssa, gesturing at Roake. The others peered down into the street at the sad lonely figure pacing around.

"Who is he?" asked Tammy.

"He's no one," said Zannah. "He should be dead, but he won't stay that way."

Balfruss was staring at Roake and his perpetual frown deepened. "If he's one of the Forsaken, why does he look so sickly and frail?"

"We don't know," said Alyssa. "He always arrives separately and never works with them."

Roake stared up at them and the intense scrutiny of so many people at once seemed to unnerve him. "I'll be back!" he squawked and shuffled off down the street.

"Should I stop him?" asked Balfruss, gesturing towards Roake with one hand.

"Let him go," said Zannah. "He's an annoyance, nothing more. Save your energy for the fight."

Alyssa knew that wasn't why Zannah didn't want Balfruss to intervene. The Battlemage could have picked Roake out of the air and let him dangle like a kite. She'd heard what he'd done to the mercenaries who'd tried to rob them on their way into the city.

Zannah liked having Roake around because he served as a constant reminder of what she'd done. He was a physical embodiment of her guilt. Zannah could have killed him and cut off his head, but she'd never once gone down into the street with him.

"Put these on," said Zannah, offering Alyssa a pair of woollen gloves. Alyssa was about to refuse when she noticed she couldn't feel the tips of her fingers. "You can take them off later if you need to use your bow." Zannah shoved them at her again and Alyssa quickly pulled on the gloves and turned to face the street.

The cool air increased visibility across the city, and above their heads a plethora of stars glimmered like diamonds in the black void.

"You look tired," said Tammy to the Battlemage.

"I found who I was looking for," he said and then offered a wry smile at their surprise. "He was waiting for me."

"Who is he?" asked Tammy.

"I don't know where he came from, but Kaine has been in Voechenka for many years. He was here before the war and the fall of the city. He taught the Warlock and the Flesh Mages."

Alyssa saw Tammy frown at the mention of the Flesh Mages, so it obviously meant something to her. Everyone knew who the Warlock was and what he'd done. Oddly, the people of Shael didn't blame him or even Taikon, the Mad King, for what had happened to them during the war. The Morrin and Vorga were the ones who had held the weapons.

"Kaine sacrificed four of his own students," Balfruss was saying. "He wanted to see how I fought. He even said our struggle would be like a game of Stones."

Tammy mused on his words for a minute while Zannah kept watch on the street. Even so, Alyssa knew she was listening just as intently.

"Do you play Stones?" asked Tammy, and Balfruss inclined his head. "What do you think he will do next?"

"Test me again, with stronger pieces using different tactics," said Balfruss. "He came at me directly. Next time it will be unexpected and more difficult."

"Do you think you can defeat Kaine?" said Tammy.

Balfruss didn't respond for a long time. "I'm not sure," he said eventually. "I know he's ruthless, incredibly skilled and he has learned many lost magical Talents. How do you prepare for the unexpected?"

"If you need my help, you just have to ask," said Tammy, touching the hilt of her sword.

Much to Alyssa's surprise Balfruss smiled. "I'm grateful. You remind me of an old friend from back home, Vannok Lore. There's no one I trust more to watch my back."

"I'll take being compared to a big hairy Seve as a compliment," said Tammy, with a wry smile. It was the first time Alyssa had seen either of them look vaguely happy since they'd arrived, but their smiles faded all too quickly.

"I think I'll need your help before long," said the Battlemage. "But what about you? Did you discover anything useful today?"

"No. I searched the eastern part of the city, but found no trace of the Forsaken. The largest buildings seemed the most likely hiding places, but they were all empty. The Forsaken must be hiding somewhere else. Beyond that I need to know more, about where it all started and how it spread. Alyssa told me where to find the mercenary bases, so I'm hoping someone there can help me, although getting inside is going to be tricky. I need something to barter with."

Zannah turned away from the street to stare at Alyssa and raised one eyebrow. "You didn't tell her?"

"No, not yet," said Alyssa. "I didn't have time."

"I found time to show the Battlemage," said Zannah. "You can show her."

"Show me what?" asked Tammy, turning her scrutiny on Alyssa.

"I'll stay up here," said Balfruss with a chuckle. "We'll send word if anything happens."

Alyssa gestured for the big warrior to follow her and she led the way down through the first two corridors where most people slept. She lit a lantern and passed another to Tammy before setting off. The steps were unforgiving and she couldn't afford to fall and break a limb or, worse, snap her neck.

As they descended deeper into the earth the temperature dropped and she avoided touching the stone walls as much as possible. When they reached the wine cellar their meagre light didn't even reach a third of the length of the cavern.

"Do you have any bottles?" asked Tammy, eyeing the stacks of barrels. "Because I don't fancy carrying one of these across the city."

"We have hundreds."

"It's perfect. The wine is worth more than gold."

Money no longer had any value. Not in this city at least. In a place shrouded in nightmares people did their best to forget. In the beginning a few had sought peace in oblivion, by taking their own lives and that of their families. Alyssa had seen a few of them after they returned as one of the Forsaken. The misery etched on their faces could not be erased by any nonsense about it being a blessing, nor could the horror in their eyes at finding themselves alive again. Part of Alyssa liked to believe that when Zannah took their heads and they died a second time they found some form of peace.

Drugs to expand the mind had been popular with some artists, but much had been destroyed with the city. That left only sex and alcohol to help people forget the world around them, and the former never lasted for very long. After a few months alcohol was becoming as scarce as food and since moving to the winery Alyssa had considered trading wine for supplies with the mercenaries. Unfortunately the risk was too great despite them having so much to spare.

"You'll need to be careful," warned Alyssa. "If they realise we have all of this, it won't just be the Forsaken we'll have to worry about. The other bases will tear down our walls ahead of them."

"That's good advice," said Tammy, her voice echoing in the dark. "Can you choose something fairly plain? Then I can tell them I brought it with me from outside."

"In the morning," said Alyssa, not liking how their shadows danced across the wall. "Let's go back upstairs."

By the time they got back to the surface and then climbed the stairs, several more people had joined Zannah and Balfruss on the wall. All of them looked worried, but when Alyssa looked into the street she saw nothing to cause alarm. It took her a minute before she realised what was amiss. There was nothing to see. Roake had fled but no one had followed in his wake.

"What's wrong?" asked Tammy, scanning for danger.

"It's already late and no one has attacked us."

"When was the last time that happened?" asked Balfruss.

"I don't remember," said Alyssa. "The Forsaken always come. Every night. Even if we only see them on their way somewhere else, they're always here."

"What does it mean?" asked someone else on the wall.

Alyssa wished she had an answer. Some would take it as a good sign, others as an omen of ill tiding. Further along the wall Zannah met her gaze and then glanced significantly at Tammy and Balfruss. She knew what the Morrin was thinking. That despite all the food and medicine they'd brought to the camp, and their efforts last night against the Forsaken, they were to blame for this.

Alyssa wanted to disagree, but their arrival coincided with a distinct change in behaviour. A small voice inside told her it was a good thing, to hold on to hope, but the louder voice was afraid.

Chapter 16

As he stared into the glowing heart of the campfire Tom pretended that nothing had changed since the war. He was just another warrior in the army. Just another sword who had answered the King's call and signed up to do the right thing. During the war it had been about fighting for his home and country. Now the war was done, but the echoes were still being felt and the people of Shael needed protection. Raiders, mercenaries and even some locals who'd gone mad on power, were trying to make little kingdoms of their own. They didn't respect the crown or the law and something needed to be done.

That was some of what he'd said to those in the army when he'd asked for volunteers to travel all the way here. Knowing what they were fighting for made it a lot easier than just having your name drawn at random.

No matter how just the cause, coming to Shael meant months away from home, and that was tough for those with families. It was bad for those left behind as well. Not knowing. Waiting to hear if their loved one would come back on their feet or if they'd just get a letter. So far Tom had not written many of those, as the bandits were desperate but no match for well-armed and well-fed veterans of the war.

Making speeches was just another part of his new life. Normally he didn't mind giving them, but today was different.

Given his role during the war, it made perfect sense. He could relate to the soldiers, since he'd stood beside them on the front line. He had the scars and the stories to prove it. Tom had also been part of Vargus's unit and had fought beside the man everyone said was responsible for starting the Brotherhood. The old bastard had never wanted that. He'd told them not to keep his name mixed up with it, and for a time they'd separated the two. But then he'd gone and died on the wall, and that was that. His name and the Brotherhood became the same thing.

Now Tom wasn't sure what to think. Vargus had died and yet he was alive again. He was also something inhuman and timeless. It was days after his encounter with the old warrior in Oshoa and yet the vision he'd seen still haunted him.

"They're ready for you," said one of Tom's royal guards. So much for pretending.

The warriors from home were all assembled. They'd been here for a few months and this was supposed to be where he gave them the good news. They were going home. That was what he was supposed to say.

Tom didn't like it but he had to stand on top of a couple of boxes to be seen by everyone in the crowd. There were a lot of tall Seve men and women from home. The sea of faces in front of him all blurred into one. Each of them was different, but they all had the same look. They were veterans. Toughened by the war or just by their time here. Even those who'd signed up after the war and come to Shael on their first posting weren't fresh faced any more. They were lean and hard, like old leather. Food was scarce, and not even the work they'd been doing entitled them to double portions. Tom felt the weight of their eyes on him and he stared back unafraid, showing them that despite his fancy title and rank, they were still the same.

"I'm supposed to make a speech about duty," said Tom, pitching his voice so it carried to those at the back. "About how you've served your Queen well and done a good thing for the people here. I'm supposed to say a lot of nice things so you can go home proud, but I can't."

Tom sensed his royal guards shifting restlessly beside him. They didn't like it when he didn't follow the script.

"Why not?" someone asked.

"Because I need your help. It's not fair, given what you've all been through, but it has to be done."

It sounded like a confession. As if he'd been caught stealing and needed an alibi from a friend. Something in his words, or perhaps his face, communicated a different message to those in the crowd. A tense silence settled across them and once more he felt the combined weight of their eyes resting upon him.

"I'm not here as your King. I'm here as someone who fought on the wall during the war. I was there at the beginning, when Benlor first gave it a name, and I was there at the end. I saw him die." Tom was still looking at the crowd but now he was seeing the past again. That awful feeling of helplessness swept over him as once more Vargus went over the battlements and he was too far away to help.

"I need the Brotherhood."

"You have it," said a familiar voice, bringing Tom out of his reverie. It took a few seconds but eventually he realised he wasn't still lost in memory. The past and the present collided as he stared at his old friend. It was Hargo.

"What's the matter, rich boy? You look like you've seen a ghost," said the big man with a grin. He looked exactly the same. A silver ring in each ear and that same cursed Yerskani cleaver hanging from his belt. He'd diced up so many with it during the war that after a while Tom had stopped counting.

"I've seen plenty of those," Tom finally managed to mutter. "Did you mean it? Will you help?"

"It's what we agreed, isn't it?" said Hargo. "To help each other."

"It's a bad situation," warned Tom, raising his voice so the whole crowd could hear him again. "I won't hold it against any that don't want to come. You can rest here until it's done, one way or the other."

"It's all right, Tom," said Hargo, clapping him on the shoulder. "They might not have been there at the start, but everyone here is my brother. Where are we going?"

"Voechenka."

A shadow passed across Hargo's face and he nodded grimly. "I thought so. We've heard stories. Who's with me?" he bellowed at the gathered soldiers.

Moving as one the crowd stepped forward.

CHAPTER 17

The following morning, with a cool winter sun on her back, Tammy travelled west towards the first mercenary camp. It was still early, but no one in the city slept much and most of their camp had been awake when she left.

Alyssa had insisted on coming with her, but before they'd left the winery Tammy made her promise she wouldn't go inside the mercenary camp.

From the way she'd spoken about them, Alyssa didn't really understand what kind of men and women they were. She wouldn't truly know the mercenaries until she'd been in a tight spot with them. Long before she'd been a Guardian of the Peace in Perizzi, Tammy had dealt with their kind, and worse.

It was likely a few were half decent, but the rest had made coin their master and the bedrock of their faith. Protecting their own skin and the money in their pocket were the only things they really cared about. Not one of them would think of anyone else when things became difficult, but Alyssa thought otherwise. Tammy hoped she never had to find out the hard way.

"If you see anyone being abused—"

"I can't interfere," said Tammy, cutting Alyssa off. "I'll be outnumbered twenty or thirty to one. Starting a fight will only make things worse. Going in like this will be delicate enough as it is."

"I wasn't going to say that."

"But you still want me to offer the people something," said Tammy, and Alyssa's jaw tightened. It was the reason she could never be allowed to see the inside of another camp. At the very first sign of abuse Alyssa would intervene, even if it cost her own life.

"Offer them shelter with us," insisted Alyssa. "We've had others come to us from time to time, but only out of desperation. Let them know there is something better. They don't have to be slaves. They need to know they'll be safe with us."

Tammy kept scanning the street as they talked. It wasn't only the Forsaken she was worried about. "The food we brought will help for a while, but it won't last forever. If I tell every person they can stay at the winery, how will we feed them?"

"The Blessed Mother will provide," said Alyssa, grabbing Tammy gently by the arm. "Offer them sanctuary."

The look in her eyes told Tammy everything she needed to know. Alyssa's faith, even in this terrible place, was unshakable. Nothing would change her mind.

"I will make the offer," promised Tammy. Only then did Alyssa let go of her arm.

A few minutes later they arrived outside the mercenaries' camp. The smell of smoke had faded since their last visit, but soot still covered a large portion of the brickwork. Behind the bars on the ground floor the windows had been boarded up. The front door was more dented, but it had been reset in its frame and there were a number of fresh scratch marks on its surface. It looked as if some massive beast had tried to claw its way into the building. If she were in the mercenaries' position Tammy would have bricked up the door and all ground-floor windows from the inside. As they drew closer she could see solid brick behind the door through some of the holes. Perhaps they'd make it through the night after all.

"Hello?" said Alyssa, calling up to the roof.

Less than a minute later three bearded faces appeared. All three men were dressed in mail or leather armour and Tammy could see each carried a weapon. All three looked worn out, dirty and hungry. Even so, there was still a glimmer of defiance in their eyes.

"Back again already?" chuckled one of the mercenaries. "Just couldn't stay away."

"It must be your smile, Graff," said one of the others. "It's what gets me out of bed in the morning."

They were putting on a good show with their banter, but Tammy could see the strain of maintaining the charade was beginning to show. Their eyes darted up and down the street several times, even during their brief conversation with Alyssa. They were scared and exhausted.

"My friend would like to come inside," said Alyssa. "Just for a short visit."

The three mercenaries studied her closely and Tammy met their gaze evenly. She expected a bit of leering but saw none. Their eyes were cold and calculating. They were trying to work out how much of a threat she posed.

Zannah was right. This city had stripped away much of the gristle and fat, leaving behind only the meat and bone. It reduced a person to their most basic parts. Tammy wondered what they saw when they looked at her. Did she still carry the mantle of a Guardian? Or had it already been scraped away? Did they see something familiar in her face? Did they see her as an easy target or a threat?

"Why do you want to come in?" asked one of the mercenaries.

Tammy shrugged. "I just want to talk to a few people. An hour of time where I can talk to anyone. In return you get what's in here," she said, pulling the heavy pack off her shoulder. A few bottles inside clanked together loudly enough for the mercenaries to hear.

"What have you got there?" asked Graff, although he clearly already knew, as Tammy could see him licking his lips. She opened her pack and took out one of the eight bottles of wine she'd decanted from a barrel. She knew nothing about wine but had been told by one of the locals it was a full-bodied red. It was also sold abroad so Tammy hoped they wouldn't speculate about its origin. Then again, looking at their faces Tammy didn't think they'd be able to tell the difference.

"Eight bottles, for an hour," said Tammy, holding up the bottle. She tilted it from side to side, the wine clinging to the glass, so that they could see it wasn't just coloured water.

The three mercenaries conferred briefly but Tammy knew it was only for show. She sent Alyssa away even before they'd finished.

"You'll have to climb up," said one of the mercenaries. Tammy had been expecting that, which is why she'd left her armour and sword back at the winery. She didn't need the extra weight on top of the bottles.

A knotted colourful rope, made from several pieces of carpet sewn together, was thrown down.

"Careful," said Graff as she was halfway up the front of the building. Tammy was under no illusions that he was concerned for her health. He just didn't want her to slip in case the bottles shattered in the fall.

When she reached the top, Graff moved to help her up but she stopped him with a look. He backed away slowly with hands raised until she pulled herself onto the roof.

Unlike the winery, there had not been any access to the roof of the bank and they'd had to improvise. Looking around her, she could see that several crossbeams had been taken out and patched with a wide assortment of material. Roughly sawed-off joists protruded, like the ends of broken bones. A hole had been ripped in the middle and a network of metal slats criss-crossed the roof, to make it more secure.

"One hour for the wine," said Tammy, standing up slowly. The mercenaries frowned slightly as she towered over them by at least six inches. "A fair trade and then I'm gone. I'm holding you three to it, understand?"

She casually rested a hand on the dagger at her waist. Her sword was back at the winery, but Tammy had three daggers on her person. Only a fool went into unfamiliar territory without any weapons.

The mercenary called Graff took the hint and nodded in understanding. The other two were not far behind in accepting her terms. If they tried anything she would gut them.

"Done, but one of us goes with you," said Graff.

It was a smart move and something she'd been expecting. Tammy consented by taking out a bottle and pulling the cork with her teeth. She offered the wine to Graff, who grunted and took a long pull. He closed his eyes and sighed with pleasure before passing it on to the others.

"So, how long have you been here in the bank?" said Tammy, handing over the pack.

"Couple of weeks now," said Graff, moving to the edge of the roof. "Our last place was bigger, but not nearly as secure. We lost a lot of people."

The other two mercenaries disappeared into the building with the wine. It would keep them distracted for a while, and before they even thought about double-crossing her she would be long gone.

"That's a story I keep hearing," said Tammy. "Now that there are only a handful of camps each is getting attacked every night."

Graff grunted and started pulling up the rope. "Then we're the lucky ones. They don't attack us every night, but we can always hear them, scurrying around in the dark. Sometimes there's only one or two and they just come and watch."

Tammy raised an eyebrow. "They watch?"

Graff was neatly folding the rope and seemed to be concentrating on it, but Tammy thought he was avoiding eye contact. "It's always people we used to know, before they were changed. They just stand there on the street for hours, out of range, otherwise we'd shoot them. They never say anything, never move, just watch. The first time it happened I thought it meant a big attack was on the way. Every now and then they show up when it gets dark, and stare at us. The others pretend it doesn't bother them or that it doesn't mean anything, but I think the Forsaken are just waiting."

"Waiting for what?"

Graff finished with the rope and went back to staring at the city. "For us to drop our guard. Maybe fall asleep. Maybe the one time we do that they will swarm this place."

"So you stay up and stare right back at them."

"Every time," said Graff with a hint of pride. "I might get taken one of these nights, but it won't be in my sleep."

Like everyone else in the city, Graff was pale with hollow cheeks from a lack of decent food and shortage of sleep. The shadows under his eyes were so purple they were almost black and he smelled ripe. He was determined never to be caught unawares but Tammy knew no matter how tough a person was, everyone had their limit.

"Do you ever talk to the other camps?" asked Tammy, after the silence had stretched out for a while.

"Why would we do that?" asked Graff. "Those bastards would only try to steal our food or kill us."

Tammy sensed a partial lie. "But you keep an eye on them, don't you?"

Graff shrugged. "We know where they are, but we keep our distance. If one of our squads sees one of theirs during the day, we walk away. That's the only agreement we all made without speaking."

"I'd like to speak with a few people inside," said Tammy.

"Give me a minute." Graff went down into the building and his two friends came up to the roof to keep watch.

At the bottom of a roughly fashioned ladder Tammy found herself on the top floor of a once-grand building. The black lacquered hardwood floors were now grimy from mud and an assortment of filth from many people living together in a small space. Grand metal railings twisted into fanciful designs on every floor were now decorated with damp clothes drying in the fetid air. A heavy miasma of unwashed bodies and partly cooked food flooded Tammy's nose. It hung in the air like a cloud and she had to breathe through her mouth for a few minutes until she adjusted to the smell.

"Ripe, isn't it?" said Graff. "You get used to it."

Peering into a few rooms Tammy saw a lot of what she'd initially expected to find in Voechenka. In a place where money meant nothing, people had to earn their place in the camps in a variety of other ways.

In one room she saw a lanky mercenary sitting on a mountain of grimy pillows like a king idling on a throne. Arranged around him were several almost-naked women, each wearing only a scrap of cloth across their hips. All of them looked cold and were bone thin, but their needs didn't seem to matter. One knelt behind the mercenary gently brushing his hair while two more rubbed oils into the skin on his hands and forearms. In one corner another sat polishing his sword and yet another was furiously working to clean the rust from his armour. The room stank of sex and body oil.

In another room she saw several local people huddled together while a mercenary held a collection of sticks towards them with one hand.

"They can't fight, so whoever draws the shortest straw goes out to scavenge for food," explained Graff with a shrug. "It's either that or they earn their keep in some other way," he said, jerking a thumb towards the mercenary and his harem.

"Give me a minute with them," said Tammy, stepping into the room with the huddled group of locals. The mercenary looked at Graff for guidance and then up at Tammy. She could practically hear what he was thinking and she grinned, daring him to try.

"We've made a deal," said Graff, a note of warning in his voice. "There's some wine if you want it."

Tammy kept her eyes on the man and one hand on her dagger until he'd moved downstairs.

After asking the local people a few questions it became clear that they knew very little about the murders or where the Forsaken had come from. There was a general consensus that it had started after that first winter, but no one knew more than that.

As she'd promised Alyssa, Tammy made them an offer of sanctuary in return for nothing. As expected they didn't believe her. It had to be a trick to tempt them into a situation worse than they currently endured. Tammy attempted to reassure them that the offer was genuine but they remained unconvinced.

In other rooms she found more groups of wan locals performing a variety of tasks to earn their keep. Each time the answers they provided were vague. After all that they had endured over the last few years most were keen to forget the recent past.

Tammy did her best not to show her shock at their living conditions but some of it must have leaked out, as Graff shrugged apologetically.

"What else can we do?" he asked. She bit her tongue and reminded herself there were at least twenty-five armed mercenaries in the building.

"Your hour's nearly up," said Graff, glancing up at the sky through the hole in the roof. Here on the ground floor the smell was worse and there were groups of mercenaries gambling, eating, sleeping and already making good headway on the wine. "Time to get moving," he warned, as a fight broke out between two women over a half-empty bottle.

By the time she had climbed back down the rope it was getting on for midday. Tammy walked away from the camp without looking back but her mind lingered on the terrible conditions inside. When she was a few streets away she paused to see if anyone had followed her. She waited in the skeletal remains of what had been a shop, hunkering down in the cool shadows, but no one came after her. Even so, she went on a winding path to where she'd stashed the next bag full of wine.

There were more camps to explore and she needed to be back at the winery before dark. Tammy wasn't sure if any of the other camps would provide useful information, but she had to try. She knew it wasn't much to go on, but in this city hope was in short supply. All you could do was keep moving forward and try to make it to the next dawn.

CHAPTER 18

A cold wind blowing in from the west made Balfruss pull on his pair of multi-coloured woollen gloves. Every day more gloves were being produced until eventually everyone would have at least one pair and probably a scarf as well. After that he suspected each person would receive a woollen cap or jumper.

It gave people in their shelter something to focus on and a way for them to contribute, if they were unable or unwilling to fight. He'd noticed Alyssa did her best to make everyone feel useful and valued. Even if it was just drawing water from the well or washing the floors, it was all seen as important. With so many people living close together, cleanliness was vital, and he was amazed at the lack of disease.

As the wind cut through his clothing Balfruss appreciated the gloves even more. Further along the wall others huddled against the cold while doing their best to keep their eyes on the street. There was still some daylight clinging to the edges of the sky and if the Forsaken returned to their old pattern it would be a couple of hours before they showed up. Normally only a few lookouts would be on the wall so early, but last night's absence had everyone worried.

"Go inside and warm up," said Alyssa, gesturing at her people

on the wall. Balfruss saw Zannah frown but she didn't contra-
dict the order and went back to her silent vigil with Tammy.
The tall Guardian had been quiet and contemplative since her
return, and from the deep furrows in her forehead he suspected
she'd seen a few unpleasant sights during the day. As the last of
the defenders went down the stairs, Kai, the plague priest, came
up onto the wall. He was a peculiar man who seemed to unnerve
the other priests to the point that they did their utmost to avoid
him at all times. If it bothered him it didn't show. Even now
he seemed completely at ease, lounging on the wall with one
foot dangling over the side and a wry grin on his face. He held
a glass of wine in one hand, a half-empty bottle in the other.

"What did you find in the other camps?" Alyssa asked
Tammy. "Anything useful?"

It took the Guardian a few seconds to reply and Balfruss
sensed she was choosing her words carefully. "Sadly not very
much. I visited two and in each the story was the same. They
have vague recollections of when people started disappearing,
but nothing precise. They don't know where it started in the
city. After a few months of living like this, I can't blame them."
Tammy gestured at the desolate city surrounding them. "When
every day is identical to the last, it makes it difficult to measure
time."

"Was nothing they said helpful?" asked Alyssa.

"A few things," conceded Tammy. "But I need to visit the
other camps to corroborate their stories."

"How were the people faring?" asked Alyssa. As always she
was trying to look after everyone in the city. Balfruss had seen
Zannah shove food into her hands and wait until Alyssa had
eaten some before leaving her alone.

"Much the same as here," said Tammy, taking out a whetstone. She held up her dagger to the fading light, spat and

started honing its edges. "They're hungry, desperate and scared. People are forced to scavenge or serve the mercenaries in other ways. In return they get to stay behind the walls."

Alyssa frowned at the Guardian, no doubt sensing there was more to her words than she was saying, but didn't press for details.

"What about the Forsaken?" asked Zannah, her eyes scanning the deepest shadows for signs of movement.

"Again, a similar story," said Tammy. "Every night the Forsaken either attack, or a few come by and stare at them. The defenders can't risk going to sleep with them close by, so they spend all night watching each other."

The whisking of steel against the whetstone triggered a memory and Balfruss fondly touched the axe at his waist in remembrance.

"None of the bases talk to each other, as they're all afraid of losing what little they have. So it's impossible to know how many Forsaken are out there."

"The numbers are always changing," said Zannah. "Every night they try to take people away and create more Forsaken."

"True, but that could also mean they have fewer than we think," suggested Alyssa, ever the optimist. "Why else would they only attack some bases and just scare others? Why not attack all of the bases at once with hundreds of Forsaken?"

It was a good question and one that none of them could answer. Alyssa waited for Zannah to explain it, but the Morrin could only shake her head. Much to everyone's surprise Kai offered them an answer that no one had even considered.

"They're separating the herd," he said, sipping his wine.

"Meaning what?" asked Balfruss.

The plague priest drained his glass then topped it up again before answering. "When a predator is hunting, it doesn't attack the whole herd. It will scare and scatter its prey, keeping them separated and clueless as to its strength. The prey has no idea if it's acting alone or with a pack. It makes prey easier to kill. It also stops the herd from grouping together and stampeding the predator to death."

Balfruss and the others looked at the priest with some alarm but he didn't seem to notice. He just kept drinking his wine and staring off into the dark as if it were an old and familiar friend.

"With everyone scared all the time in Voechenka, it stops them going on the offensive. It keeps each camp isolated," said Tammy, and Kai raised his glass in salute.

"Exactly. Together you might have a chance, and whoever is controlling the Forsaken knows that. You have to stop thinking it's the same as you. Whatever is behind all of this . . . " said Kai, flinging his arms wide and nearly toppling off the wall in the process. The half-empty bottle of wine went sailing off into the dark, but he managed to hold on to his glass and his perch. "It's not like you and probably never was. People coming back from the dead. That's a good first clue. Stop pretending it's a person."

"It's against nature and ungodly," said Alyssa, placing her right hand over her heart in remembrance of the Blessed Mother. Kai's mocking laughter echoed across the city and Alyssa looked at him askance. He was the most peculiar priest any of them had ever met. Not once had Balfruss seen him say any kind of prayer or offer thanks to his god.

"Whatever the thing is," said Kai, "it wants something, but don't try to assign human reasoning. It might want something you'd never consider."

The plague priest drained his glass and looked surprised that he wasn't holding the bottle any more. "I need more wine," he said, stumbling away down the stairs.

An odd silence settled on the wall for a minute. "He's a very peculiar man," said Alyssa. Balfruss could only agree. There was something very strange about Kai compared to every other priest he'd ever met.

An hour after full dark Balfruss briefly left the wall to get something to eat. The stew was rich and spicy, with a mix of pulses and herbs, and the bread was fresh and warm. Like everyone else he ate every mouthful and scraped the bowl before heartily thanking the cooks. He'd barely made it back to the wall when they saw the first Forsaken stumble into view. In the base there was a strange sense of relief at seeing them. Then came the familiar feelings of dread.

Alyssa sent several teenagers running to fetch others to defend the wall, and by the time they arrived and had strung their bows, the Forsaken were almost in range. Taking a deep breath Balfruss cleared his mind and let it drift into a quiet space. As the first bowstrings sang he heard with clarity the voice of his father and recalled the countless lessons in the distant jungle of the north. He'd performed the same moves over and over, so many times until they were ingrained not only in his mind, but also his muscles.

As the first ladders rattled against the stone wall Balfruss loosened his neck, rolled his shoulders and looked at the enemy. There were more Forsaken in the street than he'd ever seen, racing out of the shadows to besiege them. They attacked with such fury he wondered if their arrival and investigations had triggered this response. Or perhaps the Forsaken had finally decided it was time to eliminate another camp. Either way the time for thinking was over.

With a practised swing, using the full weight of his hips and shoulders, Balfruss brought his axe down on the skull of the first

Forsaken. It split the woman's head open and she toppled off the ladder with a scream, hitting two more people on her way down. To his left Zannah fought with renewed energy, a grim smile on her face as she took the Forsaken apart with skilled efficiency. Previously she had been dangerous, but now that he had restored her youth, she had become a force of nature. Every move was precise, every swing and counter timed perfectly so that it ended with her opponent losing a hand, an arm or sometimes their head. Her speed had also increased compared with two nights ago and now the Forsaken never came close to wounding her.

To his right Tammy rivalled the Morrin for skill and brutal efficiency. Her blade, *Maligne*, flashed through the air and seemed to be in constant motion, cleaving, slicing and generally dismembering the Forsaken as fast as they reached the top of the wall. With a roar Tammy hurled a woman over the edge and then kicked a man in the face, destroying his nose and cracking his cheek. He squawked in pain and fell out of sight, but she didn't seem satisfied. Whatever Tammy had seen during her visits to the other camps had affected her more than she realised.

A burly man dressed in ragged leathers climbed onto the wall beside Balfruss and the Sorcerer calmly turned to face him. Once, he may have been a mercenary, but now he was a hollow-eyed thing. The man raised a sword above his head and wasted time by bellowing a war cry. Balfruss whipped the haft of his axe into the mercenary's neck, crushing his throat and turning his cry into a choking gurgle. Before the man had a chance to retaliate Balfruss switched to a one-handed grip and shattered his right knee with the flat of his blade. The mercenary dropped to the ground, screaming and gasping for air, and with two hands Balfruss took off his head. It bounced once and then fell off the wall into the courtyard.

The man was quickly replaced by another body and another, to the point where the muscles in Balfruss's shoulders and arms began to burn.

The waves of Forsaken seemed to be endless but the defenders soon began to turn the tide. The Shael people didn't have the training, but the arrival of the priests had offered them a glimmer of hope which they clung too. Whether it was actually a matter of renewed faith or simply more energy from a few good meals Balfruss didn't really care. Many Forsaken were hacked apart and crushed by local people, where previously only a few would have been wounded or pushed over the wall.

As Balfruss dodged a crude overhead attack a terrified scream ripped through the air. His opponent overbalanced and stumbled forward, nearly dropping his mace in the process. Balfruss severed the man's spine just above the hips and turned towards the noise.

Several Forsaken had grabbed a young woman and she was being passed from one to another down a ladder towards the street. Bows were taken up again and several daggers thrown at the Forsaken, toppling them off the ladder, but several more in the street took hold of the girl. Her screams rattled the other defenders and several froze in terror. One or two dropped their weapons and ran, but a brave few kept fighting. With all their focus on the girl, more were knocked unconscious by the Forsaken. They dropped to the ground and the Forsaken reached out for them, ready to carry them away.

It was starting to fall apart.

As Balfruss prepared to rush forward something flashed past him in a blur. He stared in amazement as Zannah sailed through the air and then over the wall.

She landed hard on both feet and seemed to collapse, but turned her momentum into a forward roll before coming out fighting. Forsaken surrounded her but Zannah didn't wait for them to attack, lashing out with a dagger in each hand. She stabbed and gutted four of them and slit the throats of three more before they forgot about trying to carry away the sobbing girl.

On the wall Tammy rallied the defenders into action then charged into a knot of Forsaken. They were trying to carry off a man and she killed two in the first few seconds and maimed the others a moment later. Her sword cut through flesh and bone with ease and no one was able to stand against her.

Balfruss added his voice to the din, shouting encouragement and laughing in the face of the enemy as he cut down whoever stood in front of him. Slowly the locals started to find their feet again and the collective spark of courage was rekindled. Gradually the Forsaken were either maimed or thrown over the wall until only a few were left.

In the street Zannah was still dispatching those who dared get too close. All the while she remained standing over the girl, a bloody dagger in each hand, covered in gore to her elbows. Eventually the Forsaken retreated, and when the last of them was out of sight some of the defenders slid down the ladders to rescue the girl.

The fight had been brief, but Zannah had shown herself capable of terrifying brutality on a level they'd not seen before. Even as the girl was carried away Balfruss could see people were staring at the Morrin.

She scared them as much as the Forsaken, if not more, because she lived with them inside the walls. Rather than earning their respect or admiration she'd only made them even more afraid of her.

Jumping from the wall like that would have crippled or killed most people, but Zannah seemed unaffected and had just resumed fighting. Balfruss knew she would soon have to borrow more energy to repair her injuries. How long would it be before she had only months to live again?

She was killing herself for them every day and not one of them knew about her sacrifices.

Once the adrenaline faded and she realised the danger had passed Zannah sheathed her daggers. That was when she noticed how they were looking at her.

Retrieving a sword from one of the injured Forsaken she went about the grisly business of beheading every twitching body on the street. Zannah didn't wait for the others to leave the wall and this time several of them saw what she was doing before they could escape inside. From his position on top of the wall Balfruss could hear the crunching sounds of breaking bone.

When it was done Zannah approached the wall, turned the Forsaken's crude ladders into kindling, then waited until Alyssa threw down the rope.

The Forsaken were gone for now but Balfruss knew they would return, and probably in greater numbers than before. It made him wonder again what they really wanted with the people they carried away. Even trying to think beyond normal desires, as Kai had suggested, he couldn't work it out. Regardless, they had won a battle and would celebrate, because tomorrow could be much worse, and tonight might be all the time they had left.

Chapter 19

The Forsaken didn't attack again that night and for once Alyssa managed to sleep for seven hours without waking up. The nightmares were still there, lurking in the shadows of her mind, but no matter how disturbing they were, she'd seen the images many times before and now a part of her was immune to the horror. This upset her as much as the visions, as she felt as if a piece of her humanity was being eroded.

The others didn't see it. They thought she was someone to be admired and Alyssa did nothing to change their minds. In this place, no matter how thin the reed of hope that someone clung to, she would never take that away from them. Most often it was all they had.

Last night, though, she'd felt so proud to stand beside her people. As usual Zannah, as well as Balfruss and Tammy, had fought with great skill, but for once her people had done more than the usual poking and prodding. She'd seen them lose hope, but then they'd dug deep and rallied again. Perhaps it was because they were starting to fully understand the odds stacked against them. Perhaps they'd found their inner strength and had decided it was time to fight back. Or perhaps they'd been inspired by the example of the others. Alyssa's smile was more than a little wry at that thought. Not even she believed that.

Despite what Zannah had done to save the girl last night, Alyssa's people still loathed her. The act itself had been miraculous, but it just didn't matter to them. Nothing she ever did would ever be enough, and yet it didn't stop her from trying. Zannah claimed to be without faith and yet she continued to try and win them over despite it being impossible. Alyssa wondered if Zannah saw the irony.

She descended the many flights of stairs, going deeper and deeper into the earth until she finally came to a short corridor packed with many small rooms. They'd been used for storage at one time, but now had various functions. A queue had formed beside one of the six deep wells and Alyssa waited her turn, despite protests that she go straight to the front. People smiled and generally seemed happier when she was around, so she made time for everyone that spoke to her. Eventually she reached the front of the line and was handed a bucket one-quarter full of water, which she carried away to one of the small rooms.

Long curtains had been hung up in front of many and she went inside one and drew the curtain. The material was partially transparent, letting in enough light from the candles to see what she was doing, but not so much that it was immodest. After what she had endured in the camps alongside many of them during the war, Alyssa thought it a little childish. Nevertheless she said nothing and complied with their rituals of modesty. It was another reed they clung to. In truth she would have liked nothing better than to have a wash in warm sunlight. Down here in the caves it was always chilly, and the water drawn from the wells was icy.

Alyssa stripped off her clothing, took up one of the rough bars of soap Tammy and the others had brought with them, and cleaned herself from head to toe. There were still some sore patches on her skull and hips that she washed with care, but the rest was muscle, scar tissue and bone. There were a few places that had been burned so badly she couldn't feel her skin at all, so she made sure to clean those thoroughly as well.

The water drained away into a narrow channel that had recently been cut into the stone floor. It would be used again to water the mushrooms and rhubarb growing in the deepest caves. With so little water to spare they tried to find a way to reuse as much as possible.

By the time she had dressed in clean clothing and eaten a quick breakfast, Tammy and Balfruss had left for the day. Alyssa found Zannah alone on the wall, staring out across the city with a peculiar expression.

"What is it?"

The Morrin didn't answer for a long time but eventually she asked, "Were you a sculptor?"

Alyssa knew that wasn't what Zannah had originally wanted to ask. She thought the Morrin was afraid, but didn't know of what. Nothing seemed to scare her and yet this wasn't the first time she'd changed the subject when they were alone. "No, but I knew a few over the years."

"I'll get it one day," promised Zannah, but she didn't sound confident.

"Zannah . . . " said Alyssa, trying to find the right words to broach whatever it was, but the Morrin turned away to watch the street.

"You should get some rest. It's your day off."

"What about you?"

"I'm fine," said Zannah. She was alone on the wall and would remain that way until nightfall when others would come to guard the shelter.

The thump of many feet announced the arrival of a small army of children. They ranged in age and height but all were golden skinned and in far better health than many of the adults. The skin of a few actually shone and looked golden in the winter sun. "You promised us a story," declared one small girl with dazzling blue eyes. "I want my story!"

Alyssa hesitated for a moment while several children pulled on her arm, trying to lead her away. Some of the older children frowned at Zannah, but the youngest were oblivious and didn't see her as different from anyone else.

"You should go," said Zannah.

Alyssa could do little but consent as she was led away by the hand to one of the children's play areas. A slightly larger room had been decorated with brightly coloured paintings on the walls, the floor covered with layers of carpets and cushions until it was a warm and cosy space. Not even the drab sunlight filtering through the two high windows was enough to diminish the cheery mood of the room.

"Tell us another story about the Blessed Mother," said one of the children.

"Were you one of the Faithful?" asked another. Alyssa bit the inside of her lip to stop herself from laughing at the idea.

"No, but I knew someone who was." Her smile faded as she thought of Monella, only a few rooms away. Once, she had led a congregation that numbered in the hundreds. Now the former priestess said very little and every other word seemed to be soaked in vinegar and bile. "Have I told you about the story of the Blessed Mother's rebirth?"

"Is it a scary story?" asked one of the younger boys, hiding behind a big cushion.

Alyssa gave the boy a warm and generous smile. "No, it's a wonderful story about the cycle of life and death."

For a while, the rest of the world drifted away until all that existed for Alyssa was a sea of eager faces. They were rapt, hanging on her every word, and she felt a mix of joy and sadness at the attention. When she reached the end of the story several children clapped and a few of the older ones quickly wiped away tears, pretending it hadn't affected them. It saddened her that they thought showing emotion was a weakness.

Promising them another story very soon, Alyssa wandered away down the corridor with no particular destination in mind. As ever, after retelling one of the many tales about the Blessed Mother, she felt an inner peace. The bright spark inside, that so often these days seemed as if it would be extinguished, had been rekindled. It swelled her breast, lifted her chin and, despite everything, she felt a smile tugging at the corners of her mouth.

Her feet guided her back to the courtyard where Zannah maintained her lonely vigil. It would be good to spend some time together without any interruptions. Perhaps Zannah would finally ask the question she kept avoiding.

Alyssa had no sooner made it back to the top of the wall when she spotted several people coming into view at the end of the street. Zannah squinted at the distant figures and then gestured towards the stairs.

"Get the others," she said, picking up a recurve bow, bracing it against her foot and stringing it with one quick flex.

"Why would the Forsaken attack in the day?"

"Hurry," said Zannah, not taking her eyes off the street.

Alyssa raced down the stairs and gathered as many people as she could who were willing to fight, then left orders to pass the word around and went back outside.

An attack in the daytime was unprecedented. Last night's defeat must have been a more painful blow than she'd realised. By killing so many Forsaken they'd made them desperate enough to try something new. Perhaps they were hoping to catch everyone asleep in the base and wipe them out. Alyssa's heart was pounding in her ears as she took the stairs two at a time.

Zannah was where she'd left her, casually leaning on her bow, but now she seemed perplexed.

"What is it?"

Instead of answering, Zannah simply pointed down at the people in the street.

At least twenty or thirty were stood in a loose huddle not far away, all clutching weapons in a way she recognised. It suggested that until today none of them had ever held a blade or bow before. They seemed uncertain about what to do next and, looking at their faces, Alyssa thought she vaguely recognised one or two of them from her old life. Their homes, jobs and all of their wealth and influence were gone. Now they were ragged, dirty, almost skeletal figures with no name and nothing except the filthy clothing on their backs. Instead of a zealot's gleam burning in their eyes all she saw reflected was hunger. If they were Forsaken, they were like none she had ever seen before.

Defenders armed themselves quickly in the courtyard, before fanning out along the wall. Bows were strung and arrows nocked, ready for Alyssa's command, but no one fired.

Eventually a brave woman with filthy tangled brown hair stepped forward from the crowd in the street. Once she might have been beautiful, but now her dark eyes were too large in a hollow face, and her skin was blistered and cracked.

"Open the gates and give us your food," she declared, waving her borrowed short sword for emphasis. "Or we'll come in and take it."

A ragged cheer went up from the others in the street. It was ludicrous, but no one on the wall was laughing or even smiling. Zannah's grim expression turned even more sour as she looked past the rabble for the real perpetrators.

"What's your name?" asked Alyssa.

"Pella Rae. Are you going to open the gate?" she asked, not noticing that twenty bows were held at the ready. If the crowd was nothing more than it appeared, they would be dead long before any even made it to the top of the wall.

"Who sent you, Pella?"

"Fenne. He said we had to earn our place."

His was the mercenary camp with the worst reputation. Alyssa had never been anywhere near it, but the stories she'd been told by the few that escaped were horrible.

"If you lay down your weapons, you can come inside," said Alyssa.

Zannah hissed between her teeth and Alyssa felt a few others on the wall looking at her askance. "They can't be trusted," warned the Morrin. "This could be a ruse to get them inside. They could be working for him."

Alyssa shook her head. "They're hungry and desperate. They need our help."

"I can drive them off," said Zannah, nocking an arrow. "If I kill or wound one of them, the others will scatter."

"Put down your bow, Zannah. Go back to your families," she said, addressing the other defenders on the wall, but they hesitated. "I'll deal with this. You've trusted me so far."

"The Morrin is right," said Monella, stumping up the stairs. There was more vinegar in the former priestess's words than normal. She passionately hated Zannah, and Alyssa could see that it had cost her greatly to agree with the Morrin. "We trust you, but we don't know them."

"We can't turn them away," said Alyssa. "Fenne won't let

them back inside his camp and if we do nothing they'll starve or freeze to death tonight. Or something worse could happen."

Monella flinched but didn't back down. Several tears ran from her rheumy eye but she didn't notice or care. "That's true."

Alyssa turned to face the older woman. "Are you saying you don't care what happens to them?"

Everyone on the wall was waiting for her to speak. Several emotions flickered across Monella's face and it took her a long time to answer. "We can't lock them up, but letting them just walk in doesn't sit right. They need to swear an oath."

"What kind of oath?"

"One of fealty, to you."

"They're not servants, Monella."

"They need to swear a blood oath," she insisted. "To do no harm to anyone here and to follow your orders. If they all agree to that, they can come inside."

"That seems fair," said Zannah. Alyssa was alarmed to see several people on the wall were nodding in agreement.

"I'm not royalty," protested Alyssa. "And a blood oath is not something to be sworn lightly."

Monella's crooked smile was unnerving. "Then it shouldn't be a problem for them to make it."

"This is wrong. Don't do this."

Alyssa looked for support to oppose this absurd idea but everyone was staring at her with the same adoring expression. She offered guidance to others but that didn't make her their leader. She tried to explain this but they would not change their mind.

To make matters worse, Monella sank stiffly to one knee, and in front of everyone swore a blood oath in a loud, clear voice. The rest sank to their knees and repeated the words until Alyssa was looking at Zannah over a sea of kneeling heads. For a second

Alyssa thought the Morrin would also kneel, which would've been more than she could bear, but thankfully Zannah didn't.

It took Monella a while to explain to the group outside the gate but once they realised they wouldn't be turned away several wept with joy. Zannah collected every weapon and secured them in a safe location before Alyssa was allowed down onto the street.

Under instruction from Monella, and with several others watching from the walls, one by one the new arrivals knelt in front of Alyssa. Each swore a blood oath of fealty and when one woman tried to kiss her hand Alyssa drew back in horror. When it was finally over she hurried into the main building, suddenly desperate to be away from the adoring faces and grateful smiles.

The corridor swam in her vision as tears clouded her eyes and she swallowed a desperate hitch in her throat. This wasn't right. She wasn't a leader. She wasn't a member of the nobility. No one should be bending their knee to her. She didn't want this. Until now she'd let people hold on to whatever rituals made them happy, but this was a step too far. She had to stop it before it could spread any further.

Turning on her heel Alyssa wiped her eyes and intended to march back up to the courtyard when she saw the faces of other people around her in the corridor. All were looking at her with the same adulation as the new arrivals. It had always been there and she'd just not seen it. Pride had made her blind and now it was too late.

Biting her lip she managed to make it to her room and close the door before the first sob escaped her lips. She curled into a ball and wept, praying through floods of tears to the Blessed Mother for wisdom.

CHAPTER 20

Tammy had spent the morning visiting other mercenary camps and now only one remained. She'd left it until last on purpose because it had the worst reputation. Several people she'd spoken to had fled from the camp, which was run by a Morrin known as Fenne. Although the conditions they endured in the other bases were not comfortable they preferred it to Fenne's camp. This time Tammy had left the winery in her leather armour, armed with two daggers and her sword.

With a heavy pack of wine clanking on her shoulder she approached the final camp with some apprehension. The building must have once been a temple, as she could see a golden dome rising above what had formerly been a white stone wall. Now it was black and grey, smeared with what looked like dried blood and ash.

The neighbouring buildings on either side had been torn down and all rubble cleared away. A series of metal spikes driven into the ground formed a tangled web of sharp edges and blades along both sides of the temple. The wall looked as if it had originally been intended to be decorative. It had not been designed to protect worshippers from a siege, but now Fenne had turned the temple into a fortress.

At the front of the compound the only gate remained clear of spikes. The thick wooden doors looked new and had been banded with iron. Fenne had created a choke point and no doubt behind the gates he had a nasty surprise for any Forsaken that managed to make it through. Whatever else, the man was obviously devious and well prepared.

Long before she approached the entrance Tammy realised she was being watched. She'd spotted at least two lookouts positioned in buildings on either side of the street. Brief flashes of light from pieces of a mirror relayed a message back to the main camp so by the time she arrived four mercenaries were watching her from atop the wall. All were hard-faced men and women and each carried a bow held at the ready.

Moving slowly Tammy slid the rucksack off her back and took out a bottle of wine. Much to her surprise the gates started to open before she had a chance to make the offer. Four more mercenaries came out to meet her, three men and a woman with spiky red hair. Their leader, a well-built Seve dressed in ragged grey furs over chainmail, rubbed at his greying beard as he craned his neck to stare her in the eye. Though he was slight for a Seve, at only six feet tall, with a craggy face and eyes so dark they were almost black, Tammy thought he looked familiar. The most unusual feature about him that stuck in her mind was that he carried a sword on his back. It was a peculiarity normally reserved for Drassi warriors.

From the way he was looking at her it seemed as if he also recognised her from somewhere. "Perizzi?" he asked, and she nodded. "We all end up passing through there eventually."

"Do you know why I'm here?"

"We keep an eye on the other camps," he said by way of explanation. "I'm Kovac. If you want to come inside we'll need your weapons."

Tammy didn't try to argue the point or even threaten them if they reneged on the deal, but as she passed *Maligne* over to Kovac she paused. "Take good care of this blade. It was a gift from a friend."

Kovac took the sword from her and held it carefully. "You have my word."

She didn't think his word was worth much, given his profession, but again she kept her mouth shut. One of the others reached for the pack and she handed it over, then offered the bottle in her hand to Kovac. He passed it on to someone else, who pulled out the cork and took a sip.

"That's good shit," said the woman with spiky hair.

"How would you know, Sylla?" asked one of the other mercenaries as he reached for the bottle but she snatched it away.

"I used to sell this stuff," said Sylla, staring at the bottle with a frown and then smelling the wine. "Where did you get it from?"

Tammy said nothing. If Sylla was telling the truth and she knew her wine then any information could be dangerous. Anything she said might give them a clue as to where the wine had really come from.

"Fenne agreed to the same deal," said Kovac, steering her towards the open gate. "The wine for one hour inside the camp. I strongly suggest you don't linger."

Tammy accepted the warning and then there was no time for further conversation as she had to watch carefully where she was walking. Just beyond the gate was a huge yawning pit, maybe ten feet deep, lined with more metal spikes. Stones that had probably been poached from neighbouring buildings formed two high walls on either side, creating a long tunnel.

A narrow wooden gangplank lay across the middle of the pit and she waited until Kovac had crossed before following. Even then the plank wobbled up and down with just her weight and Tammy had to raise her arms to maintain her balance. One wrong step and she'd plunge to a grisly death. The pit was too long to jump and there was no space on either side to walk around. It was devious and it told her much about Fenne.

"One hour," said Kovac, gesturing around the courtyard. Unlike the other camps the temple was all on one level. There were several small outhouses built into the walls of the courtyard, two large stables and beyond them three long narrow buildings. Finally, at the back was the temple itself, its golden dome reflecting some of the meagre winter sun.

Tammy spotted several local people hard at work, fetching and carrying water from a large central well, cleaning weapons, repairing arrows and sharpening a massive pile of metal spikes. One woman worked the crank while two more held a crude metal bar against the grindstone and a shower of sparks erupted. A woman dressed in leathers stood over them, yelling instructions as sparks burned their skin.

Elsewhere she saw more people being brutalised and not one of them fought back or even glared at their tormentors. Shael was a land of broken people and those in front of her had come to accept such treatment, as if it were just their lot in life.

Tammy heard horrendous sounds of what could only be torture coming from one of the outhouses. Kovac flinched as the screams reached fever pitch and then suddenly cut off. The door of the small building flew open and a lean Morrin emerged, stripped to the waist.

Fresh blood dripped down his face and neck and more covered his furry chest and arms. His horns and hair were doused in it and he spat a huge red wad onto the ground. Everyone in the courtyard stopped what they were doing to stare as a heavy silence fell.

"Get back to work," snarled the Morrin. As if whatever he'd been doing hadn't just happened, everyone turned their faces away and went back to their tasks. As long as it wasn't them. After all, as they probably kept telling themselves, worse horrors were waiting for them outside the gates at night.

Tammy took a deep breath to try and maintain her calm. She managed it eventually but it took a while for the adrenaline to fade. Time was short so she went to work, approaching the nearest person.

After speaking to several locals, once they were given permission by whichever mercenary was lurking nearby, Tammy had very little new information. All of them had lost friends and relatives in the last few years and the pattern of disappearances seemed random. Whenever possible she mentioned Alyssa's offer of sanctuary in a whisper. Each time the person listened but never agreed to anything. One woman laughed and said she wouldn't be caught out by such a trick, and that she was loyal to Fenne.

Tammy was beginning to worry that none of the locals knew anything when she came across an old man scrubbing potatoes. At a second glance she realised he wasn't actually that old, but his skin was so pale it was almost translucent. He was so skinny Tammy could see every rib of his body. One of his eyes was swollen shut and a purple bruise ran down one side of his face.

"I'm Tammy."

"Perron."

"What happened to your face?"

"I got caught eating a potato," said Perron with a grin that showed several broken teeth. "I was just so hungry."

Time was getting on and Perron was her last chance to ask any questions about the Forsaken. "I'm here to offer you something better than this."

"That's what he said."

The words make Tammy's scalp prickle. "Who?"

Perron resumed his scrubbing and his voice dropped to a whisper. "They don't want us to talk about it. This was a few months ago, before it turned really bad. Jambral was a decent sort. He used to hunt and fish, so they sent him out to scavenge for food. One day he went out and didn't come back." Perron finished scrubbing the potato and picked up another from the pile. "We thought he was dead. A few people had disappeared or run off, except the next day he turned up. He just walked up to the gates with a deer slung over one shoulder."

Perron's eyes misted over and he started drooling, probably at the thought of venison. He smacked his lips together and went back to work, keeping one eye on the mercenary lurking nearby. Without looking around Tammy knew Kovac was stood not far away. He had shadowed her the entire time but oddly had not stopped to talk to any of the other mercenaries.

"One night Jambral told me what had happened. He went out hunting and was just so tired he fell asleep. By the time he woke up it was nearly dark. The Forsaken found him and they took him."

"Took him where?" said Tammy, as gently as she could. It was the one question that she kept coming back to which no one could answer.

"I'm not sure," said Perron. Tammy smiled through her teeth, trying not to let her frustration show. "They hit him on the head and carried him off the street, but he woke up on the way. They took him somewhere cold and he said it smelled damp. The cold seemed to seep into his bones, but after a while none of that mattered any more."

Tammy had a good idea of what Perron was going to say next but she wanted to hear him say it. "Why not?"

"They changed him. After that he felt stronger and he was always so warm. He wasn't tired, and hunger wasn't twisting him up inside any more. He wasn't alone either as he was connected to the others. Jambral tried to explain it to me, but he didn't really have the words."

"Did he say how he was changed?"

"No, he didn't."

Despite his current predicament, the broken teeth, swollen eye and fear of the mercenaries, she knew Perron was lying. Working as a Guardian, and even before, Tammy had developed a talent for knowing when someone wasn't telling the truth. She thought about explaining her offer of sanctuary to Perron, but knew he wouldn't believe her. Instead she tried a different approach.

"If you could have anything in this world, what would it be?" she asked. Her question was unusual, but from Perron's expression it was almost as if he'd been expecting her to ask it. At what seemed like the end of the world, when death was so close, it must have been a question he'd asked himself many times before. It didn't take Perron long to think of an answer.

"My daughter, Rheena. She's all I have left."

Tammy gripped one of Perron's hands until he looked at her. "I swear I will do everything I can to get her somewhere safe."

She sat back and for a few moments just listened to the scrape of his brush. Eventually Perron collected his thoughts but still spoke in barely more than a whisper, as if afraid of what might happen when the words found purchase in the world.

"Jambral said the Embrace wasn't something beautiful. It was painful and horrific. They forced his mouth open and made him swallow something. He nearly choked to death. Worst of all he said that he could feel it moving. It was alive." Perron shuddered at the thought and covered his heart with one hand, in remembrance of the Blessed Mother. "This creature they made him swallow, it became part of him. Eventually he didn't know it was there any more. It nourished him and made him stronger and healthier. After that he didn't care."

"What did it want in return?"

Perron shrugged. "He didn't know, but the Forsaken needed him to be strong."

"What happened to Jambral?"

"Something went wrong," said Perron. "The Embrace was supposed to bring him peace, being one and many together he said, but it didn't work properly. That's why he came back. He could still feel the other Forsaken, but he was different. That didn't matter to them," said Perron, gesturing towards the nearest mercenary. "Jambral couldn't hide what was happening and soon they noticed he looked far too healthy. When they realised he'd been changed they ripped him apart and burned the pieces."

"It's time to go," said Kovac, glancing around nervously.

"What's wrong?" asked Tammy, but the mercenary just shook his head.

"I won't forget my promise," she said to Perron before hurrying after Kovac across the courtyard. The gate was closed and the gangplank over the pit had been taken away, but the guards inside the gate picked it up at their approach.

"Open the gate," said Kovac and three mercenaries moved to follow his order.

"Wait," said a voice from behind her. All of the mercenaries paused in what they were doing and Tammy saw Kovac's shoulders slump. She turned around to see Fenne walking towards her, flanked by a dozen mercenaries. He'd cleaned off most of the blood and pulled on a shirt, but there were still patches on his face like war paint. The Morrin's smile was unnerving and Tammy felt her pulse begin to race as her body anticipated an imminent outburst of violence.

"We had a deal," said Tammy. "One hour inside your camp for the wine."

"That's right, and you've had your hour," said Fenne, with a feral grin. "Now, what are you going to give me for your freedom?"

CHAPTER 21

Despite the city being saturated in bleak memories and strong emotions, Balfruss was determined to find Kaine using his magic. He'd thought about trying to make contact with the lingering dead, but quickly discounted the idea. There were simply too many of them, and even if he managed to isolate one and ask for its help, its activities wouldn't go unnoticed by the others. After that he'd be hounded by hordes of them, day and night, and would probably be driven mad or forced out of the city.

He'd thought about using his magic to try and trace Kaine's path through the streets, but that proved impossible as the whole city was cross-crossed with traces of energy, both old and new. Kaine's pupils had been in Voechenka, presumably for years, training to use their power, and remnants of it stretched across the city like a giant spider web. That meant he had to rely on more traditional methods to find Kaine and employ only his natural senses and intellect.

After wandering through the city for an hour looking for clues without success, Balfruss began to realise the scale of the challenge ahead. Something brushed the edge of his senses, making him stop suddenly.

Long before he felt the sudden build-up of energy, Balfruss was alerted to the presence of another magic user by an echo from the Source. Summoning his will and instinctively weaving a shield, Balfruss spun in a circle to find the direction of the Battlemage.

Making no attempt to conceal his location or what he was doing, a young man marched down the street towards Balfruss, drawing power from the Source as he approached. Rather than fashioning it into some kind of weapon, or manipulating the energy, he just kept drawing more and more power into his body. A few seconds later the young Battlemage reached his capacity as blood ran from both nostrils and his steps faltered. With a scream of rage he flung one arm out towards Balfruss and released all of the raw energy in one concentrated burst.

Balfruss immediately dropped his shield, held both hands out towards the Battlemage and opened himself up to the Source, but without siphoning any energy. The wave of power from the young mage made him rock slightly on his heels, but then it passed through him without causing any damage. Focusing his will Balfruss channelled the energy back down into the earth, sending it deep into the ground, where it dispersed naturally.

The young mage just stared, his mouth hanging open in shock and awe. Throwing all of his strength at Balfruss in one go must have drained him, but he stubbornly tried to pull together something else.

"Do you really think that will work?" asked Balfruss, walking slowly towards him.

"The Master has tasked me with killing you," he said, wiping away the blood from his nose.

"You can't touch me with your magic."

"You're here to kill the Master, kill us all."

"You've been lied to," said Balfruss, coming within arm's

reach. Up close Balfruss could see he was just a boy, perhaps seventeen years old.

"Stay back!" cried the boy, crossing his arms in front of him as if he expected an attack. When nothing happened he opened his eyes and stared at Balfruss.

"What's your name?"

"Why? So you can bind me with it? I'll never tell you my name!"

"That doesn't work," said Balfruss, talking very slowly. "Even if I knew your full name I couldn't make you do anything against your will. That's a myth."

The boy remained sceptical. "Really?"

"Really. I'd rather not call you boy, but I can."

"What about shape-changing into animals? I've always wanted to fly."

Balfruss shook his head. "Myth. I lived with several tribes across the Dead Sea and none of them knew how. None of their ancestors ever referred to it either. They can do many things we've never imagined, but no one can do that."

The boy thought about it for a while and his shoulders slumped. "I'm Willem," he said eventually.

"Balfruss."

"What about flying? Is that possible?"

"Sort of," explained Balfruss. "It's possible to bond with an animal and share in its experiences. So, if you bonded with a bird, you could fly in a way."

Willem stared up at the sky, probably imagining what it would be like to soar through the grey clouds overhead. The air was cool and Balfruss could see his breath in front of his face. There would be a frost in the morning.

"Why didn't it work?" said Willem, gesturing towards Balfruss with one hand. "My attack."

Balfruss sat down on a pile of rubble not far away from Willem and got comfortable before speaking. The cold of the stone started to seep into his backside. He wouldn't be able to sit here for long without it going numb.

"Because I'm a Sorcerer."

"A what?"

Balfruss took a deep breath and tried to remember that Willem was very young. He also knew the boy had no interest in a history lesson or an explanation that took too long.

"A long time ago, people who wielded magic were called Sorcerers. People forgot what that meant and what was possible with magic. Battlemages are living weapons, trained only to fight. Sorcerers can do so much more. Sorcerer is not just a word. It means to have a deeper understanding of the Source."

"I don't understand," said Willem, which made Balfruss smile. He'd said the same thing many times to his teachers.

"Let's just say Sorcerers have knowledge of Talents not seen for decades or even longer."

"Like skinwalking," said Willem, trying to be helpful. "The Master teaches that to a few and if they survive they become Flesh Mages."

"Do you know where he sends them once they're trained?"

"I won't betray the Master," said Willem, getting to his feet and threatening to bolt. Despite being sent to die against an opponent he could never beat, he remained loyal to Kaine. Balfruss would have to move very slowly. Nevertheless the boy had not run away. He suspected it was because he represented someone with knowledge and Willem was burning with curiosity. He'd been the same at Willem's age, desperate to learn more than the small pieces of information being doled out in class. It was one of the reasons pupils at the Red Tower competed in illegal duels. They wanted to push themselves to the limit.

Balfruss held up his hands in surrender. "All right, can I ask how long you've been his student?"

"About two years." Looking more closely Balfruss realised he'd miscalculated the boy's age. Willem was closer to fifteen and was just a tall and gangly adolescent.

"Did you really think you could beat me?" asked Balfruss.

The boy at least had the grace to shrug. "I thought I might catch you off guard."

"You tried and failed. So what happens now?"

"I have to try again," said Willem, and Balfruss raised an eyebrow. "If I go back without your head he'll kill me."

Part of Balfruss's arse had gone numb and he quickly got to his feet, startling the boy. Willem jumped back and looked in all directions in alarm. When nothing happened and no one attacked, he started to calm down. He was jumpier than a newborn colt, startled by every shadow and loud noise.

"Go home," said Balfruss.

"I can't."

"I meant your real home."

"Can't do that either," said Willem. "The whole village got torched during the war. I was scavenging in one of the towns when the Master found me. This is my home now."

Balfruss surreptitiously rubbed his arse, trying to get some feeling back into his cheeks. "Then you should travel to the Red Tower. You're still young and they could teach you there."

"Why can't you teach me?" asked Willem.

Balfruss was just turning away when the question caught him by surprise. "Me?"

"You said you know about lots of old stuff. Why can't you teach me?"

Balfruss cocked his head to one side and stared more carefully at the boy. Despite the temperature, a few beads of sweat were running down the sides of his face. His eyes settled on Balfruss and then quickly flicked away to one side and back again.

Even as he started to ask the question Balfruss realised he already knew the answer. Willem had been nothing more than a distraction. It was just another ploy. He'd never stood a chance in a direct fight with Balfruss and Kaine knew that. Willem had been a test, to see if Balfruss would kill a weak and defenceless opponent, or if he'd talk to him. But there had to be more to it than that. If this was a game of Stones, where was the sting in the tail?

With a scream of rage Willem drew a dagger from under his shirt and lunged at Balfruss. The edge of the blade was discoloured from some kind of poison and Balfruss smelled something sickly sweet in the air. Using the side of his right hand Balfruss blocked the blow then riposted with a fist to the centre of Willem's chest, right in the solar plexus. The boy stumbled back, gasping for air and unable to stand up straight.

There was a faint prickle of energy in the air to his left and Balfruss turned towards a hollowed-out building. Realising that they had been discovered, three young students ran out of the front door, each carrying what was probably a poisoned weapon. From his right two more students with a weak connection to the Source ran at him with raised weapons. Willem would catch his breath in a few minutes and soon Balfruss would have six poisoned weapons to deal with. All of those around him were no threat to him with magic, but their blades were an entirely different matter. They wanted to kill him and yet they were nothing more than children.

Raising his arms Balfruss spread his fingers wide and lifted his palms to the sky. A hook of energy snagged one leg of each student and they were yanked into the air. Willem went with them, snared by an invisible tether forged of Balfruss's willpower, until all six were hanging upside down. A couple of weapons clattered to the ground, but one or two stubbornly held on to their blades. One of the students even managed to throw a dagger towards Balfruss. The aim was poor but if he did nothing it might catch him on the shoulder. Balfruss suspected even a scratch from these weapons would prove deadly.

While keeping the six pupils aloft Balfruss focused another portion of his will on the blade, sending it off in a different direction before it reached him. It went sailing through the air, away from any of the figures hanging upside down. A second later he heard someone cry out and spinning around he saw a seventh figure stumbling towards him with a loaded crossbow. She was no more than nineteen years old with pale skin that quickly began to flush red. The crossbow slid from fingers that were starting to swell up as she dropped to her knees.

The red skin of her hands and face became riddled with purple and blue lines until he could see every vein and artery under the skin. The girl's scream was so shrill it sounded like a trapped animal.

The other students had stopped trying to attack him or escape and were now staring at their friend. They'd probably had no idea what the poison would do, only that it would kill him. The girl was someone they knew and, by the horror on their faces, obviously cared about.

There was nothing any of them could do except watch as the girl's terror reached new heights while her veins started to turn black. It started at her fingertips and she frantically tried to stop it moving up her arms, scratching and then clawing at the skin. As it crept up her forearms she was whimpering and digging her nails into her flesh until sludgy black blood dribbled out. It hardened like clay as it made contact with the air, and her screams increased to fever pitch. Her head was whipping from side to side as the veins in her neck changed colour. She clawed at her face, digging channels in her flesh until she wore a mask of black blood. After a few seconds it hardened, freezing her expression of agony in place.

Balfruss thought it was over, but he could still hear a faint wheezing coming from her throat. She was still alive. The sound of her breathing continued for a few more seconds, echoing loudly in the street, until with one final rattle she died. Her eyes remained open, staring at her friends, who were still dangling upside down by one leg. Two were crying and praying at the same time, while the others were utterly silent, their expressions of horror a near match to that of the dead girl's.

The simplest way to deal with the six students in front of him would be to cut off their heads. Or crush them with his will until they were nothing more than red smears on the ground. He thought about it briefly, but knew he couldn't slaughter them because it would be just that. Slaughter. It didn't matter that they had been sent to kill him. They were children with very little power and almost no training.

At the Red Tower they would have been given a choice. Here, the Master had sent six of them to kill him or die trying, knowing full well that they had no hope of success. Six lives thrown away as nothing more than a distraction for the girl with the crossbow.

"You all tried and failed. If I ever see any of you again, I will kill you," said Balfruss, adding a little power behind his words until his voice rattled loose stones. "Do you understand?" he bellowed.

Any trace of bravado was gone. All of the students had been reduced to frightened children in the face of an implacable enemy.

Fear was all they knew from the Master, and now Balfruss was using the same tool against them. He loathed himself for doing it but the offer of sanctuary or compassion would be pointless. This city had sickened them, and unlike him they wouldn't even realise what had happened. After only a few days of exposure he could feel darker emotions trying to bubble up to the surface. Such desires and feelings had become second nature to them. A blunt response was all they would understand.

With a snarl Balfruss cut his magic and they all crashed to the ground.

"If you're not out of my sight by the time I count to five, I will gut you all," he said. He didn't even make it to four before he was alone on the street.

Kaine couldn't keep hiding forever. Eventually he would run out of pawns to throw at Balfruss and then he'd either come out of hiding or, if this was a game of Stones, put a different piece onto the board.

Balfruss had to find Kaine before any more people were made to sacrifice themselves out of loyalty or fear. And when he did there would be a reckoning beyond what he'd done to the Warlock.

CHAPTER 22

In the deepest cavern under the winery Alyssa knelt on the soft damp earth and tried to pray. It was warmer down here than she'd been expecting, something to do with hot air coming up through the cracks, but more importantly it was quiet. Normally when alone she had no difficulty meditating, but today stray thoughts prevented her from finding any peace.

Everywhere Alyssa went in the winery people asked her opinion and wanted her to make decisions on their behalf. It had started with the new arrivals but once others learned of the blood oath they also wanted to swear loyalty. Alyssa had refused to let anyone else kneel, but it didn't stop people treating her as if she were royalty. All day they pursued her with an endless series of questions. Even on the wall, with Zannah's glare to contend with, they wanted her to make choices for them.

Alyssa had hoped it would be peaceful down here, away from their constant demands, but a disturbing and erratic noise kept intruding. Row upon row of bright pink stalks rose above her head and every now and then one of them would creak as it stretched upwards trying to find the light. Candles dotted around the cave provided enough ambient light to find her way between the rows, but heavy shadows still pooled around the edges of the cave. In the gloomy corners, and in a small cavern off to one side, mushrooms were growing in the earth.

To her left another rhubarb stalk groaned and Alyssa flinched at the sound. It was a peculiar noise and being alone in the cave surrounded by the creaking rows of vegetables wasn't nearly as serene as she'd hoped. Turning her back on the eerie place Alyssa retraced her steps and went back up through the levels, aiming for the courtyard. Perhaps she'd find some peace on the wall with only the taciturn Zannah for company.

On the way she wanted to ignore every request, but she couldn't just walk past people when they approached her. No matter how it had been done, they needed her. Alyssa slowed down but never completely stopped walking, gave what brief advice she could, often amounting to nothing more than common sense. She suspected all of them already knew the answers, but they still seemed grateful.

Eventually she made it to the courtyard where an icy wind was blowing the dust around. The late afternoon sky was lead grey and she thought it might snow. As she paused to pull on a pair of woollen gloves, the sound of raised voices drifted down from above. Zannah was stood on the wall in her usual spot with Balfruss leaning on the wall beside her, staring out at the city. As snatches of their conversation drifted down Alyssa slowed her ascent, not wanting to interrupt but also curious about their disagreement.

"You're pushing yourself too hard. Taking too many risks," Balfruss was saying. "How much did that last stunt cost you?"

"A few years."

"A few?" scoffed Balfruss. "I heard your bones pop when you landed. How many did you break?" When Zannah didn't answer he shook his head in dismay and ran a tired hand over his face. He looked more drawn than when he'd set off that morning. "If you keep this up, you'll die, and there's nothing anyone can do. Not even me. I can't repeat it. Do you understand?"

"I'll be fine."

Balfruss's laughter was mocking. "You were days away from death when we arrived. How will you help these people if you're dead?"

Alyssa hurried to the top of the stairs and the sound of her footsteps halted the conversation.

"Are you dying?" asked Alyssa. Zannah frowned at Balfruss as if he were to blame. "Answer me!" said Alyssa, gripping her friend by the arm.

Zannah glanced down at the hand on her forearm but Alyssa ignored her glare. The Morrin's stare might intimidate others but she knew Zannah would never hurt her. Zannah tried to pull her arm away but Alyssa gripped one of her hands with both of hers. It was only then that she realised how warm Zannah was. Even through the gloves she could feel heat radiating from the Morrin's body.

"Zannah, are you dying?" she asked again.

"No. He . . . helped me," said Zannah vaguely, gesturing with her chin at Balfruss, who harrumphed but said nothing.

"Tell me what's happening," said Alyssa.

She looked between them, waiting for one of them to say something, but neither spoke. Zannah never shared anything about herself without being asked the same question repeatedly, and even then what she said was brief. Alyssa thought about asking Balfruss but knew that it would put him in a difficult situation. It was Zannah's secret to share.

"I'll find out," she promised. Zannah pulled her hand free and Alyssa thought a smile briefly touched her lips.

"Another day," said Zannah. "Today you should worry about wizards."

Alyssa turned towards Balfruss, who stood with his shoulders hunched from fatigue and something else. The muscles in the side of his face jumped as he clenched his jaw.

"Kaine sent more of his students to kill me." The Battlemage was furious, but after taking a few deep breaths his posture relaxed. "They were just children."

"Are they dead?"

Balfruss glanced at Alyssa, a look of surprise on his face that she would ask such a question. "No, not by my hand, but my fear is I've killed them all the same. One of them said if they went back without my head Kaine would kill them."

"You're not responsible for his actions," said Alyssa. "You didn't make him do it."

"No, but I hold some responsibility for them being here in the first place."

"Why?"

Balfruss waved a hand dismissively. "It's a long story about the Red Tower, for another time." He glanced at the sky and frowned. "It'll be dark soon. Where's Tammy?"

"She went to the last mercenary base. The one ruled by Fennetaris," said Zannah. Alyssa realised she'd only heard other people refer to the mercenary as Fenne.

"Do you know Fenne?"

"He was here, occupying Shael during the war." Zannah's voice had become rougher and her eyes had drifted somewhere else into the past. The guilt she carried weighed her down far worse than any suit of armour. Every day she was made to remember all of the things she'd done. All Zannah needed to do was look at the face of anyone in their shelter to see the scars of her people's work.

"One day we received an order to sail home and most of my people went. A few stayed behind. They had become gluttons."

Zannah's expression turned sour. They both knew she wasn't referring to eating or drinking too much. There had been rivers of blood and stacks of bodies piled as high as buildings.

"What happened to them?" asked Balfruss.

"I hunted them down and killed them," said Zannah, matter-of-factly. "Fennetaris was the last one, and the worst. He hid from me."

"If Fenne is as bad as you say then Tammy may need help. Can you give me directions to his camp?" asked Balfruss, turning towards the stairs.

"By the time I've drawn a map and explained the route I could be halfway there," said Alyssa. "Besides, I'm far less of a threat. By now your reputation will have spread. They might try to kill you before you have a chance to speak."

"You cannot go," said Zannah. Alyssa rounded on the Morrin and was surprised to see her smiling. "People here depend on you. They swore an oath."

"Don't remind me."

"When I suggest something that might save their lives, they ignore it. They would continue to ignore it as someone slit their throats and smile at me as they died. When you say the same thing they listen," said Zannah, checking her sword and pulling on a pair of leather gloves. "Whether you want it or not, you are now their leader."

Alyssa hated to admit it but part of her knew that Zannah was right. She was aware that her people could cope perfectly well without her, and if she died they would find someone else to lead them, but in the interim there would be chaos. Without her they might actually succeed in murdering Zannah. Even so, stubbornness, and a chance to get away from the endless questions, made her try one last time.

"I should be the one to go."

"They won't let you," said Zannah, gesturing at the court-yard. A group of people had gathered in the doorway of the main building. Every face was staring at Alyssa and she could feel the immense weight of being responsible for all of them settling on her shoulders. "You give them hope." The Morrin retrieved the knotted rope and threw it over the wall. Before Alyssa could wish her good luck or offer a prayer, Zannah went over, and a minute later was running down the street away from the winery.

So far the people in the courtyard had not followed her onto the wall. Alyssa wondered if part of their reluctance had been because of Zannah. Now that the Morrin had gone she feared they would swamp her.

"You can't hide up here all night," said Balfruss, scratching at his beard.

"Watch me."

"I know it feels heavy, but it does get easier."

"What's that?"

"Being responsible for others." The Battlemage sounded as if he were speaking from experience. "At one time we all felt it during the war. There were only six Battlemages and without us there would not have been a war between Seveldrom and the west. The Mad King and the Warlock would have marched in and slaughtered thousands. A great deal was expected of us."

Alyssa knew some of what had happened, but this was the first time she'd spoken to someone who had been there on the Seve front line.

"What happened?"

The look of sorrow that settled on Balfruss's face was so intense Alyssa reached out and laid a hand on his arm. He tried to smile but couldn't manage it. Instead he turned his face away so she couldn't see the old pain in his eyes.

"We did what was needed," said Balfruss, his voice thick with emotion. "But the other Battlemages, my friends, they all died."

"I didn't mean to open old wounds," said Alyssa, suddenly desperate for something to distract Balfruss. She brought up the first thing that came to mind, mostly because it had been niggling at her. "During the war, did you ever meet any plague priests?"

"No, none. I didn't even know they existed until this year. I've heard stories of them curing illnesses since the war ended, but Kai is the first one I've met. Why do you ask?"

Alyssa bit her lip, wondering if she was overthinking things. "It's probably nothing."

Balfruss shook his head. "Your instincts are good. It's one of the reasons people follow you. Tell me."

"It's Kai," said Alyssa, glancing around to make sure he wasn't standing below them in the courtyard. Even so she lowered her voice, slightly afraid for some reason that he might hear what was being said. "There's something odd about him."

"I know," admitted Balfruss. "He's a very strange man."

"It's not just that." Alyssa was struggling to put into words what she felt but the feeling in her gut would not leave her. "He unsettles me, and a few others."

"Has he hurt someone or said something?"

"No, nothing like that. He's been kind with all the sick and injured. It's something else. It's hard to describe, but every time he's in the room it's like having an itch inside my head."

"You have more experience of it than me. Do you think he's been changed? Is he one of the Forsaken?"

Alyssa had considered it as a possibility, but he'd exhibited none of the usual behaviour. Also he spent more time alone than with other people, which again wasn't like any of those who had been changed. They wanted to spread the word of their new gospel, not sit alone drinking wine.

"It's not that, I'm certain of it," said Alyssa. "He's got a dark sense of humour and he's a strange man, but there's something more that's out of place."

"I'll look into it," he promised.

She had thought Balfruss might challenge her more and disregard her feeling as nothing more than paranoia. Alyssa had hoped that in some ways. Instead he was going to investigate, and that worried her. What if she was right?

"Where is she?" he muttered. Tammy had been gone for a long time now.

Alyssa joined Balfruss in his vigil and together they silently watched the darkening sky. The light was beginning to fade and no doubt more Forsaken would soon follow. After last night's slaughter Alyssa wondered if they would return in even greater numbers seeking retribution for their dead.

As much as that worried her she couldn't stop thinking about Zannah all alone out there in the darkness. She offered a brief prayer and watched with a growing sense of dread as the shadows lengthened and the sun drifted below the horizon.

When darkness fell they lit the torches on the gate, and others took their places on the wall, preparing themselves for another long night. Zannah still hadn't returned. They were on their own.

CHAPTER 23

"What is your freedom worth?" asked Fenne. He was completely at ease inside his camp, flanked by a dozen mercenaries and with more dotted around the temple grounds.

"Stay calm," muttered Kovac from the corner of his mouth. "Don't let him rattle you."

"You broke our deal," said Tammy, her voice carrying around the courtyard.

"I've honoured it," insisted Fenne. "No part of the deal mentioned you getting back out."

"What do you want?"

Fenne spread his arms wide. "What do you have to offer?"

"Nothing of value besides my sword, and you can't have that."

Fenne waved that away as if it were nothing, for which Tammy was glad. During their voyage Balfruss had told her how the sword had been forged and who by. It was one of a kind and priceless. Perhaps if Fenne had looked at the blade closely he might have noticed something unusual about it, but he hadn't bothered.

"Swords don't interest me."

"Then what does?"

"There's so little to do around here," he said, idly walking towards her. "So few distractions in this dying city. Every day and night is the same, scrambling around for food. It becomes tedious very quickly. People need entertainment, otherwise they might go mad."

Tammy studied the Morrin more closely, noting the many faded scars on his face and arms. There was a hint of grey in the hair over his ears and one of his horns was slightly crooked. He could be mistaken for a normal middle-aged Morrin, if it were not for his terrible yellow eyes. They held no trace of empathy or compassion. An intense fire burned behind them. A seething rage tempered by something Tammy couldn't identify, but she thought there was a hint of madness. Reading people was normally easy for her, but Morrin were not human.

Instead she switched her attention to the other mercenaries around Fenne. They were scared, terrified in fact, and after only hearing a little of what he'd done Tammy guessed they'd seen a lot worse. She was only a temporary visitor but they had to live with the insane Morrin every day. It would be the same as living with a rabid dog and wondering every morning if today would be the day it finally ripped out your throat in a frenzy.

"What kind of entertainment do you have in mind?" she asked.

Fenne's grin was more than a little unnerving but she tried not to show that it bothered her. "Bring your sword and you'll get a chance to find out." He turned and gestured for Tammy to follow.

"What's the deal?" asked Tammy.

"You'll find out," said Fenne, calling back over one shoulder.

With Kovac walking beside her they headed towards the domed temple at the rear of the compound. Three mercenaries fell in beside Kovac, two feral-looking women dressed in hunting leathers and a tall pale-skinned Yerskani man with a shaven head. Kovac nodded amicably at them but he said nothing. Tammy wasn't sure if they were there as Kovac's back-up, or to make sure she followed Fenne to the temple.

"How good are you with a sword?" asked Kovac in a whisper. His lips were barely moving and he kept staring straight ahead.

"Better than average."

"I hope you're a lot better than that. He'll offer you a new deal. Beat one of his men in return for your freedom."

"Sounds fair, if he honours it."

Kovac frowned but didn't look at her. "It's rigged. His champion is lethal with a blade. Best I've ever seen. He'll also stretch it out, make it entertaining and bloody. Fenne always wants a show."

Tammy wasn't sure why Kovac was helping her, and putting himself at risk in the process, but she was grateful. In this sort of situation where she was the outsider, she needed a guide.

As they approached the temple more people joined the party in front of them, streaming out of the long buildings. Some were locals being herded along by mercenaries until Tammy was following a crowd of at least sixty people.

"Anything else I should know?" she asked.

"The best way to get out of this alive is to make Fenne happy. Even if you're winning, make it look good."

The temple had been devoted to the Blessed Mother and once it had been beautiful. Now the doors had been ripped off and probably burned for fuel. The walls were painted with colourful frescos but were now covered with layers of grime, soot and dust, blown in from outside until they were no longer recognisable. All she could see was a face here or pair of hands there amid the muck.

Inside there were no chairs or benches, and half of the floor had been converted into a shanty town of tents where a crowd of smelly, dirty people slept in cramped and unhygienic conditions. The smell of so many unwashed bodies crammed into such a tight space made her gag. Every face was thin and their bodies bordered on the skeletal. Many just lay on pallets or directly on the tiled floor, staring at her with huge eyes. Tammy knew that disease would come hand in hand with famine in such a desperate place.

The other half of the temple was completely clear except for a large circle that had been marked on the floor. At first Tammy thought it was ash or paint, but when she got closer it became clear the substance was dried blood.

The assembled onlookers began to file around the edges of the circle. All of them were careful not to step too close to the line. There was only one chair, a wicker monstrosity filled with cushions, which Fenne sat down in, surrounded by his group of flunkies. The crowd fell silent and the Morrin gestured for her to step into the circle.

"To earn your freedom, all you have to do is beat someone of my choosing. That's the deal." Fenne made it sound so easy.

"I have a counter offer, since you broke our first deal," said Tammy.

The silence in the temple grew oppressive, but she'd waited until this moment to pursue her grievance. Even though he ruled by fear it would become more difficult to maintain control if they knew he couldn't keep his word.

"Pick whoever you want and I'll fight them," said Tammy. "But in return I want my freedom and I want a servant of my own. You have plenty to spare."

Fenne threw back his head and laughed. Those around him smiled as well, easing their hands away from weapons.

"Of course," insisted Fenne. "One less mouth to feed would be a blessing, yes? It's a deal. So, do you want your sword back, or will it be knives?"

Tammy's grin made a few mercenaries twitch. "Neither. Let's make this interesting. How about a fist fight?"

Fenne cackled and rubbed his hands together. "Wonderful. Someone go and fetch Grennig."

Tammy moved to one side of the circle nearest Kovac. "Give me a hand with this," she said, gesturing at her leather armour. He helped her out of her leather vest and unbuckled her bracers, keeping his face bent to the task. She noticed those stood closest to Kovac were the two feral women and the Yerskani with an almost regal bearing. A small pool of space remained around them.

"Are you sure about this?" muttered Kovac.

"It's a little too late for that. Tell me about Grennig."

"He's vicious and I'd say he fights dirty, except there are no rules. He'll try to gouge your eyes, fishhook your mouth, bite you, anything to make you scream."

"You'd better help me with this as well then," said Tammy, taking off her padded vest leaving only a thin shirt. "Cut off the sleeves."

Using a dagger from his belt Kovac cut the sleeves off at the shoulders, giving her plenty of room to move without leaving anything to grab. His eyes widened slightly as he saw the thickness of her arms and shoulders, but he didn't say anything.

"Pull my shirt tight," said Tammy, turning around.

Kovac pulled the material until it was stretched tight across her breasts. He then knotted the remaining fabric on her back, giving her opponent nothing to hold. If Grennig managed to get behind her then it wouldn't matter, but at least this way she wasn't giving him anything, besides the obvious, to grip for leverage.

With a small strip of leather Tammy bound her hair up at the back of her head. The wise decision would be to cut it all off or even shave it, but she didn't think Fenne would wait. It would have to do.

A rumble among the crowd announced the arrival of Grennig and people quickly created room for him to enter the circle. Now that she was practically stripped to the waist Tammy saw a few people glancing at her physique. A few were eyeing her up appreciatively, Kovac among them, who was trying his best not to stare.

A few others around the circle were looking at her speculatively. Some of the mercenaries kept glancing at her hands, noticing the old scars, and then furiously whispering to their neighbours. They were beginning to wonder why she'd asked for this type of fight. There was a flurry of activity in the crowd as people started making bets on the outcome. Just like old times.

Grennig stepped into the circle and Tammy felt the years slip away, back to when she'd worked for one of the crime Families of Perizzi. Don Lowell had looked like everyone's favourite grandfather, but was in fact a ruthless, clever old bastard. She'd collected overdue debts and brawled in the pit fights for money because she'd enjoyed it. The cheering of the crowd and the sound of breaking bones. The domination of another human in the most primal fight for survival. No weapons, not even a sharpened stone, just a closed fist.

It had been a dark and dangerous time in her life and now she was taking herself back there. Voechenka dragged old feelings that were deeply buried back to the surface. It felt as if an old version of herself was trying to re-emerge. For now she let it happen, but also tried to temper the fury of that younger woman with her wisdom and experience.

Grennig was about six foot, which made him shorter than her, but not by much. Even so, his reach would be shorter, which gave her at least one advantage. With him stripped to the waist and with a shaven head, there was nothing for her to grab onto either. He had dusty brown skin and nearly jet-black eyes, indicating a descendant from somewhere in the desert kingdoms.

Grennig's body had few scars, but his knuckles were battered and his nose had been broken several times in the past. The skin around his eyes and mouth looked wrinkled, but as he came closer she could see lots of scar tissue. A veteran. Tammy expected he was doing the same kind of assessment of her and she felt an eager smile from her old self make its way onto her face.

"You know the rule," said Fenne. "Only one of you can step out of the circle. Apart from that there are no rules."

Tammy ignored the Morrin and kept her eyes on Grennig, watching how he moved, looking for weaknesses.

"Begin," someone said, but she didn't rush to attack and neither did Grennig. They started circling each other and although the temple and the crowd were still there on the periphery of her senses, she let them drift away into the background.

Tammy finally raised her hands and Grennig did the same. He met her in the middle of the circle and went on the offensive, jabbing and testing her. Tammy dodged and bobbed from side to side, barely moving her feet, before retaliating with a fast right towards Grennig's face. It slipped past his guard and caught him on the chin, snapping his head down. She followed up with a flurry of left and rights towards his face before stepping in close, grabbing him around the head with her arms and kneeing him in the chest.

Grennig went down backwards but turned it into a roll. He came up onto his haunches breathing hard but wasn't winded as she'd hoped. When he came forward again it was more cautiously, but Tammy didn't give him time to recover. Kovac had told her Grennig was cruel and Fenne had probably thought to make this fight another bout of sport. He was in for a rude awakening.

Keeping him at the edge of her reach Tammy hounded her opponent, going after him with vicious blows and occasionally catching him. One hard left split Grennig's bottom lip, another crunched into his left cheek and a third bruised his right eye. When he tried to pull back and take a breather she followed up, stepped inside his reach and hammered her forehead into his face.

A spray of blood landed on the ground and the first dull crack of broken bone rang out. Grennig's nose was now askew but it didn't slow him down much because he'd broken it before. If anything it made him angry, as Tammy had hoped. She took a few blows to the stomach and ribs then caught Grennig on the left temple with an elbow, which sent him reeling.

He quickly recovered and came at her hard, his fists a blur, which caught her by surprise. The punches were badly timed but remembering what Kovac said, Tammy pretended they had hurt her. Fenne wanted a show, so she would give him one.

Grennig followed up, going after her ribs, then switching to her head as she tried to hunch over her body. The volume of noise from the crowd was so loud it began to penetrate her bubble of concentration. After taking a nasty left hook on the side of her face Tammy blocked the next blow and retaliated with two hard jabs that surprised Grennig, stunning him and stopping him cold.

Before he could recover she targeted his left side, going after his ribs, then switching and rattling his jaw with an uppercut that rocked him on his feet. Next she unleashed a left hook that split the skin over his eye. Screaming in rage he tried to grab her in a bear hug but she seized his wrist, twisted his arm and tossed him over her hip. He landed badly on his back and she danced away from his clawing hands. Somewhere in the back of her mind she could hear the roaring of the crowd.

When Grennig came back to his feet she let him go on the offensive, soaking up blows on her arms, taking some to the body and one or two to the face. Grennig grinned, thinking she'd used up all of her stamina and now the fight was his. When he tried to move in closer she slammed him in the middle of the forehead with an open palm, snapping his head back. Dazed he stumbled back, just in time for her to slip behind him and land three heavy punches to his kidneys.

Howling in pain he lashed out, staggering around like a drunk, but Tammy just kept her distance and waited. Wiping blood to clear his left eye Grennig didn't see her until she was already too close. Two hard jabs rattled his teeth and there was another crack. Almost blind in one eye from the trickling blood, and with the other swelling shut, the first hints of fear began to set in. Tammy grinned fiercely at his expression and in that moment they both knew the fight was already over.

Piece by piece she took him apart, breaking him down until he was just a hunk of bloody meat.

She rattled his kidneys and ribs until he was hunched over, barely able to catch his breath. She repeatedly hammered his left eye, opening the cut even wider until half of his face was painted red. Next she seized his right arm, twisted it and tossed him halfway across the circle. He skidded across the tiled floor out of the circle, only to be shoved back in. With a grunt of effort Tammy grabbed him by the throat and crotch, lifted him overhead and threw him the other way. He landed badly on his side, one arm beneath him. Grabbing him around the throat she picked him off the floor, choking Grennig until his face turned red and then purple. When she dropped him he stayed there, on hands and knees, bloody and bruised, but still moving.

Two voices inside Tammy were telling her different things. The voice of experience told her to finish it quickly, but the other voice was telling her to hurt him. To make him suffer so that he would always remember her, and this moment when she had broken him. Now that she had opened herself to the darkness within it was difficult to suppress.

Snarling she kicked Grennig in the ribs, knocking him onto his back. A heel to the crotch made him squeal and curl up but she didn't relent, sitting astride him and hammering blows into his face over and over until her hands were covered with blood. It splashed all over the floor, her arms, her face. Grennig was mewling, trying to shield his face, but Tammy kept punching until she heard something break.

Grennig's hands stopped moving and flopped to his sides. The world swung back into focus and Tammy became aware of her surroundings and the sound of her frantic breathing. The roar of the crowd had not been in her head but now as she stood up, covered in blood, it drained away until an awful silence filled the temple. Looking down at Grennig she saw the shattered remains of a man. She didn't know if that snapping sound had been his neck. He might be dead or just unconscious.

Appalled at what she had done Tammy gritted her teeth and forced the old rage away. Stumbling towards Fenne she crossed the circle until she stood before him, trying to catch her breath. The mercenaries surrounding the Morrin had all drawn their weapons and were looking at her with a mix of fear and awe. The people beside the mercenaries were less enamoured and Tammy found she couldn't look at them as her shame was too great. Only Fenne seem unperturbed and was grinning. He applauded and his clapping rang out, echoing over and over around the dome.

"Is that it? Is that the best you have?" spat Tammy, trying to slow her breathing.

"Maybe you'd like to try another opponent?" suggested Fenne.

"That wasn't the deal," shouted one of the spectators. Fenne stood up, looking for the speaker, but with the crowd packed in so tight it was hard to find the source.

"We made a deal," said Tammy, drawing the Morrin's attention back to her. "Are you going to keep your word this time?"

Tammy knew Fenne wanted nothing more than to kill her, or pit her against another fighter, but now everyone was watching him. "Take your sword and get out," he snarled, turning away until her voice stopped him.

"And I want the girl, Rheena. You promised me a servant."

For a brief moment she considered fighting again and asking for Perron. Last time Fenne had not expected her to win, but now he had the measure of her skill. He would not give her a fair fight a second time. She had made a promise to the girl's father and she intended to keep it.

Fenne paused with his back to her and Tammy felt the atmosphere in the temple change. The whole crowd seemed to be holding its breath and she saw a few mercenaries start to draw their weapons. It had been part of the deal, but Fenne never thought he'd have to honour it. She knew he didn't care about the girl. It was more that she was taking something from him.

"Here," said Kovac, shoving a young woman towards Tammy. Rheena was tall and gawky, somewhere on the border between a girl and becoming a woman. Tammy offered a smile to try and reassure the girl but she looked unsettled. After a second she realised it was probably the blood splattered across her face and hands.

Fenne glared at Kovac and then turned away, gesturing for his flunkies to follow. The tension eased and the crowd slowly began to disperse. After wiping off the blood and dressing quickly in her armour, Kovac and his friends escorted them to the gate. The plank was already laid out across the pit and Tammy sent the girl ahead. Overhead the sky was almost completely black, a few clouds obscuring the moon.

"Will you be all right?" asked Kovac as Tammy resettled her sword. She glanced at the sky and shrugged. Hopefully they could make it back before the Forsaken started to emerge.

"We'll find out." She offered Kovac a hand, which he shook. "Thank you."

"Travel safe."

With fatigue starting to set in from the fight Tammy crossed the pit back onto the street. As the gates closed behind her the last thing she saw inside the temple was Kovac. He raised a hand in farewell and the gates boomed shut.

Rheena stared at the temple and Tammy could see the tears standing out in her eyes. Her father was still in there and no matter how horrible it had been, at least she had been safe from the Forsaken. Now she was alone in the city and nightfall was almost here.

As they set off down the street Tammy heard someone approaching from up ahead. Their footsteps were loud in the oppressive silence and, much to Tammy's surprise, Zannah walked towards her.

"Save your questions for later," said the Morrin. "We need to get back before the Forsaken attack and we're trapped outside with them."

"Lead the way," said Tammy, forcing herself to keep up with Zannah's pace. They weren't out of danger yet.

CHAPTER 24

Zannah stared at the bruised and battered face of Tammy, glanced at the girl and then turned away from the old temple. Her questions could wait.

She set a fast pace and knew the others would do their best to keep up. They understood the level of danger and Zannah would only slow down if they started to lag behind.

The streets were empty at the moment but that didn't mean anything. Any second, the Forsaken could crawl out of the shadows. In her experience where there was one, more were always lurking nearby.

At the next crossroads she turned right and then quickly stopped, one hand instinctively going to her sword. On the left side of the street one of the buildings had been completely shattered and now all that remained was one crumbling wall. It created a black pool of the deepest shadows, and despite there still being some daylight, none penetrated this pocket of night. Zannah's eyes adjusted and the black peeled away until she could see everything in the shadows. The bricks, the rotting corpse of a small animal, broken furniture.

Discarded objects leapt into sharp focus, but the woman did not.

As ever it was difficult to see her clearly, as if Zannah was looking at her through a low fog or heat haze. She was a wraith. Incredibly tall and beautiful yet so thin that it made her look out of proportion and inhuman. Her shoulders were too wide for the rest of her body and the waist too narrow, as if she'd been cobbled together from different people. Zannah tried to focus on more details but all she could see was that the wraith wore something black covering most of her body. Only her hands and feet were bare and the skin on them was white as snow. A deep cowl sat on her shoulders and bright white hair tumbled down across it, glowing with its own light.

"What is it?" asked Tammy. Part of Zannah had hoped that Tammy might be able to see the wraith, but other people never could. "Why have we stopped?"

The wraith put a long graceful finger to her cherry-red lips and smiled. Zannah felt a prickle of fear run across her scalp and down her back.

"I thought I saw something," said Zannah, turning her face away. The wraith didn't disappear like a lost spirit. There were plenty of those drifting around the city. Sometimes at night on the wall, when it was quiet, a few spirits would walk past as if they were still alive. The following night the same spirits might appear again, going through the same ritual, caught in a place between life and death.

When Zannah moved past the wraith she could still see her waving. Gritting her teeth and telling herself it was nothing, Zannah pressed on. She resumed her punishing pace as she looked for trouble, and in some ways, hoped for it. At least the Forsaken were something she could fight. Even if she didn't understand what they were, they could still be killed.

*

When they were more than halfway back to the winery she heard something in the distance. There was a brief shout of surprise followed by the roar of a crowd and then the screaming began. It was coming from somewhere to the west, towards one of the other camps.

"Keep up," she told the others. The girl looked terrified, her eyes wide and innocent. Tammy was in pain and exhausted, but she just grunted and waved for Zannah to get moving. The Morrin immediately turned down an alley and started jogging, dodging around fallen masonry and broken roof tiles. Despite moving with speed her eyes picked out the safest path in the gloom and she heard her companions mirroring her route around obstacles. After a few minutes the sounds of battle fell away and she slowed to a fast walk. The streets around her seemed deserted but that only made Zannah more nervous. Her senses were stretched to the point where she could hear the heartbeat of the two women behind her. In the next street a loose stone slid down a pile and her sword was instantly in her hand, her eyes scanning the surrounding area.

Rather than moving away Zannah stalked towards the fallen stone, expecting trouble. It would be far better to deal with it now than run with the others trailing behind. She reached the fallen stone and looked up and down the street, but there was nothing there. Not even the wraith stared back at her this time.

With a slight shove of her foot the whole wall wobbled and then collapsed. Satisfied that it was nothing more than natural instability, Zannah returned them to their original path.

By the time they arrived at the gates of the winery the sky was completely black overhead. She was pleased to see someone else had lit the torches above the gate, and that several people were standing on the wall.

"Where have you been?" said Alyssa, chiding her, yet obviously relieved to see they were safe.

The rope came down and they sent the girl up first. She was weak and climbed with some difficulty but eventually managed it. All the while Zannah stood with her back to the torches, maintaining her night vision and view of the street. After staring at this part of the city night after night she knew every rock, every shadow, every fallen stone. Nothing was out of place. Then the wraith appeared again in one of the upstairs windows of a building halfway down the street. She grinned, pulled up her hood and, once she was sure Zannah had seen her, moved out of sight.

"Are you all right?" asked Tammy. Zannah tried to relax her shoulders. "Is it the Forsaken?"

"You go up next," said Zannah, ignoring the questions.

Grunting with effort Tammy climbed the rope. Zannah kept watching the street but the wraith didn't return and there was no sign of the Forsaken.

"Your turn, Zannah," said Alyssa, from above.

Zannah turned and quickly scaled the rope, mostly using her arms and barely bracing her feet against the wall. Ever since the Battlemage had healed her she felt younger and stronger. A week ago she would have been much slower. Alyssa gave her a peculiar look as she slipped over the top, but if she'd noticed any change she didn't mention it. More surprising was when Alyssa hugged her, pressing her skinny body against her.

"I'm so glad you're safe," she whispered. The others on the wall were staring in shock and Zannah could feel a few glares, as if she were to blame for Alyssa's action.

Alyssa pulled away before Zannah could say anything in return. The girl and Tammy went inside and Zannah resumed her post on the wall. The others didn't make space for her and they continued to pretend she wasn't there. Only Balfruss seemed pleased to see her and he offered a smile before a worried frown settled back on his features. Zannah thought about asking him about the woman in the shadows. It would have to wait until they were alone.

"Will the Forsaken return tonight?" asked Balfruss, bringing her back to the present.

"Always. Last night's attack didn't work, so they'll try something else. Maybe several waves to wear us down."

Somewhere in the distance they heard a scream echo across the city. It sounded like an animal, but Zannah knew it was the feral scream of a dying human. Driven to despair and backed into a corner, a human would fight and keep fighting, even as their heart gave out. She'd seen it first-hand.

Elsewhere in the distance came the answering cry of rebellion and the clash of steel. It was coming from several directions and occasionally she saw a bright flash of light. The Forsaken were attacking other bases but not theirs. Not yet anyway. She was certain they would come in time.

Half an hour later Tammy came up the stairs. Her wounds had been treated and her hands bandaged, but there was a grey sheen to her skin from exhaustion. She clutched a steaming bowl of stew in one hand and a hunk of bread in the other.

"What's happening?" she asked with her mouth full of food.

"The Forsaken are attacking," said Zannah. Tammy tilted her head to one side and listened to the sounds of battle.

"We need to know what's going on."

"What is there to know?" asked Zannah. "The mercenaries are being attacked. Soon it will be our turn."

"How many Forsaken are there?"

Zannah frowned. "You've asked this question. The numbers always change. No one knows the answer."

"I've spoken to local people in every base, and none of them knows where the Forsaken come from or what they really are." Tammy gestured at Balfruss with her spoon. "Is there a way you can track them with your magic? Find out where they go when the sun comes up?"

The Battlemage considered it before shaking his head. "No, not really."

"We don't know enough about them. We don't even know what they want. The only way we'll find the answers is from one of them. We need to capture one of the Forsaken alive." Tammy's words hung in the air between them and Zannah heard a few people on the wall fidget in discomfort at the thought.

"Even if we caught one, I don't think it would willingly give up the others," said Balfruss.

Tammy shrugged. "Maybe, maybe not. But they may not need to."

"What did you find out?" he asked.

Tammy lowered her voice so that it didn't carry to the others further down the wall. "I spoke to a man called Perron in Fenne's camp. A friend of his became one of the Forsaken, but something went wrong. Even so he told Perron that he could feel the other Forsaken and that they're all connected. Like a beehive or an ant colony."

"There was something there," said Balfruss, almost to himself. "Before we beheaded the Forsaken, I felt an echo of something tying them together."

"If you had more time to study one of them, do you think you could trace the echo?" asked Tammy.

"Perhaps," said Balfruss. "It's worth considering."

"The risk is too great," said Zannah, not caring if anyone else heard her. "I will not bring a live Forsaken inside our shelter."

Tammy spread her hands. "I'm open to ideas."

Zannah waited for someone else to say something. The Battlemage would know of some other way to find out what they needed. He was more powerful than any wizard. He had changed the course of the war and killed the Warlock. Instead of providing an answer he remained silent and drummed his fingers on the wall.

Zannah grunted. Everyone had their limits.

Somewhere to the west there was a crashing of stone and a cheer from many voices.

"We still need to know what's going on," said Tammy, finishing off her food. "The best way is to watch the Forsaken."

"You can't go back out there," said Alyssa, coming up the stairs. "You're in no condition."

Tammy looked as if she wanted to argue but whatever had happened in Fenne's camp had exhausted her.

"I will go," said Balfruss. "I can protect myself if the Forsaken try to attack me."

"They will attack you," said Zannah, earning a frown from Alyssa. "You move like a pregnant sow, noisy and slow. The darkness holds no secrets from me. I can see everything and move silently when I must."

Alyssa stepped in front of Zannah. "You've only just come back. You don't have to do this."

"The plague priest was right," said Zannah, remembering what the weird little man had said about them. "We have become sheep, frightened into waiting for the butcher."

"I can tell by the stubborn set of your jaw that nothing I say is going to change your mind, is it?" said Alyssa and Zannah shook her head.

A smile tugged at the corners of Zannah's mouth. "I will watch and listen. I will not fight unless I must."

Part of her wanted to jump from the wall and start running

but she knew it would be reckless. Zannah caught Balfruss staring as if he knew what she had been thinking. Perhaps he did. Instead they fetched the rope and she went down, feigning caution.

As soon as her feet touched the ground Zannah turned and ran down the street, heading for the nearest mercenary base. A few minutes later she heard a disturbance up ahead. Someone was shouting angrily but there were no sounds of fighting.

Slipping into a nearby building Zannah navigated through the ruins, going up a flight of stairs and climbing through windows until she stood looking down into the street by the first mercenary base in the old bank. Much to her surprise the street looked abandoned but then she noticed two figures stood in the middle of the road. The two men were perfectly still, their faces tilted up towards the roof where three mercenaries watched them. They had to be Forsaken to stand out in the open like that, and yet they didn't attack. Each group watched one another, waiting for something, but neither of the Forsaken moved or even seemed to breathe. One of the mercenaries shouted something and wasted an arrow that fell short. The Forsaken didn't react. Zannah left them to their staring match and moved on.

At the next base she found something similar but equally worrying. A handful of Forsaken were roaming around outside, endlessly circling the mercenary camp. Like Roake they kept calling out names of people inside, telling them to come out and join them. They claimed it was much better to be with them, to be Embraced, than to be a slave to people who didn't care. It was another stalling tactic, to keep those inside scared. The six Forsaken could be easily dispatched if any of the mercenaries came out from behind their walls, but they didn't want to take the risk. Fifty more Forsaken could be waiting in the shadows. Zannah left them to their mind games and turned away.

Before she reached the third base Zannah heard the frantic sounds of battle. Taking her time to avoid being spotted, she crept through the rubble until she could look into the street from a first-floor window. Twenty or more Forsaken were trying to break down the front door of the building with a battering ram while others stood waiting with bows. Every time a mercenary attempted to drop something onto the Forsaken in the street, several bowstrings twanged and one or more defenders were wounded or killed. One man was hit with three arrows and he tumbled from the roof into the road. As soon as he landed, three Forsaken spirited him away. Zannah saw the terrified look on his face, more so from what they might do to him than his injuries. He would soon discover that sometimes it was better to die in battle than live and have to deal with whatever came next.

This base would fall tonight. The Forsaken were determined. The others were being harried by only a few, while the majority seemed to be focused here. It was probably the same at Fenn-etaris's base, one or two Forsaken keeping a hundred or more frozen with fear.

As her eyes scanned the street Zannah picked out more figures waiting in the shadows of surrounding buildings. If the mercenaries inside panicked and opened the front door to dispatch this first wave of Forsaken the others would rush in. It was over, no matter what happened.

Retracing her steps, Zannah moved back through the building before pausing in the open doorway. The wooden door itself had been stripped away long ago, so she stayed further back in the shadows, watching the street. Once she was certain no one was there she stepped out with her sword drawn.

A few seconds later three people came around a corner. Two carried bows and the other a sword on her hip, but these were not mercenaries. As they opened their mouths to scream Zannah rushed at them, cutting down one of the bowmen before he could reach for a weapon. The other man discarded his bow and managed to draw a dagger from his belt just in time for Zannah to hammer the pommel of her sword into his face. She followed up with a kick to the chest that sent him reeling backwards.

By now the Forsaken woman had drawn her sword and she came at Zannah with a scream. With a frown of disappointment the Morrin stepped to the side and casually tripped the woman with one foot as she stumbled past. Being Forsaken might make them stronger, but it did not imbue them with any sword skills. Using both hands Zannah drove the tip of her sword through the woman's back. It burst from the front of her body, spraying gore across the street. She gasped once and then slid off the sword, falling to the ground in a crumpled heap.

As the other man stumbled upright Zannah kicked him in the face again and he collapsed. The fight had lasted barely a minute. Nevertheless she paused and tilted her head to one side, listening for the sound of anyone lurking nearby. Apart from the endless pounding of the battering ram in the distance there was nothing. Not even the faintest scurry of vermin or insects.

The woman cried out once as Zannah cut off her head and the bowman made no sound at all. More Forsaken could find her at any moment. She needed to hide the bodies. Gripping them by the feet she was about to drag the corpses into one of the empty buildings when she had an idea. A vicious smile slowly crept across her face.

She beheaded the third Forsaken but instead of hiding the

bodies she left them where they were, tossing the heads into one of the buildings. Being Embraced and becoming one of the Forsaken might change a person, inside and out, but it wasn't a total transformation. The essence of who the person used to be was still there and they still had emotions.

Fear was a useful weapon and in their hands they had held the entire city to ransom. Now it was time to use it against them.

Chapter 25

The chilly night air started to seep into Balfruss's body despite his woollen gloves and scarf. His hands and feet were warm, but he felt weary after his time fighting more pupils of Kaine.

Zannah had been gone for over an hour now and still there was no sign of any Forsaken in the street. Occasionally the faint sounds of battle reached his ears from somewhere in the city. A distant cry, the clash of weapons, but it never came any closer to them at the winery.

A dozen people, plus Tammy, were stood alongside him on the wall, staring into the dark. Tammy had briefly told him what she'd found in the camp run by the last rogue Morrin. She'd skipped over the details but he knew the weary slump of her shoulders came from more than just fatigue. The cuts and bruises on her face told a story of their own but right now she didn't want to talk about it.

"They'll call us if anything happens," he said, touching her on the arm and startling her out of a reverie. "We should go and lie down."

The furrows in Tammy's forehead eased and she raised an eyebrow. "That's quite an interesting proposition."

"I didn't mean," he spluttered before realising Tammy was teasing him.

"Maybe tomorrow, when I've got a bit more energy?" she said and he chuckled before it became a full laugh. It felt good to laugh. It was the first time he'd properly done so since arriving in Shael.

"I'm going to get some sleep," he said, pretending to storm down the stairs. "Alone!"

"Sounds like a good idea," she called after him.

Balfruss went to his room and lay down but despite it being warm under the blankets he couldn't rest. His mind kept turning over what the boy, Willem, had said and how ruthless Kaine must be to put them in that kind of situation. They were just children and because the Red Tower was no longer what it used to be, a different kind of Seeker had found them. Instead of learning about the joys of the Source and all of the things it could create, they'd been taught how to kill while living in a city of sorrow and death.

Giving up on sleep Balfruss walked the hallways of the winery looking for a distraction. It was fairly gloomy at night so he summoned a blue ball of light to chase away the shadows. He descended one flight of stairs and slowly walked the full length of each corridor, glancing into open doorways. Some people were asleep, others sat reading by meagre candlelight, and the rest were playing games or just talking quietly to distract themselves from another long night. Many of the adults had weapons close to hand in case they were called to be on the wall and defend the base.

When he passed Kai's room Balfruss glanced in and then stopped in surprise. The door was almost closed but through the gap he saw it was pitch-black inside. It was as if the deepest shadows had been pulled together and a solid wall of nothingness erected on the threshold to the room. Pale blue magical light from the orb in Balfruss's hand touched the edge of the void and the darkness recoiled as if it were alive. Nudging the door open with his free hand he saw the interior of the whole room was swallowed in an unnatural black and dense fog.

Sending more power into the orb Balfruss pushed his arm forward and the black receded then vanished as if it had never been there. Suddenly he could see inside the room as normal. There was a pallet in one corner, scattered empty wine bottles on the floor and Kai was hunched in one corner where the last traces of darkness resided. His eyes flashed red and then returned to their normal colour.

Kai offered a friendly smile, trying to cover up what Balfruss had seen, but it was too late. He knew the priest was talking but he wasn't listening. He drew more power from the Source, which he fed into the orb of light until it blazed like the sun. The magical fire spread across his hand and beyond until his arm was aflame, eliminating all darkness from the room. Kai flinched at the light and his smile wavered.

Balfruss remembered what Alyssa had said about the priest being unsettling and now he felt that same unease in his gut. Reaching out with his senses towards Kai he searched for something out of place. Kai's smile disappeared as if he knew what Balfruss was doing, which was impossible. Only someone who could feel the Source would know.

"I wouldn't do that," warned Kai, his voice taking on a commanding tone. Instead of withdrawing Balfruss moved closer to the priest, amplifying his senses with even more power. The room flickered before his eyes as he concentrated on Kai. At first nothing seemed different but then he noticed the shadows in the room had returned and were now gathered around Kai as if he was the source of all darkness. His eyes started to glow red and the shadows behind him merged and swelled into one massive shape. Part of the shadow started to writhe, like the many arms of a giant squid.

When Balfruss looked at Kai again the image of the man flickered for a second. For a brief moment he saw something else. A monstrous creature with writhing tentacles and dozens of glowing red eyes that glared at him. And there was something else too. A terrible weight started to press against his mind.

"What are you?" whispered Balfruss, summoning a shield and drawing more power into him.

"Enough," said Kai, standing up quickly. He made a cutting motion with one hand and the world around them changed.

Balfruss barely managed to hold on to the Source as suddenly he found they were not standing in the winery any more. Instead they were in an enormous hall with a stone floor and a long banqueting table running down the middle. Identical wooden chairs were spaced out equally along its length and at the head sat a massive chair far bigger than the rest. Cold stone fireplaces, large enough for Balfruss to walk into, were spaced out along the walls and there were no doors or windows anywhere in sight. The room was utterly lifeless and he could hear nothing except his own echoing heartbeat.

"Where are we?" asked Balfruss, summoning power into his hands and crafting it into a ball of something deadly. "What are you?"

"I'm not a threat," said Kai, holding up both hands and making a show of them being empty. "I was sent to Voechenka to investigate the darkness, just like you."

When Kai took a step forward Balfruss moved backwards, maintaining the distance between them. His hip brushed up against one of the chairs and vivid colours and images of bright summer days flashed through his mind. Stumbling back he moved away from the chairs while trying to keep his hold on the Source.

"I wouldn't do that again if I were you," suggested Kai.

"You're not human," said Balfruss.

"No, I'm not."

"Are you working with Kaine or the Forsaken?"

"You're not listening," said Kai. "I was sent to find out what the Forsaken really are."

Balfruss was listening but at the same time he was also looking for a way out of the room. There had to be a door hidden somewhere in one of the walls. Maybe a secret panel inside one of the fireplaces. The high ceiling above his head was criss-crossed with thick black wooden beams like the bones of a monstrous beast. He also realised there were no lanterns or candles anywhere in the room and yet there was enough light to see normally.

"Who sent you?" asked Balfruss.

Kai winced. "That's difficult to explain."

"How do I get out of here?" Balfruss touched one of the stone walls and found it was cool and the surface was rough against his fingertips. It felt real enough and yet as he applied some pressure he felt the wall bend ever so slightly. "What is this place?"

"It's nowhere and everywhere," said Kai. "We're still in the winery. This place is just between moments."

Balfruss stared at him without comprehension. "Take us back."

"Wait—"

Stalking towards Kai, Balfruss summoned more power while channelling light into the glowing sphere clasped between his hands. Kai squinted at the brightness of the orb and involuntarily took a step back.

"Take us back now!" demanded Balfruss, his voice echoing around the room.

"Hello, Balfruss," said a calm voice from behind him.

The Sorcerer spun around and this time his concentration did fall apart. All of his summoned power vanished and the light in the room returned to normal.

It was Vargus.

He looked exactly the same as when Balfruss had seen him last, in Charas. Except that was impossible, because Vargus was dead. Balfruss had heard the story from many who were there during the warrior's final moments. They'd seen him fall from the walls of the city. That was over four years ago.

"What are you?" was all Balfruss managed to say.

"What do you think, Sorcerer?" asked the warrior. He said the title with an odd inflection and it sparked a memory in Balfruss's mind. A memory from their time together during the war when a drunken Vargus had described the Warlock as nothing more than a child playing with fire. He'd also talked about meeting Sorcerers in person when no one had used the title in centuries. At the time Balfruss had put it down to Vargus being drunk and confused, but now as he stared around the banqueting hall, he knew it was something else.

"You're not human either," said Balfruss. Vargus smiled and gestured for him to continue. "You're old. Very old in fact. When we first met you knew about ancient and obscure religions like the Twelve and the Triumvirate."

"Kai shouldn't have brought you here, but now that he has there seems little point in denying it. I cannot tell you everything, so please do not ask for more than I'm willing to share." Vargus waited for Balfruss to agree before he continued. "There are beings in the world, far older than mankind. Older than the Vorga and even the Sull, that live among you. Kai and I are two such beings."

"Are there more like you?" asked Balfruss, and Vargus raised an eyebrow. "Sorry," apologised the Sorcerer. "It's just with so many chairs I guessed there had to be more."

"Yes, there are," confirmed Vargus, "but don't ask anything else."

"I can't help asking questions."

"That's one of the reasons mortals are so dangerous," said Kai, moving around the room until he stood on the other side of the table. "You're always asking why, what and how. Why is the sky blue? What's over that hill? How do we build this thing bigger? That looks dangerous, how do we kill it?"

Balfruss was glad they were both standing where he could keep an eye on them. Part of his mind was screaming at him to run or attack, but there was nowhere to go and he doubted his magic would hurt them. After all, Vargus had died and yet he was alive in this nowhere place. To make matters worse there was also the troubling shadow Balfruss had seen behind Kai and his glowing red eyes.

It was a lot to take in and Balfruss felt light-headed. He was about to suggest sitting down when he noticed both Kai and Vargus stayed away from the chairs. In fact there was a distinct gap between them and the furniture.

"What he means is that's one of the reasons mankind has flourished," said Vargus, frowning at Kai.

"I know what I meant," was all he said.

"By the Maker," hissed Balfruss, and both Vargus and the priest winced.

"Don't say his name," said Kai, glancing at something behind Balfruss. "Especially not here."

The pieces began to slot into place. Balfruss glanced at the massive chair at the head of the table and then back at Vargus. He felt as if the world were spinning and yet he knew nothing had moved. Stumbling he moved to one of the walls and leaned against it, hoping it didn't give way. Pressing his forehead and hands against the stone Balfruss took a moment to collect his thoughts. He tried to speak several times and had to swallow hard before he could manage it.

"Is he out there too?" asked Balfruss, pointing at the huge chair. "Walking around as one of us?"

"Not that it matters," said Vargus, "but yes he is. Right now you need to focus on the fallen city."

"Do you know what has infected Voechenka?" asked Balfruss.

"For all of our knowledge we only have theories. If you could tell me about what you've found we might be able to help." Vargus gestured at himself and Kai, who didn't look very confident.

"The city has been poisoned," said Balfruss, scrubbing a hand over his face as he tried to collect his thoughts. He casually studied his surroundings at the same time, trying to record every detail. "There is no life anywhere. No birds or rats, not even any insects in the earth. Something has drained it all away. I suspect if you planted a seed in the soil nothing would grow."

"Do you know where to find this thing?" asked Vargus, a frown creasing his weathered face.

"Tammy is trying, but it's proving difficult to locate. It's also affecting everyone in the city. It presses on the mind, bringing up dark thoughts and feelings that are normally buried. The longer someone is exposed to it, the worse it becomes. I suspect most people in Voechenka don't even realise why they're so angry or despondent all the time."

"It's another tactic to keep its prey subdued," said Kai, earning a frown from Vargus, but the priest just grinned, showing off sharp teeth that made Balfruss take a step back. "It's also building an army."

"Why?" asked Balfruss. "What does it want?"

Vargus and Kai exchanged a look and the priest shrugged, leaving the decision up to the warrior.

"Whatever this creature is, I believe it's almost outgrown Voechenka," said Vargus. "The Forsaken are its foot soldiers and I think it's nearly ready for an invasion."

"I felt something when I studied one of them," said Balfruss. "There was a delicate whisper of something. If I could study one for a while, I might be able to find where it's hiding."

Vargus walked towards him and Balfruss had to fight hard to suppress his instincts to run. The warrior smiled as if he understood the conflict and laid a hand on Balfruss's shoulder. "I know all of this is very strange, but trust me when I say that we want the same thing. I fought in the war alongside you because I wanted to save lives. If the Mad King and the Warlock had been unopposed the world would've been a different place. If the poison in Voechenka spreads it will kill thousands, maybe more. That cannot be allowed to happen."

"What do you suggest?"

"Stick to the plan. Try using one of the Forsaken to track down the source and then kill whatever it is, but remember, Kai is there to help." Vargus glanced sideways at the priest, who offered what he assumed was meant to be a reassuring smile. Balfruss had glimpsed what he really was and couldn't easily forget. "Call on him if you need help."

Balfruss wasn't sure that he would ever turn to the priest for help, but he agreed, to placate Vargus. The grizzled warrior smiled and thumped him on the shoulder.

"We were right about you."

Before Balfruss could ask Vargus what he meant, the world around him shuddered. The light changed and Balfruss suddenly found himself back in Kai's room at the winery amid a collection of empty bottles.

The priest looked human enough and his shadow had returned to normal, but now Balfruss could see an inhuman gleam behind his eyes. Moving carefully he backed out of the room but Kai made no attempt to follow. Instead he started looking through the bottles, searching for one that still had some wine left in it.

Balfruss retraced his steps to his room and wedged the door shut. He didn't think it would make any difference but he didn't know what else to do. Sleep had evaded him earlier because of thoughts about Kaine, but now he was afraid to doze in case he saw in full what his mind had glimpsed. Every time he closed his eyes all he could see was a massive writhing shadow on the wall and glowing red eyes.

It made him reassess a great many things that had happened during the war. Most of all, he wondered, if Kai was really that creature underneath, what did Vargus truly look like?

CHAPTER 26

It had been another long and tiring night for Tammy. She'd intended to follow Balfruss's suggestion of getting some sleep, but seeing the locals standing alone had made her hesitate. Normally Zannah was there to lead them, and as much as they hated her, each person in the shelter knew she was an implacable force against the Forsaken. But now the Morrin was out there in the city, trying to find out what the Forsaken were doing at the other camps.

Tammy was about to stay when Alyssa approached and gestured for her to follow a little way along the wall away from the others.

"They need this," Alyssa whispered, so that her voice didn't carry to the others. "Zannah has always been there to protect them. If they're ever going to stand on their own they need to build some confidence."

It made sense. If she stayed they would simply defer to her experience instead of Zannah's.

Back in her room, wrapped in a huge pile of woollen blankets, Tammy drifted in and out of sleep. In her dreams the fight with Grennig at the temple kept coming back to her in snatches, except now it had become even more bloody and violent. Instead of tossing Grennig across the ring she lifted him above her head and then brought him down against her knee, shattering his spine.

Tammy came awake, looking around the tiny room for a distraction to slow her frantic pulse. Eventually the weariness pulled her back under and this time she dreamed she was pinned to the floor, struggling to breathe as her opponent strangled her to death. Except this time it wasn't Grennig, but a heavily tattooed man from the desert kingdoms. In desperation she bit into his neck and ripped it open with her teeth. Hot blood sprayed all over her face, in her eyes and mouth, and she gagged on it.

Tammy came awake again, trying to understand the source of the intense imagery. It had to be this cursed city. It had dredged up a lot of emotions she'd long since shoved into the darkest corners of her mind. With them came memories of real fights that had actually taken place. Years ago she had fought a man from the desert and beaten him, but she hadn't bitten out his throat.

Unable to sleep she went down to the lower levels which were abandoned at this hour of night. After drawing water from one of the wells she stripped and had a cold shower. The water sharpened her mind and helped chase away the remnants of the nightmares. By the time she'd dressed and eaten some porridge it was almost dawn.

As she stepped into the courtyard a flurry of light snow was drifting down from the grey sky overhead. It was definitely getting colder every morning and soon the whole city would be covered with a blanket of white. If only it were that easy to transform the city from a ruin full of despair into something new and wonderful.

The people around her tried to pretend that all would be well, but Tammy saw how quickly their smiles slipped away. They all felt it. Time was running out.

Even though it was early the wall was still busy with local defenders. Alyssa was absent but Balfruss was leaning against it and staring out across the city with a mug of tea in one hand. He glanced at her and she saw dark shadows under his eyes from a sleepless night. The Sorcerer had something on his mind as well that had kept him awake. Much to her surprise the yawning defenders were smiling and clearly pleased with themselves about something. They had been here all night then. Peering over the wall into the street she saw a few arrows but no Forsaken anywhere.

"We chased them off," said a woman. "They thought they could scare us or get over the wall, but we showed them."

Tammy said nothing, remembering what the mercenary Graff had said about two Forsaken keeping everyone in the entire base on alert all night.

Alyssa joined them on the wall with a mug of tea as they waited for Zannah to return. As the sky changed to a dull grey overhead the defenders decided their vigil was over. Without any outside help they had defended their home. That was what they would tell themselves but Tammy knew it was only an illusion. If the Forsaken attacked tonight and the locals survived, then their newfound confidence would be real. Half a dozen fresh faces took their place on the wall to keep watch in case they were attacked during the day. It was unlikely but Zannah had always done it and in her absence they would too.

A short time later Zannah came jogging down the street towards them. Alyssa heaved an audible sigh of relief and some of the tension eased from her shoulders. The Morrin climbed up the rope with ease and wasn't remotely out of breath when she reached the top. In fact Tammy thought she looked refreshed, as if time away from the wall or perhaps whatever she'd been doing had invigorated her.

"I've seen the Forsaken," said the Morrin.

"You must be tired," said Alyssa, trying to steer Zannah downstairs.

"That can wait," said Zannah, gently shaking off Alyssa's attempt to look after her. "It's as we expected. We've killed so many that the Forsaken are now outnumbered."

Zannah described what she had seen at the other camps; tactics to delay and distract while the majority of the Forsaken assaulted one base.

"It will have fallen by now. They were determined."

"Blessed Mother watch over them," said Alyssa, placing her right hand over her heart. "Those poor people."

"They're gone," said Zannah, frowning as the plague priest came up the stairs to join them. He smiled amicably but Tammy noticed Balfruss had tensed up and was staring at Kai. "The Forsaken needed more foot soldiers for whatever comes next."

"And now they have them," said Balfruss, resting one hand on the axe at his waist.

"And one less base to worry about," said Tammy, thinking about it strategically. "The Forsaken were splitting their forces six ways, now it's five. How long before they do the same thing and attack another base?"

"How many people were in that base?" Tammy asked Zannah.

"Maybe fifty or sixty."

"And now they could all be Forsaken," said the Guardian.

"The change, the Embrace as they call it," said Zannah. "It seems to take a while. When people were abducted in the past they didn't return for two or three days."

It was a short amount of time to do something. Tammy didn't know what just yet, as they still were no closer to finding where the Forsaken came from. Perron, the old man from Fenne's base, had given her a clue as to what was done to a person when they were Embraced, but she still didn't know where they were hiding.

"I'm hungry," said Zannah, turning towards Alyssa. "Is there any porridge left?"

"Probably."

"Could you check for me?" asked Zannah.

"All right," said Alyssa, giving the Morrin a pointed look.

"I'll be right down," said Zannah, ignoring the unspoken question. Alyssa went down the stairs and before she had even crossed the courtyard Zannah gestured for Tammy and Balfruss to come closer. Kai included himself in the huddle and seemed unperturbed by the Morrin's unwavering stare.

"What is it?" asked Balfruss.

"At the last base I visited I was chased by several Forsaken," said Zannah in a whisper. "I killed all of them except one. He's tied up in a building not far from here."

"Why?" asked Tammy.

"Because you were right. We need to know more about them and dead men tell no stories. I will not risk bringing one inside the walls, but you can question him out there. Do not bring him back. Promise me this." Zannah was adamant they swore an oath before she would tell them where to find the Forsaken. She gave them directions and then went in search of something to eat.

"I wouldn't mind stretching my legs," said Kai as Tammy and Balfruss prepared to go over the wall.

Tammy expected the Sorcerer to disagree but instead he just shrugged a shoulder. "He might be useful. He knows more about diseases and infections than anyone."

It wouldn't hurt to have a third set of eyes, and Kai's disturbing insights had proven useful in the past. Even so there was something else going on that Balfruss wasn't telling her. She decided to play along for now and keep an eye on the priest.

They went over the wall and followed Zannah's directions to a building that was in better condition than many others around it. At first glance Tammy thought it was intact but as they came closer she could see cracks running across the façade. All of the windows had been broken and as they stepped inside she saw huge gaping holes in the roof. What had probably once been an elaborate wooden staircase had been stripped for fuel and only a decorative curved railing remained. It was delicate metalwork, which explained how part of it had been fashioned into a temporary prison.

A middle-aged balding man with a broken nose was hanging in a makeshift web of bent metal bars from the staircase. By itself each metal bar wasn't very strong, but Zannah had secured him in several places across his arms and legs so that he couldn't move. Another misshapen bar had been twisted around his neck, forcing the man to keep his chin up to avoid strangling himself. His feet barely touched the floor and every few seconds he had to pull himself upright or risk choking. It looked incredibly painful but Tammy made herself remember this wasn't an ordinary man.

As they came into the room he tilted his head so he could see them, before raising his chin again.

"Who are you?" he asked. "Why have you imprisoned me?"

"I'm asking the questions," said Tammy. "Let's start with your name."

The other two spread out around the room, moving to her left and right so that the Forsaken couldn't watch all of them at once. It was a basic distraction technique she'd used several times while questioning a suspect. It was also one of the many reasons Guardians usually worked in pairs. While the suspect spoke to one of them the other would be looking for the lie.

"Yorris. I was a sculptor before the war."

"And now you're one of the Forsaken."

Yorris tried to shake his head and gagged as the metal pressed into his throat. "Being Embraced is glorious. It's a blessing, not a curse."

On her right Kai was staring at Yorris while on the other side Balfruss had one hand held out towards him. She couldn't feel or see anything but from his look of concentration Tammy knew he was doing something with magic.

"If it's so wonderful then why do you need to abduct people?" she asked.

"Change is always difficult, and being Embraced is a rebirth. Once you've gone through it you'll wonder how you ever lived before." Yorris spoke with the passion of a zealot who was unconcerned by ideas like freedom and choice. It was also clear he thought everyone would inevitably be transformed. The problem was, Tammy didn't know if he had always been easy to persuade, or if being changed had eroded his willpower. How much of the original Yorris remained?

Kai drifted closer, staring hard at Yorris, and in the dim light of the room she thought his eyes had changed colour. A second later she decided it must have been a trick of the light.

"It's not an infection," said Kai, gesturing at the exposed skin on Yorris's face, neck and arms. The dried blood on his face had turned brown, giving him the illusion of a goatee. "I don't think it's a virus either. His blood isn't tainted with anything familiar. It's something else."

"How can you tell?" she asked.

Kai didn't seem to hear but then he answered, almost to himself. "I'd be able to smell it."

The words made Tammy's skin crawl and she saw Balfruss grimace. He definitely knew more than he was saying about the priest.

"Let me go," said Yorris, testing his strength against the restraints. The metal bars around his arms moved a little but there were too many for him to break free.

"By the Maker," hissed Balfruss, pointing at Yorris's neck. A lump under the skin bulged outwards then writhed and flexed as if alive before vanishing beneath the surface.

"What is that?" said Tammy, drawing her sword.

"I know it must seem strange, but it's perfectly natural," said Yorris, beseeching Tammy as he tried to pull his arms free without any luck. Zannah was a lot stronger than she'd realised, to have bent the bars with only her hands.

"Can you sense anything?"

Balfruss spoke between gritted teeth. "I'm trying, but it keeps slipping away. It's like trying to hold on to a shadow. It's not magic."

Yorris was still preaching. "All my life I felt like an outsider. I was desperate to be part of something greater, but I was looking in the wrong places. I tried venthe and black crystal. I even went to an orgy once, but it was all fleeting and meaningless. The answer wasn't in religion or something I did to my body. It was there for me to find all along."

"He's really starting to get on my nerves," said Kai. "How much more of this do we have to endure?"

"I'm trying," said Balfruss. "This isn't easy."

"Can we at least gag him? Will it still work if he's silent?" asked the priest. Tammy was inclined to agree. Yorris's speech was similar in style to many sermons she'd heard over the years, most often spoken by people on street corners, proclaiming theirs was the one true god.

"Haven't you ever felt like you didn't belong?"

Tammy started to answer and then caught herself. She was used to asking questions, not sharing personal information with strangers. He was doing something to her, to all of them, judging by the peculiar reaction of the others.

"Hurry up," muttered Kai, pressing one hand to his right temple as if he were in pain.

"Everything else is just a shadow by comparison. Now, I'm truly part of something greater. Something more—" Yorris suddenly stopped talking when Tammy punched him hard in the face. It rocked his head back against the metal frame and his eyes rolled up in his head.

"Blessed be," said Kai, sighing with relief. "Another minute and I would've ripped out his tongue or confessed my darkest secrets."

Tammy ignored him and turned towards the Sorcerer. "Is the connection still there?"

"Yes. Now let me work." Balfruss closed his eyes and held up both hands towards Yorris. As the silence deepened in the room Tammy thought she would feel some relief. Instead there was a faint prickle along the back of her neck that told her she was being watched. Spinning about she glanced out the door into the street but there was no one there.

"I see it," said Kai, drawing her attention back to their prisoner. He was pointing at Yorris's torso on the left-hand side. "It's there. Some kind of parasite, but it's merged with him. There are so many tendrils it's become part of him."

Tammy started to ask how he knew, but then she saw a red glimmer pass across his eyes again. It had to be magic, but unlike any she'd seen or heard about.

"I can feel it. The connection is somewhere to the east," said Balfruss, opening his eyes and staring at their prisoner. "What's in the east of Voechenka?"

"Nothing," said Tammy. "I've already scouted the area and there are no bases out that way. It's abandoned."

If Balfruss was right then the Forsaken were better at hiding than she realised. She'd searched all of the largest buildings but not looked inside every one. That would take days by herself. Perhaps the Forsaken were scattered across the whole area rather than concealing themselves in one location.

"Can you be more precise?" asked Tammy.

Balfruss shook his head. "I'm barely able to do this."

Across the room Kai took a step away from the prisoner.

"If we let him go, could you follow him?"

"Maybe," said the Sorcerer, although he didn't sound very certain.

Yorris's head snapped up and he stared around the room, glaring at each of them in turn. Tammy was surprised he was awake so quickly given how hard she'd hit him.

"If you start preaching I'll knock you out again," she promised him, but Yorris just kept staring, as if seeing her for the first time. When she started to move closer, Kai shouted a warning.

"Get back!" yelled the priest. "That's not Yorris."

"What?"

Yorris pulled against the metal bars on his arms and this time she heard the metal groan as it moved. Before Kai could answer, Balfruss recoiled as if he'd been slapped. He stumbled back and shook his head like a dog trying to get rid of a fly.

"Are you all right?"

The Sorcerer's eyes were open but his mind seemed elsewhere and his hands were making a strange series of gestures, over and over. It reminded Tammy of a game she and her sister had played as children, creating a web of wool between their outstretched fingers. Balfruss scrunched his eyes closed and kept weaving some sort of net with his magic, right in front of his face.

"Kill it," said Kai, gesturing at her sword. "Kill it quickly, before it escapes."

Yorris's left arm pulled against the metal bars and three of them started to unravel. His newfound strength was remarkable as two more of the bars wrapped around his legs started to bend. With another surge Yorris pulled his left arm free and tried to get his right arm loose as well.

The tip of *Maligne* sliced off the first two fingers of his left hand. They fell to the floor like bloody sausages and Yorris paused in his attempt to escape. But he didn't scream and seemed unconcerned about the blood coming from the severed stumps. He kept staring at the fingers on the floor as if he couldn't understand why they didn't work any more. When he turned to look at Tammy she felt an icy hand grip her heart.

Something was staring at her from behind Yorris's eyes. His expression was utterly alien and insidious. It was one of the Forsaken, unshackled by its human host.

Balfruss had stumbled to one knee but now she could hear him growling like an animal. On her right Kai seemed to be faring better, but he was staring at Yorris with his mouth hanging open.

"Kill it," he said again, almost to himself.

Right before her eyes the bloody stumps of Yorris's fingers on his left hand closed over until they were utterly smooth, as if he'd always been born without them. With a screech of metal the bars holding his right arm began to stretch and unwind.

Several things bulged in unison under the surface of Yorris's skin, moving independently of each other, before they resettled. But now she could see thick purple lines across his arms and up one side of his neck, as if he had been badly bruised.

Zannah's warnings about the Forsaken being dangerous rang in Tammy's mind as she raised her sword on high. Whatever was happening to Yorris would have to remain a mystery for now. As she brought her sword down in an arc to slice off his head the Forsaken managed to pull itself free of the metal bars holding its torso in place. Her sword struck the metal railings and before Tammy could riposte something struck her in the chest.

She skidded backwards across the floor and collided with the wall. As she scrambled to her feet she heard another meaty thump on her right. It turned towards Balfruss but the Sorcerer was ready and unleashed something towards the Forsaken. A fine blue mist drifted over Yorris's entire body, outlining it with a glowing halo of white in the gloomy building. It vanished a second later and the Forsaken froze in place as if locked in stone.

"I can't hold it long," said Balfruss through gritted teeth.

As the Forsaken struggled against whatever magical net held it, its skin began to darken all over until it was the colour of a ripe plum. When it tried to pull free of the metal bars Tammy sliced off its right arm just above the elbow. Blood gushed as normal but it showed no signs of discomfort or pain, merely annoyance that one of its arms was no longer attached. With only one mutilated hand remaining, the Forsaken tried to hold her in place with its vicious gaze. She felt something pressing against the fringes of her mind and a great shadow passed across her eyes.

"Fight it!" shouted Balfruss.

Moving with instinct and muscle memory Tammy swung her sword in a lethal series of cuts. On the third sweep of her blade the darkness lifted from her eyes and she saw Yorris's body was bleeding from several deep wounds. She had partially decapitated him but the wound was trying to stitch itself back together again. With a quick cut from left to right she separated the Forsaken's head from its shoulders.

As soon as the head hit the floor the weight pressing on her mind vanished. Balfruss recovered as well, coming to his feet with one hand held out towards the body. Kai was grumbling to himself but otherwise seemed unhurt.

Tammy stared at the body, almost expecting something, but it didn't move.

"It's dead," said Balfruss. "The thread is gone. I can't sense anything."

They left the corpse where it had fallen and went back out into the street. She still had little to go on, just a direction. Perhaps she'd missed something during her first search. Tammy had no knowledge of the city, but maybe Alyssa could help.

As they made their way back to the winery in silence she tried to picture what the city had looked like before the war. Staring around at the empty streets and broken buildings it was hard to see this place as anything but a haven for despair and darkness.

Part of Tammy knew that even if they succeeded in destroying the Forsaken Voechenka would never again become a thriving community for artists. It was a ghost town, and if she stayed too long she feared for her sanity. If her sister Mary-Beth were here she would say a prayer to the Maker or claim there was a plan for everyone.

Tammy offered no prayers and didn't believe in fate, but she did rest one hand on her sword. Faith would not save her in this place but steel could make all the difference. A wry smile stretched across her face. The city hadn't beaten her and it wasn't over yet.

CHAPTER 27

By the time Alyssa made it back onto the wall it was almost midday. She'd spent the morning helping other people, which consisted of offering suggestions to problems they understood better than her. Nevertheless they were grateful and seemed happier for her guidance.

Before she'd gone very far down the corridor someone else intercepted her with a matter that needed her immediate attention. With more people to feed food was starting to become a problem and rationing would only get them so far. They had plenty of water, as the deep wells were connected to a vast underground lake, but their food was not without its limit. As the nights became colder the woollen blankets, scarves and gloves would become more important, but they still needed fuel for fires and cooking. For now they were gradually chopping up the racks and distilling wine, but the process took time and neither would last forever. The obvious idea was to bring logs in from the old wood outside the city.

Her offer to go into the countryside to forage was met with surprise and shock. A team of ten armed volunteers offered to go over the wall instead, to check her traps and cut down a few trees. Normally people were reluctant to leave the safety of the walls, but suddenly the idea of stepping out of the city, even for a short time, had become appealing. Alyssa knew the reason why, even if they didn't. She could feel the darkness inside her trying to push its way to the surface, but she wouldn't let it be her master. Whenever she felt her temper begin to fray at the endless questions, she took a moment to breathe and pray.

Her people were changing. Guarding the walls by themselves for one night had given some of them a jolt of courage. It was untested and wouldn't last long once they'd endured a night with the Forsaken, but she knew it was a beginning. With a mixture of fear and pride she consented for the party to visit the old wood.

As she made it to the top of the wall someone pressed a bowl of stew and a chunk of fresh bread into her hands. The woman smiled at Alyssa and then carelessly set another bowl on the wall a few feet away from Zannah. Alyssa carried the bowl to her friend and split the bread in two. As they ate in silence she poked the lumps in her stew with her spoon until she could recognise them. Mushrooms and rhubarb. There were still plenty of both and thankfully she wasn't tired of the taste just yet.

"Where are the others?" asked Alyssa, her mouth half full of stew.

"The wizard went out into the city again and Tammy is asleep."

Movement caught Alyssa's attention on the street and a few seconds later she saw several people stumble into view. All were bruised, bloody and battered. Several bore wounds and most were local people. There were also three mercenaries and they were in an equally bad state, limping along and wrapped in bloody bandages.

Before Alyssa could stop her, Zannah raised the alarm and a dozen people came running to join them on the wall.

"There's no need for this," said Alyssa, gesturing at the other defenders to lower their weapons. "They need our help, not more violence."

"Who are they?" asked Tammy, coming up the stairs, followed closely by the plague priest.

"Survivors from last night's attack," said Zannah, staring at the twelve people shuffling towards them. She didn't need to say what had happened to the rest. They were either dead or, worse, had been taken by the Forsaken.

"Throw down the rope," said Alyssa, but for once no one moved to follow her order.

"They could be infected," warned Zannah.

"You didn't say that in the past when people sought shelter."

"That was before a whole base was destroyed in one night. We need to be sure."

"How?" asked Alyssa.

"I can test them," said Kai, glancing at both Tammy and Zannah. A message seemed to pass between them and to her surprise Zannah grunted in assent.

Some of those in the street were too badly hurt to climb and had to be hoisted up one at a time, but none complained. Once all the newcomers were brought inside, each was made to stand in front of Kai. Alyssa couldn't see what he was doing, but it looked as if he just held their hand for a moment. Tammy was visibly unsettled and Alyssa noticed she had one hand resting on her sword. Her whole body was taut with tension until Kai had cleared them all.

"They must swear an oath," said one of the other defenders. More people had come out of the main building to greet the new arrivals and Alyssa's protests were drowned out by noise from the crowd. Perhaps it was because they were desperate for protection and had nowhere else to go, but all twelve sank to their knees and swore an oath of fealty to her. Alyssa tasted bile in the back of her mouth as they spoke, but she managed not to vomit. It seemed to last forever but eventually the brief ceremony was over and the injured were taken downstairs to have their wounds treated.

Now that the danger had passed the others drifted away, leaving only six defenders and Zannah to guard the wall.

"Leave it," said Alyssa as Zannah went to pull up the rope. "I'm going out." The other defenders started to protest until Alyssa stopped their tongues. "No one here is a prisoner, or a slave. That sort of treatment is reserved for those in the mercenary camps. Anyone can leave at any time."

A few of the others on the wall looked towards Zannah, perhaps hoping she would object. "Be careful," was all the Morrin said.

As she lowered herself to the street Alyssa could feel several people staring at her but she ignored them. It was only when she was a few streets away that she properly began to relax.

It wasn't just her people who were changing. Living in the winery over the last few weeks had been difficult, but the familiar routine brought a form of comfort, as she'd always known what to expect. In the day she would spend time on the wall with Zannah, or leave the city behind and forage in the woods. At night they would watch and wait for the Forsaken, balanced on a knife edge. Long days and longer nights, but those too were changing.

Now she had become a leader who people looked to for guidance and hope. Alyssa had thought the priests of the Holy Light would share some of the burden. A few had sought them out for spiritual guidance, but most had lost their faith in the face of overwhelming despair, and it had not yet returned.

Every day the priests tended to the sick and injured and

carried out whatever chores they were asked to perform, never once complaining. At first Alyssa had been suspicious, but over time she'd come to realise they were nothing more than they appeared to be. If anyone asked, they offered a prayer, but whenever the children wanted a story they always came to Alyssa to hear about the Blessed Mother.

It was at her worst moment, slowly dying of starvation in a prison camp during the war, that Alyssa's faith had crystallised. With her death no more than days away she found a form of acceptance and peace. Her belief in the Blessed Mother mattered more in that place than ever before. It was her armour when they'd tortured and killed her people, and a soothing balm for those in their final moments. She held them in her arms and blessed them as they died. She spoke about the peace and beauty of what came next, offering them some comfort at the very end.

While her faith remained intact, she now struggled to find any peace inside the camp.

Her feet seemed to know where to go because when she looked up she realised they'd been taking her east. She picked streets at random following her nose until the stones beneath her feet changed to huge slabs of weathered granite. Many had been worn smooth by waves on the lake, and as the lapping of water reached her ears, Alyssa felt the remaining tension ease from her shoulders.

The waterfront bars and shops were empty and long ago had been stripped of anything valuable. Even so as she walked past the scarred buildings she found herself pausing to look inside. In one she found a mobile hanging from the ceiling made from pieces of orange glass. The clever glassblower had shaped them into different animals and she put it into her pack for the children. In another shop she discovered a small painting of a woman holding a cherubic baby. The tenderness in the woman's face made her heart ache in a way she'd not felt in a long time.

Once the docks had been home to dozens of brightly coloured pleasure craft designed for jaunts and short trips. Now the stone piers were all but abandoned and the only remaining vessels were used for fishing. A group of four men were huddled together at the end of one of the six piers. A small boat bobbed in the water below them and the men seemed to be having an argument, which was cut short as she approached.

All four were gaunt, dressed in ragged clothing, and they looked scared. One held two straws in his hand and another was deliberating, his hand hovering over which to choose.

"Which camp did you come from?" asked Alyssa.

"Fenne sent us," said a man with a grey beard. "He said we had to come back with a full catch or we can't get back inside."

"Do you know where the old Messu winery is?" asked Alyssa.

"Yes," said the bearded man.

"Go there, and tell them Alyssa sent you. They'll let you inside."

All four men looked sceptical. "What's the price?" asked grey beard.

No one gave anything away for free in Voechenka any more. Alyssa knew that the truth wouldn't serve her, no matter how earnest or sincere. Fenne had probably made similar promises until they were inside his walls. After that it was serve or die.

"You have to swear an oath of fealty to their leader. And you must protect the walls at night from the Forsaken. We all must do our part."

Grey beard chewed his bottom lip, searching the faces of the other men for their thoughts. One shook his head and the other two shrugged.

"I don't know if you're playing some game, but we'll go back there with you. Then we'll see what this leader of yours has to say. What's his name?"

A smile tugged at the corners of her mouth. "Her name is Alyssa. It's a pleasure to meet you."

The four men stared until she gestured at the boat. "Can I borrow it?"

Grey beard sucked at his teeth. "Why go out there?"

"Because we still need to feed everyone and our supplies aren't unlimited."

Grey beard cocked his head to one side.

"What's your name?" Alyssa asked him.

"Crinn."

"I'm not forcing anyone to go with me. Wait here if you like."

"We will."

Alyssa descended the worn stairs cut into the pier and climbed into the little fishing boat. Shoving the heavy net to one side she grabbed the oars and set them in the oarlocks. Crinn jumped into the boat and seemed as surprised as her that he'd done it.

"I'd already drawn the short straw," he said with a shrug.

The other three waited at the end of the dock, looking uncertain about whether they should risk going back to Fenne empty-handed, or wait for her to return. Alyssa dipped the oars into the water and put the men from her mind for now. She settled into a rhythm, feeling the muscles in her shoulders and arms pull as she took the boat out onto the lake.

Today the water was a mix of murky blue and slate grey and there was little wind. The surface of the lake was fairly still, which made it easier to cut through the water. Here and there patches of fog clung to the surface, obscuring their view, and after a little while she couldn't see the docks any longer. A few voices drifted to her ears announcing the presence of other fishermen, but they were somewhere out of sight.

Crinn offered no conversation as his attention was focused on the water. His eyes darted across the surface, looking for anything unusual. Alyssa had heard the stories but had yet to meet someone who had personally experienced trouble on the lake. Large bodies of water held a certain level of fear for most people, especially once they couldn't see the shore. It was perfectly natural given not everyone knew how to swim.

When their boat was far enough out they worked together to unravel the net and then cast it wide across the water. As they waited in silence a wonderful calm came across her. Their boat bobbed in the water, gently rocking from side to side. Before the city's fall she would have heard the mournful cries of seagulls, but they were long gone. Instead the only things she could hear were the lapping of the water and a faint murmur of the wind.

Something stirred in the lake and Crinn's gasp made Alyssa open her eyes. The boat wobbled alarmingly from side to side for a few seconds before settling. Staring out across the water she could see that the passage of something to her left had created some shallow waves. Nothing broke the surface but the wave continued moving further away from them as something under the water continued on its path.

"We need to go. Now!" whispered Crinn, afraid that the sound of his voice would draw its attention. There was definitely something big in the water and Alyssa didn't want to find out if it was dangerous or not.

Moving slowly and carefully they started to draw in the net, always keeping one eye on the lake. To her left the wake continued to spread, steadily moving away from them. Something cold and wet flapped against her leg and Alyssa recoiled, scrabbling backwards. A moment later she realised it was a fish. In fact the net was completely full of them, almost as if they had been fleeing from a predator. Her arms began to burn as the net seemed impossibly heavy, and it was only half hauled in.

"We should cut the net," said Crinn, drawing a crude knife from his belt.

"No. We need this," she said. Crinn looked as if he were about to argue but, against his better judgement, he changed his mind. Instead he put the knife away and redoubled his efforts. By the time they'd pulled the last of the net in the bottom was flooded with fish of all shapes and sizes.

The sound of raised voices caught their attention and turning her head Alyssa saw something break the surface. She had a brief glimpse of something long and black before it disappeared again. From the size of the fin, if that's what it was, it could have been a whale. Except that the lake was completely landlocked and the fin was the wrong shape.

Crinn must have seen it too as his face turned incredibly pale. He fumbled but managed to set the oars in the oarlocks and immediately started rowing with vigour. When the oars slapped the water they both cringed but nothing happened.

Then came the screams. She didn't want to turn around but part of Alyssa couldn't help looking behind her towards the noise. The patchy fog hid most of it but she saw something massive burst out of the depths. The snapping and crunching of wood that followed seemed impossibly loud. A man screamed and she heard a heavy splash as something hit the surface. Next came the pleading and sounds of choking, gurgling water and then silence.

Alyssa offered a prayer to the Blessed Mother for the safe journey of the fisherman's soul.

Crinn was wheezing and muttering a litany with each breath

as he pulled on the oars, gliding the boat along with long, smooth strokes. He could have gone faster but he was trying to make as little noise as possible. They were making good time and Alyssa hoped their luck would hold out just a little while longer.

Something stirred the water again and now the wake was moving towards them. At first it was barely noticeable, just a slight increase in the rocking from side to side, but soon Crinn noticed. His eyes widened and he looked as if he wanted to scream but swallowed it instead.

It was definitely coming towards them.

She saw the question on his face before he asked it. Should he stop rowing? Would it be better to be motionless and hope that it didn't notice them, or keep going?

"Keep going," said Alyssa, peering over his shoulder towards the bay. She couldn't see the docks but they couldn't be that far away by now.

Crinn leaned into the oars even more, pulling harder and faster, caring less about silence and more about speed. Alyssa split her focus, watching behind Crinn for the docks as well as looking out across the water. The wave moving towards them continued to build as the thing approached. Soon, without realising it, her own voice had joined with Crinn's, murmuring an almost inaudible prayer to the Blessed Mother to protect them and keep them safe from evil.

A large black fin broke the water moving directly towards them. A moment later Alyssa saw a second one appear in parallel and then a third and fourth a little distance back. The water was too dark to see beneath the surface so she couldn't be sure if there was one huge creature or a pod of them swimming in formation.

The fins closed the distance between them with alarming

speed and then swerved away and disappeared beneath the water again.

It could have taken them. It could have flicked them out of the water with little effort and yet it hadn't.

It was playing with them.

Alyssa turned her attention back towards the shore and was relieved to see the shadowy outline of the docks. Crinn saw her smile but didn't turn. He maintained his pace and rhythm, praying and rowing.

Something slapped the water to the left of their boat, sending them off course and breaking Crinn's stroke. He flailed, dropped one oar, and the other jumped out of the lock and started to slide over the side. Alyssa dived towards it and managed to grab it in time before it disappeared into the water. The boat tipped alarmingly to one side but Crinn moved to balance the weight and it quickly settled.

They reset the oars and then waited for any sign of the creature, staring out at the water. All was silent and utterly still. Even the faint wind seemed to have died.

"Keep going," said Alyssa, no longer bothering to whisper.

"But—"

"It's playing with us. Toying with its food. I am nobody's prey." Alyssa focused her attention on Crinn and he immediately regained a semblance of calm. "Row."

At her command he leaned back, adjusted their course and resumed rowing towards shore.

Alyssa didn't need to see the creature to know that it was waiting somewhere close by. She could feel it deep in her bones. It was probably watching the little boat amble along on the surface, letting them create an illusion of hope as safety came within sight.

When the next attack came they were close enough to shore

that she could see the three men standing at the end of the dock. They started to wave but she saw their arms drop as hands pressed to their mouths. A mighty splash behind her actually pushed the boat forward, instantly soaking her and Crinn to the skin. His eyes were wide with terror as he'd been looking directly at it. If only they had some kind of a weapon, but Alyssa wasn't sure if anything would harm it.

A massive shadow passed under the boat and she heard the wood creak in alarm. Water began to trickle into the boat from a hole in the bottom, but it was a slow leak for now. Crinn was frozen, hands still resting on the oars.

"Row!" she screamed, urging him to do something, but he didn't move. Shoving him to one side Alyssa sat down beside him and grabbed one of the oars with both hands. Whether it was her proximity or physical contact Crinn started to move again. Keening like an animal he grabbed the right oar and they worked in unison, driving their boat towards shore with a rhythm born of desperation.

The three men were shouting, but whether it was prayers or a distraction she couldn't tell. The sound of her heart and Crinn's frantic breathing filled her ears. Her gut told her the creature wasn't far away now. The next attack would come at any moment.

As she'd expected, a wave started to build towards them. Alyssa saw it coming this time. The dock was so close now. Just another minute and they would be safe. Bracing her legs on either side she stood and pulled the oar from its lock. With a sharp motion she brought it down against the side of the boat, snapping the wood in two.

Crinn screamed at her and tried to pull her back down but she shook him off. The oar was ruined and now tapered to a sharp point. It wasn't much but it was better than nothing.

Their momentum and the wave moving ahead of the creature would drive their boat to shore or dash it against the stone dock. Perhaps that was what it wanted. For them to feel safe only to be snatched out of the water as they flailed towards the stairs.

Four fins appeared above the water, moving towards them with incredible speed. Two more and then yet others joined them until what was apparently a whole school of the creatures was coming towards them. The shadow of the stone pier fell over her and a second later something started to rise out of the water. Pushing off with her feet Alyssa leapt the short distance from bow to stern, driving the wooden spear downwards with all of her strength and weight. She heard the wood begin to splinter and pieces sheared off, cutting her face and digging into her head. To avoid looking her doom in the eye, she closed her eyes as it attacked.

A sound unlike any she'd heard before passed through her. It made every part of her body ache, moving across her skin like a wave of agony. Alyssa dropped the spear and fell back into the boat on top of their catch. In the wake of the sound she couldn't move but she could still feel and hear.

Crinn was screaming over and over until something seemed to tear in his throat and he fell silent.

Slowly the pain eased and Alyssa managed to roll over and make it onto her elbows and knees amid the fish. She looked around and saw Crinn clutching the remaining oar to his chest.

Behind him something massive and black fell over them and the temperature dropped. Crinn's mouth opened to scream but no sound emerged. In unison they looked behind him.

It was the docks. They were safe. Without waiting to see what Alyssa did, Crinn dropped the oar and scrambled up the steps. He ran the entire length of the dock and didn't stop until he'd disappeared from sight. Alyssa stared out into the lake but couldn't see anything. With help from the three men she carried the fish up the stairs and dumped them onto the dock.

Looking out across the water from the end of the pier, she waited for any sign of the creatures. She waited a long time, but saw nothing. Just as she was turning away something struck the stone pier hard enough for it to knock her down.

Frantically she looked for the cause but part of her already knew. Lying flat on her stomach she crawled to the edge of the pier. Staring down over the edge she saw something monstrous and black withdrawing into the water. Alyssa had no idea what she was looking at. All she knew for certain was that the multitude of fins didn't belong to several creatures. It was all one enormous monster.

Scrambling backwards she urged the men to pick up the net and together they ran back into the city.

CHAPTER 28

Zannah rubbed her hands together in an attempt to chase away some of the chill. The temperature had dropped again and the sky was a uniform lead grey that promised snow or sleet at the very least. Fighting on the wall tonight could be even more difficult with slippery footing.

The sky was starting to darken around the edges when Alyssa finally came into view at the far end of the street. Even at this distance she could recognise her friend. Zannah's relief was short-lived when she noticed the three men accompanying Alyssa. All four were carrying something between them but it wasn't that which alarmed the Morrin. Long before they reached the gates Zannah heard the loud wheezing breaths of all four echoing off the broken buildings. They had been running as fast as they could for quite some time.

The rope was thrown down but before any of the men could scramble up Alyssa tied it to their burden. Staring down into the street Zannah was amazed to see a net full of fish. She was about to pull it up when Tammy came up the stairs with Balfruss a step behind her.

"Let them do it," whispered the big warrior, gesturing with her chin towards the other defenders. Zannah had heard about how the local people had defended the wall without her last night. Many of them now strutted about with their weapons, believing themselves to be warriors. Previously they had only picked up a blade or bow when it was absolutely necessary and always at the last minute. For the rest of the day, the weapons were kept in a little shed in the courtyard. It had been up to her to keep the swords free of rust and salvage as many arrows as possible. Now they had begun to try and care for their own weapons.

Zannah said nothing and made no move towards the rope. Three women and one local man bent their backs to the task. Slowly the heavy net of fish was dragged up the wall and then carried down into the courtyard. A dozen men and women came up from the lower levels and the fish was taken away to the food store.

The three men came up the rope next and Alyssa followed them. All four looked terrified and Alyssa's clothes were wet and musty. She was shivering in the cold and her fingers had turned red, but Zannah didn't think her trembling was because of the temperature. A deep terror had taken up residence behind her eyes and the three new arrivals carried it as well.

"We went onto the lake," she said, her teeth chattering.

"Get warm and then you can tell us," said Zannah, but Alyssa wouldn't move. She grabbed hold of the Morrin's arm and her eyes were wide.

"I saw it," she whispered.

"Saw what?" asked the Sorcerer. "Was it the Forsaken?"

"No, it was . . . " said Alyssa, trailing off. Several times she tried to describe it, but she didn't have the words. All that emerged was a terrified babble about something huge in the water.

"Who are they?" asked Zannah, gesturing at the three men.

"They were sent by Fenne to fish on the lake." Alyssa

gratefully accepted a blanket from one of her people, which she pulled around her shoulders. The three men still looked terrified but now they were staring at Tammy.

"We saw you at the temple," said one of them. Zannah noticed the men flinched when Tammy put a hand on the hilt of her dagger.

"You must have made quite an impression," said Balfruss. They'd all seen her bruises and how stiffly she moved, but so far she hadn't told anyone what had happened inside Fennetaris's camp. The girl, Rheena, had said very little as well since her arrival. Perhaps Alyssa could speak with her later to discover the truth of why the men were so scared of the Guardian.

Monella, the grumpy woman with one blind eye, came up the stairs with more blankets. "No oaths," said Alyssa, glaring at Monella as if she knew what the older woman had been about to say. "They can stay here without that."

Monella was not appeased. "Everyone must play their part."

To Zannah's ears, it sounded like a familiar saying, or perhaps it was a piece of their scripture. Whatever its origin Alyssa's reaction was not what Monella wanted. Her back straightened and that regal bearing swept over her again. The blanket held loosely around her shoulders could suddenly have become a cape.

"You're right. Monella, I'm putting you in charge of new arrivals." Alyssa waited for her to protest but instead she bowed her head. "I want you to see that they're fed, clothed, given blankets, and find somewhere for them to sleep. We've not touched the lower level. It seems that will have to change. Find six people and get them to clean out the rooms."

"As you wish," said Monella, her face twisted into something halfway between a smile and a grimace. Zannah couldn't tell if she was pleased or not. It was so hard to keep up with how quickly human emotions changed. Perhaps it was because their lives were so short.

"Zannah." The imperial tone of voice was still there. "You're in charge of the armoury. Make sure everyone who can fight has a weapon. If they don't know how to look after it, show them. Bows stay in the shed until they're needed, but everyone else is to keep their weapons on their person at all times. We need to be ready." Alyssa said this more loudly than was necessary, to make sure every person on the wall heard her. A few looked unsettled at the decision but it was too late. They had raised her up and now Alyssa was wielding her authority with both hands.

"If we don't have enough weapons, tell me. I know where there are several caches in the city."

"It will be done." Zannah didn't bow and Alyssa flashed a brief smile of thanks. She disappeared inside and even from on the wall Zannah could hear her giving more orders.

"That's quite a change," said Tammy, and Balfruss just grunted. Something had unsettled him. Since coming back mid-afternoon he'd been quiet and kept rubbing the tattoo around his wrist. Zannah noticed this was something he did when he was thinking something through.

An hour later Alyssa reappeared, dressed in dry clothes, but her new attitude remained the same.

"There's someone in the street," called one of the women on the wall. Zannah glanced at the sky, noting it wasn't dark enough yet to warrant the torches. Four figures jogged towards them in the gloom. Defenders scrambled to string their bows in case it was the Forsaken. They'd not attacked this early before, and never with so few, but Zannah saw no point in trying to predict what they would do next. It seemed as if their technique would continue to change until they succeeded in getting inside and everyone had been hollowed out.

As the four figures came closer to the wall it was difficult to see their features until Balfruss summoned a ball of pale blue light.

"I know them," said Tammy. "His name is Kovac. He helped me at Fenne's camp."

"They look like mercenaries," said Alyssa. Zannah was inclined to agree.

"They are," said Tammy.

The one she had called Kovac wore grey furs and chainmail armour, but she noticed it was well cared for. Behind him came two women, who looked like sisters, with black hair that stood up like the spines of a hedgehog. Their leather armour fitted perfectly and their weapons were without elaborate decoration. Zannah also noticed that neither of them had any scars on their face, which told her they knew their business. The last stood a little behind them, a tall white-skinned Yerskani. He didn't have the same swagger as the others and looked very out of place. They were trying to pretend they weren't scared of being trapped outside as night approached, but Zannah could see it. She could almost smell the fear coming off them in waves.

"Fenne exiled us," said Kovac. "He waited until it was near dark before forcing us out."

"Why?" asked Alyssa.

"For helping me," said Tammy before the mercenary had a chance to speak.

"That, and a few other things," admitted Kovac, nervously scanning the street.

"Can they be trusted?" said Alyssa, addressing the question to Tammy.

"I think so."

"Throw down the rope." Alyssa's tone of voice brooked no argument and no one muttered under their breath. As the fourth mercenary made it to the top of the rope Zannah noted that it had begun snowing. A light shower of flakes was drifting down, briefly clinging to everything before they melted.

"Tammy, you're in charge of them and the other mercenaries in our camp," said Alyssa, not waiting for the big Seve to respond before she faced the four armed mercenaries. Alyssa carried no weapon but she faced them down with only her will and her words. Most surprising was that they suddenly seemed uncomfortable with her staring at them, as if she had power over them.

"Everyone here plays a role and so will you. We have dozens of people who can fight, so we don't really need you, but I won't turn anyone away." That sounded like the old Alyssa and yet the four mercenaries continued to squirm under her gaze. "As long as you fight you're welcome to stay. If you steal or hurt anyone here, I will have someone rip out your lungs. Any questions?"

The mercenaries shook their heads and their relief was palpable when Alyssa went back inside.

A minute later Monella appeared, to fulfil her new role and find the mercenaries somewhere to live. Although they went with the old woman Zannah could see they were still startled by their abrupt welcome. Perhaps they had expected something less organised, with someone more pliable in charge. Zannah knew they would not be the last people to be surprised by Alyssa today.

When it was fully dark they lit the torches above the gate and Zannah prepared herself for a long and uncomfortable night. The light snow continued to fall, soaking into her clothes, trickling down the back of her neck. The hazy sky obscured much of the city and everything else was wet and grey. It was difficult to see very far and they all squinted through the shower as the torches continually fizzed.

"This might help," said Balfruss, touching his hand against the top of the wall. Light blossomed between his fingers and a pale blue orb the size of a small melon appeared, glowing steadily like a lantern. Leaving the orb where it was he moved down the wall a short distance and deposited another magic lantern. The defenders stared with some concern at the magical lights but once it was done they could see most of the street, even with the snow shower. More people came up to the wall carrying weapons, but Zannah made sure they kept their bows unstrung until the last second.

Movement caught everyone's attention and Zannah watched as a familiar bedraggled shape shuffled into view. Roake looked much worse than when she'd last seen him a few days ago. His pale skin was so washed out it was almost translucent and his clothing was more ragged than before. The snow made it stick to his skin, outlining every bony joint of his body. Hollowed-out cheeks and black-rimmed eyes made him resemble a corpse more than ever. Perhaps whatever cruel trick had kept him alive was starting to wear off. It looked as if he was very close to a final and painful death.

"Come down, Zannah!" he shouted. Even his voice was weak compared to what it used to be.

"Maybe we should put him out of his misery," said Zannah. "Could you burn him to ash?" she asked the Sorcerer. She doubted Roake would be able to come back from that.

"Yes, if that's what you want."

"If he used to be one of the Forsaken, maybe we can use him," said Tammy. "He might be able to lead us to the others."

"I doubt that," said Zannah. "He runs away whenever they're in sight. He's afraid of them."

"Even so, there might be a connection," said Balfruss. "If we capture him I might be able to use him to find the others."

"Maybe we should try something less direct," suggested Tammy. "It didn't go well the last time we captured one of the Forsaken."

Zannah hadn't spoken to them yet about what had happened, but judging by their reaction something had gone very wrong.

"I'll be back," shouted Roake, hurrying off into the dark.

A few minutes later Zannah saw a crowd begin to build up at the far end of the street. A quick headcount told her it was a force unlike any they'd seen before. While the locals gawped and began to tremble she grabbed the nearest person on the wall and shoved him towards the stairs.

"Tell Alyssa we need everyone who can fight."

The Sorcerer was squinting at the crowd of Forsaken. "Perhaps I should use magic to get rid of them all."

"Can you do that?" asked Zannah, glancing at the snow-filled sky.

"I could, but it would need to be something fairly significant to destroy so many at once."

"I thought you said that would draw attention," said Tammy. "Won't the Master and all of his pupils know where you are?"

"I don't think it matters any more. They know I'm in the city."

"You can protect yourself, but what about everyone else?" asked Tammy, gesturing at the other defenders. "What if they come here when you're elsewhere? You'd be putting their lives at risk."

Balfruss considered it for a long while before finally drawing the axe from his belt. "Then we do it the hard way," he said, hefting the weapon.

Alyssa came marching up the stairs followed closely by at least two dozen people until the wall was packed. Among them were Kovac and his three friends, plus mercenaries from the other camp. More people were waiting on the stairs and in the courtyard as well.

"It's too crowded up here," said Zannah in a quiet voice to Alyssa, knowing that people wouldn't listen to her. "Send at least a dozen to wait in the courtyard. We need room to fight and we'll need reserves. And clear the stairs too."

Alyssa listened to her advice and then ordered people off the wall. It seemed as if the time when she made suggestions was over. Those remaining on the wall spread out a little and Zannah found herself with Balfruss on one side and Tammy on the other. The big warrior ordered the mercenaries to spread themselves along the wall in pairs, creating pockets of people with skill to shore up the locals.

Staring at the approaching horde Zannah cocked her head to one side, trying to listen for sounds of fighting elsewhere in the city. Despite the constant shuffling of people on the wall beside her, she couldn't hear any distant screams. It seemed as if tonight the other camps would be harassed by just a few Forsaken and theirs was the one destined to be destroyed.

The thump of many approaching feet brought her back to the immediate problem. The Forsaken were a mix of people, locals and a few mercenaries, and for once there were no familiar faces. Unfortunately she heard cries of alarm from others further down the wall as people recognised former friends or relatives. That familiarity might be what killed them. It would make them hesitate and in that moment the Forsaken would strike.

Most of the Forsaken carried makeshift clubs fashioned from lumps of wood and bars of metal, but several carried swords and axes. Zannah knew they would do their best to incapacitate the defenders without killing them. Usually that meant clubbing them about the head until they were unconscious, but sometimes that wasn't possible. If it meant they had to cut off an arm or a hand they would do it. Their power to heal meant that even severe wounds could be regenerated over time.

The Forsaken horde picked up their pace, moving to a sprint as they rushed the walls with their homemade ladders.

"Fire!" shouted Alyssa. All along the wall a chorus of bow-strings hummed in response. A dozen Forsaken stumbled and went down, only to be trampled by those behind. The rest of the Forsaken raced on and people began firing at will, picking individual targets. Several metal ladders rose up into the air before coming down with a heavy impact against the wall. A few defenders tried to shove one of the ladders backwards but their combined efforts barely moved it. Kovac stepped in with the two feral women and they slid it to one side instead, where it collided with another ladder, sending them both tumbling. That trick only worked once though. As soon as the Forsaken started to climb a ladder the weight became too great to move.

The locals screamed at the Forsaken, cursing them and doing anything to fire up their blood, creating an illusion of courage where none existed. The mercenaries remained silent, conserving their energy for the fight. Beside Zannah, Tammy and the Sorcerer wore grim expressions and both just watched and waited.

A ragged face appeared above the top of the wall to Zannah's left and she immediately attacked. Her sword split the man's skull in two down to the bridge of his nose, pulping his brain in the process. The Forsaken tumbled away, but was swiftly replaced by two more, and then the time for thinking was over.

Grunting and sweating Zannah moved from one strike to another, rarely having to worry about parrying, since those she faced had little skill. The Forsaken, though, had the advantage of numbers, and almost immediately it began to tell. Bodies forced themselves onto the wall and several defenders fell, collapsing to the ground in stunned and silent heaps. Some fell into the courtyard below where they were quickly pulled out of the way by those waiting in reserve.

To her left Balfruss hacked away, severing arms and splitting skulls with ruthless efficiency. On her right Tammy fought more stiffly than usual but her ability was nonetheless greater than her opponents. Blood sprayed across over the stones as her peculiar sword cut through the Forsaken with ease. When one woman tried to swing her club at the big warrior Tammy took off the woman's hand with a flick of her sword and then split her in two with the follow-up. The two halves of the Forsaken slid off the wall and her organs rained down on those below.

The snow had built up a little underfoot, creating slush that was quickly churned from grey into pink. It made finding footing a little difficult but if someone slipped they were quickly pulled upright by the defender beside them.

Six Forsaken burst onto the wall to her far right and in a rush they overpowered the defenders. But rather than continue to fight the Forsaken threw themselves forward into the courtyard. Those waiting in reserve did what was instinctive. They attempted to catch the falling bodies, noticing at the last second they were not friends. Several defenders were knocked down and more were stunned before they started to recover and fight back. The Forsaken ran for the main stairs and five made it to the main entrance. The sixth was cut down in the courtyard.

"I saw it," said Tammy, moving to the stairs. "I'll go after them."

The big warrior raced after the Forsaken and a second later Kovac followed.

The breach on the wall was closed and several reserves came up the stairs at Zannah's frantic gesturing. But the Forsaken were not done yet and still more of them were scrambling up the ladders. Looking along the wall she couldn't tell how the fight would end. The locals were barely holding on. Their brief spurt of courage had abandoned them and their anger had worn thin in the face of such an unrelenting enemy. All it would take was one person to run and the rest would follow.

It was time to change the odds.

Zannah reached into the energy reserve within and forced herself to move faster. She whirled from one Forsaken to the next, slicing off pieces until they fell away. Their screams started to fill her ears until it became the only sound in the world.

Space opened up around her on all sides as no Forsaken seemed willing to get too close. Moving one step at a time she began to work her way down the wall, killing Forsaken as she went.

As she'd hoped, the defenders saw the Forsaken fall back from her assault and it gave them a boost. The mercenaries were smart enough to follow her lead, a few laughing at the Forsaken while others mocked and jeered. The defenders rallied and started to force the Forsaken back, screaming their own insults. The tide of the battle began to turn.

CHAPTER 29

Tammy followed the screams and the trail of felled bodies lying in the corridor. All of the people she passed in the first hallway were either huddled in corners or unconscious on the floor. Several doors were closed and she could hear frantic breathing coming from the other side. Only a few had seen the Forsaken coming and none had been fast enough to protect themselves.

At the end of the corridor Tammy found a man bleeding from his scalp with a second wound in his leg. A dagger lay on the ground not far away but he was more concerned with trying to stem the bleeding. It didn't look too deep but even so she paused to help him.

"Keep pressure on it," she told him, folding both of his hands on top of the wound and pushing down hard. The man groaned in pain and blanched, but he gritted his teeth and nodded with determination.

Tammy heard footsteps coming up behind and a few seconds later Kovac came into view. A woman screamed below them, long and shrill. They took the stairs two at a time and on the next level found more of the same. The Forsaken had left a trail of unconscious and bleeding bodies in their wake. A scuffle in the doorway of one room and more shouting led them on.

One of the Forsaken, a woman with red hair, was trying to drag another woman away by the hand. Two local people had taken hold of her other arm and a tug of war was taking place.

"Come with me," said the Forsaken. "It's so much better now."

Tammy didn't hesitate. She brought her sword down on the Forsaken's arm, just above the elbow. *Maligne* seemed to glow slightly in the gloomy corridor as it severed the arm. The Forsaken screamed but before she could raise the axe in her other hand, Kovac stabbed the woman in the chest, pinning her to the wall. They left the body where it fell and ran on, following the sounds of raised voices.

On the next level down four women were fighting off a Forsaken with pans and broom handles. Tammy stepped up behind the man and stabbed him through the back. She held him upright for a second then yanked her sword free.

A short distance ahead a burly man stepped into view. He carried a short sword in either hand and Tammy saw a look pass between him and Kovac.

"Friend of yours?"

Kovac shook his head. "No, but we've run into each other a few times. I didn't realise he'd been taken."

"All these years, Kovac," said the mercenary as they walked towards him. "We've been chasing stories, hoping to find something life-changing. And it was here all along."

"Do they ever shut up?" said Kovac.

"Listen to me. It's worth more gold than any job you've ever had." The mercenary was almost pleading. "Just let me explain."

Tammy's instincts told her something wasn't right and quickly realised what he was doing. "He doesn't want to convert us. He's just trying to delay us."

Realising that his ruse had been uncovered the mercenary grinned and raised his weapons. With Kovac on her right

Tammy stayed to the left side of the corridor. Just as she was about to reach the mercenary someone burst out of an open doorway.

She turned and managed to get her sword up just in time to block a cut towards her head. The two swords sheared together and a shower of sparks rained down. A leather-clad mercenary came at her again with a broadsword, driving Tammy back. She could hear Kovac fighting the other mercenary but couldn't risk looking away from her opponent. The Forsaken was skilled, and her face was tight with concentration. In the narrow corridor their struggle became more of a brawl than a sword fight. With little space to move they resorted to jabbing, trying to kick, punch, or smash each other against the walls.

The woman's fetid breath made Tammy's eyes water so she quickly pushed her away and followed up with a kick at her opponent's leg. She caught a knee and the mercenary stumbled back, bounced off the wall and came back with an underhand cut. Tammy's momentum was already carrying her forward and with no time to reverse she threw herself to one side. Despite her efforts the tip of the Forsaken's blade scored a line up one thigh, making her hiss in pain. Tammy lashed out with an elbow, snapping the woman's head to one side.

The Forsaken cracked the pommel of her sword into Tammy's side, catching her bruised ribs, and she fell back wheezing as fingers of pain jabbed into her side. Using a double-handed grip she blocked a slash then leaned into it, forcing the Forsaken back with her weight and strength. They collided with a wall but not enough to stun her opponent, so Tammy smashed her forehead into the woman's face. It bought her a couple of seconds, which she used to step back and swing at the Forsaken's stomach. The mercenary saw it coming but was too slow to block it in time.

Tammy's sword entered the woman's body just under the ribcage and emerged out the back, severing her spine. With her last breath before she toppled over, the Forsaken tried to curse Tammy. Her lips formed the words but she had no air in her lungs to say anything out loud.

"A little help," said Kovac. A second later he was thrown past her and skidded down the corridor on his back. He scrambled to his feet but the mercenary hadn't followed to finish him off. This was still part of a delaying tactic but she couldn't work out what it was for. Five Forsaken could not take over the whole base by themselves, let alone one, so what would a few minutes buy the remaining Forsaken?

"Together?" suggested Tammy.

"Together," agreed Kovac, hefting his sword. "On three."

"Three," said Tammy and they both charged at the mercenary.

As the sounds of violence drifted down to his ears Kai moved towards the disturbance while the other priests shied away. Far above his head people were screaming and fighting for their lives. Kai closed his eyes and smiled at the chaos and rich surge of dark emotions flooding his senses.

He could smell fresh blood in the air but the delicious bouquet was soured by a bitter and familiar tang. It came from whatever creature had sucked all of the life and joy from this once-thriving city. A piece of its essence infused every one of its people. He could feel it now, which meant there were Forsaken inside the building.

The sound of heavy feet moving away down the corridor drew his attention. The intruder stank worse than if he'd been soaked in vinegar and sprayed with shit. There was also something unusual about this Forsaken.

Kai followed the man at a distance into the most secluded

part of the winery. At first he thought the Forsaken was heading towards the caves but he stopped near to the first of the deep wells. The fighting on the wall must have been intense for one of them to make it all the way down here. Kai was curious about why they would mount such an attack, just so that one man could make it all this way. He slowly drew closer, observing the man and waiting to see what he did next.

Judging by his armour and weapons, which looked better than most, he was a former mercenary. Kai extended his senses towards the man and picked up some of his surface thoughts. The dream of riches and a quiet life spent idling in luxury were still there in the back of his mind, but now all he cared about was his mission. The man's thoughts were jumbled for the most part, but they seemed to be completely his own. Kai felt a vague presence of the other, whatever piece of the creature he carried inside, but it seemed asleep.

The former mercenary dropped his weapons and started to pull off his armour, casually throwing it away. Next he opened his shirt, exposing his chest, and closed his eyes, tilting his head back with his mouth open wide.

Something moved under the skin of the man's stomach. Kai saw several strands probing and pushing outwards, perhaps testing how pliable the skin was without ripping it. The tendrils settled and then the man's whole stomach and chest started to swell outwards as if he were being filled with too much air.

The skin stretched and then began to rip in places. The man tried to scream but his voice was muffled, as if there were something lodged in his throat. A faint wisp of something green drifted up from the Forsaken's gaping mouth and he choked, creating another fetid cloud. Shuffling slowly to one side he inched towards the well.

The creature's plan was ingenious in its simplicity. Trying to capture all of the local people one at a time was proving difficult. They fought back. They died and they beheaded those already turned. Its numbers never increased significantly because the humans refused to accept the gifts it offered. This way, whatever was gestating inside the mercenary would soon escape and poison the water. Over the next few days it would infect everyone and probably incapacitate them. Then it would be easy to take all of them at once without the need for violence.

It was devious and ruthless and exactly what Kai would have done.

With his eyes on the ceiling the Forsaken didn't see the plague priest approach, but he felt the dagger taken from his belt as it entered his groin. The man's head snapped down and his mouth clamped shut as blood began to pour down his leg. With claw-like hands the man lurched towards Kai and tried to rake his eyes. Kai tried to bat the man's hands away as he waited for the inevitable, but when that didn't happen fast enough he sliced off a few fingers.

He danced back, careful not to get the dagger anywhere near the bloated man's torso. The slightest cut and whatever was festering inside could be released. As the man's lifeblood drained from the artery in his leg his attacks became less aggressive, until Kai barely needed to move to evade them. Realisation dawned on the man, and the parasite within him, as he turned from Kai and staggered towards the well on shaky legs.

"I don't think so," said Kai. He kicked the man in the side of one knee and a meaty crack echoed around the cave. With a scream the Forsaken toppled over, falling hard onto his left side. In a normal human it would have been over, but only a few seconds later the man hauled himself onto his belly. Dragging himself forward with his shattered leg dangling behind, he continued to inch across the floor, leaving a growing trail of blood in his wake.

Kai easily kept pace with the dying man, looking down on him, the dagger held loosely in one hand. The Forsaken managed to make it to the base of the well but his six remaining fingers weren't strong enough to pull him up the stones. He continued to claw at the wall until the nails were ripped off and his finger-ends were bloody.

Finally the death of the body caught up with whatever urged it forward as the man's hands stopped moving. Kai sat down beside the corpse, closed its eyes and laid a hand on its shoulder. When someone eventually stumbled across the tableau they would think he was praying for the man and offering some final words for his recently departed soul. In reality, direct skin contact allowed him to look deeper into the dead man and study the parasite.

The meat was completely dead, but deep inside there was a faint spark of something that could be described as life. Even as the flesh cooled and the blood congealed he could feel it slowly reaching out and probing the limits of the damage to its vessel. The Morrin always insisted on cutting off the head and now he could see why. Eventually, if left unattended, the parasite would regenerate the damaged tissue until the only essence that animated the body was its own. It would utilise the memories and skills of its meat puppet, but the person it wore would be gone. The mercenary had died the moment his heart stopped beating, but the parasite didn't need him, only his flesh.

Pushing the dagger deep into one of the man's eye sockets Kai scrambled the cooling brain. Although the man's flesh didn't move he felt a subtle shift inside and a spasm of shock ran through the creature. Without a brain to move it around the body was useless and soon the parasite would die. Once that happened perhaps he could find a way to take the body somewhere private and cut out the parasite to study it in more detail.

The sound of heavy footsteps and loud breathing reached him long before Tammy and a mercenary came skidding into view. They stared at the dead man and then the bloody dagger in his hand. A hundred questions were on their lips but he answered the most important one.

"He was going to poison the well," said Kai. "I had to stop him."

While the mercenary seemed appeased by his answer the big Seve just stared at him. She was better at concealing her emotions than others but Kai could see the distrust. He looked away, knelt beside the corpse and bowed his head.

"I will stay here and pray for him. He was human once." It sounded like something a priest would say at this moment. He could sense Tammy's continued suspicion and knew she would not stay silent forever.

"We need to get back to the wall," said the mercenary.

"We'll send someone to take care of the body," said Tammy. Kai nodded and continued to pretend he was praying over the dead man. The pair's footsteps receded and he heard them race back along the corridor and then up the stairs.

The sounds of chaos filtering down from above were beginning to fade. The fight was nearly over. He was almost out of time.

Turning back to the corpse Kai flipped the body over onto its back. Plunging the dagger into the man's chest he sliced open the flesh, pulled the wound wide with both hands and rooted around inside for the parasite.

By the time Tammy made it back into the courtyard the fight was almost finished. The defenders heavily outnumbered any Forsaken in sight and were now working in pairs to take them down. What the local people lacked in skill they certainly made up for in heart as they battered and beat their enemy to the floor.

Several injured people were lying on the ground, and a few more had been knocked unconscious, but they were being tended to by the priests. Under the direction of Alyssa the injured were carried into the main building.

As Tammy made it to the top of the stairs she saw something in the street that made everyone on the wall spontaneously cheer. The Forsaken were retreating. Many were running and others dragging themselves and the wounded away.

"We need to stop them," said Zannah. "Otherwise they'll just come back again when they're healed."

"There could be more waiting for us," warned Balfruss, using a strip of cloth to clean the gore off his axe. He had blood spattered across his face and clothes but either he hadn't noticed or didn't care. All of his attention was focused on the axe.

"He's right," said Tammy.

"I could go after them," suggested Zannah.

"No," said Alyssa, coming up the stairs. "The fighting is done for tonight. Now it's time to celebrate our victory."

Zannah ground her teeth but said nothing. She looked down the wall and, following her gaze, Tammy saw that the local people looked happy. They had stood their ground and won. For the first time in years the people of Voechenka had faced an invading enemy and driven them back.

"Don't rob them of this," whispered Alyssa. "We both know tomorrow night will be worse."

"As you wish," said Zannah. "But I will finish those left behind."

This time when the Morrin went over the wall to behead the injured Forsaken, Tammy noticed the defenders didn't look away. Their smiles stayed in place despite the horrors they had just witnessed.

Just as Zannah made it back to the top of the wall, and the first bottles of wine were being passed around, a sound reached Tammy's ears. It took a few seconds for the others to hear but gradually the sounds of merriment faded until silence gripped the camp again.

It didn't take long before the others heard it as well. People were screaming and fire blossomed on the horizon as another base was attacked by the Forsaken.

CHAPTER 30

While some of the soldiers were getting annoyed or complaining about the snow, Tom couldn't stop grinning. The last few years had fallen away and once more he was sat around a campfire with his old friend Hargo. Even when a trickle of snow ran down the back of his neck, it couldn't dampen his spirits. He shifted closer to the fire, warming his feet, and sipped his mug of tea.

Captain Rees had been delighted when Tom and two hundred Seve warriors showed up at his garrison. His men had too much ground to cover and they were already exhausted from trying to hold the line. Vargus had not given him many details about what was trying to escape from Voechenka, but Rees held nothing back. The Forsaken sounded horrific and Tom could see why Vargus had called on him for help. He wondered if Vargus had known he would find an old friend among the crowd of Seve warriors.

In the light of the sputtering campfire Tom studied Hargo's battered face. He had a few more scars, a few more lines around the eyes, but little else had changed. When he'd thought of asking the Brotherhood for help, he'd never imagined that he would meet someone from his old life.

"What happened?" asked Tom, stirring Hargo from his doze. "Where did you go after the war?"

"Home," said Hargo, sounding wistful. "Thought I could settle back into my old life in Tyrnon. Zera welcomed me back as well. It was good."

"What changed?"

"Me. After all that I'd seen, good and bad, I couldn't go back to sitting idle. Zera said I'd done my part and that others would take their turn." Hargo forced a smile, trying to pretend that it didn't hurt, but they both knew different.

Tom had felt much the same. The idea of raising cattle and following in his father's footsteps hadn't appealed to him much before the war. Afterwards, it was the last thing he wanted.

"There was no going back, not after what we'd seen," he said aloud and Hargo nodded.

"I tried, but in the end I had to leave. It was making us both miserable." Hargo wiped at his face and Tom pretended the big man was brushing snow out of his eyes. "I travelled for a bit, working here and there, but in the end I came back to the Queen's army. I'm home with the Brotherhood," he said, gesturing at the surrounding campfires. "Look at you, though," said Hargo. "From rich boy to royalty."

It was Tom's turn to force a smile. At first it had felt like the worst kind of trap. He'd ignored letters from his father for years, but when a summons came from the palace he couldn't refuse. Tom had done his best to distance himself from his family name and all of the responsibilities that came with it. But there were some duties that went beyond those to his family.

Alliances were made and deals struck between his father and other Lords in the south of Seveldrom. In return, the country remained well fed and well supplied with leather for armour, and the Queen got herself a husband.

To say that their first meeting had gone badly would be putting it mildly. Over time they'd grown close, but it had taken a long while before they found anything in common.

"I can honestly say I never imagined I'd be here," said Tom, scratching at his stubble. He'd have to shave the beard before he got back home. She wasn't fond of facial hair.

"Rider coming in," said someone to Tom's left. Thoughts of his wife and son were pushed away as Tom drew his sword. All around him warriors were pulling on helmets and strapping on shields.

"What's happening?" asked Tom. It felt peculiar not knowing what was going on. He'd grown used to being among the decision makers but now he was back on the front line. The information would come in time, but first there would be orders that he and the others would be expected to follow without question. It was both irritating and a relief to have someone else making the decisions.

"Kasha, on Tom's left," said Hargo, to a scarred redhead. She grunted and picked up her battle-axe, a vicious-looking weapon with two blades. "I'm on his right. You two, stay back unless you're needed. You're not part of the Brotherhood."

The royal guards didn't like him fighting alongside the others but Tom had insisted. He wasn't in any immediate danger and was also surrounded by two hundred veterans. No one knew he was there and the Forsaken would have no reason to target him specifically. Now all he had to worry about was getting killed at random or because he did something stupid. The royal guards were there, just in case, to save him from himself.

Captain Rees himself approached Tom, looking more worried than usual. "Rider spotted a large group of men and women moving this way. Maybe a hundred."

"Are they Forsaken or refugees?" asked Tom.

"They're all armed, and there's something wrong with their faces. It's them."

"Have they ever done this before?"

"No."

"Then why now?"

"They must be desperate. Or something has changed in the city. Get ready." Captain Rees moved away without another word and the story was spread from one squad to the next.

The snow continued to drift down, making it difficult to see more than a dozen paces in every direction. Tom could just about make out blurry spots of colour where fires were burning in the distance.

"Everyone grab a torch," said Hargo. Each warrior took a flaming branch from the fire, which they held aloft, trying to drive back the gloom and see the enemy before they were too close.

Dozens of shadowy figures appeared ahead, shuffling forward with a peculiar gait. When they stepped into the light from the torches they stopped. In the gloom Tom could just make out their surprised expressions. Instead of a handful of tired warriors from Shael they were facing two hundred grizzled Seves. Captain Rees was right about there being something wrong with their faces. The skin was purple in places as if bruised, and black veins pulsed beneath the surface. It didn't matter. Vargus had told Tom he had to stop them escaping from Voechenka and that's what he would do.

"All right, let's see what colour these fuckers bleed!" said Hargo, raising his shield. With a mighty roar he led the charge and Tom added his voice to the din as he raced towards the enemy.

*

Strong as they'd been, possessed by whatever dark magic or devilry, the Forsaken had died like any other. Outnumbered two to one they'd fought like cornered rats but in the end it made no difference.

Tom managed not to do anything stupid, like getting himself killed. He'd even managed to kill two of the Forsaken, with some help from Hargo. In the aftermath of the fight he experienced a sense of belonging he'd not felt in years since the war. As he shared a smile with those around him Tom could see why the big man felt at home in such company. He felt it too, the bond between them, and yet his first thought was when he'd next see his wife and son.

He'd changed more than he realised. Hargo was right. You couldn't go back.

Under strict orders from Captain Rees the bodies were beheaded and then piled up, soaked in oil and burned. Thankfully the wind was blowing away from where Tom and the others made camp, tending their wounds and cleaning weapons. As he shared a skin of ale with Hargo and others around the campfire, Tom glanced over his shoulder into the hazy snow.

He didn't expect to see anyone out there and was surprised when a single figure emerged from the shadows. A shout built up in his throat until he saw the man's face. Vargus smiled then raised his hand in farewell before disappearing into the falling snow.

"Do you think they'll come back?" asked Hargo.

"No, I think our work here is done," said Tom, feeling confident that the Brotherhood was no longer needed in Voechenka. He considered telling the big man about Vargus but quickly changed his mind. The Brotherhood was doing just fine without him and Tom knew they would always be there if he needed them again.

CHAPTER 31

Fenne stared at the distant wisps of smoke rising from the ruins of what had once been another mercenary camp. At first light he'd sent a dozen men to check the ruins for anything they could salvage. At first all they'd found were blackened stones, charred timbers and a few scattered lumps of bone and burned human meat. Every other body in the camp was gone. They'd left behind clothes, food, blankets and weapons, which his mercenaries brought back with them. Fenne had enough weapons to arm everyone in his camp twice over. Not that it would make a difference.

This morning the sky was so blue it hurt his eyes and, even worse, there was no cloud or wind. The smoke from the fallen base hung over the city like a black cloud of doom that would not disperse. The air was bitingly cold and frost glittered on hard surfaces like a scattering of diamonds.

As Fenne moved around the former temple grounds he noticed the changes in how people were reacting to him. Some were subtle, sly glances from eye corners, where before the local people had not dared look at him at all. Others were far more direct and showed a clear lack of respect. A few of the mercenaries didn't stand up when he approached or even stop what they were doing and acknowledge his presence. Occasionally their answers to his questions were terse and bordering on insolent.

So far, they'd continued to follow his orders, but he suspected it was only because they hadn't decided how to get rid of him. He knew they were planning something. But in a city with few choices and little to gain from being in charge, no one was willing to take on his responsibility. Not just yet anyway. It would happen though, and very soon. Someone would step forward and try to wrestle control from him. Then they would have a target painted on their back.

It had all started to change with that woman. The Seve fighter. Her victory and insolence in front of everyone had led to others thinking they could show him disrespect. Her presence had infected everyone, and some of the mercenaries, like that weasel Kovac and his friends, had supported her from the beginning. Perhaps they'd hoped she would end up in charge and make everything better.

Fenne had done his best to stamp it out. He'd made a public spectacle when getting rid of Kovac, forcing him out as night fell to send a clear message to the others. They should have been more afraid of him after that, but for some reason it hadn't worked. In fact, somehow, it made things worse. A lot of people had liked Kovac, although he didn't know why. So far he'd not come back as one of the Forsaken, but it was only a matter of time. When Kovac tried to drag one of his old friends away they would soon forget.

Fenne completed his circuit of the base and his eyes alighted on one of the local women. She was just skin and bone, they all were like that after being in the camps, but this one still held a vague shadow of beauty. When she saw Fenne staring at her she should have cowered or run away. She knew what was coming and should've been afraid for her life. Instead she lifted her chin and glared at him. She dared to openly defy him. Fenne was so surprised he turned away, pretending he hadn't noticed her. Even the former slaves were rebelling.

The war had been a glorious time. He'd indulged in such wonderful sport here in Voechenka, pitting the locals against each other for money. Feasting on the best food and wine until his stomach was swollen and his head swimming. At one point he'd fought and killed until he became lost in a blood haze, only to emerge days later to find himself surrounded by a sea of bodies. When the war ended he'd stayed behind and thought the best time in his life would continue.

Now the country was a rotting corpse and he was just another maggot crawling through decaying flesh, looking for nourishment.

Two bases had been destroyed in two nights and only four remained, including his. One of those was protected by that traitorous hag, Zannahrae. Fenne ground his teeth and spat, feeling his temper flare as he thought about her. She'd betrayed her country. She'd hunted down her own people, choosing to side with the yellow-skinned slaves. Fenne started to shake with anger as he remembered stumbling across the butchered corpses of his friends.

Someone said something behind him and in a rage he span around and lashed out. It was one of the local women, offering him some breakfast as she did every morning. The woman went flying and so did his food, landing in the dirt.

The woman's wounded expression made him even more furious. It was almost as if she expected him to apologise. Drawing his axe Fenne brought it down on the woman's head, splitting her skull open and spraying brains and blood everywhere. Howling in rage he hacked away at the woman but she'd been dead from the first blow. The fire was still burning inside and he didn't feel satisfied. Even now, as he started to force himself to calm down, everyone was staring. Fenne was used to that, but he wasn't used to seeing disappointment in their eyes.

That doused him in cold water and helped make his decision. He cleaned his axe on the woman's clothing and stormed back to his room. After pulling on his armour, he stalked towards the gate.

"Open it," he said to the men lurking nearby. When one of them hesitated, Fenne moved towards him, and the man quickly leapt into action. Another few seconds and Fenne would have thrown him into the pit.

They were probably wondering why he was going out into the city. He'd not done it in weeks and never went alone. If they thought he was going to make it easy for them they would be sorely disappointed.

"Do you want us to come with you?" asked one of the few who were still loyal.

"No. I need you to wait here and make sure they let me back in."

Fenne didn't wait for a response. It would be a sign of weakness and it was critical he showed none at this stage. He needed the mercenaries to think that he remained unaware of their disloyalty.

The gates were cranked open and the gangplank laid out. Fenne walked across the pit as the plank was settling and marched down the street without looking back. He headed west to the end of the street and paused after turning the corner. In the heavy shadows between two tall buildings he took a moment to calm his frayed nerves and get his bearings. It had been some time since he'd last explored the city and several buildings had fallen down in the interim.

He travelled east and stuck to narrow streets until he was certain no one from the temple walls could see where he was going. After that, Fenne strolled down once-grand avenues that were now nothing more than dirty and barren pathways that echoed with the sound of his footsteps. There was nothing else to hear in every direction. No birds or dogs barking. No merchants standing in doorways shouting about their wares. No priests on street corners bragging about theirs being the one true god. Not even the trickle of water in the fountains. They were empty, rusting and forlorn like everything else in sight. The whole city had become a ghost town that reeked of despair and abandonment.

Further to the north-east Fenne smelled the lake, but he turned away from it and angled deeper into the city. No one had come to this area in months. There was no reason to come here. At least that's what everyone said and what they told themselves. The rumours said this was where it had all begun. Where the first of the Forsaken had abducted someone during the cold winter after the war. Whether it was true or not, some sort of disease had swept through the neighbourhood and lots of people started to die and disappear. It seemed like a good place to start his search for them.

After that many locals had fled the city, trying to outrun whatever stalked them in their homes. Others stayed behind and fought on but it proved pointless. They'd all died until no one wanted to live here. Until only death stalked the streets. Even the criminals moved out. It should have made a perfect hideout for them. An entire area with no patrols and no law, where they could live like kings in homes full of luxury. But even the rats knew when it was time to flee, and the killers and thieves had scurried away.

Fenne stopped in front of a huge mansion with two columns

on either side of the front door. This was where he'd lived for a time. Now it was a rotting husk, stripped bare of anything that could be sold, burned or melted down. Glimpsed through the open doorway it now resembled a mausoleum.

Without him realising it, his feet began to drag and a prickle of fear became something else. A cold hand on the back of his neck. A gnawing sensation, telling him to turn around and leave. Next came the smell. A sulphurous stench of rotting eggs, decaying flesh and rivers of shit. The further he went the worse it became until it clogged his senses and he felt as if he were tasting it with every breath.

Finally his feet stopped of their own accord, as though he'd walked into a solid barrier.

"I want to talk," he tried to say, but nothing more than a croak emerged. Fenne tried to wet his lips but found his mouth was horribly dry. He couldn't summon any spit and even though his heart was racing there was no sweat on his skin. All of the moisture in his body had abandoned him. He struggled to speak as the silence of the city pressed down on him. The stench filled his nose and mouth and all of his senses were screaming at him to turn back.

He tried to cry out in defiance but made no sound. He would not turn back. He would not be bested by this sorcery. It was all in his mind. Going back would mean sitting and waiting to die. Waiting for someone to stab him in the back or cut his throat while he slept. He would not be hunted again. Zannahrae had stalked all of them, but only he had survived. He would not go back to living in fear like that.

Pulling up his right sleeve Fenne bit into the flesh of his forearm until the blood flowed, wetting his mouth.

"I am here!" he bellowed, his voice echoing off the stone façades of the once-great homes. "Here!" he shouted again.

Blood trickled down his arm and dripped off his fingers onto the street. The arid ground greedily drank up his offering as the blood quickly disappeared into the cracks between the stones.

The feeling of being watched increased and the stench of filth diminished slightly. He sensed movement at his left eye corner and turning that way saw something flitting around inside one of the buildings. There was more movement to his right and then all around as the itch between his shoulder blades increased. He was dimly aware that several pairs of eyes were staring at him.

He licked the blood from his arm to wet his mouth before speaking again.

"I'm here to make an offer."

"Why would we need anything from you?" asked a sibilant whisper. A golden-skinned local woman with short red hair sauntered towards him. She was plump with rosy cheeks and her lazy swagger showed how at ease she felt. Part of Fenne itched to take off her head to teach her a lesson. But he could feel the others watching even if he couldn't see them.

"I want protection. I want to live, without being changed."

The woman came close enough to touch him but Fenne didn't flinch or turn his head as she circled him. He knew she was looking him up and down like a cow at the meat market, trying to assess his worth.

"I should just take you now. Make you one of us." Fenne said nothing and kept staring straight ahead, ignoring the rising tide of emotions the woman brought to the surface. Some of it came from him, but there was some outside force at work in his mind. He could feel it dragging its nails through the shadowy parts of his memory, pulling the worst to the surface for inspection. The woman chuckled at something and continued to walk around him, trailing a finger across his shoulders. Maybe she delighted in the things he had done, or perhaps she laughed because she thought him foolish. Without the others to protect her from his wrath she would not laugh. She would scream and beg him for mercy.

"Once you feel the Embrace, you will thank me."

"I am here to make a deal, in return for my safety."

"Tell me, Morrin man, what do you have to offer?" asked the Forsaken. "What do you think you can give us that we cannot take?"

Fenne's sneer made her pause in her endless circuit. "How many die every night? How many heads do you lose?" The woman said nothing but he could see she was listening, her head cocked to one side like a stupid dog. She was that. A lapdog for whoever was really in charge. "In two nights you have taken two of the remaining camps. I wondered why at first, but the answer was not hard to find. The city is dead. There is nothing left to claim. Desperation forces you to attack. But the cost of taking each camp is high."

"We have enough to destroy you."

Fenne laughed in her face because he already knew he'd won. "No, you don't. Or we wouldn't be talking. You would have claimed me already."

The woman was quiet for a long time but eventually she stopped directly in front of him. There was now a stiffness to her posture and her eyes were pinched. "I am listening."

"You will not claim me. In return I will work with you."

"And what do you offer?"

"My people. If we fight together we can take the other bases more quickly and fewer will die."

The woman moved closer and stood on her toes until her nose was almost touching his. Fenne's instincts told him to kill her or run, but he fought both urges and remained, staring into her eyes. "And what do you get from this?"

"You cannot stay here. Once the camps are gone you must move on. I want you to leave."

"Why? So you can remain and be the ruler of this city of bone and ashes?" Her tone was mocking, which made his hands twitch. Instead of reaching for his axe Fenne clenched them into fists. She saw the movement and grinned. "Do it."

He ignored her goading. "Do you accept my deal?"

"No. I have a different offer to make." The woman finally stepped back and made a series of flicking gestures with both hands, as if trying to shake the water from them. Boots scraped on stone and a dozen people walked towards him from all sides. They all looked well fed, rested and each carried a blunt weapon.

The circle of bodies tightened slowly and this time he did draw his axe. He would kill them. He would not be taken. He would make them hurt him so badly he could not be turned and hollowed-out like the others.

"Your offer is not good enough." The woman's voice drew his focus back to her face. "Your people could turn on us at any time. We cannot trust you."

Fenne licked his lips and tasted blood. "What is your deal?"

"Your life for theirs. We will spare you, but in return we want you to give all of them to us. Every person in your camp will be Embraced." The Forsaken stepped closer until they were just outside the reach of his axe. "Or we will take you now. Choose now, and choose wisely."

Fenne looked at the eager faces around him. None were familiar but all had the same eyes. Some thing lived inside them and he sensed that it was watching him. It had made them more and yet less than what they had been before.

He knew they wanted him to fight. Hands tightened on weapons and eyes strayed to his axe, waiting for his first strike.

"I accept."

The others were visibly disappointed but the woman seemed delighted. The circle of bodies immediately moved away, disappearing into the shadows, leaving him alone with her.

"When?" he asked.

"As soon as darkness falls. Open the gate and we will be there."

Fenne waited for her to say more but she just stared at him with those empty eyes.

By the time he reached the temple gates he'd regained his self-control. The gates were closed and at first it seemed as if his efforts had been for nothing. They would leave him outside until nightfall. Then he would be taken instead and become one of the Forsaken.

Slowly though, the gate began to open and Fenne did his best to hide his relief. None of the mercenaries spoke to him, but many who saw him turned their faces away. Part of their fear of him had returned. Perhaps it was the dried blood smeared across his face or the look in his eyes.

When night began to fall he returned to the gates and stared out into the empty street. At first he thought the woman had lied but he could think of no reason why she would have done so. Then, although he could still see nothing, Fenne felt the familiar prickle of someone staring and with it came the awful smell of rot and decay.

"Open the gate," he told those closest, as he went to stand in front of them. They hesitated and just stared. "New allies have arrived. Open the gate or I will kill you and do it myself."

Still they hesitated, casting fearful looks at the darkening sky overhead. The sun had not yet completely dipped below the horizon but it would not be long. Drawing his axe Fenne pulled back his arm and prepared to kill one of the men with it, which finally prompted them into action. The gate was opened and the plank laid out, but the street remained empty.

Fenne had not counted to ten heartbeats when the woman appeared. Behind her came a few, then two dozen and then more. All of them were Forsaken. All of them had been tainted and transformed.

As the woman crossed the gangplank and came into the grounds, he saw the confusion in the faces of those surrounding him. That changed into fear and then terror as the first person was clubbed over the head. The Forsaken began to flood into the temple grounds and the screaming began. Weapons were drawn and people tried to fight back but it was too late. There were too many of them and there was nowhere to run.

Fenne watched as those around him fought for their lives against the inevitable tide. Clubs rose and fell, knocking people down until the ground was littered with a sea of unconscious bodies. The locals fell first as they had so little fight left in them. Soon afterwards, blood was spilt as the mercenaries fought back, but it was a retreating battle and eventually they too were outnumbered and pulled down.

The screaming continued, on and on until Fenne thought it would never stop. Finally the last body fell to the ground. Silence should have returned but he could still hear them in his mind. Screaming and pleading for their lives.

CHAPTER 32

Balfruss and Tammy stood side by side on the wall, staring into the dark. Both were wrapped in silence, lost in their own thoughts.

Last night the attack on their camp had been the worst yet. Alyssa's plan to arm everyone who could fight had been a good one. The problem was that most weren't ready to use their weapon to take a life. It wasn't until Forsaken were running through the corridors of the winery that some of them had been faced with such a difficult choice. Now everyone with a weapon was being shown the basics by Zannah. Some had protested but Alyssa had overridden their complaints and told them this was how it had to be. They wanted to survive and the Morrin could show them how. The alternative was they die screaming, aimlessly waving a sword around. Alyssa told them that if they chose not to listen then their deaths would not be on her conscience. And when they came back from the dead that she would not hesitate to put an arrow in their eye. There was a steel core to the woman that everyone was only just discovering.

Thankfully Tammy and Kovac had taken care of the Forsaken inside the camp before anyone was killed. Most troubling was the attempt to poison the well. Tammy mentioned this had been stopped by Kai.

Balfruss shied away from that. He wasn't quite ready to speculate what that thing was who pretended to be a man. There was something in the back of his mind, an old scrap from history, that gave him a vague notion of what Kai might be, but he didn't pursue it.

His meeting in the banquet hall with Vargus was starting to feel like a dream. He could remember what had happened, but the images in his mind were slightly foggy, as if he were being made to forget. With such powerful beings, anything was possible.

So far the city had been quiet tonight and there'd been no sign of any Forsaken. Everyone knew that could change at any moment, so they stood ready. More people waited below out of the cold and those in their rooms now clung to their weapons.

Glancing at the warrior beside him Balfruss noticed her bruises were starting to change colour and the swelling on her face looked painful. Pushing his own troubles away he unclenched his jaw and rubbed the sides of his face, suddenly realising how tight it felt.

"You've been grinding your teeth for over an hour," said Tammy, her eyes still on the city.

"And your shoulders are so hunched they're practically touching your ears," he observed. She smiled and her shoulders eased. "Do you want to talk about it?"

Tammy leaned forward, resting her hands on the wall. Frost still clung to all hard surfaces but at least it wasn't snowing like last night.

"Following up on the connection you felt, I visited the east part of the city, in the Dureen district. I spent half of yesterday and all of today searching the area. And in all that time I found nothing."

"Nothing at all?"

"There are so many places to hide that even with help from the mercenaries, it will take two or three days to search everywhere."

She didn't need to say it. They might not have two days. Two bases had fallen in two nights and after last night's assault on the winery they both knew it would only get worse.

"How do you feel?" asked Balfruss.

Tammy looked at him askance at the question, but nevertheless she eventually answered. "I'm hungry and bruised, why?"

"I can help with the bruised part if you want," he said, gesturing at her injuries. It wasn't the first time he'd offered but she'd previously turned him down. "But what I meant was, how does this city make you feel?" Before she looked away, Balfruss saw something in her eyes that told him she knew what he was talking about.

"It dredged up some feelings from my past that I'd buried."

"Let me guess," said Balfruss. "Rage, jealousy, even strong sexual urges have been rising to the surface."

"At the temple, when the fight began I started to lose myself." Tammy gestured at the bruises on her face. "It was so difficult to push down the anger."

"I have an idea." Balfruss rubbed the side of his jaw again, trying to ease the aching muscles. "It's more of a theory."

"Tell me."

"Whatever is behind all of this, the darkness, the Forsaken, I think it's stayed hidden for so long because in the beginning it was weak. However it was created, or spawned, it had to hide and slowly build its strength. Then it started reaching out with surrogates, slowly claiming people, changing them until they became the Forsaken."

"And now it's strong enough that it no longer has to hide in the shadows," said Tammy. "It's built up an army and is taking the city, one camp every night."

"Yes, but I think I know how you can find the Forsaken."

Tammy sensed his hesitation and put a hand on Balfruss's arm, making him face her. "I'm not going to like this, am I?"

"No," he said. She chewed it over for a minute before gesturing for him to continue. "Go back to the Dureen district and open yourself up to everything. Dig deep into those raw emotions, immerse yourself in them and feel it all."

"And then?" asked Tammy.

"Use it. Listen to your instincts. Like calls to like. It is responsible for a river of blood, agony and death. It thrives on darkness and despair. Use the darkness within to guide you. Then you will find it. Or . . . " Balfruss trailed off, not wanting to say what could happen.

"Or it will find me," said Tammy.

While his idea might work there was also great risk, but from her expression Tammy was already thinking about it. If she immersed herself too deeply in that darkness, she might not be able to come back.

There was something more that worried Balfruss, which he doubted Tammy had considered. The Forsaken transformed people, making them healthier and stronger. Up to now the most dangerous people it had claimed were mercenaries. Tammy was something else. Whatever darkness lay in her past was part of a different life. She'd moved on and buried the past, becoming a Guardian of the Peace. That meant a lot of hard work as only the best in Yerskania were promoted from the Watch to the Guardians. She was a soldier, a fighter, an investigator and she'd years of training. If she was taken and transformed, she might become a terrifying General at the head of an army of Forsaken.

"What about your hunt?" said Tammy, startling Balfruss from his reverie. "Have you had any luck?"

Balfruss grimaced. "Yes, and that's the problem."

He'd spent most of the past two days searching for Kaine, but instead he'd stumbled across more of his students. Three of them had been on an errand before taking a winding route home. At first it had seemed more like a trap than coincidence. Wrapping himself in magic to camouflage his appearance he'd trailed them at a distance, waiting for more students to attack him from the shadows.

"How did you follow them?" asked Tammy, interrupting his retelling. "And how did you hide yourself?"

"It's easier if I just show you," said Balfruss, reaching for the Source. Whenever he did this it took him back to his time in the emerald jungle. As ever, his memories were tainted with sadness and he rubbed the tattoo around his wrist.

Holding up his left hand Balfruss placed it on the wall. The stones were mostly grey but there were flecks of blue and white, plus a layer of frost. Weaving a fine mesh of magic around his hand and then his arm, Balfruss focused on blending it into the background. Slowly his hand started to disappear as it gradually took on the appearance of the wall. As long as he didn't move too quickly it was almost invisible.

After a minute he released the magic and was pleased to see a look of wonder on Tammy's face. It was a good sign that she could still be amazed. It gave him hope that the poison of this city had not dug its claws in too deeply.

"I used this to hunt in the jungle across the Dead Sea." He saw the next question on her lips but waved a hand. "A story for another time." She didn't press him but gestured for him to continue. "There's also an echo of magic, a pulse that comes from every person who can touch the Source. It's how Seekers test children to see if they have the ability to wield magic. I used this echo to follow them."

"Let me guess," said Tammy. "They should have known you were following them, but somehow you can conceal yourself from them."

Balfruss grinned. "Exactly. It's another form of camouflage."

"So where did they lead you?"

"To their home. Nearly a dozen of them are holed up in a run-down building. They sleep in the basement, huddled together under blankets, and they cook their meals there as well."

"What about Kaine? Did you see him?"

Balfruss shook his head. "I heard them talking about him, but he never appeared. Even worse, they don't know where he is. He just shows up and gives them orders then disappears again. If they fail he kills them in front of the others as an example."

"Why don't they leave?"

"I thought it was because they were afraid. Or because we're in the middle of nowhere. But it's worse than that."

"How?" asked Tammy.

Balfruss realised he needed to tell her everything. She wouldn't be able to help with only half the facts.

"During the war, did you know the Warlock had several apprentices?"

"I remember they had a strange title," said Tammy. "But no one ever knew their names or who they were."

"He called them Splinters. They were hollowed-out shells that looked like people. He imprinted himself on them, giving them a set of rules, and that was all they knew. They had no other thoughts in their heads. They were just small pieces of his mind in their bodies."

"By the Maker," hissed Tammy.

"Using magic to change someone's mind is one of the foulest

uses of the Source. To rob someone of their free will is abhorrent. The Warlock learned this ability from Kaine."

"And he used this power on his students," said Tammy, seeing where he was going.

"Kaine's pupils never think about leaving because he's altered their minds. It took me a few hours to see what he's done, but all of them have been changed. Any kindness or sympathy in these children has been scrubbed clean. I showed some of them mercy, but this morning I heard them discussing how best to kill me. They don't care or feel because they can't. They have no free will."

Balfruss's hands sought a distraction. Setting his axe on the wall he took out a whetstone and began to sharpen the edge. The rhythmic motion was soothing but it also brought back memories of his father. Every night just before sleep as they sat across from one another with a fire between them, his father would sharpen his blade. Other men drank, read or prayed. He always made sure he was ready for the day ahead and to him that meant being able to fight.

"Can you help them?" asked Tammy. "Can you undo what's been done to them?"

"I wouldn't know where to start. Even if I tried it could take me months for each one. There's also a good chance that I'll kill them in my fumbling around. The mind is incredibly delicate. Healing the body is complex, but the mind, that's completely different. Especially with children, when the mind is not fully formed . . ."

Balfruss took out his frustrations on his axe, tilting it towards the light from the torches before working the edge again with the whetstone.

"Kaine is playing a game of Stones with me."

"I've always hated that game," said Tammy. "So many pieces

that move differently. Trying to think ahead eight or nine steps. As a child my father tried to teach me."

"What happened?"

"I used to sweep away all of the pieces."

"I never liked it as a child either. I'd flip the board in frustration."

Tammy put a hand on his, drawing his focus to her eyes. "You're missing the point. You're trying to be careful, to out-smart him, but ultimately you're still playing his game. If you clear the board of all his pieces, then he'll have to face you."

"Do you have any children?" he asked and felt her hand tighten on his before she let go. The answer was in her eyes as clearly as the unshed tears which she quickly wiped away.

"Do you?" she whispered.

"A daughter." Saying it out loud was difficult, and it took Balfruss a while to clear the lump in his throat.

They both knew what she was suggesting. In his heart he already knew there was no other course of action, but it was hard to comprehend.

"Will you let me help you with those?" he said, gesturing at her bruises. Tammy looked as if she would turn him down again but changed her mind. Perhaps she could see that he needed to do something. For many years now those with magic had been treated as nothing more than living weapons. Even the name, Battlemage, was merely a shadow of what someone could accomplish with magic. Ever since he'd come back to the mainland Balfruss had felt himself slipping back into the old and familiar rut. Some days it felt as if his time in the north belonged to someone else. It was time for a reminder that it had not been a dream and that he had become more than a weapon.

"After this you'll be hungry and tired, but you'll feel much better."

"All right. What do you want me to do?" asked Tammy.

"Just close your eyes."

Balfruss put aside his axe and stepped close to Tammy until he was within arm's reach. Reaching up with both hands he placed one on either side of her face and bent his head towards her.

Power from the Source flooded into Balfruss, washing away all of his aches and pains, sharpening his senses and filling him with a deep joy. It was the power of creation, the fountain of all life, and he was a part of it.

Slowly he extended a fine golden mesh of healing energy that flowed outwards until it touched Tammy. He felt her flinch in surprise and saw her head tip forward until their foreheads touched. The golden light travelled throughout her body, knitting bone, mending tissue and reducing swelling. As the Source healed Tammy they stood together, wrapped in a cocoon of magic, and for a time the city and its taint could not touch them. A feeling of peace and contentment settled over him and Balfruss felt his mind drift.

He imagined he was back home in Seveldrom, walking through a field of long grass with the sun on his face. At the end of the field he came to a house where a familiar woman stood in the doorway, a child on her hip and another clinging to her knee. The scent of wild flowers and fresh bread filled his nose. In the real world he felt himself smile at the image.

All too soon the glow started to fade and he gradually withdrew the net of magic. He gently took his hands away from Tammy's face and stepped back, but she remained with her head bent forward and eyes closed. The smile on her face was not something he'd seen before. Looking more closely he saw the bruises and swelling had completely gone and he knew her cracked ribs had also been fully healed.

Finally she opened her eyes and they both heard her stomach rumble.

"You should get something to eat. Someone will find you if you're needed," he said, gesturing over the wall.

"Thank you, Balfruss," she answered, and he realised it was the first time she'd used his name.

As she went down the stairs he turned back towards the city and contemplated the difficult choice that lay ahead.

CHAPTER 33

Just after breakfast Tammy and the mercenaries left the winery to scout the Dureen district again. All of them were armed to the teeth and Alyssa thought Tammy looked more determined than ever. She walked with purpose, as if she knew that today she would find something. Balfruss left shortly afterwards, looking equally driven, although he had the appearance of a man about to do something distasteful.

Last night there had not been any sight of the Forsaken. The whole city had been silent and still, wrapped in a freezing fog. They'd listened all night for anything that might indicate the other camps were being attacked, but no one heard anything. Alyssa wasn't sure which bothered her most, the silence or the screams.

She spent the next couple of hours organising people, assigning tasks and observing Zannah drilling groups in the courtyard. There was no wood to spare for training weapons so they had to use real steel. Alyssa had little experience with swords but it was obvious most had never held one before. Their movements were incredibly slow and clumsy but Zannah made them repeat the moves over and over until they could barely lift their arms. Then she moved on to another group while the first rested. The frost in the courtyard made their footing slippery, but it was good practice. It would be the same on the wall from now on as the nights would only get colder.

With a shiver Alyssa pulled on a pair of gloves and adjusted the scarf around her neck. If the Forsaken didn't kill them this winter then the cold would. At least if she froze to death she would know what to expect. She'd seen it happen several times to friends during the war. Closing her eyes she murmured a prayer to the Blessed Mother, asking for relief from the darkness that pressed on her mind. It made her thoughts bleak and she could almost feel it trying to leach all of the joy and hope from her heart.

The familiar sound of heavy feet coming up the stairs told her it was Zannah, even before she opened her eyes. The Morrin had been awake for most of the night on the wall and up early this morning. Alyssa wondered if the others would ever appreciate all that Zannah had done for them.

"I'm going into the city," she said, waiting for Zannah to object. To Alyssa's surprise she just shrugged.

"You'll go over the wall no matter what I say, so why argue?" As ever the Morrin was being incredibly practical.

"I'm going to the old wood."

"Will you try to stop me if I come with you?" asked Zannah.

Her question caught Alyssa by surprise because she had been about to ask Zannah to come with her. "No, of course not, but what about them?" She gestured at the lines of people training in the courtyard.

Zannah grunted. "They have no stamina. They're exhausted after a few hours of practice. If I push them any more today they'll be asleep on the wall tonight."

Ten people kept watch on the wall, wrapped in layers of clothing and blankets. It had not yet snowed today but it was cold enough to start at any time. However, the weather would not deter them from taking their duty seriously. Several bore scars from fighting with the Forsaken two nights ago and they wore them with pride. A few even sneered at those practising in the courtyard, as if they were veterans of many wars.

"That arrogance will get them killed," said Zannah, tossing the rope over the wall. In their minds they were the reason the Forsaken had been driven back. Alyssa had seen them frozen in place with fear, teetering between fight and flight. It was Zannah who had rallied them.

The Morrin went down first, watching the street for signs of trouble. Alyssa saw her gaze linger on one building longer than the others but she couldn't see anyone hiding in the ruins.

"Zannah? Is there something wrong?"

"No. Let's go."

Alyssa knew her friend was lying but didn't press the subject as it only made her dig her heels in. She would talk about it or she wouldn't. Perhaps it was Zannah's stubborn streak that had rubbed off on her lately.

Following her usual route, Alyssa led the way.

When the city had been thriving, shops had put little stalls out every day, displaying a range of fresh crafts, paintings, seasonal fruit and freshly baked bread. The streets had been awash with noise and colour. With so many people creating music not all of them were sponsored by wealthy patrons. On every street corner a musician would stand with a bowl or hat, adding their latest tune to the hubbub.

Now only silence rang in Alyssa's ears. The crumbling ruins and empty shells of once-beautiful homes and shops loomed on either side. When she thought about what had been lost the ache in her heart was overwhelming. This pain didn't come from whatever had infected the city. It was her own heartache and she accepted it because she understood the reason.

Whatever happened with the Forsaken a part of her knew that Voechenka was lost. Perhaps it would be a kindness to tear down every building and let the area return to nature. In a hundred years or so, a forest or fields of grass would cover it and there would be nothing to show for all of the lives that had been lost. At least it would then be more than just a graveyard and a place of sorrow.

"Keep up," said Alyssa, turning off the main road and cutting down a narrow side street. She took the most direct route west through the city, passing through Debrussi square, and carried on, heading towards the bank. Zannah must have realised where she was heading but remained silent and watchful, one hand resting on her sword.

When they reached the bank Alyssa was surprised to see no one on the roof watching the street. Picking up a handful of stones she started lobbing them at the roof, from where they clattered down noisily. When that failed to attract anyone's attention she picked up a large rock and hammered on the battered front door. The metal rang loudly and she felt the vibrations up both arms but persisted until someone appeared.

"Are you crazy, girl?" yelled the familiar voice of Graff from the roof. "We could have killed you."

Half a dozen mercenaries were watching her and Zannah with bows in hand. All were dishevelled and red-eyed. They were probably exhausted after a long night of waiting for the Forsaken to attack, only for them not to show up.

"What do you want?" yelled Graff, grumpy at being woken up.

"You know what's coming. Do you think you'll be able to hold out against the Forsaken?" Her direct approach caught them by surprise and sullen faces turned thoughtful. The time for banter and pretending everything would be well was over.

"We've managed so far."

"That was before they started destroying one base every night. Do you think they left anyone behind? Do you think they killed anyone if they could help it?" The only way to get through to them was with cold hard facts. Alyssa had done her best to avoid the ugly truth in the past, but the city had forced her to change. It was the only way to survive. Now they had to change too or die.

"Have you got a present for me today?" said Graff with a wry smile. It was something he used to say to her but today there was nothing suggestive in his voice. He looked wrung out and utterly exhausted. She knew they were all hanging on by their fingernails.

"Sooner or later, they'll come for you," said Alyssa. They already knew that, but she felt it needed to be said. "Maybe you'll keep them out on the first night, and if you're really lucky, the second night. Eventually they'll get in. If you stay here and try to fight them by yourselves, you'll end up dead or worse."

Graff started to say something, maybe to make a joke or curse her, but in the end he said nothing. When one of the men beside him started to mutter, Graff gave him a look and he fell silent.

"What are you suggesting? An alliance?"

"No." Alyssa knew she had to make her position very clear from the start. The mercenaries understood a chain of command but if she asked them to work with her, then sooner or later they would take advantage of her kindness and try to take over.

Swearing an oath wasn't the right approach, but Monella had been right about one thing. In this sort of situation people needed someone to follow. Someone to tell them what to do and where to go. It gave them the illusion that the person in charge knew what they were doing.

Graff and the others were confused. "Then what's the deal?"

"You all work for me. I lead and you follow."

In spite of everything the mercenaries laughed, hooting and howling, their voices echoing down the street. The only one of them not laughing was Graff. He didn't even crack a smile.

"Blessed Mother, we needed that," said one of the other mercenaries, wiping a tear from his eye corner.

"Tonight, when the screaming starts and you hear people begging for death, think about my offer." Alyssa's voice cut through their good humour like a razor. "If they come for you instead of someone else, see if you feel like laughing then."

With that she turned and walked away, never once looking back. She desperately wanted to but kept facing forward, working hard to keep her breathing level and her emotions in check. Zannah walked beside her, a solid and reliable presence from whom she drew strength. If Zannah noticed her wiping away tears, she didn't say anything.

By the time they reached the west gate Alyssa was starting to feel more like herself, which made her laugh.

"What's funny?" asked Zannah.

"I was just thinking about who I am now and who I used to be."

They followed the path beyond the gate, walking on what had once been a muddy track. It had frozen in the last few days and Alyssa heard it cracking under Zannah's unrelenting boots. After a few minutes she began to notice subtle changes in her friend and was pleased to see she was starting to relax. Zannah probably didn't even realise she was doing it.

At the top of a gentle hill they reached the edge of the old wood. Apart from patches of frost it looked much the same as the last time she'd visited. A couple of trees had been chopped down as she'd instructed, but the area was still beautiful. Above their heads a few little birds flitted among the branches, looking for food. The trees swayed gently in a mild breeze, creaking and groaning as if speaking in a language of their own.

Zannah was transfixed. She stared up at the birds with a child-like look of wonder. The area was so peaceful Alyssa felt some of the tension ease from her mind. It would be waiting for her when she went back, but for just a little while she wanted to pretend that it didn't exist.

"You did well with the mercenaries," said Zannah, following her through the wood towards the stream.

"Do you think they'll listen?"

"I don't know, but if they don't it's not your fault. You've already taken on too much."

"I was about to say the same thing to you," said Alyssa, smiling at her friend. Zannah said nothing, but in her silence Alyssa heard many questions. The Morrin was good at burying her emotions and keeping her mouth shut, even when she burned to ask a question. She would rather say nothing and wait to see if the answers came out by themselves. She never asked for anything for herself, as if that were a shameful thing.

"Tell me about your life, before the war," said Alyssa.

"There's little to tell."

"That's not true. Who were you? What did you do?"

"I was a soldier, like now. Only back then I followed orders." Zannah said it matter-of-factly, as if what she had done by disobeying those orders was nothing. As if it hadn't cost her everything. Her people. Her country. Her family.

"I'm not who I used to be," said Alyssa. "Although there are moments when I remember."

"I've not guessed in a while," admitted Zannah. They'd had little time for their game lately. "I'm not certain I will ever get it right."

"I'll tell you one day," said Alyssa, gesturing towards the stream. The water had slowed with the cold and there were drifting patches of thin ice, but it hadn't frozen solid. Alyssa sat down beside the stream, observing how the weak sunlight created a kaleidoscope of colours as it passed through the ice. When she realised they weren't going to walk any further Zannah sat down but she looked uncomfortable. It was a long time since she'd nothing to do or anyone to protect. The only thing to do here was talk and she usually avoided that if possible.

"You never asked me about the lake," said Alyssa.

"No."

"Why not?"

"You saw something terrifying. You survived and returned safe. That's all that matters."

"No, it's not," said Alyssa, shaking her head. What she'd seen mattered, although she tried to avoid thinking about it as much as possible. What was more important was what the experience had done to her.

"Do you know why I went to the lake?" The best way to find out what Zannah was thinking was to ask her direct questions.

Zannah picked up a loose stone and flicked it across the water. It hit a small patch of ice, cracking it, and immediately sank into the water. The hard exterior was thinner and more fragile than it looked.

"Because you were running away from what needed to be done. From what people wanted you to be."

"That's part of it," admitted Alyssa. "They needed someone to be strong for them. To show them the way. I thought they wanted my advice, but really they wanted the illusion of order. I have no power, no authority, but asking permission gave them comfort and I was shying away from that. I was selfish and I nearly died before I realised that."

Zannah looked at her askance. "You do more than that for them."

"I don't understand."

The Morrin was quiet for a while and Alyssa could see she was trying to find the right words. This was probably the most she'd spoken in weeks. They used to talk a lot more when it was just the two of them guarding the wall late into the night.

"For your people, hope used to be a good thing, like their faith. It brought them comfort and a promise that tomorrow would be better. They went through the war and the camps, and then they were left alone in a dying city. This place strips away all the fat and gristle, leaving behind only skin and bone. It eats away your dreams, your future and finally your hope. Many of your people were just waiting to die."

"And now?"

Zannah's laugh was both unexpected and slightly terrifying. In all their time together Alyssa had never heard her laugh in such a way. "Do you really not know? Do you not see?"

Alyssa shook her head. "Know what?"

"You give them hope for the future."

"It's not just me," said Alyssa, gripping one of Zannah's hands with both of hers. "We light torches every night, but you're the one who drives back the darkness. You've saved countless lives and you helped them find their courage."

"They hate me."

"They need you and would be dead without you."

"I bring death. That's my only gift."

"Now who's being blind?" Zannah tried to pull her hand away but Alyssa held on more tightly. "I need you to do something for me."

"Name it." Zannah didn't hesitate, not even for a second, which only made Alyssa love her more.

"I need you to stop taking risks." Zannah tried to move away but Alyssa persisted and squeezed her hand. "I won't let you go. Not without a fight."

Alyssa knew that Zannah thought her fate was to die fighting to protect people who hated her. Everything she'd done since the war was part of her penance, but in her mind redemption was for other people.

"My people will never forgive the Morrin for what they did during the war. I don't think they know how," said Alyssa. "But I forgive you. I forgive you, Zannah."

At first she didn't think the Morrin had heard her, as she didn't react. After a long silence she withdrew her hand and this time Alyssa let go.

Then Zannah started to shake, hugging herself with both arms, and began to cry. Loud wracking sobs erupted from her throat, making her whole body tremble.

Alyssa held Zannah to her chest, as tears ran down both their faces, and she waited for the storm to pass.

CHAPTER 34

For the last two days Tammy had been methodically search-ing the Dureen district of the city for signs of the Forsaken. She had used logic and common sense in an attempt to find some clues as to where they hid during the day. Given their numbers there had to be some physical signs of their passage, but so far her efforts had produced nothing. She'd previously started with the largest buildings as the most obvious hiding places. Once those had been cleared she moved to a systematic sweep, street by street, and still there was nothing. Not one body or drop of blood. Nothing.

Now, with seven nervous mercenaries walking behind her, Tammy was leading them through the area, relying only on her instincts.

Right now they were screaming at her to turn around and run in the opposite direction. There was something else. Judg-ing from how closely they were watching the streets she knew the mercenaries could feel it too. A tingle along the spine as if they were being watched. But there were no faces observing them from empty windows. No scuttling sounds or the patter of footsteps on stone. Not even a flicker of movement half-seen from eye corners, because there was nothing to see or hear.

The city echoed with a silence as deep and profound as the grave. Maybe that's what the chill was. The absence of life and the flutter of restless spirits on the edges of her perception. Maybe hordes of the dead watched them even now. The streets could be choked with people, but they were the only ones who were still alive.

"Do you know where we're going?" asked Kovac.

Tammy didn't realise she'd stopped at a crossroads until he spoke. The others were looking at her expectantly while keeping one eye on the surrounding buildings. Instead of answering she picked a direction at random and set off.

She'd been delaying the inevitable. Hoping that somehow she'd find the Forsaken by chance, despite their previous lack of success. Probing her reasoning more deeply Tammy realised she was afraid of what might happen.

"Kovac." She gestured for him to follow her into the nearest building. The others spread out and took up positions without being asked, watching all directions. As she stepped into the front room Tammy saw it had once been a clothing shop. Racks of shirts, dresses and brightly coloured scarves were crowded on racks and shelves. None of them were covered in cobwebs and not one had been chewed through by moths. If not for the fine layer of dust it might seem as if the owner had just stepped out the back door.

"They're hiding in here?" asked Kovac, raising an eyebrow at the small building.

"I'm going to try something to find the Forsaken. It might be dangerous," said Tammy.

"How dangerous?"

"Do you remember what happened during the fight with Grennig?" she asked and Kovac nodded. "I lost control. I can blame whatever has infested this city for some of it, but part of that darkness came from inside me. There are things in my past I've tried to forget and make up for. This place dredges it all to the surface."

"We all have regrets." Kovac looked into the distance and she saw something familiar touch his weathered features. Sorrow and remorse. Tammy couldn't help asking about it. The Guardian in her just wanted to know.

"What did you do?"

Kovac's laugh was bitter. "Trusted the wrong man, and here I am, living as a king, drowning in riches." He gestured at their barren surroundings and then dropped his hands.

The more time she spent with him the more she realised he wasn't a typical mercenary. Now wasn't the time to ask for more details but she knew he was carrying a heavy burden of guilt. There was a lot more to him than his rugged appearance.

"Balfruss had an idea about how to find the Forsaken." Kovac looked uncomfortable when she mentioned the Sorcerer's name. She'd seen how all of the mercenaries glanced at him when he wasn't looking. Mercenaries weren't known for being polite and good-mannered, but not one of them had said so much as a harsh word to anyone in the camp since their arrival. Tammy wondered how much of it was due to the Sorcerer's presence rather than Alyssa's promise of repercussions.

"You can do magic?" said Kovac.

"No, it's difficult to explain. I need you to do something for me."

"What is it?"

"If I start to lose control, I want you to stop me before I hurt anyone." Tammy knew she was being vague, but explaining it would just cause another delay and her nerve was already wavering. Kovac might try to talk her out of it and then she would have an excuse not to try.

To her surprise Kovac didn't ask for more details.

"I'll try," was all he said.

"Promise me."

"I can't," said Kovac. "You're damn strong and I've seen you fight with that," he said, gesturing at her sword. "I'd be lying if I said I could beat you by myself."

"Then just try your best," she said. "Give me a minute and I'll be out."

Closing her eyes Tammy focused on her breathing and tried to empty her mind. Years of training in the Watch and then the Guardians had taught her how to control her emotions, but since coming to Voechenka it had proven difficult. Now, instead of holding them at bay, she began to let all of her strongest emotions come to the surface.

Tammy turned her thoughts back in time, focusing on her bloody days as an enforcer and fighter. Once again she heard the cracking of bones, the popping of joints and the screams as she twisted flesh beneath her hands. The wet smacking of fists on flesh. The baying of the crowd as it screamed for blood and the addictive rush of adrenaline as her opponent fell to the ground. Reaching down into herself she tried to peel back her self-control and shrug off the chains of morality and ethics.

Buried, deep inside, was her primal self. As strong urges started to fill her mind Tammy tried to hold on to them and not let them control her. Normally such a struggle wouldn't be necessary, but she could feel something in the air calling to her to just let go. To draw her sword and kill the first person she saw. To bathe in their blood. To run wild through the streets howling at the sky. The urge was so strong she had partly drawn her sword before she realised and quickly shoved it back.

Stumbling out the door Tammy felt as if she were teetering

on a tightrope. She felt drunk and hungry, horny and angry, as the urge to kill swelled in her chest.

Someone slapped her across the face and she turned, snarling at the man dressed in grey furs. Tammy could see he was talking but the words just didn't make any sense. She could smell his fear and see the concern on his face, but his name evaded her. There were others close by, staring at her, and all of them were armed for a fight. The odds did not look good but she would make them bleed.

"Tammy!" screamed the man. The word, her name, penetrated the fog in her mind. She felt his hand on her chin and started to pull away, but then another stronger urge started to overwhelm her at his touch. Tammy pulled him tight against her, forcing him onto his toes so that she could kiss him. A growl started deep in her throat as she tasted him and felt his body start to respond. When she grabbed his crotch the man stumbled back, wide-eyed and confused. He wanted to play. Well, she could play.

"The Forsaken," he jabbered and something shifted at the back of her mind. She was supposed to be doing something. "Where are the Forsaken?" he said.

Tammy felt the darkness recede for a second and she managed to regain control, but it was tenuous. She felt as if she were barely holding on.

Balfruss had been right. Something in the city rejoiced at everything that she'd done and she knew it wanted more. It wanted her.

Turning slowly in a circle she tried to concentrate on the city rather than the emotions within. The streets echoed with violence and the whisper of spirits, but there was a strong and familiar pulse from something still alive. It called to her with a siren song, telling her to walk blindly into the dark and embrace the primitive version of herself.

"This way," she said, moving at a jog. She hoped the others would follow and that she could stop it overwhelming her again. The closer she came to the source the stronger the urges became. Tammy had to fight her own body not to draw her sword and kill everyone. Another part of her mind told her to tear off Kovac's clothes, shove him to the ground and mount him. The images of sex and violence were so powerful her breathing became loud and ragged. With every step she had to fight her own nature and repress the animal inside.

Stumbling along, forced to pause from time to time to centre herself, Tammy led the mercenaries across the city. It felt as if the struggle had been going on for hours by the time she found the church. It wasn't large but even a cursory glance showed it was considerably older than the surrounding buildings. The doors had been ripped off, allowing her to stagger inside and collapse on all fours.

Kovac started to move towards her but she waved him back, sitting on her haunches. She couldn't bear for anyone to get too close in case of what she might do to them. There was a fire raging inside. It surged along her veins and beat in time with her heart. The echo of that madness and thirst for violence had drawn her to this place.

Closing her eyes Tammy tried to repress everything she'd dug up inside, but images of the past flashed before her mind's eye. Instead she looked around the church for a distraction. The pews had been taken away and probably burned, along with any tables or chairs. All that remained was a huge stone table at the far end of the room, a heavy metal bench and a pile of mouldy cushions stacked in a corner. The stone floor was built from a mosaic of tiny red and white tiles, but kneeling so close to them she couldn't see a pattern.

Weak winter sunlight poured in through the windows and

Tammy felt faint warmth on her face. Turning towards the light she stared up at the stained-glass windows which somehow remained intact. This was an old church of the Maker. One window showed him labouring beside the First Men in the fields, planting a row of tall crops. The First Men were supposed to be massive beings, but still He towered over them as if they were young children. The expression on His face was one of benevolence and yet she thought it was tinged with sorrow, as if He could foresee the many horrors the tribes would commit against each other in the future. He had created and raised them, teaching them about love and compassion, and yet they had still killed their neighbours. Out of greed, out of jealousy, out of fear.

In the next window a man stood with a flaming torch, bold and defiant against the dark while the Maker looked on with pride. Each window showed a miracle where He had given the people a gift to help them live and grow.

Tammy didn't believe in the Maker or the Blessed Mother. Everything she'd ever accomplished had been because of her own perseverance and determination. She owed her success to no one and equally there was no one to blame for her failures. She was responsible for it all and was not about to give up now.

Digging deep within herself again she faced everything she'd done head on. All of the lives she'd taken. All of the families she'd ruined. All of the pain and heartache she'd caused. But not all of it had been bad. With the unpleasant memories came others. Lives she'd saved as a Guardian. Families reunited and justice meted out. The scales might not be balanced yet but she was moving in the right direction. Whatever controlled the Forsaken, it had nothing new to show her that she'd not thought about by herself. It did not control her. She knew her own worth.

Tammy stood up and looked around at the church with fresh eyes. The mercenaries were still wary, Kovac most of all, but she tried to appease him with a smile.

"It's all right. I'm in control again."

He didn't look convinced but slowly edged into the church. Three stayed outside to watch the street, while the others helped her search the room.

"What are we looking for?" asked the tall mercenary, the one they called the Prince.

"I don't know but the Forsaken were definitely here." Tammy was certain. She could still feel a faint echo of their presence as if someone were running a finger across her scalp.

A search of the main hall revealed nothing so they moved to the back. A few rooms had been used for storage and living quarters for the priests. Two rooms had metal doors and the rest were missing, which Tammy assumed meant they had been made of wood and carried away. Both of the remaining doors were locked and the dents and scratches showed people had unsuccessfully tried to break them down several times.

"Give me a minute," said one of the sisters. Kovac had told her their names, Teela and Teeva, but Tammy couldn't tell them apart. One knelt by the lock and took out a set of picks while the other held her sister's sword. "Someone's made a mess of this," she tutted, probing the lock with several long metal pins. After another minute there was a loud click that seemed to echo very loudly in the short corridor.

Everyone drew their weapons and on Tammy's signal Kovac pushed open the door. Inside the room they found the former occupants. Both priests were dead, a dagger buried in each of their hearts in what appeared to be some sort of suicide pact. Their faces had sunk and the skin was tight, but they showed little sign of decay, making it difficult to know when they'd died.

The sister went to work on the other lock and as she worked Tammy felt something brush against her skin. She glanced at the others to see if they had noticed. Kovac was staring at the door and the others were fidgeting. He held one hand against the edge of the closed door where there was a small gap next to the frame.

"I can feel air moving," he whispered. The lock clicked open and once again they proceeded with caution.

Beyond this door was a short set of stairs that led down to an empty basement. Tammy and the others stared at a hole in the floor that fell away into a black pit. The flagstones had been ripped up and finally she saw some evidence of the passage of many people. There were numerous scuffmarks on the stones as well as mud and drops of old blood. Rising up from the hole was a musty and damp smell that she couldn't identify, and yet it was familiar.

One of the sisters stripped some of the clothing off the dead priests, which she then lit with flint and tinder. It made for a poor torch and would burn out quickly but it was all they had. The light revealed what looked like a cave or tunnel under the basement. A set of crude steps had been created with chunks of stone which Tammy considered as she drew her sword.

"Are you sure?" asked Kovac, still talking in a whisper.

"We can't turn back now."

Tammy went first while other makeshift torches were fashioned until they had one each. At the bottom of the rough steps Tammy found she was standing in a long tunnel that extended in both directions. The walls were so cold they felt almost damp to the touch. The mildew smell was much stronger but she still couldn't see anything rotting.

Choosing the left tunnel at random she moved down it before it curved out of sight. The mercenaries followed, the sisters staying at the steps and watching the tunnel in the other direction.

Around the bend the tunnel extended in a straight line for a while before it came to a crossroads. Faced with three options she chose the left fork, determined to at least map the edge of the cave system. It was completely black in the tunnel and there were no natural sources of light, not even any phosphorescent fungus clinging to the walls.

When they reached the next junction Prince stopped suddenly, cocking his head to one side. Kovac tapped her on the arm and they all stood in silence, listening to the crackle of the fire as it ate up the material of the priests' old robes.

Prince tapped his ear and pointed down the passageway on his left. Straining her ears Tammy tried to blot out the pounding of her heart and focus on the darkness beyond. Her breathing and that of the others seemed to be incredibly loud, but there was nothing else to hear. Just the silence echoing over and over. She was just about ready to move on when she heard something. A faint huff of breath.

There was someone else down here. There was no way to know how close they were or how many were hiding in the dark.

Kovac moved to her side until he could whisper in her ear. "We've gone far enough. The torches won't last very long and we don't want to get caught down here in the dark."

Prince tapped Kovac on the arm again and this time gestured down a different passageway. This time she didn't have to wait long to hear the scuffle of movement against stone.

"Move," she said, urging Kovac back the way they'd come. He didn't need to be told twice and neither did the others. They raced back, taking the right turn at every junction, shoving the others ahead of them.

She followed the others and tried not to focus on whatever

was lurking in the dark behind her. Perhaps spurred on by their sudden flight, something was moving closer and closer behind her. It wasn't trying to hide its presence any more and the rhythmic patter on stone told her it was walking on two feet.

By the time she reached the last bend in the tunnel the sisters and Prince had already gone up the steps into the basement. Each had dropped their torch as they went, creating a pool of light.

Tammy waited until only Kovac was left in the tunnel before moving slowly towards the steps. Taking a risk she threw her torch behind her, hoping to catch a glimpse of whatever was pursuing them. The torch bounced off the wall and then fell to the ground, where it lay for a moment before someone picked it up.

The man who held it was a stranger but Tammy recognised the writhing black tendrils moving beneath his skin. More surprising was that the Forsaken's skin had started to turn purple in places, as if badly bruised. Even more startling was that when their eyes met he snarled, revealing a set of pointed teeth and a black tongue. She raised her sword and he took a step back, only to collide with something. Looming over his shoulder Tammy caught sight of another face and beyond that several more. All of them had pale purple skin and some had peculiar growths that had erupted from their face and neck.

Turning her back on them Tammy ran for her life. She could hear them giving chase, but it was only a short sprint to the steps and she had long legs. Hands pulled her up the steps and then she span around and waited with the others in a ring around the hole.

When the first Forsaken tried to come up the steps Kovac split open the woman's skull with his sword. She fell back with a scream but three more replaced her and then they started to boil up out of the tunnels like a rising tide. It was a good chokepoint, but after a few minutes of stabbing and shoving them back, Tammy's shoulders and arms were burning and fatigue began to set in.

There wasn't much room to fight, which stopped the Forsaken from overwhelming them, but their numbers seemed to be endless. There appeared to be sufficient bodies to keep this up all day, but she and the mercenaries would eventually tire and slip up. They had to fall back before it was too late.

"Pull back slowly," said Tammy. "Get ready to lock the door," she yelled at the sisters. One of them nodded grimly a second before jabbing her sword into a man's face through his right eye. He screamed and fell back into the darkness but others scrambled forward to take his place.

The others withdrew until only Tammy and Kovac held the Forsaken at bay, swinging more wildly now that they had room to attack. Sweat ran down her face and she was breathing heavily, gasping for air in the stale basement as the Forsaken crawled out of the darkness like a walking plague.

"Get out of there!" yelled the sister from the top of the stairs.

"Go!" yelled Tammy, but Kovac shook his head before stabbing a man in the throat.

"We go together," he said. "Now."

They both cut into the Forsaken with a final burst of energy and then fell back together, running up the stairs. The moment they were both through the door it slammed shut and the sister went to work on the lock. The other mercenaries piled in, pressing themselves against the door to try and keep it in place. Tammy added her own weight, pushing as hard as she could in readiness for the first assault. Something hit the door from the other side, hard enough to make her grunt, but the door barely shifted. Several people were shuffling around on the other side but by the time they pushed again, one of the sisters was done with the lock. She made a savage twisting motion and snapped her pick. This time when the Forsaken hit the door it didn't move.

Not waiting to see how long the lock would hold they ran out of the church and kept up their pace until they were out of the Dureen district. They slowed finally to a fast walk but no one relaxed until they saw the familiar wall of the winery.

Now that Tammy knew where the Forsaken were hiding, she would normally make a plan to study them. But just as the plague priest had said, assigning human motivations was pointless. They only wanted one thing. She would have to respond in an equally direct fashion.

Right now, the only plan she had in mind involved a lot of fire and smoke to choke them to death in their underground burrow. Failing that, she would call on the Sorcerer, who she was confident could summon fire hot enough to roast them to death.

As they reached the gates of the winery Tammy knew they were safe for now, but she wondered how the Forsaken would react to having their territory invaded. She suspected they wouldn't have to wait long for an answer. It was going to be a long night.

CHAPTER 35

As soon as he left the camp Balfruss took precautions, hiding the echo of his connection to the Source. If one of Kaine's students saw him, it wouldn't make any difference, but at least this way they wouldn't be able to feel him getting closer.

It was one of the earliest things he'd learned from the First People. Just after the war he'd left Seveldrom with his father and travelled to live with the tribal people in the north. In less than a year they'd taught him so much about the nuances of magic that he felt like a child again. The majority of what he learned was not anything anyone at the Red Tower had ever been taught. When someone hired a Battlemage they wanted powerful and aggressive magic to force back an enemy. The First People had taught him subtlety and finesse and how to weave magic so delicate a person wouldn't even feel it unless they concentrated.

The First People believed that all life was connected to the Source and that, on a primal level, animals could feel that link. Beyond their normal senses many animals seemed to possess unusual intuition, which helped them avoid predators. People able to wield magic were broadcasting their connection so loudly it made them useless as hunters, unless they could hide the echo of their power.

Weaving a fine net he'd memorised years ago, Balfruss laid it over himself, starting at his heart before miming pulling it tight over his head like a hood. The tribal teachers had laughed at his gestures, as they weren't necessary, but they helped him picture things in his mind. The memory of such a different time in his life brought a sad smile to his face.

Physically nothing had changed but now anyone trying to find him with magic would look right past him.

While holding the net in place he drew a little more power from the Source and extended his senses, stretching his hearing and eyesight beyond that of a normal person. The buildings around him swung into sharp focus until he could see every crack in the stonework and every grain of dirt on the windows. He could hear the faint sighing of the wind through gaps in the stone and smell a change in the air. More snow was definitely on the way.

Holding both weaves in place while reaching for a third would have been impossible for him until after the war. The Grey Council had abandoned their posts as teachers and leaders of the Red Tower, which ultimately led to its downfall. Long before that, they'd undermined the school and its students by hoarding their knowledge. They had known about so many Talents, but very few of them were taught.

Across the west, mages became nothing more than living weapons. In other parts of the world they were teachers, scholars, and people of learning whose counsel was highly valued. The failure of the Grey Council was one of the reasons many students left the Red Tower with a deep sense of wanderlust as they were still hungry for knowledge.

Taking a slightly roundabout route Balfruss retraced his

steps towards the ramshackle building from the previous day where he'd found Kaine's students. He checked the direction of the wind and circled the area until he was upwind, just in case they had scouts. Part of him still thought this was an elaborate trap set up by Kaine using his own students as pawns. A little caution wouldn't hurt and could save his life.

Balfruss closed his eyes and scanned the area with his magic, moving very slowly across the buildings. All of them were empty of people and there were no signs of the Forsaken. There hadn't been any indication up to now that Kaine's pupils were working with them, but he was taking nothing for granted. Once he was certain the area was clear Balfruss edged closer to the students' building.

When the building came into sight he hunkered down behind a pile of rubble. At this range he would need to be extremely careful, as even though the students couldn't sense him, they would feel him using magic if it wasn't subtle. It was painfully slow work and it required a lot of concentration, but Balfruss had learned patience while hunting in the emerald jungle. Whether a magic user or not, his tribal hosts had expected him to do his share and that meant putting meat on the table. Now he was hunting quarry of a different kind.

With a filament of magic as fine as a spider's thread, he touched the outer stones of the building. Numerous echoes of magic immediately rang in his ears, like a multitude of heartbeats, but each was slightly different in rhythm and tone. Every person's connection to the Source was unique.

As before, he counted twelve people but took no aggressive action. Instead he expanded the magical threads a little bit further until he could sense more about each individual.

Some of the students were sleeping in a curtained-off corner of the basement. They were more active during the night, shielding the building and running errands for Kaine despite the threat of the Forsaken. They were also the strongest and oldest students, which made it easier to see a peculiar synchronicity to their dreams. Kaine's fingerprint on their minds had remoulded them into something similar, though this wasn't obvious when they were awake. The others were younger, so the imprecise joins of what their Master had done to their thoughts were easier to see, like weeping sores in the mind. Eventually the wounds would heal over and they would become slaves to him without ever realising it. They would follow his orders and never question them because the idea of doing so would never occur to them.

Hardening his heart about what had to be done, Balfruss seeded more filaments of magic in the building. Instead of extending them towards the people he passed them into the stone walls. The columns supporting the basement had once been well made, but now they were old and one was cracked. Balfruss found pockets of damage in all of them, which he reinforced with magic, pressing it deep into the stone like wet clay. It was delicate work that had to be done slowly so that those inside didn't realise he was there. After an hour of concentrating and gradually trickling magic into the building, Balfruss was sweating and a headache was starting to form behind his eyes. Cramp had set in from sitting in one position for so long that his legs and hips ached, but he persisted and ignored the pain. Sweat was also starting to freeze against his skin as the temperature was falling as the day wore on. The snow was almost here.

Finally the last tiny thread of magic was in place. An earthquake could hit the entire city and Balfruss knew this building wouldn't fall. His magic had shored it up in so many tiny places it was almost indestructible. Drawing more power from the

Source he flexed the magical filaments throughout the building, as if clenching a fist, and then quickly withdrew them all simultaneously. The people inside were immediately aware of his presence but not of what he'd done.

Balfruss stood up in plain view of the building and forced himself to watch. The tiny fissures and pockets he'd dug into the building's structure were torn open. The damaged support column cracked even further, then began to slide sideways. Pieces of stone started to trickle into the basement, first a few and then more as the other columns deteriorated, suffering decades of damage in an hour.

With a grinding of stone and a loud rumble, all of the support columns collapsed at once. Tons of stone from the two floors above dropped down onto the basement and a huge cloud of dust rose up into the air. It took only a few minutes but eventually the rubble settled until all that remained of the building was a huge mound of stones and one jagged wall.

Even though he knew what he would find, Balfruss had to make sure. Using magic again he extended his senses into the basement, searching for any signs of life. There were none. Everyone inside would have been killed almost instantly, crushed beneath the rubble before they had a chance to protect themselves.

Bile rose up in the back of his throat but Balfruss forced it down.

The Stones board had been cleared. There was no one left now, just him and Kaine.

Just as he started to turn away he sensed something, a faint prickle of life. At first he thought someone had survived, but after only a few seconds the pulse of life became much louder and stronger. Something was moving towards him with incredible speed. The echo of magic was unlike anything he'd ever felt before. In fact it didn't seem human.

"That's impossible," he whispered, moving to one side of the street. He stood just inside the open doorway of a building that was moderately intact, checking there was a back door before weaving a shroud of camouflage. Slowly, as the alien pulse of magic became a throbbing drum in his temples, he faded from view and blended in with the stones behind him.

Balfruss heard it long before it arrived, skidding to a halt at the end of the street. The creature was unlike anything he'd ever seen before and he struggled to recognise anything familiar. It was only when it turned to sniff the air and paw at the rubble that he thought there was something vaguely canine about it. It was roughly the size of a bull but it seemed to be part bear and part jackal with huge shoulders and short hind legs. Its leathery skin was deep purple, the same colour as a ripe aubergine, and its whole body was corded with lean muscle. Worst of all was the face. It had an unnaturally long muzzle, dripping with saliva, and a dangling black tongue that lolled as it caught its breath. A heavy bone ridge protruded from its forehead and its deep-set eyes were a pure emerald green that looked human.

As it scanned the street Balfruss could see it was looking for him as much as using its other senses. With its nose held high, tongue tasting the air and flappy ears tilting one way and then the other, he didn't think it would be long before it found his trail.

Kaine had created this creature. Balfruss could feel the familiar echo of Kaine's magic at work. It should not have had any sort of connection to the Source and yet the heavy thump in his ears told him that part of the creature had once been human.

Using the blackest of magic, Kaine had blended beast and man to create something new and abhorrent. With his students dead he had sent this bloodhound monstrosity to finish Balfruss off.

As he drew a little power from the Source the bloodhound's head whipped around. Balfruss released the power but held on to the weave that concealed his appearance. The bloodhound kept sniffing the air as if it could smell him, or perhaps it had sensed him using magic. It started to drift down the street towards him, glancing in doorways in a very human fashion before moving on to the next. It would reach him in less than a minute.

Balfruss considered a number of options. He didn't think hiding from it would work for very long. Dropping his camouflage Balfruss drew heavily on the Source and immediately released it, directing all of the energy at the bloodhound in a broad wave of force. It hit the bloodhound just as it was turning its head.

The creature was thrown sideways off its feet where it collided with the side of the nearest building. The amount of energy he'd thrown should have been enough to send it through the front wall and out the back. Much to Balfruss's surprise the bloodhound merely slammed into the front wall, shook its head to clear away the grogginess, then turned its eyes on him. It was shielded. Somehow it had shaken off the full force of his magic. His first attack should have killed or at least severely wounded it, but instead it merely looked angry.

Wasting no more time on speculation Balfruss slipped through the door into the building and ran towards the back. The bloodhound crashed into the doorway a second later with enough force to shake the building. Its broad shoulders prevented it from getting inside, even when it tried turning sideways. From the rear doorway Balfruss watched as its massive claws started tearing the stone to create an opening.

Dashing out the back door he ran down a narrow lane between two roads, cut down another alley and continued to zig-zag across the city using the smallest roads possible. The drumbeat of the bloodhound's connection to the Source faded only slightly before he heard it draw closer again. Its long powerful legs meant it was gaining on him.

Running into the nearest building Balfruss went up the stairs to the top floor and then out onto a flat roof. Making a sharp twisting motion with one hand, he ripped out the stairs on the lower floors. The stone cracked and tumbled away leaving him staring down into a void.

He needed a moment to think but the bloodhound had other ideas. It appeared beneath him in a matter of seconds. Undeterred by the lack of stairs it dug its claws into the outer wall and started to climb.

Taking a couple of seconds to settle himself, Balfruss changed tactics. Drawing more power from the Source he focused it into a tight ball, no bigger than an egg, then poured more energy into it until it glowed like the sun. He could hear the snarling and gnashing of the bloodhound, but didn't let it distract him. When the pain from drawing power from the Source outweighed the drumbeat at his temples he let go, driving the ball of energy down with several tons of force.

Burning as it went, the energy entered the bloodhound's chest and continued to travel down the length of its body before exiting its flank. Screaming in agony and thrashing about, the creature lost its grip on the wall. Dark purple blood gushed from the holes in its chest and back and Balfruss smiled grimly. He was about to finish it when something changed.

The wounds began to close up, black tendrils writhed beneath the creature's skin and he sensed a strange whisper in his mind. It was the same connection he'd felt when Zannah had captured one of the Forsaken. The bloodhound was far more of an abomination than he'd previously imagined.

It shook off the wounds, climbed back to its feet and snarled at him. A dozen ideas ran through Balfruss's mind as it resumed its climb. The parasite possessing the bloodhound was not without its limits. It could heal wounds, but it could not bring the dead back to life.

"Let's see just how tough you are," said Balfruss, rolling up his sleeves. Fire had always been something he'd used as a weapon, but since the war he'd avoided it. After what had happened to so many of his friends on the walls of Charas, he couldn't bring himself to wield it. Now as he contemplated using it to save his life a snowflake drifted down to land on his hand.

A smile touched Balfruss's face and he grinned at the creature. Drawing heavily from the Source, he reached into the sky for what he needed. Above the mist thick clouds were gathering and he focused on one, watching as tiny drops of water fell, froze and then drifted towards the city. Scooping them up with his magic, he reshaped them while they were still pliable, blending dozens together without having to summon any ice of his own.

The bloodhound was almost upon him. Its breathing was loud and he could smell its rancid breath. It didn't matter. All he had to do was stand in one spot and let nature take care of the rest. Weaving a shield around his head and body, Balfruss sat down on the roof and waited.

The bloodhound climbed out of the hole and paused, its sides heaving from the climb. The once-human eyes stared at him with hatred but it was also being cautious. It tilted its head to one side and looked at the area around him, as if it could see his shield. When it snarled at him and prepared to charge Balfruss began to laugh.

The creature's snarl faded and it seemed puzzled by his reaction. Perhaps it was the look on its face or that he was simply tired, but it only made Balfruss laugh even harder. Tears ran down his cheeks and his eyes hurt as the tears started to cool on his face.

The creature's muscles tensed as it prepared to pounce but Balfruss knew it was already too late. The first ice spear pierced the bloodhound through its left shoulder, pinning it to the roof. It yelped in pain and pulled back, snapping the icicle in two. A second later two more were driven into its back, stabbing huge holes in its skin. The parasite started to respond, driving out the shards, closing up the wounds and doing its best to maintain its host. Six more spears hammered into the creature's back, severing its spine and flattening it on the roof. Before it had a chance to recover, the rest of the shower fell in a single wave, peppering every inch of the building with countless icy spears.

They bounced and shattered as the ice collided with Balfruss's shield, but he maintained his grip on the Source and not one of them touched him. The creature's screams tore at his eardrums as the daggers fell from the sky. Every inch of the creature's back was covered and more hit it every second, ripping open wounds before they could close, tearing flesh and piercing organs beneath its malformed muscles. As the creature tilted its head to one side an icicle slammed into its face, popping one of its eyes like an overripe tomato.

A growing pool of purple blood started to cover the roof. Despite its injuries the bloodhound inched towards Balfruss. It seemed determined to kill him with whatever remaining strength it had. Finally the shower tailed off, the last icicle pinning one of its forelegs to the ground as it reached towards him.

Balfruss stared at its one remaining eye and waited. Its body was a mass of open wounds, some so wide that he could see pink muscle and even white bone in a few places. Black wires ran throughout the creature's innards but they were limp and lifeless.

The remaining eye glared at him balefully but then even that glow faded until the creature was just a misshapen monster freezing in the falling snow.

Taking no chances Balfruss drew the axe from his belt, raised it high overhead and brought it down with both hands on the back of the creature's neck. It took him three swings but eventually he severed its head from the body.

Raising his bloody axe on high Balfruss screamed at the sky in defiance.

All of Kaine's students were dead and he'd butchered his abomination. It was almost over and they both knew it. There was a chance that Kaine might try to run, or even continue to hide, but Balfruss didn't think his arrogance or his pride would let him. Soon Kaine would call him out and they would battle until one of them was dead.

Since he'd first learned about the Warlock at the start of the war, everything he'd done had been leading up to this moment. Kaine was responsible for it all. The Warlock, the Splinters, the Flesh Mages and now all of the deaths here in Voechenka. For years Balfruss had been playing a game of Stones against Kaine's pawns without even knowing.

Every struggle, every triumph and loss, every lesson he'd learned about magic and the Source. All of it was for this fight.

This was his crucible and he was ready.

CHAPTER 36

Alyssa stared into the dark, desperately hoping that someone would walk down the street. As night fell they lit the torches above the gate and her shoulders slumped in defeat.

"They're not coming."

On her way back from the old wood with Zannah, she'd visited the other mercenary camps. She'd made the same offer and once again they'd rebuffed her with bravado that barely masked their terror. Alyssa had hoped at least a few people would change their mind, but it seemed that no one had.

The Forsaken ruled the night. Everyone else would be huddled behind their walls by this hour, praying and waiting for the dawn. Praying that the terror in the dark would come for someone else. But with each base that fell, the odds became much smaller. Tomorrow she would try again and even make the longer journey to the temple where Fenne ruled. Alyssa despised him but she knew that there were many innocent people trapped inside his base. She owed it to them to at least try and help.

Since coming back from the woods Zannah had retreated into herself again. Her behaviour hadn't changed. She still barely spoke and not once did she smile, not even at Alyssa. If she hadn't been there with the Morrin it might seem like she dreamed it.

Stood beside her were Balfruss, Tammy and Kovac, who looked warm in his grey furs. Zannah stood nearby, wrapped in silence, all of her attention seemingly focused on the city. She didn't join in the conversation but Alyssa knew she was listening.

It seemed as if today marked a significant change for all of them. Balfruss had spoken briefly about what had happened to Kaine's students. He clearly loathed what he'd been forced to do, but no one offered him any sympathy. He didn't want any and it had been a difficult decision to make, but in this city, that was all that remained. Despite his calm exterior Alyssa could feel a river of rage bubbling just under the surface. She was reminded of the stories she'd heard during the war about his final battle with the Warlock. She wondered if any part of the city would be left standing if he and Kaine went to war with one another.

"It was an abomination," said Balfruss, talking about Kaine's monster. Not that long ago the very same beast had pursued her through the streets. They had wounded it but she'd never really believed it was dead. "He'd blended an animal with a man and one of the parasites."

"I'm just glad it's dead," said Alyssa. He'd made sure by cutting off its head. Nothing could heal itself from that. It also made her wonder if the creature in the lake was another of Kaine's creations.

"I think he's out of tricks and puppets," said Balfruss. "Tomorrow, he will have to face me alone."

"What if he just hides instead?" asked Tammy. "Can you find him?"

Balfruss's smile was wintry. "I will find him."

Kovac shifted uncomfortably but said nothing. Although he did his best to hide it, Alyssa could see the Sorcerer made him very nervous. It was one thing to hear the stories about what

Balfruss had done during the war. It was something very different meeting him in person.

Alyssa could see why Kovac was standing with them on the wall, while the other mercenaries were inside in the warmth, even if Tammy couldn't. She hid a smile behind her hands as she blew on them to try and stay warm.

"We found something as well," said Tammy, including Kovac in her gesture. "I know where the Forsaken have been hiding."

Over Tammy's shoulder Zannah stared at her in shock for a few seconds before turning away again.

"Where?" asked Balfruss.

"It was in the Dureen district, right under our noses." There was a lot Tammy wasn't saying. She'd only been gone for a few hours but Alyssa thought she looked more than just weary. It was almost as if the experience had sapped not only her body but also her spirit. Kovac's shoulders were also slumped from exhaustion, but his eyes were full of concern for Tammy. Something had happened to her that worried him.

"You were right about how to find them." Tammy spoke directly to Balfruss and her voice quivered with anger. Her hands curled up into tight fists and it took her a while to regain control.

"I'm sorry," said Balfruss. He reached out towards Tammy but then changed his mind and dropped his hand. She also wanted no sympathy from anyone for what she'd been forced to do. The city was leaving an indelible mark on all of them.

"The Forsaken are hiding in a network of tunnels beneath the city," said Tammy. "It was old but looked man-made. Have you ever heard of anything like this before?" The question was directed at Alyssa and she took a minute to think about it.

"No, never. I thought I knew this city's history. Perhaps someone else might know."

"I've heard of them before," said Kovac.

Tammy rounded on the mercenary, who swayed back slightly under her glare but to his credit stood his ground. Even when she and the Sorcerer were staring at him Kovac didn't flinch.

"Why didn't you mention this before?" asked Tammy.

"Because I thought the tunnels were a myth until we saw them." Kovac shook his head and laughed at himself. "It's the main reason so many mercenaries came to Voechenka when the city fell."

"What reason?" asked Alyssa.

"Why do mercenaries do anything?" said Tammy rhetorically. "Money."

Kovac winced but didn't deny it. "There's an old story floating around about a city that was here before Voechenka. This was long before people with golden skin came to this country and called it Shael."

As he spoke Alyssa noticed Monella had come up the stairs with two of her assistants. Each carried bowls of steaming stew. Alyssa was about to interrupt the mercenary when she noticed how Monella was looking at him.

"It was supposed to be a glorious place full of riches," continued Kovac, unaware of his new audience. "People used to come from all over the world to visit. We thought they might have left some of their riches behind. The problem was we couldn't find anything."

"Do you know what happened to the city?" asked Tammy. Balfruss was listening intently, his brow furrowed in concentration. The story sounded totally unfamiliar to Alyssa and she'd lived here all her life. Not once had she heard even a whisper of such a thing.

Kovac shrugged. "No one knows. It could've been a plague or an earthquake. The story says that one day the people were here and the next they were all gone. Just wiped clean."

"There was treasure here, but not the kind you're after," said Monella, handing out bowls of stew. Alyssa tried not to make a face when she saw lumps of rhubarb floating on the surface. At least it was filling and would warm her up. "Voechenka was the birthplace of the Blessed Mother. The first church devoted to her was built here hundreds of years ago."

Followers of the Blessed Mother claimed it to be one of the first religions in the world. Alyssa had always known that it was an old faith, but people with golden skin had been living in Shael for centuries. How could Monella know such a thing?

"What happened?" asked Tammy, before Alyssa could ask.

"What always happens," said Monella, shoving a bowl into Kovac's hands with more force than was necessary. "War. One tribe didn't like the new religion. They fought and tried to kill everyone who followed the Blessed Mother. Some escaped and they spread the Faith."

"If it's not gold or riches, what was the treasure?" asked Tammy.

"The original sacred text," said Monella with more than a hint of reverence. "All eight books of the Harvest written on stone tablets. The divine word passed down from God through a true Oracle. It was so precious they built a maze and hid the books at its heart to keep them safe."

Alyssa saw that Monella was taking perverse pleasure in telling Kovac that his treasure hunt had been for nothing.

"How do you know this?" asked Alyssa.

Monella's expression darkened and she didn't answer until she'd ushered her two aides away down the stairs. "I suppose it doesn't matter now. I used to be one of the Faithful. I devoted my life to the Blessed Mother. The origin of our faith is a secret that has been passed down through the generations of priests here in Voechenka. It has been this way since the old city fell."

"The High Priest. Other members of the Faithful elsewhere. Do they know?"

Monella shook her head. "No one knew outside this city. There are dozens of stories out there, but they're all fake. All of the Faithful in Voechenka are dead. Now, you are the only ones that know this secret."

"Did you ever try to find it?" asked Alyssa. "Find the heart of the maze?"

Monella started to turn away but paused with her back towards them. "No."

"Why not?"

"My faith wasn't strong enough." With that the old woman stumped away down the stairs.

"A maze," said Balfruss, poking at his stew with a spoon. "That could take weeks to map."

He didn't need to say it. They were all thinking the same thing. They didn't have time. The Forsaken were destroying a different base almost every night. Their power and strength would be growing, so too would their numbers. They left no bodies behind unless they were truly dead. It wouldn't be long before they came to the winery. For all Alyssa knew, they could be next.

Even as she thought about the Forsaken Alyssa heard a scream drift through the air from elsewhere in the city. Next came the roar of battle and the clash of steel as people in another camp fought for their lives.

Part of her was grateful that it wasn't their turn tonight and she immediately felt guilty for such an unworthy thought. The Forsaken would come for them soon enough.

Closing her eyes Alyssa offered a prayer to the Blessed Mother to watch over them all. If she couldn't protect them then perhaps she could gift them with a swift and merciful death. The more

Alyssa learned about the Forsaken the less terrifying she found the alternative.

Knowing that others would be looking to her for strength and hope, she went to her room to pray.

This time, as she sank down on her knees in the silence of her own room, she found other thoughts didn't intrude. Other noises in the building were muffled but she could easily block them out. Despair and fear about what might happen to them all caused tears to run down her cheeks, but she didn't wipe them away. Lying down and just waiting to be consumed by the tide would be so easy. They'd fought long and hard, but now it seemed pointless. You couldn't fight the ocean and the Forsaken seemed as implacable and relentless as the waves.

Alyssa knew a small portion of her fear came from the city and its taint, but the rest was all of her own making. It was she who had given comfort to her people in the death camps when all hope was lost. It was she who had taken on the role as spiritual leader when others lost their faith. And now it was she who had been chosen to lead her people and inspire them. But for all of her people's recent accomplishments and their spark of defiance, she was afraid it was far too little, too late.

Here, in one of the darkest corners of the world, Alyssa wondered if the Blessed Mother still listened to the prayers of her Faithful. Surely, if this was truly her birthplace, then she would hear.

"Blessed Mother, help me." Alyssa choked back a sob. "Blessed Mother, guide me. I didn't want it, but I have become the leader of my people. I try to offer them hope in the darkness, but the evil surrounding us is so strong. I have given everything and now the well is dry. I need something. I need help."

She bowed her head and tried to find even a spark of something that would lift her up. But she was hollow inside, scraped clean by years of terrible experiences, and now more was being asked of her. Behind the closed door of her room, Alyssa began to cry. She did her best to muffle the noise, clamping a hand over her mouth, but her body still shook. It hurt so much she felt as if her heart was going to explode from the anguish inside.

The Forsaken would win and everyone in her camp would die or be taken. Every child would scream and beg for mercy, but none would be given. Everyone would be dragged away and the betrayal in their eyes would cut deeper than any blade. She would see their faces right up to the moment she too was hollowed out and became one of the damned.

When a hand fell on her shoulder she stopped crying, afraid that someone had overheard and come to investigate. Then she noticed the door was still locked. Looking up from the hand on her shoulder to the person's face Alyssa's heart skipped a beat. Her mouth stretched wide in a cry of joy but no sound emerged.

A pure white light began to fill the room, driving away all of the shadows, wrapping her in a cherished warmth she'd not felt since being a child. It was so bright it hurt her eyes but she didn't look away or blink. The light passed through her skin and filled her being with joy unlike anything she'd ever known.

A voice told her to rest but she fought it, desperate to stay awake. But she was so tired, right down to her bones, that eventually her eyelids began to droop. Slowly, she drifted into a dreamless sleep, but Alyssa knew someone was still there, watching over her and protecting her from the darkness, within and without.

CHAPTER 37

The next morning Tammy made sure her armour was on tight, checked her weapons and even considered taking her shield, but in the end she left her room without it. It would be too heavy if they needed to run and she was better using her sword with both hands.

Balfruss had only loaned her the blade fairly recently and already she thought of *Maligne* as hers. Normally she wasn't someone that grew attached to objects. Weapons were merely tools. The sword she'd carried for years as a Guardian was simple and had done its job well, but if it were stolen or broken, she wouldn't mourn. She'd simply buy another.

This sword though. It was something else. At night, when she honed *Maligne* Tammy often found herself staring into its surface as myriad colours danced across it. Her training and experience made her dangerous, but when she wielded this weapon she felt unbeatable. She needed to be careful that feeling didn't become the death of her, especially as so many emotions were still bubbling away under the surface. Balfruss's idea about how to find the Forsaken had worked, but it had left her feeling raw and she had to work harder than normal to control her moods.

Quickly she sheathed the sword and left her room. The sooner she left this damned city the better. One way or another, it would all be over soon.

She was the last to arrive at the main gate. Alyssa and the mercenaries led by Kovac were waiting for her. All were rubbing their hands or stamping their feet, trying to stay warm as a light shower fell. The snow had settled enough to paint the whole area in a brilliant white sheet, hiding the dried blood from previous nights.

Without a word they went up the stairs and then down the rope. As soon as they were all in the street they drew their weapons. Alyssa carried none but she didn't need any. The sisters took the lead but it was Alyssa who directed them towards the nearest mercenary camp. Tammy noticed that everyone now followed Alyssa's lead without question. She didn't want to be responsible for everyone in the winery and yet they all instinctively looked to her for guidance. Last night she'd been unsettled by the distant sounds of battle in the city, but this morning she was serene.

Alyssa walked through the city as if it belonged to her or she was a visiting dignitary and they her bodyguards. In a way that was true as she'd insisted on coming on this trip. Tammy had thought someone on the wall would argue but not one person had objected.

Half an hour later they arrived at the remains of the mercenary camp that had been attacked during the night. There was very little to see. Scorch marks showed on one of the outer walls from where the Forsaken had tried to smoke out the mercenaries, but the fire had been quickly extinguished. Dried blood and churned mud marked where the battle had taken place but there was little else. No bodies. Not even a stray limb. Broken arrows and shattered weapons littered the ground outside. The front door and part of the front surrounding wall had been broken down.

While the mercenaries kept watch outside, the rest of them went into the building. There was more of the same, splashes of blood on stone, stray weapons and signs of a struggle. In some places the blood had frozen to form red sheets of ice. Given the choice of death or being taken by the Forsaken some people had taken their own lives. Daggers and swords were buried in throats and hearts, and in one room they found one man and six women. The women's throats had been slit, frozen blood forming red necklaces. The man had died from the dagger buried in the side of his own neck. None of the dead looked peaceful.

The air was bitingly cold but they didn't hurry their search. Alyssa walked ahead of everyone going into each room first. She paused beside each body to murmur a quiet prayer before moving on to the next. Her face was without expression but Tammy could see the grief in her eyes. Kovac stalked from room to room, teeth gritted, knuckles white on his sword.

When they'd searched every room and found no one alive, Tammy and the others followed Alyssa to the next base. There were only two remaining, apart from the winery, and one of them was controlled by Fenne, the Morrin. Tammy had no desire to go back to the temple, but she doubted arguing with Alyssa would change her mind. She intended to make the same offer again to each base, regardless of personal feelings and what had recently transpired. Not for the first time Tammy wondered who Alyssa had been before the war.

The mercenary camp at the old bank had been attacked at least once since Tammy's last visit. There was more rubble in the street outside. The previously dented front door was now covered with deep craters and dozens of scratches. One section in the top left corner had been gouged away and temporarily repaired. The Forsaken had clearly tried extraordinarily hard to get inside on their last attempt. A few bars on the ground-floor windows had been removed, but not enough for a person to squeeze through. Those that remained looked battered and in desperate need of repair.

Alyssa was also studying the new damage. She touched the sheared-off remains of an iron bar on one of the windows and her fingers came away red from old blood.

"They tried their best," said a rasping voice from the roof, "but they didn't get inside. Not one of them."

The mercenary, Graff, looked even more drained and exhausted than the last time. His pale skin was waxy, his eyes completely bloodshot and he had a blood-soaked bandage around his head. Alyssa regarded him and the street for a minute.

"You can see what's happening, Graff," said Alyssa, gesturing at the destruction in the street. "The Forsaken are getting stronger. Almost every night they're overrunning a base. If you stay here tonight, you'll die. Or worse, you'll be taken." Her voice wasn't cold but Tammy had expected a gentler or more compassionate approach. "If you want to stay, go ahead, but I'm here for those you're trying to protect. I can offer them a chance."

Graff ran a hand over his tired features, scrubbing it back and forth as he tried to wake himself up. "You've changed, girl," he muttered.

"In this place, what choice do any of us have?" said Alyssa.

Graff grunted and looked off into the distance. He was on the edge and at his wits' end, but Alyssa didn't soften her approach.

"There are only two camps left besides mine. Once we're done I'm going to speak to Fenne. If we stand together there's a chance we might survive until tomorrow. You have until nightfall to decide."

"Do you really think that we can win?" asked Graff, staring down at Alyssa.

Alyssa shrugged. "We're stronger together. The Forsaken know that. That's why they've kept us separate and scared. Now, I don't think they care what we do, but it's not over yet."

With that, Alyssa set off towards the old temple and they hurried after her, the sisters racing ahead to scout the streets. Kovac fell in step beside Tammy, a troubled look on his face.

"Say it," said Tammy.

"Do you really want Fenne and his people in the camp?"

"No, but they might be all that stands between us and the Forsaken."

"Fenne might play nice at first, maybe even appear all meek and humble, but he'll turn on us," said Kovac. "It's just his nature."

Tammy didn't disagree but she wasn't sure they had a choice. She knew Alyssa had some of her people keeping a close eye on all of the mercenaries in the winery, just in case one of them stepped out of line. It would be no different with Fenne and the others. Things would be a lot more crowded though, and she'd have to work extra hard not to punch him in the face whenever she saw him.

Tammy didn't realise she'd muttered the last part out loud until Kovac chuckled.

"I think we all feel like that. He has one of those faces."

When the old temple came into view at the end of the street Tammy's shoulders tensed. She tried to unclench her muscles but the place was clearly having a similar effect on Kovac and the other mercenaries.

As they came closer the sisters spotted something and ran ahead. The mercenary called Prince took up the front position, putting himself between Alyssa and any danger. She started to move forward but Prince urged her back and they paused as the sisters checked for any danger.

"What is it?" asked Tammy.

Kovac squinted at the temple and clenched his teeth. "Look at the gate."

It took Tammy a few seconds to realise what was amiss. The gate was open. The sisters disappeared through the gate while the rest waited in silence, listening for the first sounds of trouble. Tammy scanned windows and doorways, convinced that someone would come racing towards her at any second. A few minutes later they came trotting back down the street, armour rattling and spiky hair waving.

They still held their weapons ready but the urgency had faded from their movements.

"Whole place is empty," said Teela. "Not one body inside."

"Any signs of a battle?" asked Tammy.

Teeva shook her head. "Doesn't make sense. How'd the Forsaken get inside without a fight?"

"I might be able to help," said a voice to their left. A figure stepped out of the shadows between two buildings. Prince shoved Alyssa behind him and the others formed a protective line.

The ragged figure of Roake stepped into the street and slowly raised his hands in surrender. His clothes were ripped and covered in filth, and his pale golden skin was now green and blue in places. Parts of his scalp had come away revealing bright pink flesh underneath. His soiled clothes hung off a body so bony he resembled a freshly dug-up corpse.

"Kill it," hissed Teela, starting to move towards Roake, her sister a second behind her.

"Wait!" shouted Alyssa. The tone of her voice carried sufficient authority that the sisters froze, their weapons inches from

Roake's face. He didn't seem alarmed and when they stepped back he looked genuinely disappointed. Alyssa gently moved the others aside until she stood facing the dead man.

"Do you know this creature?" asked Kovac.

"This is Roake," said Alyssa.

"He's one of the Forsaken," said Teeva. "We should kill it."

"When was the last time you saw a Forsaken so ragged?" asked Alyssa. "What do you want, Roake?"

He lowered his hands but there was really no need. It was clear he didn't pose any kind of threat. "I know what happened to them," he said, gesturing at the temple. "Fenne invited the Forsaken inside."

"He wouldn't do that," said Kovac, although it didn't sound as if he really believed what he was saying.

"I was here when he opened the gates," said Roake. "He gave everyone to the Forsaken. In return he kept his own skin and wasn't Embraced."

"This could be some kind of Forsaken trick," said Teeva, and her sister nodded emphatically, readying their weapons for a fight.

"All he had to do was let everyone else die to save himself," said Roake. "He gave them an army."

"What are you?" asked Tammy.

She felt slightly sick when Roake grinned, showing off black and yellow gums with a few remaining rotting teeth. "I was taken and the Forsaken tried their Embrace on me." He lifted up one side of his shirt to reveal an open wound in his right side below his ribs. It was the size of two fists and it looked as if something had exploded out of his chest. "It didn't work."

"Blessed Mother save us," murmured Alyssa.

"That's impossible," said Kovac.

"He might be telling the truth," said Tammy. "This is the second time I've heard a story like this."

"You didn't answer my question," said Alyssa. "What do you want?"

"I'll tell you, but only you," he said, gesturing at Alyssa. Despite protests from the others she moved them aside and boldly walked right up to Roake. It wouldn't take much for him to reach out and snap her neck. If he truly wanted her dead he could do it quickly and they wouldn't have time to stop him. Alyssa knew the risks but she stared him straight in the eye, almost daring Roake to try.

Instead he merely leaned closer and whispered something in her ear. Alyssa flinched, either at the smell of him or at his words. She considered his request for a minute and then nodded.

"He's coming with us," she said, holding up a hand before anyone could argue. "He has information that might prove valuable."

Tammy was remembering what the old man, Perron, had told her in the temple about his friend. Roake might be a lot more useful than even Alyssa realised.

They set off the way they'd come, Roake walking in the middle of the circle beside Alyssa. The sisters resumed their position at the front while Kovac and Tammy followed at the rear.

"Do you know what happened to everyone?" asked Kovac, gesturing at the temple behind them. "Have they all been changed?"

Roake's rotting smile was grim but his words were more chilling. "Oh no, it's worse than that. The time of the Embrace is over."

"I don't understand," said Alyssa. "I thought the Forsaken wanted people for their Embrace."

"They do, but the Embrace was only temporary. It was an incubation period while the parasite grew to maturity."

Tammy could see Alyssa was afraid to ask but they had to know. "What happens next?"

"The balance of power will shift and the outer shell will be remade."

"Into what?" whispered Alyssa.

Roake shook his head. "I don't know and I pray we never find out."

CHAPTER 38

As Balfruss walked through the empty streets of Voechenka he found himself thinking about the Warlock.

Long before the war, the Warlock had been a young man named Torval who was driven by a thirst for knowledge and then later, a hunger for power. He'd claimed to have visited every country in the world during his travels, but Balfruss knew this to be a lie. Torval had never spent time across the Dead Sea living with the jungle tribes. But he had come to Voechenka and studied under the tutelage of Kaine, who'd taught him dangerous magic that should have remained lost.

During the war the Warlock had felt no guilt about anything he'd done and Balfruss suspected Kaine would feel the same way. They both did it because they could and they wanted to. To them it was just that simple. The consequences didn't matter. In their minds they were the centre of the world and everyone else was less important.

While the world turned Kaine had been lurking in the shadows of Voechenka, delving into the darkness and uncovering magical Talents few would want or even consider. Not content with damning himself, he had taught others and sent them out into the world. Each Flesh Mage had been responsible for many deaths and the Warlock had helped drag most of the world into a war where thousands had died.

Kaine shared the blame for each of those deaths, for every warrior killed on the battlefield and every friend Balfruss had lost fighting the Splinters. He had to pay for all of the innocent blood that had been spilled.

Balfruss also wondered about the nature of the Forsaken. The parasites were not natural and even Kai had said as much. It seemed plausible that Kaine was also responsible for summoning them. Perhaps he had opened a rift to somewhere beyond the Veil, just as the Warlock had done. If so then there was even more blood on Kaine's hands than Balfruss had realised.

The old rage, the legacy from his father, was still there simmering under the surface. Long ago he had learned to control it and had sworn it would not be his master, but in this city it was becoming more difficult by the day to rein it in.

As he normally did when he needed to calm his mind Balfruss traced the fine tattoo on his wrist. He ran a finger over every whorl and twist, over and over, the design forming an eternal chain that could never be broken. Not by distance or death. He pushed away his fury and buried it deep under layers of control where it wouldn't interfere with what had to be done.

Reaching out, Balfruss delved deep into the Source, then cast a fine net across the city, stretching it as far as he could in all directions. Now that he and Kaine were the only two people able to touch the Source, Balfruss hoped it would be easier to find the other Sorcerer. Despite their differences, Balfruss could not deny Kaine the honorary title and all that it entailed. They had both become more than weapons, more than Battlemages.

The battle between them would not be one of raw strength. It would be a complex game of attack and counter-attack, feints and tricks intended to catch the other unawares.

Balfruss had no idea if a simple echo net would help him find Kaine, but it was the easiest approach. After that he would have to try more elaborate means to locate him.

Much to his surprise Balfruss felt an echo almost immediately. Kaine was very close. He tightened the net to a narrow area ahead and to his left, while using more magic to amplify his senses. It was far too easy. He suspected a trap and moved forward with extreme caution. When he entered Debrussi square and saw Kaine sitting on a pile of rubble it merely confirmed his suspicion. It would be madness to idly sit out in the open and wait for the enemy.

Balfruss paused at the edge of the square and carefully studied each building for traces of magic. Using the finest filaments of power he could manage, narrower than a human hair, he crawled through every window and doorway with his senses. A first pass revealed nothing, but he knew that some magical traps could be crafted so that they remained dormant until triggered. If Kaine had noticed his presence he showed no signs of alarm and seemed content to doze, chin resting on one hand.

Balfruss's second and third searches revealed nothing as well, which only made him more nervous. It would be unwise to underestimate Kaine. There could be elaborate traps hidden in ways Balfruss couldn't even begin to imagine.

Finally, after weaving a dense shield around himself and with his heart beating loudly in his ears, Balfruss set foot in the square.

Nothing happened. Kaine continued dozing and nothing sprang at Balfruss. It was only when he scuffed his boots against a loose pile of rubble that Kaine woke with a snort, glancing around with bleary eyes.

"Ah, there you are. I thought you weren't coming."

Balfruss ignored him for a moment. There had to be something he was missing.

"There's no one else here," added Kaine. "You killed all my pupils."

"You left me no choice when you broke into their minds. You took away their free will."

Kaine waved a hand dismissively. "They were idle children who had no ambition. I forged them into something useful for my purpose."

The Warlock had said almost exactly the same thing when he'd created his Splinters. They were men and women born with the ability to wield magic who'd never had the opportunity of being trained at the Red Tower. The Warlock had hollowed out their minds and made them nothing more than walking puppets who fought with magic at his command. Kaine's invasion of his pupils' minds had been worse, as they still thought they had free will. They had been living in a prison they couldn't see or feel and yet they had been enslaved by him.

"Do you know how many people died because of the Flesh Mages or the Warlock?"

"No, but does it matter?" asked Kaine.

Balfruss forced himself to stay calm. It wasn't just that Kaine lacked empathy for the dead. He seemed to be completely without a conscience. Even so he couldn't accept that Kaine would do all of this for no reason.

"Why do any of this? Why spend so many years delving into mysteries if not for some purpose? Why send Flesh Mages out into the world? What is it that you want?"

Kaine sat upright and seemed to focus on Balfruss for the first time. "That is the right question."

When the silence between them had stretched out for a while Balfruss realised he wasn't going to get an answer. Kaine was looking straight at him but he was completely motionless. "Are you waiting for me to guess?"

"No. I considered telling you, but really, I don't see the point. You're stuck in the past, in the old way of thinking. You still belong to the Red Tower. I can see their thumb resting firmly on your head, Battlemage."

"And you? Who do you belong to?"

"To the future. I will create it here, in the shadows. I will build my own Tower if I must. A Black Tower."

Balfruss laughed and shook his head sadly. "With what? Rubble and corpses? That's all this city has to offer. You have no pupils, no resources, nothing but your arrogance and your mania."

Kaine shrugged. "I can always find more pupils. The Red Tower is broken and a lot of children never find their way there."

"That's changing. It's being rebuilt."

"It will fail. The Grey Council are gone and cannot be replaced."

Balfruss was growing tired of Kaine. The more he talked the more Balfruss realised there was no changing his mind. He had lived this way for decades and no matter what Balfruss said he would never accept reason. There was nothing that would make Kaine reconsider his decisions.

"Did you wait here for me just to argue? Or do you want something?"

Kaine smiled and Balfruss readied his shield. "I want everything."

There was a subtle shift in the air and Balfruss felt something brush against his skin. "Everything?"

Kaine stood up and his air of nonchalance faded. "I know all about your travels to the desert kingdoms. I know about what happened during the war and how you defeated the Warlock. I even know about the years you spent across the Dead Sea with your father. I want every scrap of knowledge that you've picked up, every Talent, every drop of it."

A wall of force lashed out across the square so fast Balfruss barely had time to brace himself. It collided with his shield and the power behind it was so great he was thrown backwards. He flew several feet through the air and collided with a wall that collapsed as he landed. Stumbling to one knee, trying to catch his breath, Balfruss shook away the black spots dancing in front of his eyes.

"Give it to me!" said Kaine, reaching out with one hand and making a sharp twisting motion.

Something began to claw at the edges of Balfruss's mind, like a rat trying to burrow its way into his skull. He felt a growing pressure against both temples as if ghostly fingers were trying to dig their way through his flesh to get at his brain. The power of the attack was strong, but the method was crude, relying on brute force and surprise. Now that he knew what Kaine wanted Balfruss reinforced the shield around himself with one hand while weaving a net around his mind. He started at his heart and again mimed pulling something over his head like a cowl, covering his eyes and nose. The pressure against his skull faded as he blocked Kaine's attempt to break into his mind.

Steadying himself against the broken wall, Balfruss pushed himself upright. For a moment Kaine seemed surprised that the fight wasn't already over, but then a sneer twisted his face. Removing what little heat remained in the air, he created a shower of icy needles, which he flung at Balfruss. The icicles shattered against his shield and fell to the ground with tinkling sounds like breaking glass. Balfruss retaliated with a globe of light, which he hurled into the air above Kaine. He quickly turned around and covered his eyes as the globe exploded into a hundred burning spores as bright as the sun.

Behind his back he heard Kaine howl in pain and surprise.

Whipping round, Balfruss saw the Sorcerer stumbling about, one hand rubbing his red and watering eyes. The blindness wouldn't last for long and Balfruss needed to press his advantage.

Trying to outmuscle an opponent with brute force was something he'd done as a pupil at the Red Tower. They'd tested their strength against one another and the old adage was true about their always being someone stronger. Since then he'd learned many subtle and cunning ways to unbalance another magic user.

The earth beneath their feet was dead. Nothing grew in the soil, no seeds lay dormant waiting to grow and no insects crawled. As Balfruss lashed out with his magic he saw Kaine's shield flicker as it refracted a meagre burst of sunlight. Instead of targeting him directly Balfruss directed his will at the stones, bedrock and soil beneath Kaine's feet.

Moments later the surface collapsed, an eight-foot-wide sinkhole ripping through the square. Kaine dropped out of view without a sound.

A pregnant silence filled the square and Balfruss waited. The fall wouldn't have been deep enough to kill Kaine, but it might have broken his legs. As the seconds stretched on, Balfruss wondered if Kaine was actually dead. After all that he'd done, it would be a mistake to assume anything. Balfruss would only believe Kaine was dead when he looked into his lifeless eyes and not a second before. He inched a little closer until he could look over the lip of the sinkhole.

The air temperature turned noticeably colder and Balfruss felt a dull throb of pain in his finger ends and other extremities. A funnel of cold air was sucked down into the sinkhole in a whirling cloud of ice. Slowly Kaine emerged from beneath the ground, walking up a set of icy stairs he'd crafted, spitting and cursing.

When he made it back onto the street he was limping badly

on his left side and shaking with anger. In contrast Balfruss felt calmer than ever before and faced his enemy with an icy detachment. Without realising, Balfruss found himself smiling, not at the injury he'd inflicted, but at the ghosts of yesterday. Finally he would be rid of the Warlock's shadow that had lingered, long after his death. With the death of Kaine there would also be no more Flesh Mages. Others might rise in time, but the root of so much pain and suffering would at last be at an end.

Kaine raised a hand to the sky and started to summon a storm, pulling wisps of clouds together from nothing. With a negligent flick of his hand Balfruss severed the skyward threads of power, quickly dispelling the clouds. When he tried to summon more ice Balfruss nudged over a nearby wall, sending it toppling towards Kaine. With a squawk of surprise he dropped the ice shards and focused all of his energy on reinforcing his defences. The slabs of stone shattered against Kaine's shield and blue sparks erupted on impact. The weight of the wall drove him to his knees, burying him up to his shoulders. Once the stones had settled he emerged again unhurt, though covered in dust and dirt.

Balfruss was surprised at how ineffective Kaine's attacks had been so far. They were more like those of a student than someone who the others had called Master.

"Enough games," spat Kaine. With one hand he started to weave something small in the palm of his hand while the other maintained his shield. Instead of reinforcing his own, Balfruss focused on the air immediately surrounding Kaine's shield.

Summoning more power from the Source he drew moisture and heat from the air, drawing it towards his outstretched hands. As the energy accumulated, an icy dome began to form around Kaine. He screamed something but his words were swiftly cut off as he was sealed inside and disappeared from view.

Balfruss pulled more heat towards him and the ice prison around Kaine changed colour from white to a deep ocean blue. Blue fire kindled around Balfruss's hands and arms as the ice continued to grow in thickness. He kept drawing energy from the Source, taking all of the heat from the surrounding air until his breath frosted and a localised shower of snow began to fall in the square.

Finally he released the Source and waited to see what happened as the magical fire around him began to disperse. As the seconds ticked by, he wondered if Kaine was already dead as the ice prison around him would be air tight. After another few minutes, Balfruss ventured closer, but not before he wove a dense shield around himself so that he wasn't caught unawares.

A loud crack rang around the square and a tiny fissure started to run up the ice from the bottom. As Balfruss backed away the ice split further until it was covered with a network of tiny veins. With a loud detonation, a section of Kaine's ice prison burst open and he slumped forward and slid to the ground.

Lying on his side Kaine glared up at Balfruss and unleashed the full force of his will. It was fashioned as a crushing force that sought to squeeze the life out of Balfruss and rip his body apart at the same time. It seemed as if Kaine had run out of tricks. Now he had made it into a simple battle of willpower. Balfruss tried to force away Kaine's attack while he set about trying to strangle the life out of his enemy.

The two stumbled back and forth, gasping and choking, while flinging each other around with jerky motions like puppets with severed strings. All thought of Kaine's crimes were driven out of his mind as Balfruss fought to keep himself whole. There was no time to think, or even get angry. All he could do was hold on to the image of himself as he struggled to pull Kaine apart.

Drawing more energy from the Source Balfruss clamped his teeth together and pressed forward, stretching himself to his absolute limit. Kaine was straining to keep him back, but very quickly Balfruss felt him begin to buckle under the strain. They balanced on the edge of the razor together for a second, with Kaine teetering towards destruction. With a final surge of effort it was over. Kaine's scream was lost as Balfruss's will crushed him under a massive hammer made of pure force.

Kaine was driven into the ground and flattened as if he'd been stepped on by a giant. His skull cracked open, his brains leaked out and both eyes burst like grapes. Ribs were compressed and driven into his internal organs, which exploded from the pressure. He had no time to scream and was dead in an instant. The only noise in the square was a quiet trickling sound as a slow river of blood began to spread out across the stones from the flattened corpse.

Chapter 39

Zannah watched as Balfruss shuffled down the street, slowly making his way back to the winery. When he eventually made it to the gate she threw down the rope but he just stared at it for a minute in silence. Eventually he gripped the rope with both hands but made no attempt to climb. When he looked up at her from the street below she saw fatigue etched into his features.

"Hold on. I'll pull you up," said Zannah, and he nodded, as if speaking was too taxing. Balfruss wrapped the rope around his waist and held on with both hands. Working hand over hand she pulled him up the wall by herself. The others on the wall watched in silence but made no attempt to help until he reached the top. Then two women pulled him over the lip and supported him down the stairs, one under each arm.

A few minutes later Monella came up the stairs to the top of the wall. She stood a short distance away from Zannah and just stared out at the desolate city.

"The Sorcerer is exhausted. He practically fell asleep standing up." She spoke quietly, as if talking to herself or praying, and didn't turn her head. It wouldn't do for others to know she was talking to Zannah. "Do you know what happened?"

"No," said Zannah, which made Monella frown, so she added. "He went hunting another wizard. Maybe he found him."

Monella harrumphed, spat over the wall and turned to head back down the stairs. Their eyes met for a second and Zannah was surprised to see a mix of emotions behind the old woman's remaining good eye. The cloudy one told her nothing, but the other showed glimmers of anger and hate, which were familiar, but also something new and alien. Regret. Monella was gone before Zannah had a chance to say anything.

With little activity during the day to interrupt her thoughts Zannah sometimes lost track of time. Hours would pass by unnoticed as she stood and stared and thought about the past. If not for the unpredictable nature of the nights, her whole life could have been a reflection of this moment; standing atop the wall at her post, waiting for something to happen.

It was some time later when Alyssa, Tammy and the mercenaries returned. A ragged figure walked with them and it wasn't until they came closer that she recognised the stranger. Roake. There had to be a good reason he was with Alyssa, let alone that she was speaking to the creature, but Zannah couldn't think of it. Zannah wanted to ask Alyssa, or shoot Roake full of arrows to drive him away, but instead she said nothing and threw down the rope.

Alyssa climbed up first and then the mercenaries, one by one, until only Tammy and Roake remained in the street. Some of the others on the wall had noticed him too and were visibly disturbed by his presence. As if Alyssa sensed the unasked questions, she moved to Zannah's side.

"We need him," was all she said, and the clench of her jaw told Zannah that nothing would change her mind. Roake's arms were so weak they lacked the strength to climb the knotted rope. "Haul him up," commanded Alyssa. For the second time that day Zannah dragged someone up the wall by herself, but this time the burden was far less. Roake weighed little more than a child as there was so little meat left on his bones. His skin was rotting and discoloured in places. It was as though he were already dead as the stench was like an open grave. When he reached the top of the wall no one rushed to help him over the top. Some of the defenders even moved back or covered their noses and mouths because of the smell.

As Alyssa descended the stairs Monella came into the courtyard. Surprise and horror warred on her face at the sight of Roake. "What is that creature doing here?" she asked.

"We need him and he's our guest. Find him somewhere to sleep." Alyssa's voice carried to everyone on the wall and once more her tone was commanding.

"You cannot let that inside the building," argued Monella.

"Then find him an alternative. That's your job." Alyssa went inside without another word, leaving the older woman staring at the grinning corpse. In the end, one of the storage sheds in the courtyard was cleared out. One of Monella's people swept the room and covered the floor with a couple of colourful blankets. The woman shoved another into Roake's arms and quickly fled, gagging at the smell.

"Was it something I said?" he asked. Monella wasn't amused and just pointed at the shed. With a grisly sneer Roake obediently shuffled inside and closed the door, reducing the fetid cloud in the air.

An hour after midday and another bowl of rhubarb stew, Alyssa joined Zannah on the wall. Her eyes were red, probably from crying, and she said nothing for a long time. Other people wanted her favour, but they could see she wanted to be left alone and for once they honoured her wishes.

"We visited the remaining camps," said Alyssa, running a

hand over her freshly shaven scalp. "Another fell in the night and there was nothing left. It was as if no one had ever been living there."

It was just as they'd experienced in the past. Long before coming to the winery, they'd seen buildings hollowed out and every person living inside seemed to just vanish. No one had known where they'd gone or had seen any strangers in the area. They had just disappeared. When it began to happen more frequently, one house at a time and then whole streets, the survivors started grouping together.

The early camps had been little more than enclosures with temporary walls made from overturned carts. For a short time, the semblance of normal life continued within these small cities. But when guards started to vanish at night they knew it wasn't enough. Fortified areas followed but then fighting broke out over food and fuel to get them through winter. Separate camps followed shortly after, but over and over again they were driven from safety by a growing number of Forsaken.

The winery and any remaining camps were the last line. Everyone knew they would not fall back to a new base this time. The whole city had become like a carcass picked clean of meat. The stones would not feed or keep them warm. This was the end.

"I appealed to those who were left to join us, but I have my doubts they'll listen. Pride, or perhaps taking orders from a woman, stops them. They can see what's happening and still they ignore it."

Zannah knew Alyssa was the best person in their camp to lead and so did the others. That was all that mattered. Humans puzzled her sometimes.

Alyssa started to say something else and then stopped, briefly resting a hand on Zannah's arm. Grief and sadness clung to her like a cloak. Once again Zannah was reminded of how small and frail Alyssa seemed at times.

"You want to tell me something that I will not like to hear."

"Yes."

"Then say it," said Zannah, looking up at the cloudy sky. Perhaps it was her yellow eyes, but Alyssa and the others found it easier to say difficult things when she looked elsewhere.

"We visited the remaining camps, including the old temple."

Zannah remained silent and waited for the words that Alyssa was struggling with. There was a blade hidden among them and Alyssa knew it would cut her. It would hurt either way but Zannah always thought it was better to be quick than slow.

"It was empty. They're all gone. Roake told us what happened. Fenne was starting to lose control of his people. Their fear of him was diminishing." Alyssa bit her lip before continuing. "He made a deal to save himself. He opened the gates and sacrificed everyone to the Forsaken. I've just had to tell Rheena, the girl Tammy rescued, about her father. Some of the others had relatives inside the temple."

It was one thing to hear that relatives were dead. That was difficult, but eventually it came to everyone. The pattern was as old as time itself. People had learned how to cope, but it never became an easy thing.

To be taken, hollowed out and remade into something else that wore your skin, was a difficult idea to hold in the mind. To see what looked like your family, walking and talking, had fooled many. Those people who welcomed their former kin with open arms were then dragged away and the betrayal they felt cut deeper than any blade.

"Soon they will rise again. We have a little time yet."

"It was two or three nights ago," said Alyssa.

A thought occurred which Zannah puzzled over, trying to see it from Alyssa's point of view, but finding no answer she eventually had to ask. "Why did you hesitate to tell me?"

"I know you hunted down your people who stayed behind after the war." She was trying to speak gently but there was no way to soften such things.

"That is true."

"And Fenne escaped. Since then he's done many evil things. I didn't want you to feel guilty for those taken from his camp."

Zannah checked to make sure this was not a joke, but Alyssa's expression remained serious. Her shoulders slumped in submission and she cowered, as if expecting to be hit. Perhaps she was supposed to be angry at what Fennetaris had done because he was also a Morrin.

"His deeds and his crimes are his own. Not mine."

"But if you'd caught him, those people might be alive."

Zannah shrugged. "Perhaps. But Fennetaris is rotten inside and his heart is black. I do not share the blame for who he is and what he has done."

This time Alyssa looked closely at her to check that she was not joking. Despite all the time they'd spent together, Alyssa and the others sometimes baffled her. When Alyssa was satisfied she offered a weak smile and her shoulders rose until she stood proud once more.

"Were you a tailor?" asked Zannah, more out of habit than anything else.

Alyssa smiled and shook her head.

Any further conversation was halted as a figure suddenly appeared at the end of the street. Zannah recognised him immediately. There was something familiar about him that spoke of home. As he came closer, the others on the wall started to panic, calling for weapons and reinforcements. Zannah ignored the bustle of activity while Fennetaris sauntered closer. Soon the wall was bristling with people, all of them armed and many pointing arrows at the lone figure. There was no sign of the Forsaken, but Zannah had no doubt they wouldn't be far away. They were probably watching to see how he performed. This did not feel like an attack though. He was up to something else.

When Fennetaris finally stood in the street below they stared at each other in silence for a long time. This was the first time in months, perhaps years, since they'd been face to face like this. He looked older than she remembered. Some of the colour had faded from his hair and beard. And though he did his best to hide it, she could see he was tired and afraid.

"Speak," Zannah said, but at first he remained silent. Instead he stared at the people on the wall, one at a time, as if memorising them. All knew who he was and had heard the stories of his crimes. Many could not meet his gaze, but others stared back, angry and defiant. The grin he used on them was a brittle mask but some were still intimidated by it.

Finally his gaze rested on Alyssa. "You lead them, yes?"

Alyssa drew herself up and stared down her nose at him. "I do."

"And they listen to you? To your orders?"

"This is not the army. I guide them."

Fennetaris considered this for a moment. "If your people were walking towards a pit, would you tell them to keep walking and trust you?"

"No. I would tell them to stop."

He gestured at the city around them. "Stopping in one place has not worked very well."

Alyssa would not be baited, but she played along with his game. "Then I would tell my people to go around the pit."

"A wise decision. But you cannot go around what approaches. You cannot avoid it. You can stop and wait, but the ending will still be the same. It will only be more painful if you fight. All will be Embraced."

A faint smile lifted the corners of Alyssa's mouth. "By your masters?"

"I have no masters."

"All I see is a servant and mouthpiece for someone else." Alyssa waved him away, dismissing him like a lowly subject in her court.

Fennetaris snarled but there was little he could do. The time when he could beat to death those who disagreed with him was at an end. He might not wear a lead but he was a servant, nonetheless, of those more powerful than him.

"I am here to offer you one chance for a peaceful solution. If you resist, then many of your people will be injured. Some may even die."

"And that would displease your masters, yes?" said Alyssa, copying his way of speaking.

"You dare mock me?" said Fennetaris. Bowstrings were pulled back and a dozen arrows pointed at his chest. He glared up at Alyssa as if totally unaware of the odds. "I will kill you with my bare hands. I will crush your skull and—"

"You will do nothing. You are nothing." Alyssa's words cut Fennetaris off as if she had slapped him across the face. His mouth gaped but no more words emerged. "You have no power over me or anyone else," continued Alyssa. "In fact, I pity you."

To be loathed and feared were things he was used to, but to be pitied was more than he could bear.

Fennetaris glared up at her. "I offered the other camps the

same deal," he snarled, "but there will not be an Embrace for you. Tonight will be your last as individuals. Tomorrow all of you will be taken and changed by the parasites against your will. There will be no balance, only slavery."

Zannah called out to him. "Even if everything you say comes to be, it will not change what you are." His head snapped around and she leaned forward, hands on the wall, glaring at her former countryman. "You will always be a coward, Fennetaris."

"And I know what you are, traitor," he sneered, but his words had no power to hurt her. Deflated, powerless and alone, there was nothing more he could say.

Fennetaris turned and walked away while bowstrings relaxed and sighs of relief echoed along the wall. Nevertheless Zannah could sense they were more afraid than before. Fennetaris had succeeded in undermining their morale, and soon news of his visit would spread. He had made Alyssa's task even more difficult.

"I have to go," said Alyssa, frowning as if she realised what he had done and what now lay ahead.

A few hours later, before nightfall, a long procession of people carrying all their belongings appeared outside the gate. At the front was a group of bedraggled mercenaries. A runner was sent and a short time later Alyssa came back to the wall.

"Hello, girl," said the mercenary, trying to act brave in front of the others.

"Hello, Graff."

"Does that offer still stand?" he asked. It cost him a great deal to ask in front of everyone but Alyssa did not gloat or drag out the moment. Her warm smile enveloped everyone in the street and she welcomed them as family.

There were too many to climb the rope, so although he was physically exhausted the Sorcerer came up from his room. This time Zannah saw Balfruss struggle a great deal to lift the cart, but eventually he managed it. The spectacle gave many people hope where there had been none before.

By the time everyone was inside and the winery made secure again, it was dark. Torches were lit and a heavy guard set on the wall but the night passed uneventfully. But when dawn came without any sightings, many felt dread about the coming night, because they all knew that it could be their last as free men and women.

CHAPTER 40

It was a little after dawn when Alyssa finally left the wall. The Forsaken had not come in the night, just as Fenne had promised. She'd kept watch all night with the others, staring into the darkness, trying not to fall asleep at her post despite the biting cold.

On the way to her room Alyssa expected several people to stop her and ask for advice. Perhaps it was because she was asleep on her feet, but she made it to her door without interruption.

Sleep claimed her the moment her head hit the pillow, and it was a little after midday before she finally woke. When she went in search of breakfast she was surprised to find the corridors full of people. There was almost a festival atmosphere with people eating, drinking and laughing. A few had brought out instruments and music drifted around the winery, adding to the mood. Word of Fenne's visit must have spread, and by now everyone knew what they faced tonight.

Now, more than ever, was the time for her people to live. When the Forsaken had first appeared, her people had cowered and hidden in their rooms. Now they laughed, danced and sang in the face of the enemy and the prospect of dying. The sound of ringing steel echoed from above and when she emerged into the courtyard she wasn't surprised to see long rows of people training with swords under the watchful eye of Zannah.

Tammy had joined her in instructing them and was walking up and down the lines, correcting people with slight adjustments to their arms, legs and shoulders. A few days' training would not make them skilled, but it was better than nothing.

Balfruss sat off to one side, wrapped in a blanket, an empty bowl in front of him. Since returning from his fight with the Master the previous day, the Sorcerer had done little except eat and sleep.

Alyssa sat down on a barrel beside him and together they watched the sword practice in companionable silence. Monella appeared a short time later with two bowls of something. Alyssa didn't care what it was and neither did her stomach which just rumbled with hunger. Monella gave her a bowl and after a quick glance at Balfruss gave him the second. He tucked in with vigour and was half done with his porridge before Alyssa had eaten her first mouthful.

"It's quite the party," said Balfruss, gesturing with his spoon. A trio with two fiddles and a drum emerged from inside the main building and behind them came a line of people. Each was carrying a bowl of food, which they began passing out to everyone in the courtyard. Practice stopped for a while as people moved to sit around the edges while the musicians played.

A group of six women, in pristine white dresses edged in silver, started to dance in the middle of the courtyard. They whirled and spun, leaping from foot to foot like prancing bucks. Watching them twirl about so quickly made Alyssa feel dizzy. It was an old folk dance she'd not seen performed in a very long time. Six men in matching green and gold outfits waited at the side and when the women formed a line they ran forward. Then the spinning began anew, as the men lifted each other into the air, one at a time and then in pairs. Soon they joined hands with the women and began to spin faster and faster as the tempo increased. People were clapping along and whistling as the crowd swelled. The music built to a crescendo and with one final explosive movement all six women were lifted into the air at the same time.

The applause was immediate and spontaneous. The dancers took a bow but were not done yet. The musicians started to play a slower tune and a few people were pulled up to join the dancers in the courtyard. If they didn't know the steps they were quickly shown until two lines had formed down the middle. Everyone was clapping along and laughing in good humour, even at their own fumbles and missteps.

Zannah came around to Alyssa's side of the courtyard but instead of talking she went up the stairs to the wall. The few defenders up there were watching the dancers and clapping along in time to the music. Zannah turned her back on the dancers and kept watch on the street by herself. Alyssa joined her and together they watched the city while listening to the music behind them. There was no sign of Roake anywhere, for which Alyssa was grateful. She knew Zannah wouldn't ask until she brought up the subject first. They would have to talk about it soon, but not just yet.

"I'll give you one more guess," said Alyssa. "Then I'll tell you."

Now more than ever Alyssa wanted Zannah to know who she'd been before the war. She knew a little about her friend, about what she'd done and why, but not who she used to be. Zannah thought about the past a great deal, and was weighed down by her failures, but there must have been a time before the war when she was happy and she smiled.

Zannah pondered the question and took her time because it

was her last guess. "Were you a patron?" she asked finally. The question caught Alyssa by surprise.

"Why do you say that?"

Zannah shrugged. "All along you've said you worked with many different artists. It seemed the logical choice."

"It's a good guess."

"But it's not right."

"No." Alyssa touched her on the arm and Zannah turned to face her. "I was a muse."

"A muse?"

She was staring at Zannah but Alyssa's mind drifted back into the past. It seemed so long ago at times. "This city was full of so many creative people. Do you know what that's like?" Zannah shook her head but she barely saw her. "It was a place of miraculous accidents. They would happen every day. Sometimes three musicians would meet, sit down together and begin to play. The music they'd create in that moment would be unlike anything you'd ever heard before. Music so beautiful it made you weep. And the next day one of the musicians would move on and that music would not exist any more. Do you understand?"

Zannah shook her head in puzzlement. "What did you do?"

"The air was charged with a form of energy from so many creative people living together. Competition was fierce and sometimes an artist stumbled. They were tired, or inspiration left them at a critical moment. They hired me to help them find their rhythm again."

Zannah pondered this for a while before asking, "Did you give them your ideas?"

Alyssa smiled. "I know it's difficult to believe, but once I used to be beautiful. I had long hair down to my waist and a figure that women envied and men desired. Sometimes I posed for artists and that gave them the spark. Other times I merely sat in the room with a writer or poet and they would begin to write with intense fury. They paid me for my time."

"How did you do it?"

It was something Alyssa had pondered for a long time over the years. At first she'd not questioned her good fortune. It seemed foolish to try and unravel the reason when it could stop at any moment. But after a while, when artists and sculptors had continued to be inspired by her presence, she'd begun to explore her ability.

"The ideas are theirs. They're just stuck. I believe that inspiration comes through a small door in the mind. All I did was open the door and the ideas flowed."

Zannah's silence was long and contemplative. After spending so much time together Alyssa had become adept at interpreting the meaning of her different silences.

"They paid you well for this?"

"I was one of the richest women in the city. I wasn't a noble or a patron, but I lived like one of them." The thing Alyssa really missed from those days was her bath. It had been a glorious tiled monstrosity large enough for eight people. "I made them the best version of themselves."

"And this ability never left you?" asked Zannah.

"No."

Zannah's eyebrows shot upwards as realisation dawned on her. "Is it a form of magic?"

"I think they call it a Talent," she said, gesturing at Balfruss. "But mine is so slight, even he doesn't notice when I'm doing it."

"This Talent, did you ever—"

"No, never on you. I swear." Alyssa was adamant and Zannah accepted her at her word.

"But your magic is not why they chose you to lead. That is

just you." Once again Zannah was proving to be more astute than she realised.

"The last time I used it was when I went onto the lake. I couldn't fish by myself so I encouraged a man named Crinn to help. Deep down he was a good man, but his fear of Fenne, and of whatever is in the water, stopped him from helping me." Alyssa regretted manipulating him. If the impulse to help her had not already been there, then it wouldn't have worked on him. Even so, she wished she'd hadn't done it. Crinn had nearly died on the water because of her. He'd fled as soon as they made it to dry land and had not been seen since. She suspected he was dead by now or had been taken.

"I would never have guessed. I'm glad I knew before the end."

"Why are you so certain this is the end?" asked Alyssa.

Zannah swept her hand across the horizon from left to right. All was desolation, dust and ruin. Nothing lived. Nothing grew. Nothing breathed. There was only cold, unfeeling stone and a bloody past, littered with corpses.

"I will not be leaving this place. There is no tomorrow for me, but perhaps some of the others will escape." Zannah sounded certain of her fate, yet Alyssa smiled at her friend.

"Have faith," said Alyssa.

"After all you've seen, how can you still believe?"

"After everything you've seen, how can you not?"

Alyssa knew her words puzzled Zannah, but she couldn't help it. She didn't know what would happen tomorrow. She didn't know who would live and who would be taken by the Forsaken, but her instincts told her this was not the end. Not the end of her people. They would go from this place in some way. They were filled with purpose like never before and nothing would stop them.

*

Tammy sat down beside Balfruss at the edge of the courtyard, watching as the dancers paused to take a much needed break. He looked a little better than yesterday, not quite as frail, but still seemed remarkably pale and weak.

"I'm not dying," he said without looking around.

"Can't you use your magic to heal yourself?"

"I'm just exhausted. Once I rest up I'll be fine." Despite not knowing him for very long Tammy heard the lie. He'd avoided the question about his magic, which probably meant he'd tried to use it and it hadn't worked, perhaps because he was too weak.

"Did you stop him?"

Balfruss's smile was grim. "Yes. Kaine is dead."

"You don't seem very happy about it?" she pointed out.

"There was something peculiar about the fight. It was almost too easy."

Tammy raised an eyebrow and gestured at him, huddled in a blanket, exhausted and haggard. "This was easy?"

Balfruss shrugged. "Even after a fight like that, I shouldn't be this drained. I'm trying to recover my strength, but it's taking longer than usual. It's like pouring water into a bucket with a hole in the bottom. I think it's this city. When I drew power from the Source, a piece of the darkness seeped inside."

After what she'd experienced, Tammy could believe that. Her self-control wasn't back to normal yet and every now and then she experienced impulses that she fought to repress. Her fingers would clench into fists, or a growl would start somewhere deep in her throat, and she had to take a few seconds to calm down.

"The sooner we leave this place, the better."

"I agree," said Balfruss. "I think my strength will return once we put this city behind us. I'm certain of it."

"Now all we have to do is survive the night. It's almost too easy."

Balfruss grinned. "I'll say a prayer to Elwei for you."

"I don't believe in the gods, but given what we're facing, I don't see that it could hurt."

"You really do remind me of my friend Vann."

"I'm honoured," said Tammy, rolling her eyes.

The smile drained from Balfruss's face and he became unusually still. He barely seemed to breathe and his dark eyes bored into hers. "He's the most grounded and capable man I know. He's strong, determined, stubborn as a mule, and a canny fighter. He's also one of a handful of people that I trust with my life." A second later Tammy realised he wasn't just talking about Vann.

"Oh," was all she could think to say.

"Can I offer you some advice?" he asked, and she gestured for him to continue. "I think you should enjoy the moment. I would be dancing with the others, but I don't have the strength. Tonight, the Forsaken will come, but until then you should live."

It was good advice. Everyone else was treating it as if it were their last day and so far all she'd done was train others to fight. A number of ideas ran through her head, together with several strong urges, but there was only one she wanted to pursue.

Leaving Balfruss to watch the dancers she went inside and down the stairs to her room. With stiff fingers she set her weapons aside, unbuckled her armour and took off her padded shirt. Her hands shook but she willed them to stop and the tremors quickly subsided. Even so, it didn't stop her stomach from churning.

In the lowest level she found several groups of people gathered around the wine racks. They were tapping barrels and filling up empty bottles with rich red wine. Someone offered her a couple of bottles, which she accepted and then went in search of company to share it with.

Tammy knocked on the door and went in immediately. She wasn't sure why she didn't wait for a response. Perhaps she'd been hoping to catch him doing something unpleasant, giving her an excuse to turn around.

Kovac was sat on the floor of his small cell-like room in a shirt and trousers. His ragged furs and armour were hung up on a peg on the wall. The rest of the room was tidy and organised, giving her more clues about his past before he became a mercenary. On the floor in front of him lay his sword, dagger and an oily rag. He held a second dagger in one hand and a whetstone in the other.

"Am I disturbing you?" It was a stupid thing to say but he just shook his head. "I thought you might fancy a drink. Everyone else is enjoying themselves."

"Sounds good to me," he said, putting his weapons aside and creating some space for her to sit down. They drank in silence for a while and Tammy tried to appreciate the taste of the wine. She knew it was expensive but wine had never been her thing. It was incredibly smooth though and her head was feeling a little fuzzy.

"I also came to apologise."

"What for?" asked Kovac.

"I tried to kill you and the others, right before we found the Forsaken under the church."

"You weren't yourself," he said. Tammy wasn't used to apologising and Kovac wasn't making it easy.

"I also made assumptions about you. I said that you came here for the treasure."

Kovac grunted. "You were right. I did." Tammy sensed there was a lot more to his story that he wasn't telling her.

"Before that, you helped at the temple and spoke up for me against Fenne."

"He gave his word, then tried to wriggle out of a deal. It wasn't right."

"I'm trying to thank you. Just shut up and take the compliment," she snapped.

Kovac blinked a couple of times before answering. "You're welcome."

They drank some more in silence until she'd calmed down. "I want to ask you for a favour."

"Name it," he said.

"If the Forsaken get over the wall, I want you to make sure the children aren't taken."

It was a difficult thing to ask of him, but it needed to be done. In this city they had all come to realise there were things worse than dying. She needed someone she could rely on. Someone who would follow through and not buckle under pressure at the critical moment. They drank some more in companionable silence while he thought it over.

"What makes you think I won't run at the first sign of trouble to save my own skin?"

"You put yourself at risk for me when you had no reason to. You're a man of honour."

Kovac's laugh was bitter. "Not any more."

"Well, you're a man of your word at least."

"I am that."

"Who were you, Kovac? Before becoming a mercenary?" It was probably something no mercenary liked to talk about, but she had to ask.

"You don't think I've always been one?"

"I'm a Guardian, remember? Most mercenaries are driven by greed or bloodlust, but neither drives you."

"Then what does?" he asked.

"I'm not sure. At first I thought you were seeking redemption.

That you were punishing yourself for something in the past, but I don't think that's it either. I think something terrible happened and you were forced to start again. I think you're just trying to survive."

"I trusted the wrong man and lost everything." Kovac's eyes were angry and he took three long pulls of wine before the fury in them faded. "I can never go back. So, I came here seeking my fortune."

"I think you are a man of honour. You just hide it well from the others."

He didn't disagree this time and Tammy didn't push it.

"And you? Why did you come here?" he asked suddenly.

"To find out what was infecting the city and stop it spreading."

"I meant, why did you come to my room?"

Tammy put down her bottle of wine, which somehow was already half empty. Her hands were steady. "Because today could be our last. Because everyone is enjoying themselves. Because I don't want to be alone. And because I've seen how you've been looking at me since the temple."

Kovac tried to say something but she silenced him by pulling him close and kissing him. He tasted of wine and smelled of leather and oil. His beard tickled her face and she tried to remember the last time she'd kissed someone. The last time someone had held her. The last time she'd been at peace.

"No more words," she murmured, pulling up Kovac's shirt and lifting it over his head. Running a hand across his chest she found several old scars, but their stories and the world outside would have to wait.

CHAPTER 41

As night fell on the last camp in Voechenka Zannah lit the torches above the gate and resumed her post on the wall, perhaps for the last time.

The air was cool but there was no frost on the streets and the sky was clear of any clouds. A full moon sat fat and heavy overhead. It offered some light but it was sickly yellow and made it look as if the whole city was dying.

The darkness stretched out in all directions as far as Zannah could see. Beyond their camp there wasn't another living soul who remained free. There was only the endless night and the Forsaken.

The wraith was back. She was leaning in an empty window of a nearby building and seemed unable to stop smiling. She looked delighted by the forthcoming battle and Zannah actually saw her rub her hands in glee at one point. In mockery of the Blessed Mother she put her left hand over her heart and blew a kiss at Zannah.

It had taken the Morrin months to realise who she was. It was the only answer that made sense. Hers was a blessing Zannah had neither pursued nor wanted. Only a fool would think being regarded as her champion was a good thing. She was an immortal black-hearted bitch who cared for no one.

Behind Zannah in the courtyard Tammy and the mercenaries were handing out weapons to everyone who could fight. There were some who were too old or too scared. They would be secured on the lowest level of the building with the children.

Alyssa had ordered a temporary hospital to be set up on the ground floor, with every room being converted to care for the wounded. Those held in reserve to fight would wait in the courtyard and drag the injured away to be cared for by the priests.

Tammy was attempting to organise people into squads but it was slow work. Each team would be led by at least one mercenary in an attempt to give them some order amid the chaos that would follow. The air was thick with tension, and not just because of the forthcoming battle. Some of the defenders had been humiliated, debased and treated as slaves by mercenaries in other camps. Now they were being asked to follow their orders. It made for an uneasy atmosphere.

Alyssa had not made a speech about why they had to forget about past crimes and fight together, because everyone already knew. Tonight they would fight as one, united as the living against the undead. If anyone survived and saw the dawn, then there would be time to settle old grudges.

All along the wall more torches were being lit and stacks of wine bottles lined up. They had been distilling wine since they'd first moved into the winery. It had provided them with fuel and light and now it would be a weapon against the Forsaken. Fire cleansed and purified and none could escape its wrath.

Alyssa made a circuit around the wall, checking that everything was in place, before coming to stand beside Zannah. Together they looked into the dark for a while in silence.

"I need to tell you something," said Alyssa. "It's about Roake." Zannah said nothing and waited. "He's asked for something in return for helping us."

"He could not even climb the rope. How can he help us fight?"

"That's not why he's here. He's neither one of us nor one of them. Alive or dead."

Zannah could hear the sympathy in her voice but she ignored it. She wanted to continue feeling nothing for Roake. "Then how can he help us?"

"When the time is right, he'll tell you."

Zannah pondered this for a while. Whatever Roake was offering was not something she would like.

"And what is his price?" she asked.

Alyssa placed her right hand over her heart, which she only did when thinking of praying to the Blessed Mother. "He believes taking his own life is a grave sin. He said it has to be you."

Zannah bared her teeth but said nothing. While they fought for their lives against the Forsaken he would cower in a dark corner and wait for it to be over. Then, if anyone survived he would dole out whatever nugget of information he had. It might prove useful to them, but his help would be meaningless if everyone was taken and changed. If that happened the Forsaken would kill him, as he could not become one of them. Whatever the outcome he would get his wish.

"He is a maggot," said Zannah, suddenly feeling something more than guilt for what had happened to Roake. Her hatred of him was starting to burn away any blame she carried for his current situation. "I will make him tell me what he knows and then kill him now."

"Not yet. Besides, I think there will be plenty of death without adding one more body." Alyssa's eyes passed over those in the courtyard and she quietly whispered a prayer. Only now was she coming to terms with what Zannah had known for some time. Very few, if any of her people, would survive the night. Zannah admired Alyssa for many things, especially maintaining her faith in the face of the horrors they'd experienced, but now she had realised the truth.

Balfruss slowly made his way across the courtyard and up the stairs. Zannah noticed he still had heavy shadows under his eyes, but his face was not quite as drawn and pale. He moved like a much older man, but that wouldn't matter as long as his skill remained.

"Your magic?" asked Alyssa, and Balfruss shook his head.

"As long as I don't try to do much with it, I'm fine," he said with a bitter smile. "Once I'm free of this place I'm confident it will return to normal. For now I'll just have to let this speak for me," he said, tapping the axe on his belt. Zannah noticed he hadn't said when he left this place, only that he would be free of it.

"We could use your help leading a squad," said Alyssa.

"It's the least I can do," he answered. "I have one last errand and then I'll be ready."

He went back inside, moving through the crowd without anyone paying attention. When he had first arrived people had thought him a saviour and looked at him with reverence. Now they understood the truth. That for all of his past accomplishments he was just flesh and blood like everyone else, and he could die just like them.

Balfruss glanced into a few of the rooms on the ground floor as he went past. Stacks of bandages, towels, blankets and crude medical equipment were piled up in every room. The priests were checking that everything was ready or sat praying with their eyes closed. Over the last few weeks he'd not learned a great deal about them but he knew them all to be caring people who sought only to protect and preserve life. They were also human and he suspected several were asking for courage to get them through the next few hours.

At the end of the hall he came face to face with Kai, just coming out of one of the rooms. The plague priest stopped and offered what was probably intended to be a friendly smile. "Hello there," he said. When Balfruss didn't reciprocate he glanced around and lowered his voice. "Something I can do for you, Sorcerer?"

"Can you stop what's about to happen? Can you save their lives?" said Balfruss, gesturing behind him.

Kai's grimace was almost human. "No. It's not permitted. We can't change the course of major events. If I saved everyone here the ripples of that decision would echo for a long time."

Balfruss wondered who had made the rule and who Kai was answerable to, but he didn't ask, afraid of what the answer might reveal.

"Then can you at least protect those in the lower levels? Can you stop any Forsaken getting to them?"

"I can do that," promised Kai. He gestured for Balfruss to follow him and they went down a set of stairs to the next level. All of the rooms along the corridor were deserted.

"Stay there," said Kai, before walking to the far end of the corridor. As he passed each doorway the shadows seemed to thicken, seeping across the floor like fog. The darkness crawled and clumped together until the ground was completely obscured. Next the shadows started to rise into the air with black tendrils and spread out, becoming denser by the second. By the time Kai reached the far end of the corridor Balfruss could barely see him. He blinked a few times and the fog became a wall of complete darkness.

Somewhere in the void a pair of red eyes appeared, glowing

with an alien light. The two eyes became four, then eight, then more. A hundred eyes blinked in unison and he heard the rustling of something large brushing against the stone walls.

If any Forsaken made it this far they would soon regret it when they came face to face with what lurked in the dark. Backing away slowly, Balfruss retraced his steps and breathed a sigh of relief when he was back in the courtyard.

Despite their best efforts to appear brave, Balfruss could see that most people were afraid of what awaited them. The Forsaken were not just people from another country that sought to conquer and enslave them. They were something else entirely, alien and unnatural. Something that wanted to invade their minds and take over their bodies. The Forsaken would consume them and then continue using their bodies after death.

The thought of that, alone, was difficult for them to cope with. Balfruss thought it best they remain ignorant of what was lurking in the dark below.

Tammy finished organising the last squad and after double-checking that they knew what to do, sat down to rest and gather her thoughts. Kovac was standing with another group of local people, all of them determined to fight despite only one of them having ever held a weapon. They were all pale and scared. Everyone had been given hot food earlier in the day, but one good meal wasn't enough to build their strength. They were out of time. They just had to try and hope for the best.

Once Kovac had finished demonstrating a series of weapon moves to his squad he came across to sit down beside her. Neither of them had spoken about what had happened and while she didn't regret it, Tammy wasn't sure if she should say something. Kovac was equally taciturn and had treated her no differently than before, which she appreciated.

"Do you think anyone will survive?" he whispered, being careful that his voice didn't carry very far.

"It depends. All we can do is try."

Tammy suspected that the Forsaken had greater numbers than them, but when someone was turned it didn't make them into a warrior. They were more savage and driven, but the people in the winery had nowhere else to go and they knew what would happen if they were overrun. She also knew how hard people fought when they were defending their home and families.

All she knew for certain was that it would be brutal and bloody.

"Any regrets?" asked Kovac.

"A few, but not recent ones. What about you?" she asked.

"No, just old scores I wish I'd settled. I might not get the chance now."

A cry went up on the wall and all eyes turned towards a woman pointing and shouting. Her words were lost in the clamour that followed but Tammy didn't need to hear what she'd said.

She already knew. They all knew. The Forsaken were coming.

CHAPTER 42

In the gloomy light provided by the two torches above the gate, Tammy stared down at the horde of Forsaken filling the street. Many were deep in the shadows but those at the front were not what she had been expecting.

Below the old church of the Maker she'd seen Forsaken whose skin was turning purple, but otherwise they'd looked human. Roake's words came back to her about the Embrace being temporary while the parasite grew to maturity. Every single person on the street had been remade into something alien and grotesque.

Their skin was the colour of a ripe plum marbled with veins of red and dark blue. Bony protrusions grew out of either side of a hairless dimpled skull that stretched backwards more than before. White eyes glared up at her from under a heavy bone ridge, and a wide jaw was filled with pointed teeth and a split black tongue. The darkness hid the worst details, as well as making it difficult for her to judge how many were out there.

Each of the Forsaken carried a bladed weapon, swords, axes and an array of pole-arms. They were not here to take prisoners and create more soldiers for their army. This was the first wave of an invasion that would destroy Voechenka and then spread to the rest of Shael like a plague.

The defenders on the wall blanched at the sight, several crying out in terror. A few started to pray, their courage wavering.

"It's time," said Tammy, nudging Balfruss.

The Sorcerer took a deep breath and closed his eyes to help him concentrate. Normally this would have been easy, but now it required a huge effort on his part. Tammy hoped he could manage it because right now they needed something to inspire the defenders and remind them that the Forsaken were mortal.

She began to worry, as nothing happened apart from sweat trickling down the sides of Balfruss's face. Then, with a loud detonation, the streets burst into light and the Forsaken howled in pain and surprise. They had used fear of what lurked in the darkness as another weapon that Tammy wanted to take away from them.

A series of barrels filled with distilled wine had been stashed in buildings around the winery during the day. With a little help from Balfruss they erupted, spitting blue and yellow flames into the air. The creatures recoiled and many covered their eyes or turned their faces away as if they were sensitive to the light. A ring of orange flames encircled the winery on all sides, illuminating everywhere.

Now it was time to show everyone that the Forsaken were mortal.

"Light them up!" shouted Tammy, and all along the wall people lit arrowheads that had been wrapped in wool and dipped in alcohol. "Fire!"

Two dozen arrows sailed through the air before slamming into the Forsaken, who screamed in pain and thrashed about, colliding with their neighbours. Those who were hit bled and died and they did not get back up again. It was important for everyone on the wall to know that despite the physical changes the Forsaken could still be killed.

"Fire at will!" Tammy bellowed, and all along the wall bow strings twanged as the creatures gathered for a charge. More fell with flaming arrows in their chests, some of them catching fire.

In the middle of the street several of the enemy appeared, holding a long battering ram. Tammy started to shout a warning, but Zannah and several others had already spotted the danger and had tossed flaming bottles at those carrying the ram. Four hit their targets, which were immediately engulfed in flames. Animal-like screams soared into the night as the creatures dropped the ram and lurched off into the dark. The ram lay forgotten in the street but it wasn't over yet. Several Forsaken carrying ladders ran towards them, and from the sounds of battle around her she knew other walls besides their own were under attack. This was only the beginning.

Prince studied the Forsaken as they ran towards the rear wall of the winery. They were unusual to look at, but no more peculiar than the Morrin who had horns or the Vorga who came from the ocean. Whatever their origin they could bleed and die like any other mortal. Their peculiar screams of pain from outside the front gate had proven that. Now he just needed to show the local people here. They needed to see it with their own eyes.

"Take out a few," he said, nudging Teela. "And laugh while you do it."

Teela raised an eyebrow but nodded as she drew back her bow and picked out a target. She'd come to trust him and was obviously interested in him, which he used to his advantage from time to time. She whooped in delight as one of her arrows went through an eye, punching one of the Forsaken off its feet. Teela took out another two targets, laughing all the while. The people of Shael took heart and their initial fear began to fade.

The Forsaken's unusual features were a blessing. On previous nights the people beside him had fought friends and relatives who had been taken and changed. Now none of them looked familiar. They were no longer people, but had become creatures. They were all made from the same mould and there was little to distinguish them.

One thing he noticed was that they were more organised than before and were almost moving in unison. A quick scan around showed him no obvious leaders who might be directing them, but there had to be someone.

As they came closer with their ladders, Prince drew his sword, but his eyes were still studying the enemy. Finally he spotted what he was looking for. Just beyond the fires he could see two figures watching the battle. He suspected they were directing this part of the attack.

"Teeva, do you see them?" he asked, knowing her eyesight was better than his. She squinted and tilted her head to one side in a manner he thought quite endearing, not that he'd tell her. She might take it as an expression of interest, which would make her sister jealous.

The ladders rattled against the wall and people beside him began lighting bottles and hurling them down at the Forsaken. Others fired their bows, and at this range it was impossible to miss. All around him was a whirlwind of activity but he remained perfectly still and calm.

"Two figures. One short, one tall," said Teeva.

"Can you hit them from here?" he asked, unsure if her bow would reach that distance. She squinted again, checked the wind against her finger and nodded.

Not far away in the street, flaming figures were running around like headless chickens, knocking ladders aside, but he ignored them.

"We need to take them both out at once."

"Then you'll need me for that," said Teela from his other side, resting a hand lightly on his arm.

He smiled at her. "I will need you both."

"Who are they?" asked Teeva, rolling her shoulders. She casually kicked a creature in the face as it reached the top of a ladder. On his other side Teela stabbed a Forsaken in the throat three times and threw it from the wall. Prince held his sword ready but didn't use it, even though the battle was raging around him.

"I think they're Generals, or whatever the equivalent is for them."

"Keep the Forsaken off my back," said Teela, moving to stand beside her sister.

"I bet you miss," said Teeva, nudging her sister's elbow.

"Do that again and I'll throw you off the wall," snarled Teela, but there was no heat to her words.

As a grinning creature climbed over the wall in front of him Prince was finally forced into action. With a weary sigh he assumed Climbing Ivy stance and from there made three elegant cuts. The Forsaken slid apart into pieces and he nimbly stepped aside to avoid the blood.

The sisters drew their bows and leaned backwards, making small adjustments until they were finally satisfied. Their two arrows flew high into the air, disappearing into the night sky. Prince was forced to kill two more Forsaken that wandered too close before he saw the arrows come down.

Just beyond the fire he heard two distant squawks of pain and both figures stumbled and then fell. One landed in the fire and its clothing burst into flames.

Almost immediately something went out of the creatures attacking them. They hesitated, looked at one another in confusion and their coordination fell apart. Several were cut down by people on the wall, who clubbed and hacked away at them. Prince gestured for the twins to go along the wall in one direction as he went in the other, clearing it of the enemy with short efficient strokes. The people around him began to cheer as the Forsaken fell before his onslaught, but his mind remained elsewhere, watching the rest of the fight and trying to calculate what they would try next.

When their section was clear he gestured for the defenders to start tipping away the ladders. They threw themselves into the task with glee, perhaps thinking the fight was over.

He knew they had a short reprieve at best. He needed to know if other parts of the wall were being directed in the same fashion.

Moments later the Forsaken gathered their wits and started to attack again. Almost immediately, Prince could see it was different from before. They were less organised and attacked as a mob again rather than as precise groups. This second weak attack was easily repelled and the remaining creatures withdrew in an almost sullen silence.

The others needed to know.

"I'll be back," he said to the twins, sheathing his sword and heading for the stairs.

Zannah watched as the tall mercenary moved from one section of the wall to the next. He spoke with several people each time and she picked out a few words in the din but little else. A moment later she was distracted by a trio of Forsaken that made it to the top of the wall.

A couple of local people battered the threesome with their swords, using them as if they were clubs. Their blows were ill-timed and did little more than dent armour and inflict superficial wounds. Nevertheless it kept the enemy distracted, allowing her to come up behind and hamstring two of them. They stumbled to their knees and slid off the wall into the winery courtyard, where those waiting in reserve made short work of them. Before the third Forsaken could attack, Zannah rammed her sword under its chin and up into its brain. It shook for a few seconds like a headless chicken and then died. She didn't know if cutting off their heads was necessary any more. They would worry about that later.

So far the Forsaken had been pushed back every time they managed to get a foothold on the wall, and the breach had been closed. But the people of Shael were not used to fighting and their stamina was already flagging. Unless something was done soon, they would be overrun.

She saw Prince coming up the steps but didn't turn towards him until he spoke.

"Someone is directing them. Giving them focus," said the mercenary. "There!" he said, pointing over the wall. Zannah followed his outstretched arm and saw a pair of figures standing at the rear of those attacking. "We took them out on our part of the wall and their coordination fell apart."

"I think I can hit one of them," said Alyssa. "I'll pick a few others, to make sure."

Normally six archers would be overkill for two targets but Zannah knew the odds were not good, given that they had so little experience. She and Prince kept the Forsaken away from the archers while they readied themselves and fired. Two arrows landed short, a third went long, but thankfully three hit the targets. The taller figure was hit in the torso and the shorter in the head and neck. As soon as the arrows reached their mark a wave of confusion passed through the creatures in front of her. They stumbled and stared around in shock.

"Press the advantage. Clear the wall," shouted Zannah, shoving people into action, lashing out with her sword, stabbing and slicing anything in her path. Other mercenaries saw the change in the enemy and urged their squads to take the initiative.

Slowly the tide began to turn and by the time the Forsaken had recovered their wits, it was too late. A ragged cheer went up around the base as the whole wall was suddenly clear of the enemy.

Wasting no time, Zannah urged that the injured be taken away and called up reserves waiting in the courtyard. They were fresh and eager to get into the fight. The Forsaken had been pushed back but it wasn't over yet.

CHAPTER 43

Rudderless and without their war leaders, the Forsaken united behind Fennetaris. He stood among them, an outcast from his own people and from the living, marshalling them like soldiers in his army.

Once, long ago, he had been a decent officer, but his cruel and vicious streak had been his undoing. Brought up on charges several times he would eventually have been hung if they'd not been ordered home. The fact he had stayed behind showed that he'd not belonged among his own people, even back then.

Now, the Forsaken were relying on his old skills and survival instinct to help them win against a stubborn enemy. His eyes met Zannah's across the battlefield and Fennetaris grinned, showing his intent without saying a word. There would be no falling back this time, no reprieve and no mercy. He intended to kill them all. Every man, woman and child.

There was a brief lull and then the creatures started to spread out around the base on all sides. A silent signal was given and in unison they charged at the winery, howling and screaming with inhuman voices, their white eyes reflecting the light from the fires.

*

Balfruss cursed and kicked out at the creature in front of him. He missed its knee but caught it on the thigh, making it stumble back hissing in pain. As it started to raise its sword he brought his axe down with both hands, swinging from the hips. The blade bit deep into the Forsaken's skull, cracking it open like an egg and spraying grey brains everywhere. He shoved it aside and buried his axe in the back of another, right between the shoulder blades. The two men it had been harrying stabbed the Forsaken and then hurled it aside, grinning with savage glee. Their moment of triumph quickly faded as two more creatures replaced the first.

Soon after, Balfruss saw one of the men die, falling from the wall with a dagger in his belly. He was too far away to help and snarled in frustration at the creature in front of him.

With plenty of room to swing, Balfruss spread his feet wide to keep his balance, and sliced at the enemy. His first swing cut a Forsaken across the chest, his second took the arm from another and his third nearly decapitated yet another. Advancing slowly and with grim determination he drove the enemy back, offering them no chances to get close.

Elsewhere the defenders were not faring as well. He saw countless people cut down as they feebly attacked, their energy and bravery gone, replaced only with weariness and desperation. The mercenaries were doing their best to keep them in some kind of formation, but weren't having much success. Lack of skill and discipline, as well as inferior numbers, was starting to tell, as the people of Shael were gradually being driven back.

Whenever the Forsaken got a foothold on the wall people raced to fill it, led by Tammy, Zannah or one of the mercenaries. Their skill and courage saved many lives but they were not without their limits. He didn't know how long they had been fighting but everyone was starting to show signs of fatigue except for Zannah. She was as fast and ruthless as when the Forsaken had first appeared, which he guessed meant she was borrowing years from her future. The Morrin could not expect to fight a war by herself and win.

Every time Balfruss had tried using his magic a nauseous feeling swept through him, followed by a cold sweat and a desperate urge to leave the city. Wielding any power from the Source was infinitely more difficult than before and holding on to it for long had proven agonising. Lighting the barrels earlier should have been easy, but it had almost rendered him unconscious.

All magic, both the subtle and the overt that had earned him the titles of Battlemage and Sorcerer, was beyond his reach. For now he was just another warrior. Someone other than him would have to be the deciding factor in this battle.

Whatever the catalyst might be, it had to happen soon or else they would be overrun and have to fall back to the main building. Then it would be a slow retreat until they were cornered in the deep caves. At that point it would be over very quickly.

Balfruss prayed to Elwei for a miracle but his wish was not answered. At least not in a way he would ever have wanted.

Zannah knew they were losing. She watched in dismay as people she'd fought to protect for months started dying around her. The Forsaken were too strong, too fast and more determined in their purpose than they were. This time the invaders were not looking to capture anyone and were intent only on murder. No blunt weapons were used. No prisoners taken and no mercy was shown.

Men and women who fled in despair were cut down, stabbed in the back and beheaded on the spot. This was not the end of

Shael and its people, but the Forsaken clearly intended it to be the end of Voechenka, once and for all. It was the completion of the task her people and the Vorga had begun during the war.

Gritting her teeth Zannah forced herself to move faster and then faster still. Wielding a short sword in either hand she cut a swathe through the Forsaken, splitting skulls, severing limbs and kicking them off the wall.

When one tried to attack she stepped aside, ripped open its abdomen, spun around and stabbed it in the back through the heart. Another came at her with an axe, which she blocked with one of her swords while taking off the woman's arm at the shoulder with the other. As the scream started, Zannah cut her throat and moved on. She was constantly moving forward, forcing each opponent to stand and fight someone who was not afraid. Someone who was just as strong and ruthless as they were.

They tried to match her speed and failed. As fast as they could be, as hard as they could force their host bodies to move, they were still partially human and she was not. When they tried to match her skill they failed, as she had been stripped of everything except this. She was a warrior. She had nothing else. No family, no people, no country.

She hoped that her assault on the creatures might inspire the people of Shael to stand and fight. The odds were against them but it was not over while they were still alive.

A whisper of sound behind Zannah made her spin about with her swords ready to strike. But instead of one of the Forsaken, she came face to face with Alyssa, who just smiled at her.

Taking a deep breath Zannah lowered her weapons and relaxed, until she saw the sword sticking out of Alyssa's stomach. Time seemed to stop. The world became just the two of them and everything else faded into insignificance.

Zannah recalled the first time they met.

Mercifully it had been shortly after the war, when she'd saved a group of locals from one of her own people. The rogue Morrin soldier had killed two local people for their food and was determined to kill the others. The only thing stopping him had been Alyssa, unarmed and unafraid, facing him down with nothing more than her will and her faith for protection. Her fearlessness made him pause, as he was baffled by her willingness to sacrifice her life to protect the others. Two seconds later Zannah ran him through from behind and their friendship had begun.

Now it was over, and a terrible pain swelled inside Zannah. It filled her whole being until she felt as if she were dying and not her only friend in the world.

A Forsaken reared up from behind Alyssa and with a savage twist ripped his blade clear of her body. With a howl of fury Zannah took off his head with both swords but she knew it was already too late.

Alyssa dropped to her knees and slid off the wall into the courtyard where several people caught her before she hit the ground. Zannah raced down the stairs, shoving bodies aside until she knelt beside her friend. Someone went to fetch one of the priests, but Zannah knew they couldn't help. Blood bubbled from Alyssa's mouth and her face was racked with agony, turning her beautiful features into a mask of pain.

Reaching out with one hand Alyssa pulled Zannah close until her ear was almost pressed to her lips.

"Promise me something," she whispered.

"Anything," said Zannah.

"Live. Live for me."

A priest shoved Zannah aside but she barely noticed. Her eyes were locked on Alyssa, who stared back while the priest tried to staunch the bleeding. Zannah was still gazing into Alyssa's eyes when she died a few moments later.

Zannah was wrong. The city had forged her into a weapon, but it had also given her something to lose. Something she cherished more than her own life, and the Forsaken had taken it from her.

Many of those on the wall were looking down at Alyssa's body. She had died for Zannah and would have done the same for any of them.

A terrible hunger began to swell in her chest until her whole body was quivering with rage. Snarling like an angry dog she ran back up the stairs and attacked the Forsaken with reckless abandon. She didn't care if they hurt her. Her own life didn't matter any more. She had nothing left to lose.

When a sword flashed towards her face she smiled, welcoming the pain, but the blade was deflected by another. Turning around, Zannah saw Monella beside her, struggling to keep the sword at bay.

"Don't just stand there, help me!" she hissed. Zannah stabbed the creature before throwing him off the wall into the street.

Below her the courtyard was emptying, every person able to wield a weapon flooding onto the wall. No one wanted to run any more. What they lacked in skill the people of Voechenka made up for in heart. Fighting in pairs and groups they pushed the enemy back, one step at a time, and whenever one of them fell two more rushed forward to take their place.

The people of Voechenka had been transformed. Not by starvation or what they had endured, but by the sacrifice of one woman who had given her life to save them. Not for fame or riches, not because she hoped to gain anything from it, but simply because it was the right thing to do.

Monella, the former priest, cursed the enemy with her vicious tongue as she fought, cutting down the creatures with an axe as though she were chopping wood. Beside her, the mercenary

Graff protected her back, throwing himself into the fight. Rheena, the girl Tammy had rescued from Fennetaris, screamed as she stabbed one of the creatures in the chest, unleashing her rage.

Pella Rae, the first refugee to bend her knee and swear a blood oath to serve Alyssa, fought back to back with another woman. It was Alyssa who had taken her and so many other people in. She had offered them shelter and a safe place away from the shadow that crept across the city. Now Pella and the others fought to honour all that they had been given. They fought to survive and keep alive the spark of hope that Alyssa had given them.

If this was the end of Voechenka then its people were determined it would be a battle that was not forgotten by history. They intended to fight until the last of them drew their final breath.

The Forsaken could not stand against such an implacable tide of humanity. They screamed and shrieked while their adversaries faced them with an icy calm. Even when the first creature turned and ran, the people of Voechenka did not cheer. They kept on fighting until there was no one left to kill.

And when the sun came up the Forsaken were gone and the people of Voechenka were free.

CHAPTER 44

Tammy stared down at the long lines of bodies laid out in the courtyard. All of them had been covered with blankets to conceal their wounds. But the brightly coloured wool could not hide the cost of their victory. Almost half of those who had fought on the wall were dead, with many more severely wounded.

Among the dead were several mercenaries, including Graff, who had died protecting two injured locals. Graff had killed the Forsaken, and three more, before he was run through. Even then he fought as if berserk until finally his strength ran out. In his final act, he'd hugged one of the Forsaken to his chest and thrown them both from the wall. Like everyone else, he had witnessed Alyssa's bravery and had done his best to make her proud.

At first when Tammy saw what remained of his body she'd thought it was Kovac. When he appeared a few minutes later from inside she was torn between the urge to kill or kiss him. She settled on the latter, much to his surprise.

The wounded had been carried inside where they were being tended, while almost everyone else was either eating or asleep from exhaustion. Tammy's limbs felt leaden but she couldn't rest, not yet.

They had driven the Forsaken away, and killed many of them in the process, but she didn't think that they were completely gone. Fenne had disappeared at some point as well, which told her it wasn't over.

Earlier, Balfruss had moved the cart laden with stone so that they could open the gate, but once again the effort had proven a great struggle. He had almost passed out and even now, more than an hour later, was sat in the same spot. As Tammy approached she thought he was asleep or in a daze but she saw his eyes were open. They were staring at something far away and he seemed completely oblivious to his surroundings. His left hand was slightly raised and the fingers were twitching ever so slightly, as if he were pulling on very delicate strings. She noticed he was facing out towards the city, looking through the open gates. Tammy peered out, expecting to see something amiss, but the street was empty.

"Did you need my help?" he asked, startling her.

"How are you feeling?" asked Tammy.

"Exactly the same," said Balfruss, and to her surprise he smiled, as if that were a good thing.

"I'm going to organise some tracking parties to hunt down the remaining Forsaken. They may have fled back to the tunnels, but they could be elsewhere since we know where they've been hiding. Are you well enough to come with us?"

Balfruss considered it for a moment and then offered her that secret smile again. "Yes, but there's something I have to do first."

Balfruss walked into what could only be described as a laboratory. On one side of the large room, shelves lined the wall from floor to ceiling. Floating in a series of jars were various animals, plants, internal organs and some things he couldn't identify. In those nearest the door he saw several lumps of purple tissue, which he assumed were human organs until he saw the black tendrils. As he drew closer he noticed that while everything else in jars appeared to be dead and in a state of decay, these specimens were fresh and still alive. A few black tendrils twitched and jerked, feebly clawing at the glass.

In the centre of the room was a massive table that ran the entire length. A vast array of books, glass tubing, vials of liquid, paper, animal skulls and all sorts of seemingly random items were scattered across the surface. Given the size of the table and the amount of space in the room it must have taken its owner years to accumulate the collection. Some of the objects were stacked so high in places they almost reached the ceiling. The whole place smelled musty and yet there were layers of other scents beneath the dust. Rotting meat and vegetables, spicy herbs and abrasive smells he'd associate with an apothecary. They were all jumbled together like the contents of the room.

The only part of the room that showed any sign of order was the far wall. It was lined with shelves full of identical red books, all with handwritten labels on the spines. A door at the rear led to what he guessed were living quarters and light came from a series of small windows set high on two walls that looked out onto the street above.

A young woman with unkempt blonde hair shuffled into the laboratory from the back. She was hunched over and muttering to herself as she held a book in one hand and a yellow bone in the other hand. Balfruss guessed she was originally from Yerskania, but her skin was so pale he suspected her lack of colour came from rarely leaving this room. It would also explain her dishevelled clothing and bare feet which were covered with grime. Her hands were impeccably clean, though, which seemed a peculiar contrast to the rest.

Moving to the long workbench she cleared a space, set down the book and tilted the bone towards the light, peering at it closely. After a few seconds she realised he was standing there, but rather than registering surprise at his presence she seemed disappointed.

"Ah, you're here," she said, before carefully setting the bone down and peering at him. She squinted and then fished around on the desk before retrieving a pair of battered glasses, which she perched on the end of her nose. "I rather hoped you'd be on your way by now, Balfruss."

Studying her face he expected to see something familiar, but there was nothing he recognised. He'd never seen her before in his life.

"On my way where?"

"Oh, I don't know," she said, flapping a hand towards the windows and the world beyond. "Somewhere, anywhere that's not here."

Despite her being a stranger to him, there was something familiar in her mannerisms and the way she talked, though he couldn't put his finger on it.

"It took me a while, but eventually I realised why I had such a strong compulsion to leave Voechenka. The feeling wasn't there to begin with," said Balfruss, moving slowly down the room towards her. "It only started after I fought Kaine. I thought I'd been infected by the bleakness of this city, but that wasn't it."

"It could have been," she suggested. "This place is a stinking tomb, full of despair and sorrow. It's reasonable to assume that whatever leaked into the bones of this city might have seeped into you."

"It was you all along," said Balfruss, and all at once the pieces in his head slid into place. The way she spoke with an air of wisdom and authority more usual in someone much older. The way she peered at him through her glasses resting on the end of her nose, as if he were a student in her classroom. The way she seemed disappointed and yet not surprised by his presence. The years peeled back and he was a boy again at the Red Tower, dreaming of being old enough to shave.

"There is no Kaine, only you. Polganna Naral, formerly of the Grey Council."

The woman tilted her head to one side and a sly smile crept across her face. "You were always a gifted student."

Many years ago Balfruss had been among the last pupils to be taught by members of the Grey Council. This was before they'd abandoned their posts and gone in search of a prophesised saviour who would change the nature of magic. At the time all of the Council had been in their mid-fifties and he had assumed that by now they'd be dead. And yet, the young woman standing in front of him was Polganna.

"How?" he asked, gesturing at her face.

"Think, then tell me the answer," she chided him, turning back to her book while he thought it through.

"You used the Source to regenerate your flesh."

"Not just my flesh," she said without looking up. "Young skin wouldn't do me much good if my organs rotted and my joints were stiff and old. It took years, and many experiments," she said, gesturing vaguely at the jars. "But eventually I unlocked the secret. It started with the Morrin, of course."

Their special connection to the Source gave all Morrin unusual longevity. A rare few could manipulate it like Zannah, who could survive normally fatal wounds.

Somehow Polganna had found a way to tap into that ability and use it to heal her body and then go beyond that and reverse the ageing process. Staring at the organs floating in the jars, Balfruss wondered how many had belonged to Morrin.

"The Flesh Mages. Were they planned or a by-product?"

"That was unexpected," conceded Polganna. "But it was such an exciting and remarkable discovery. I found an old reference to the Talent. They called it skinwalking."

"If I ask you how it was done, will you tell me?" said Balfruss. A trickle of sweat started to run down the side of his face, which he quickly wiped away before she noticed.

Polganna finally lifted her eyes from the page and raised an eyebrow. "You want to learn how to skinwalk?"

"No, I mean what you've done to me."

That sly smile came again, slower this time. Polganna was obviously particularly proud of how she'd hobbled him. "Ah, that. Are you to be my pupil again, young Balfruss?"

He didn't know if she was being serious or not, but he played along and shrugged his shoulders, forcing himself to relax. "We both know there's little I can do in my condition except listen. I can barely reach for the Source without feeling nauseous and wanting to run from this city."

"It would have faded," said Polganna, "but I had to make it a strong compulsion to ensure you had no urge to come back later. I detest interruptions."

"I'm curious, just like you," he conceded. "I was never satisfied with what I was taught. I knew there was so much more. So many secrets being held back from me."

Polganna gave him her full attention now, moving slightly towards him with a smile that was warm and almost maternal. "Yes, you were so driven and still are. My little birds have brought me many stories of your adventures over the years. Into the desert, during the war, and then across the Dead Sea. You must have seen some remarkable sights."

"A few, which I can share, if you will."

"Yes, your compulsion," said Polganna. "You said it started

when you fought my final Splinter, the old man. It actually started the minute you entered the city and used magic. What's one of the first lessons you were taught at the Red Tower?"

"A Battlemage's strength will never change over time," he replied, even though they both knew it was a lie.

"And what else?"

"That everyone's connection to the Source is unique."

"That part is true at least," said Polganna. "Every time you meet someone else with the ability, you feel a pulse from them. It is the echo of like calling to like, but if you listen very closely, you'll notice it's always slightly different in pitch. All I did was listen carefully when you used your magic and eventually found yours. I simply added something to that connection."

"Can it be reversed?"

"Of course," said Polganna, seemingly appalled by his suggestion that anything she'd done could not be undone. "Such an unnatural reflex starts to decay over time, so it would have faded eventually."

Balfruss tried his best to hide his relief, but he suspected there was very little that Polganna didn't see.

"Here, let me show you," she said, and before he saw what she'd done, a wave of energy passed through him. Tentatively he pretended to reach for the Source for the first time, drawing a large amount of power and summoning a flame on the palm of his outstretched hand. The sickness and fear had gone, as had the compulsion to leave the city.

"Is it even worth asking why?" he said and Polganna just tutted.

"Think, then tell me the answer," she repeated, just as she'd done when he was a boy.

"Knowledge."

"Exactly," said Polganna, sweeping her arms wide to

encompass the whole room. Balfruss noticed there were echoes of the Warlock in how she spoke in a dramatic fashion. He must have spent many years studying under her. Balfruss extinguished the flame but maintained a minute connection to the Source. The same one he'd been holding on to since before entering the room, only now it was much easier.

"A lifetime's work and it's still not done," Polganna was saying. "There's so much left to discover." With that she turned back to her books and Balfruss knew he had to keep her full attention on him.

"Did you actually find whoever the Opsum Prophecy referred to?"

Polganna looked up at him and laughed. It was a rich warm sound full of genuine mirth that normally he would have found endearing, but knowing who lurked under the young flesh mask made his skin crawl.

"We searched for years, travelling through every city, town and backwater village. Always we went in disguise, so as not to draw attention to ourselves. We separated to cover more ground and after a decade of searching the entire continent, do you know what we discovered?" Polganna was starting to look hysterical and her eyes were wide and manic. "Nothing!" she roared in a voice so loud it rattled the jars on her table. "They wanted to continue, even though I knew it was a fool's errand. So I came here and began my experiments."

"Did you bring them here? The parasites?" asked Balfruss, gesturing at the twitching things in the jars. "They're from beyond the Veil, aren't they?"

Polganna showed the first sign of regret, although it was so fleeting he wondered if he'd imagined it. "My experiments didn't always start out well, but I learned from my mistakes. What lives beyond the Veil is too unpredictable. The same test can produce different results three times in a row. So I moved on to focus on safer areas of study."

It was the closest thing Balfruss thought he was going to get to an admittance of regret. Polganna had brought the first of the Forsaken through to this world from beyond the Veil, destroying a city and all of its remaining population in the process.

There was a vague flicker of movement behind Polganna's head but he ignored it and focused on her face.

"Do you know how many have died in Voechenka because of your abandoned experiment?"

"If it became a problem I would have dealt with it."

"How many people have to die before you consider it a problem?" asked Balfruss.

"Don't be so dramatic," chided Polganna.

"If everyone is dead, how will your knowledge help them?"

Polganna stared at him in shock and then began to laugh again. "You're serious. Help people? I'm not going to help them," she said, appalled at the idea. "Most of them aren't worthy. They don't care what happens. They kill each other over nothing. A scrap of land. A flag. A crown. No, I'm not going to help them. Whoever is strong will survive. Eventually I would have sought out those worthy few and shared a little of my knowledge. But not yet. Not when there's still so much to do."

Polganna chuckled to herself and shook her head at what she obviously saw as an amusing and ludicrous idea.

He would almost have preferred it if she'd seemed unstable, but she wasn't at all. She was sane, but her view of the world was dramatically different to his. Everything Balfruss had ever done with his magic had been to help people and save lives. Polganna saw everyone in the world as nothing more than ignorant and unworthy children. If she had her way it would be just the same as when he was at the Red Tower. Secrets would be parcelled out but only when she decided they were ready for such knowledge, and history would repeat itself.

"I think I've heard enough," said Balfruss, gritting his teeth and readying himself for what came next.

Polganna noticed the change in his tone and posture, as she offered him a grin that showed too many teeth. "Are you really going to try and fight me with magic?"

"No. Absolutely not," said Balfruss. "Magic would be completely useless against you."

"Good," said Polganna, looking back at her book, thinking the matter closed.

"Steel on the other hand will kill you, just like any other person."

Polganna slapped her hand on the book and glared at him. "Insolent child! You dare threaten me," she hissed as he drew the axe from his belt.

She was so focused on him that Polganna didn't know about the sword until it burst out the front of her chest. Balfruss finally released the thin camouflage weave he'd been maintaining and Tammy shimmered back into view. He felt as Polganna tried to reach for the Source but the star-metal blade stopped her.

With a quick movement Tammy yanked *Maligne* free and stepped back. Polganna fell forward onto her table as blood began to spread out in a pool. Balfruss stalked towards her, both eyes alert in case of any sudden movement. But Tammy had struck true and pierced the woman's heart. It had taken her a long time to slowly creep into the room and then move behind Polganna without being seen.

"Are you sure you don't want me to finish it?" asked Tammy.

"No. I need to do this," said Balfruss.

"I'll be outside," she said, touching him lightly on the arm. "Thank you, my friend."

Tammy smiled and went out the door without looking back.

"Think about what you're doing," said Polganna, gesturing weakly at her surroundings. "Think about what you could learn."

The rage inside was bubbling up so much that Balfruss started to shake. "How many lives did one volume cost?" he said, pointing at the shelves full of identical books. "A hundred? A thousand? Ten thousand?"

Polganna remained unapologetic. "Without me it will take years for you to unravel even a fraction of my knowledge. You don't have the stomach to do what's necessary to extend your life. You'll be dead before you accomplish anything of note."

Her words had a peculiar effect, as an icy calm swept through Balfruss. He gripped his axe with both hands and felt his shoulders relax.

"I'm not going to steal it. I'm going to destroy it. Every single page of your life's work," he said. Before she could attempt to make a deal he quickly brought the axe down on the back of her neck.

The body slumped to the floor but her head remained on the table. One eye continued staring at him until eventually the light faded from it.

Leaving everything where it was Balfruss walked to the door, turned and then summoned an inferno. He started at the back of the laboratory, concentrating the fire on the books, watching as the leather curled up and blackened. The blaze quickly spread from there around the room as glass jars exploded, spraying alcohol everywhere.

He fed more energy into the fire until it was hot enough to set the timbers ablaze and the roof began to collapse. The heat from the fire was intense but he didn't move away, watching as the flames rose up into the night, burning up every dark secret.

Channelling more power he maintained the temperature until he was certain that everything inside was on fire and that the blaze would keep going by itself for a few hours. He intended to make sure that nothing remained, not even her bones. Every twisted Talent and horrific piece of magic she had ever uncovered would be lost.

CHAPTER 45

When Tammy returned to the camp with Balfruss she was surprised to see there were people standing guard on the wall. The defenders thought Voechenka was free of the Forsaken and yet those on the wall seemed nervous.

In the courtyard they found a peculiar tableau awaiting them. Roake was kneeling in the middle of the square with Zannah stood over him, her sword resting against the back of his neck. Off to one side the plague priest was sat on a barrel, watching with mild interest as he worked his way through a bottle of wine.

As they approached, Zannah nudged the skeletal form of Roake with her boot, waking him from a doze. Tammy noticed he was now so emaciated that all of the tendons in his face and neck stood out like steel wire. His skin was turning yellow in places and was so tight across his skull she wasn't sure he could speak without it tearing. His eyes seemed to have receded even further back in his skull and were surrounded by deep black pits. Air wheezed in and rattled out of his body and the pause after every breath made her think that the next could be his last.

"They've returned," said Zannah, kicking him. "Now, tell us what you know so I can cut off your head."

Roake ignored the boot digging into his back, perhaps because he didn't care or had suffered worse in the past. Tammy felt a growing sense of loathing as he worked his jaw several times before it clacked open like a rusty trap. Despite the smell they had to move closer to hear the dry rasp of his voice.

"They're defeated, but not all dead," whispered Roake.

"Tell us something we do not already know," said Zannah. She was seething with rage and seconds away from killing what little remained of the man kneeling before her.

Roake tried to speak again but this time almost no sound emerged, just a faint wheeze.

"Here," said Kai, approaching and shoving the bottle towards Roake. Moving like an old man Roake feebly gripped it with both hands and tipped the neck towards his open mouth. Red wine gushed down his face and chin, but some splashed into his mouth, making him choke and gasp. A few seconds later Tammy watched as some of it trickled out of the wound in his side, soaking into the ground.

"I can still feel them out there," said Roake, gesturing beyond the city with one hand. In doing so he dropped the bottle and it smashed on the ground, spraying the remaining wine across the stones. It was an unpleasant reminder of the blood that had been spilled, and that not very far away Alyssa had died. This must have occurred to Zannah as she pressed the blade harder against Roake's neck, nearly toppling him over in the process.

"Where?" she asked.

"Where do you think?" asked Kai, frowning down at the spilled wine. "They went back to mummy dearest."

"Mother?" said Zannah.

"The Forsaken are parasites. They were spawned by something. It's what has been feeding on the city." Kai shared a knowing look with Balfruss, who shifted uncomfortably as the priest stared at him.

"The brood mother," whispered Roake, drawing all eyes back to him.

"Do you know where to find it?" asked Tammy.

"In the maze," said Roake.

"We know where that is. So we don't need you any more," said Zannah, raising her sword.

"I can guide you through the maze. You'll never find it without me," whispered Roake.

Tammy watched as Zannah's arm shook, her anger battling with common sense. It would take them weeks to search the maze without Roake, and by then some of the Forsaken could have slipped away.

"Then we leave immediately," said Zannah. She lifted Roake to his feet with one hand. "Are you coming?" she said, including everyone in her glare.

"Of course," said Tammy, and Balfruss nodded in agreement. Now that he had full control of his magic again he would be a powerful ally against the remaining Forsaken and the brood mother.

"We need to make sure that every single parasite is destroyed," said Kai. "I might be able to help with that." He didn't say how but no one chose to argue. Tammy thought she should at least mention that he wasn't carrying any weapons, but for some reason she didn't.

"Do we even know what the brood mother looks like? Or how big it is?" she asked instead.

They followed Zannah out the gate, who was shoving Roake ahead of her down the road. "If you've been out on the lake then you've seen it," said Roake. "It's been eating fishermen for months."

*

Even though she knew the way, Tammy followed Zannah and Roake east, retracing her path towards the abandoned church of the Maker. Behind her came Kai and Balfruss, who was keeping one wary eye on the city around him and the other on the priest.

When they reached the church they followed Roake to the rooms at the back. The door that led to the underground tunnels had been torn off its hinges, no doubt from the surging press of Forsaken bodies. Beyond the door they found the empty basement and the entrance to the maze, a yawning black pit.

"Let me," said Balfruss, making a peculiar circling gesture with his hand. A small pale blue light, the size and shape of an egg, appeared in his palm. It gave off a dull glow but peeled back the shadows, almost in layers, so although it wasn't bright it helped them see quite clearly in the gloom. Balfruss passed the mage-light to Tammy, and she was surprised that it didn't give off any heat and weighed almost nothing. If she closed her eyes she wouldn't have known it was even there, resting against her palm. When she raised her hand it followed a second behind, as though it was tethered to her.

Zannah didn't need any such light as she had perfect night vision and when the Sorcerer offered one to Roake he declined.

"I can barely see, besides, I can feel them," said Roake, offering them a grisly smile that showed off his few remaining teeth clinging to black gums.

When he offered one to Kai the priest just shook his head, and whispered something which made Balfruss frown.

Zannah led the way and the others held their light as low as possible so as not to disrupt her night vision. A step behind her came Roake, who shuffled along with increasing difficulty, but Zannah did not slow her pace, not even for a second, and he never once complained. Balfruss came next, then the priest, and Tammy brought up the rear.

The mage-light never flickered, for which Tammy was grateful as without it they would have been in complete darkness after the first corner. Roake gave directions with complete certainty, never once hesitating at a junction. Tammy tried to keep track of the route they'd taken, looking for something to distinguish one tunnel from another. There was nothing to see. No markings on the walls, no moss or even a crack in any of them. Each was as mottled and indistinct as the next.

The suspicious part of her mind wondered if Roake was simply directing them into a trap but she discounted the idea. Whatever he had become, and whatever remained, Roake seemed determined to keep his promise to Alyssa. Despite being so close to death, in a way Tammy had never seen before, he forced himself on, one step at a time. Something made him keep going beyond any mortal endurance and she didn't believe it was hatred.

At the next junction Roake paused and pointed off to the left. "There's someone there," he said. "A few Forsaken. Perhaps it's an ambush, but the others are this way," he said, pointing to the right.

"Allow me," said Balfruss, stepping up to the mouth of the tunnel. "I'd suggest you all avert your eyes."

Tammy turned around, keeping her eyes on the tunnel they'd just come from. Despite that, she saw a flicker of orange light at her eye corners and felt a wall of heat against her back. A quick glance over her shoulder showed a spear of fire roaring down the tunnel from Balfruss's outstretched hand. A few seconds later she heard the scrambling of feet and then screams as the Forsaken ambushers were roasted alive. The stench of burned flesh was hideous, unlike any meat she'd ever smelled before. With a wave of his hand Balfruss summoned a small breeze, redirecting the smoke and odour away from them.

"This way," said Roake, turning towards the tunnel on the right. As Kai reached the junction he paused, sniffed the air and peered into the darkness. All Tammy could see beyond the circle of light in her hand was a solid wall of black. Kai clearly had some magic of his own, because he stared into the dark and then grunted, "They're gone. We have to make sure they're all dead. If even one escapes, this could happen all over again."

"How do you know?" Tammy managed to ask, even though something in her mind was telling her not to question the plague priest. Her instincts told her there was a lot more to him than the obvious.

"Better you don't know," he said and even though a voice inside was screaming at her to ask him another question, the larger part of her seemed satisfied with his answer.

They pressed on into the heart of the labyrinth, moving through the seemingly endless darkness. Despite her best attempts Tammy lost track of their route and then she lost track of time. Occasionally Roake would pause and point, before turning to look in another direction. Balfruss would investigate, usually with fire that illuminated the tunnel and the lurking creatures within. The magical fire he produced was so hot that after only a few seconds the Forsaken were reduced to piles of ash and a few charred bones.

When they reached another junction Roake stopped again and Balfruss went to investigate. As she peered over their shoulders to see what was ahead, Tammy heard a scuffing sound behind her. Spinning on her heel she brought her sword down in a tight arc. The blade sliced open the Forsaken's torso and it fell back, screaming in pain. Two more came for her, stepping on their thrashing friend, but in such a tight space they couldn't take advantage of their numbers. Tammy stepped forward to meet them, chopping the arm off one and stabbing another in the throat. She made short work of them after that, stabbing each until they stopped moving. To make sure they were dead she beheaded them, which seemed to satisfy Kai.

"You need to see this," said Balfruss.

They followed him a short distance down the tunnel to an opening that led to a large cavern. Green phosphorescent moss clung to the walls and ceiling, providing enough light for them to see that the ground was covered with lumpy mounds of writhing creatures. She couldn't quite see what they were, but each was about the size of two clenched fists and dark blue in colour. Each had no discernible limbs or features. It was just a wiggling lump of fleshy tissue, like a giant maggot.

A constant rustling sound ebbed and flowed like the tide as the creatures brushed up against each other. The air in the cavern was damp and there was a strong metallic smell like fresh blood. Even though the ceiling of the cave was almost three times Tammy's height, the creatures were piled so high they came up to her shoulder.

"What are they?" asked Tammy in a whisper.

"I have no idea," said Balfruss. None of them were keen to step into the cave to find out.

"It's the birthing pit," said Roake. "Each of these will become a parasite."

Tammy stared in horror at the wriggling creatures. She tried to estimate how many were writhing around there and guessed they numbered in the thousands. At the far side of the cave there was an opening in the wall. A rushing sound announced the arrival of several new creatures that slid out of the twitching orifice before plopping down on top of the others.

The brood mother was still spawning.

"Will fire destroy them?" asked Balfruss.

"Yes," said Kai. "But the moment you kill them, the brood mother will know we're here."

"She already knows," whispered Roake.

As Tammy and the others moved away from the cave she felt a change in the air. The temperature dropped and a shiver ran down her spine then cherry-red fire blossomed between Balfruss's outstretched hands. A second later the flames flew into the cave and the screaming began. It was shrill and high pitched like a child's, but no human had ever made such a keening sound. As dozens and then hundreds of voices merged together into one horrendous cacophony, pain erupted in her head.

Tammy fell to the ground, her skull pounding until the screaming finally stopped. Eventually she became aware of the sound of her own breathing and the pounding of her heart. Looking around she saw Kai was sat on his haunches not far away, waiting for everyone to wake up. Zannah was sat on the ground with her head in her hands, but was otherwise unhurt.

As Tammy pushed herself upright she saw that Roake was still on his back and, further along the tunnel, Balfruss was slumped against the wall. She was relieved to see that he was still breathing and appeared to be just a little dazed. Peering into what had once been the birthing pit she saw it had been scoured clean. Every creature had been turned to ash and even the moss on the walls had been burned away, leaving behind only a black oily residue.

"Are you all right?" she asked, offering him a hand.

"I will be," he said as she pulled him upright. He leaned against the wall for a minute but then was able to stand unaided.

Roake had recovered consciousness and Zannah had one hand under his arm. He barely seemed aware of his surroundings and one of his eyes had fallen out, leaving an empty socket. Whatever spark of life kept him moving was almost extinguished.

"Is it much further?" asked Tammy.

Roake shook his head slightly and gestured down a tunnel with his free hand. At every subsequent junction he chose the tunnel to the right and they began to spiral inwards towards the centre. The air was getting noticeably cooler and damper until eventually they arrived at the heart of the labyrinth.

It was a vast chamber about two hundred metres in length with a lake covering half of the ground and a forest of stalagmites the rest. Far above their heads rocky fingers pointed down towards the floor, sometimes joining up with their twins to create stone ribs, as if they were inside the skeleton of a giant beast. Glowing moss and lichen provided just enough light to see the outlines of objects, but they had no idea what was hiding in the shadows.

As Tammy stepped into the cave she heard a rush of movement. Spinning around she saw Fenne launch himself from a hidden ledge above their heads. Even as Tammy started to shout a warning, his sword was coming down towards Zannah's exposed back.

CHAPTER 46

As Tammy shouted Balfruss sensed something moving towards him. Dropping to the ground he rolled away before coming up with his axe in one hand, a ball of energy in the other.

Roake shoved Zannah aside, taking the full brunt of Fenne's attack. The sword entered his body at the shoulder and emerged at his hip, cutting him into two pieces. The dry halves slid to the floor and the tiny spark of life that had kept him moving was finally snuffed out. A second later Zannah's sword was whistling towards Fenne's head and the two of them began to battle each other.

"I have him," said Zannah. "Take care of the brood mother."

Balfruss left the two Morrin behind and together with Tammy and Kai he followed the narrow path towards the lake. It was a well-worn route, but it wound back and forth between the stalagmites, which were so dense that in places they were all but impassable. There were plenty of shadowy alcoves and Balfruss held his axe ready in case any lurking Forsaken should try to catch him unawares.

When they emerged on the shore of the lake he saw half a dozen Forsaken kneeling away from them towards the water.

At the sound of their footsteps the creatures came to their feet and drew their weapons, faces twisting into snarling masks of rage. This was an invasion of their inner sanctum and they had nowhere to retreat. Not wasting any time on threats or curses, the creatures attacked, two coming for each of them. Even as they did so, Balfruss noticed a huge shadow lurking under the water that seemed to be growing in size. They needed to deal with the last Forsaken quickly before the brood mother emerged.

He feinted towards one with his axe and directed a tight spear of solid willpower towards the other with his free hand. It punched a fist-sized hole straight through the Forsaken's chest, making it stumble and fall on its face. Ignoring it, Balfruss deflected a couple of wild swings from the other, sparks flying as their weapons met. He ducked one blow and lashed out with a short blast of will, catching the Forsaken on the hip and spinning it about. As the Forsaken fell to its knees Balfruss brought down the flat of his axe on the middle of its back, snapping its spine. Flipping the weapon in his hand he quickly brought it down on the nape of its neck, severing its head from the body. The other was barely alive but Balfruss wasn't prepared to take any risks and beheaded that one too.

Before he had time to react something crashed into him, sending him flying through the air. Instinctively, he wove a magic shield to cushion his impact and a few seconds later he collided with several stalagmites, shattered them into stone fragments. If not for his magic the collision would have killed him.

Tammy and Kai had finished dealing with the remaining Forsaken but Balfruss's attention now was entirely to the thing emerging from the lake. The thick black tentacle that had struck him was just the first of many attached to the monstrous beast that was slowly dragging itself out of the water.

The brood mother was an enormous creature and the bulk of its body was still under water. A horrific blend of whale, giant squid and shark, its skin was midnight black, mottled with white in places, and a dozen pointed fins covered its back. A huge gaping maw was lined with a row of razor-sharp teeth the size of swords, and one yellow malevolent eye on either side of its wedge-shaped head glared at Balfruss with uncanny intelligence. The dozen tentacles at its front allowed the creature to move on land and he could see more on the rear portion of its body. He suspected in the water it was incredibly fast and graceful, but on land it seemed clumsy.

Balfruss felt a huge presence pushing against the edges of his mind as the brood mother turned its attention towards him. He tried weaving a protective shield around his thoughts, but felt as if he were trying to stop a storm with a handful of cobwebs. He fell to his hands and knees, shaking his head like a dog as it tried to bend him to its will.

Not far away he saw Tammy fighting to keep the tentacles at bay, whipping *Maligne* left and right while steadily retreating. Chunks of black flesh and purple blood were raining down all around her, but the brood mother seemed unconcerned by such minor wounds. Balfruss gritted his teeth and focused all his effort on driving the creature out of his mind. He was no one's puppet and would not be controlled by anything or anyone.

"Time to even the odds," said Kai, walking past Balfruss directly towards the brood mother. The creature's writhing tentacles were constantly in motion but now they paused, half a dozen hanging motionless in the air above Tammy and the rest poised above the plague priest. Balfruss let out an explosive breath as the weight of its mind moved away from him. "Kill it while I keep it distracted," said Kai, slipping off his robe and walking naked towards the monster. Balfruss saw the brood mother's eyes shift, but otherwise it remained motionless, watching and waiting.

Kai's face and body began to change. His nose shrank and disappeared as something orange under the skin began to push forward in its place. Balfruss realised he was about to see in full what he'd only glimpsed in Kai's room.

With a tearing sound the skin across the priest's back split open and a pulsating mass of dark blue tentacles erupted, swelling in length and growing thicker by the second.

Kai's whole body began to ripple as if it were merely an illusion and popping sounds echoed around the cave as his joints shifted and came apart. The priest's skull split in two like an egg and a host of red eyes emerged, four, then eight, then more, all blinking in unison and growing in size. The remnants of Kai's human body vanished as the thing living within swelled and continued growing every second.

In less than a minute the brood mother was facing off against a monster of equal size. This one had a large orange beak, a hundred glowing red eyes and dozens of twitching blue arms. With inhuman screeches the two creatures slammed together and began wrestling around the cavern.

The brood mother was attempting to withdraw into the lake, perhaps where it would have the advantage, while Kai was trying to drag it onto dry land. They were thrashing about so much that the whole cavern shook, knocking Balfruss off his feet. Above his head several spikes of rock fell from the ceiling, crashing into the water.

Balfruss turned his attention to the brood mother while drawing power from the Source. Fire or lightning would be too imprecise, he might also hit Kai, and if it normally lived underwater it would be used to extreme cold. Its skin looked incredibly tough making it difficult to penetrate with anything sharp. Tammy had injured its tentacles with *Maligne,* but it was a special blade forged from the heart of a dying star. That left him with a few alternatives, but in such a fight where precision was required, there was only one choice.

After everything he'd learned and all of his lessons with subtle magic, once more a fight required the use of raw willpower. In honour of an old friend, Balfruss forged a massive hammer that only he could see, made of pure willpower.

The brood mother raised two tentacles, preparing to strike at Kai, and he lashed out, using the physical manifestation of his will. It hit the brood mother across both limbs, catching one full on and the other a glancing blow. One of the tentacles hit the wall of the cave and the bones within were crushed. The other arm was knocked aside, and the creature howled in pain so loudly it set his teeth on edge. Grinning fiercely at the monster, Balfruss watched and waited for another opening to strike again.

Fennetaris had no choice but to retreat from the intensity of Zannah's onslaught. Every breath he took was another reminder of what she had lost. It was because of him that Alyssa was dead. Without their war leaders the Forsaken had been in disarray, but he had organised their second attack on the winery.

Fennetaris stumbled back and was slow to dodge out of the way of her sword. The tip caught him across the top of his left thigh, making him bare his teeth in pain. He started talking but Zannah couldn't hear him and she just didn't care. It was another distraction. To make her angry or feel guilt. None of that mattered and nothing would stop her.

Alyssa had asked her if she felt guilty for what Fennetaris had done, and she'd said no. Until this moment that had been true, but now she thought about how many lives, including Alyssa's, could have been saved if she'd killed him sooner.

Realising his words were having no effect he tried to use his weight to shove her backwards. Zannah side-stepped and riposted with a series of sharp cuts towards his head and arms. Fennetaris was forced to block and had no time to go on the offensive. She kept up her momentum and pace, never once slowing down or being turned aside from her purpose.

Despite the cool temperature in the cave sweat was running down his face. He wasn't used to such intensive exercise and for too long had let others fight in his stead. Zannah knew he was cunning, but there was nothing left for him to use against her. No traps, no other people, no hidden weapons. He was finished.

He retreated again, dodging around some of the stone spikes, and she followed at a steady pace. As she came around a spike Fennetaris threw some grit into her face and attacked. Zannah stumbled back, spitting and coughing as she swung her sword to keep him at arm's length. She saw him coming and whipped her sword in a series of tight slashes. One hit stone, jarring her sword, and the rest hit only air, but she sensed he was nearby, watching and waiting.

Wiping a hand across her face Zannah was forced to shuffle backwards. Her left eye was completely useless and the other watering badly, forcing her to rely on her other senses. Closing both eyes and letting her tears wash them clean, she stood perfectly still and waited. In the distance she could hear the fight with the brood mother. The sounds echoed around the cave, occasionally shaking the ground, but in this part of the cave it was quiet. Nothing moved or crawled. It was just her and Fennetaris.

She heard him approaching slowly on her left, his breathing rapid and hissing through clenched teeth. A rock crunched beneath his weight and a whistle of air announced his attack.

Zannah blocked and riposted before stepping back, sliding her foot backwards to avoid any obstacles.

Blinking rapidly, Zannah realised her right eye was clear and she even had partial vision again in her left. A few steps away she could see Fennetaris creeping closer. Hiding a smile she kept her eyes open but continued to feign blindness, turning left and right at imagined sounds and swinging wildly with her sword. He grinned like the fool he was and picked up a few rocks, which he threw to one side. Zannah obligingly turned in that direction as if his ruse had worked.

Moving one careful step at a time he came forward while she watched and waited. When he was within her reach she struck, slicing him across his left arm and then the ribs before he could react. She pressed forward, thinking Fennetaris was beaten, but once again he surprised her. Snarling, he met her halfway, anger fuelling him as their swords came together.

Zannah started to channel energy from within to make her reflexes faster. It would be the easiest way to beat him. She reached towards the well inside and then stopped. She had promised Alyssa that she would live, and stealing time to win this fight would break her vow.

Pushing herself as hard as her muscles allowed naturally, Zannah took the fight to her opponent. Her sword slipped through his defence twice, cutting him across a cheek, narrowly missing an eye, and then slashing a second time across his chest. Even though he was bleeding in several places he didn't seem to care. His eyes were burning and his jaw clenched so tight that the muscles stood out in his neck and jaw. Blow for blow he tried to match her, but his skill and speed were no match for Zannah's. When he overstretched himself, she merely nudged him with her hip, sending him off balance. He stumbled off to one side and she laughed, knowing that she could have finished it. He knew it too and flew into a rage, attacking her with such ferocity that Zannah barely kept his sword at bay.

Ultimately it was Fennetaris's anger that proved to be his undoing. When he tried to take off her head his balance was off and momentum carried him forward. Zannah dropped to one knee and thrust up with her blade. Her sword entered the centre of his chest and burst out of his back. As he fell it drove the blade deeper into his body until it was buried up to the hilt. Fennetaris slumped forward until they were knelt facing one another.

Surprise and pain warred for dominance on his face. He simply could not believe this was his fate. Even though his body was dying his arrogance refused to accept what was happening. Zannah held him upright with her sword as he choked his last few breaths. Towards the end he tried to say something but his throat was too full of blood to make out the words.

Finally the light faded behind Fennetaris's eyes and Zannah released him, sitting down beside the corpse. With his death she had avenged her friend. Now all she had to do was work out what to do with the rest of her life.

Tammy ducked one black tentacle only to be gripped around the waist by another, which attempted to hoist her into the air. She switched her sword to a two-handed grip and hacked at the offending limb, managing to gouge a chunk out of it. The arm released her and quickly snaked away but more loomed above her, threatening to strike. The brood mother's skin was incredibly tough and so far all she'd done was inflict minor wounds.

With another loud crack like a thunderclap Balfruss hit the monster with his magic, rocking its whole body to one side. Meanwhile the many-eyed monster that was once Kai dug its beak into the brood mother's side, tearing off a chunk of black flesh. The resulting scream hurt Tammy's head but she grimly pressed forward, pinning one tentacle to the floor and then stabbing down with both hands. The blade slid into the flesh with greater ease but as she yanked it out the wound started to close up. Like its offspring, the brood mother had a regenerative ability, but she doubted it had ever been attacked by three such opponents.

As the flexing tentacles came at her again Tammy spotted a few white blotches on the creature's skin. At first she thought they were merely where the skin was still healing, but then she noticed each was still seeping blood. They also matched the wounds she had inflicted. Staring again at *Maligne* she saw a range of colours swirl across the face of the blade, reminding her of its unique origin.

When the next attack came she swung as hard as she could in a downwards slash. Her sword cut straight through the tentacle, slicing six foot off the end. As it withdrew she noticed it didn't heal immediately and although the wound started to close it was much slower than before.

Working in partnership with Kai, Balfruss timed his attacks to when the brood mother was most distracted. The two huge creatures had a dozen tentacles wrapped around each other and Kai was trying to take out one of the brood mother's eyes with his beak. As the vast serrated maw of the brood mother opened wide Balfruss hit it again in the roof of its mouth. Tammy heard the crunch of bone and saw a hole as big as a horse punch through its upper jaw.

The creature gave up on the idea of escaping into the water and shuffled completely into the cave. Tammy thought this a good thing until she saw its massive tail and more tentacles on its rear half. Flipping around, it struck Kai with its tail, sending the monster back, giving it a moment to focus on Balfruss.

Tammy raced forward, dodging under tentacles and then scrambling up the monster's side onto its back. As it turned, she felt huge muscles under her feet begin to flex. Tammy stabbed downwards with her sword, deep into the brood mother's body. The blade sank right up to the hilt and then she was desperately holding on as it thrashed about in pain, trying to dislodge her. Several tentacles reached for her and Tammy knew she had to move before they tore her apart.

A blast of force from Balfruss ripped off several of the creature's arms, which splashed into the water and then disappeared from view. Torn between fighting the Sorcerer and getting rid of her, the brood mother focused its efforts on what it perceived was the bigger threat. The magic user. Meanwhile Tammy held on grimly but she was aware that sooner or later it would flip over and attempt to crush her. As it started to turn she braced her knees against its body and held on to her sword with both hands. Riding the monster's back as though it were a bucking horse, she tried to maintain her balance as it rocked from side to side.

With a scream it reared up and then came down, slamming the ground hard enough to knock Balfruss off his feet. Kai was starting to recover but wasn't ready to attack, leaving the Sorcerer unprotected. Instead of sliding off its side Tammy ran forward, towards the brood mother's mouth.

The brood mother hesitated, tilting its head to one side and glaring at her with one massive eye. Tammy's sword went straight through it, bursting the eyeball and spraying jelly everywhere. As it thrashed about she yanked her sword clear and jumped from its back.

She landed badly on one ankle but scrambled to her feet and kept running as the monster's shadow fell over her. Just as she reached Balfruss's side it reared up, getting ready to crush them both.

Kai rammed into the brood mother with enough force to punch a hole in its side with his beak. Strangling tentacles wrapped around the creature's head while his beak frantically started ripping the hole wider, snapping bones and tearing out the innards. Balfruss seemed dazed but he gestured with one hand towards the brood mother.

The creature's head snapped to one side before colliding with the cave wall. It was briefly stunned but Kai didn't stop ripping at it with his beak and tentacles. Seeing an opening Tammy ran forward and hacked off several arms before it recovered. This time the wounds were much slower to heal and the dismembered limbs decomposed in seconds until they resembled bits of old leather.

The brood mother's tail slapped at Kai but he wouldn't be dislodged and all of his tentacles were now tight against its body. His head and beak were buried inside the creature's side, ripping away and spraying blood and bits of organs into the air. When it opened its mouth to try and bite, Balfruss hit it again, snapping its bottom jaw and shattering several of its blade-like teeth.

With a keening howl the monstrous parasite fell forward onto the ground but they continued their assault. Kai ripping and gobbling down huge lumps of meat and Balfruss hammering it with blunt force, crushing bone and stunning it into submission. Tammy leapt on top of its head and started chopping away with her sword as she searched for its brain, but all she found was more of its spine. Working backwards she eventually came to a massive bony plate that not even her sword would penetrate. She cut the flesh around it and then whistled to draw Balfruss's attention.

He gestured for her to step back and then brought both of his fists down as if striking with an unseen warhammer. The air rushed directly in front of Tammy's face as a huge invisible force cracked the bone plate and drove down into the brood mother's body. Lifting the thick armoured pieces aside she saw a purple pulsing mass that was either its heart or brain. Wasting no time Tammy hacked away at it. The remaining tentacles tried to reach for her but Kai held them back and ripped them off one at a time. The brood mother didn't have enough energy to scream and its pulsating heart slowed and then stopped. Tammy stabbed it a few more times, waiting for it to heal, but nothing happened. There was one final long exhalation and then silence.

She slid down its body and went around to the front. The brood mother's remaining eye was lifeless and empty. Tammy realised she was covered with dark sticky blood and that her breathing sounded very loud in the silent cave. Balfruss looked exhausted, but otherwise seemed unhurt. They both sat down and took a moment to catch their breath while Kai continued feasting on the corpse of the brood mother.

"What is that?" she asked.

"I do not want to know and I think the answer would only give me fresh nightmares," he said, grimacing as Kai pulled apart the carcass and continued eating.

Turning away from the grisly feast they retraced their steps along the path to where Roake had died. They found Zannah sat beside the two pieces that remained of him.

"Fenne?" asked Tammy, and Zannah just pointed to a blood-stained body not far away.

"Then it's over," said Balfruss. "The Forsaken are gone and the brood mother is dead. Voechenka is free."

Tammy was so exhausted she was tempted to just lie down on the ground and go to sleep. The others didn't look much better but the problem was they were at the heart of the maze and their guide was dead.

"So, how do we get out?" she asked.

"I can show you," said Kai, coming up behind them. He looked like a man again but he was much taller than Tammy remembered and he seemed to be glowing with health. "I memorised the route. It's time to go home."

The idea of following him anywhere felt like a bad idea but there was little choice. So the three of them followed the plague priest out of the maze and back into the dawn light of a new day.

CHAPTER 47

Kai was alone in the banqueting hall for only a short time before the others arrived. Nethun appeared first. As ever he felt awed and intimidated by the old sailor's presence but did his best not to show it. He stood and made a small bow as a sign of respect for his elder. Normally he wouldn't have bothered, but it didn't hurt to be polite. Nethun inclined his head and looked at him critically with one beady eye.

"You're looking well," he said.

"I had a big meal," said Kai, patting his full stomach.

"Then it's over?" asked Vargus, appearing and quickly taking his seat at the table.

"The city is clean. The original parasite was summoned by Polganna Naral, from beyond the Veil."

"That name is familiar," said Nethun.

"She was one of the Grey Council," said Vargus. "I thought she was dead."

"Well, she is now," said Kai with a smirk, before filling them in on what had happened and how she had met her fate.

"Are you sure the parasites are all gone?" asked Vargus. "If even one remains—"

"I was very thorough," said Kai, licking his lips. "Every scrap is gone. The shadow that hung over the city has vanished."

"Did any of the people survive?" asked Nethun.

"And what of Balfruss?" asked Vargus.

Kai nodded. "Our friends are alive, plus some of the local people and a few mercenaries. Even so, I doubt Voechenka will ever be anything more than a graveyard. The source of all that terror is gone but the memories remain. In time that may change, but everyone just wants to leave. It's too painful for them to try to rebuild."

"What about the land, is it still poisoned?" asked Vargus.

"No. It's strange, but life is already beginning to return to the area. You can smell something in the air, a certain freshness, and birds and insects have been seen in the ruins."

"Life always finds a way," muttered Nethun.

"Well at least Shael now has a chance at a future," said Vargus.

"Yes, they're free to murder each other as much as they want," said Kai, raising one eyebrow. "Just like the rest of the world."

"If that is to be their fate then so be it," said Nethun. There was a hint of warning in his voice. "But it's their choice to make, one without influence from us or forces beyond the Veil."

"As it should be," said Vargus.

"I'm just less optimistic than both of you about what comes next," admitted Kai.

"The old Grey Council is gone, and with them the shadow that has hung over the world for the last few years. There are Seekers abroad again and the Red Tower is in ascension once more. Perhaps this is the end of the age of darkness for magic and the beginning of something new." Vargus sounded, if not pleased, then at least satisfied with what had happened.

"But what is coming next?" asked Kai, looking towards Vargus for guidance. Nethun raised an eyebrow but the Weaver just shrugged, unable or unwilling to share what might be coming.

"Any change will not happen overnight," mused Nethun. "A large ship cannot turn quickly and mortals are the same. They will mourn their dead and talk of having moved on during the day, but in the darkest hour of the night they will hold their grudges close to their hearts and plot their revenge. The scars of the war will linger for a while."

"I fear you're right," said Vargus with a grimace. "Events will likely get worse before they get better."

"Blood will flow," agreed Nethun, "but it will not last forever."

The others brooded in silence for a while before Kai had to interrupt them. If he was to survive and thrive in the years ahead he wanted a head start.

"And then?" asked Kai, looking at them for some clues.

"Then we see what they will become," said Vargus. "Many paths will open up and different crossroads appear. For now we must simply watch and wait."

Kai had no intention of sitting back and doing nothing. He would not leave his fate to chance. He had not felt this strong in a long time and would not let his power just ebb away and risk destruction again.

If the last few years had taught him anything it was that he had to be exceptionally careful and move very slowly and quietly. The lantern boy had been stupid and rash. Now he was nothing more than a fading memory and was already being replaced by the newly revered Lady of Light. Someone had destroyed him utterly and Kai suspected it was someone sat at the table with him right now. Few others had the power or the nerve to do such a thing.

But Kai said none of that. He just smiled and nodded, playing along.

"Watch and wait. That's very good advice," agreed Kai. He would have to pay very close attention to both of his brothers at the table.

CHAPTER 48

Two days after the death of the brood mother everyone in the winery was ready to leave. It was a cold and crisp morning and every brightly coloured scarf, jumper and woolly hat was pulled on tight. Several blankets had been altered to create thick cloaks to keep people warm on the long trek out of the city. As the survivors gathered in the courtyard carrying their belongings, Tammy thought they resembled a bright bunch of flowers in an otherwise grey and white landscape. The splash of colour seemed so out of place and a welcome relief. It spoke of life in the heart of an otherwise dead city.

Balfruss came into the courtyard and joined her on the wall. He too was wrapped up for travel in a garish blue, red and yellow hat. It sat slightly askew on his head but when she mentioned it he just grinned.

"At least it keeps my head warm," he said, clearly not caring how he looked. Tammy returned his smile and pulled on her equally bright green and purple hat.

"You look much better," she said, noting the flush of colour in his cheeks. Some of it was probably due to the cold but after a couple of days' rest she felt equally refreshed.

A disturbance in the courtyard drew their attention and the general hum of conversation trailed off to be replaced by an uncomfortable silence. Zannah had emerged from inside the building and now stood at the edge of the courtyard facing a sea of faces. Since returning from the labyrinth the Morrin had said very little, although Tammy knew Balfruss had spoken to her a few times. As usual the local people had very little to do with her and went about their business as if she wasn't there. Now they couldn't ignore her and every face was staring at her yellow eyes, her horns, her alien features. She was not one of them and never would be, no matter what she did or how many lives she saved.

Zannah shouldered her pack, scanned the crowd and eventually her eyes drifted up to the wall where she had spent many long days and nights. As their eyes met, Tammy raised a hand in farewell and Zannah inclined her head, ever so slightly. As usual, the taciturn Morrin preferred to let her actions speak for her.

Eyeing the people in the courtyard Zannah rolled her shoulders and took one step forward, bracing herself as if expecting she would have to fight her way through the crowd. As one the people of Voechenka stepped aside, creating a narrow channel. She looked at the faces to the left and right, trying to discern what the gesture meant. Then, fearless as ever, she strode forward through the crowd. No one cursed or spat. No one beat her or frowned. As she walked past each person they placed their right hand over their heart, just as Alyssa had done when praying to the Blessed Mother.

Zannah was slow to notice, but when she did so Tammy saw her increase her pace, trying to distance herself from them as quickly as possible. When she reached the gate two people stood blocking the way. It was Monella and Rheena, the girl Tammy had rescued from Fenne's camp.

The girl had seen unspeakable acts of horror committed by a

Morrin, and for a moment she stared at Zannah's face and horns, a shiver running through her. She started to say something, but in the end just bowed her head and stepped aside.

Zannah stared at the weathered and hard face of Monella, waiting for the old woman to blame her for what had happened to Alyssa. Instead she covered her heart with her right hand and stepped aside. This final gesture made Zannah pause on the threshold of the camp that had been her home. A moment later she was striding away down the street and those at the gate watched until she was out of sight.

"Where do you think she will go?" asked Tammy.

"I don't know and I don't think she does either," said Balfruss. "She was a soldier and now she is not. She can go anywhere and do anything. She is free."

"You sound a little envious," she said, and Balfruss grunted.

"I am, but only a little." Balfruss turned towards her and his expression became serious. Tammy had been waiting for this moment and dreading it. Reaching over her shoulder she retrieved *Maligne,* holding it for a moment before offering it back to him.

Much to her surprise Balfruss held up both of his hands. "You should keep it. The blade is yours."

"Why?"

"You earned it, but more than that I think you may need it in the future."

"Why do you say that?" asked Tammy.

Balfruss's expression softened, becoming almost sympathetic, but she didn't know why. "Because I see a fire burning inside you. Something is driving you forward," he said, tapping her on the chest. "It's why you left everything behind to come here. I don't know what caused it, but I sense you're not ready for a quiet life in Perizzi, being a Guardian for the rest of your life."

"You're right," said Tammy. It had been on her mind since the moment the brood mother had exhaled its final breath. The Khevassar was expecting her to return and give a full report of what had happened. After that she would be thanked and then put back to work on the streets, hunting down murderers and chasing criminals. It was important work, but after being out here it seemed so small.

"Do you know what you will do?" he asked, and Tammy could only shake her head. "Well, you'll have a long trip back to think about it."

"You're not coming?"

"No. My path leads to the Red Tower."

Given what Balfruss had told her about his years studying at the Red Tower and Polganna, she was surprised by his decision.

"Why now?"

Balfruss looked out at the city for a moment as he collected his thoughts. As she studied his profile Tammy noticed that the scar tissue on his face stood out as livid white marks against his rosy cheeks. He ran his fingers around the tattoo on his wrist and a strange smile touched his face.

"Ever since the Grey Council abandoned their posts I've spent a lot of time worrying about the future of magic and the Red Tower. At first I thought the Council would reappear, admit they'd left on a fool's errand and everything would go back to normal. As the years passed I realised they weren't coming back and I watched the school begin to decline, but I did nothing. I saw magic become a shadow of what it used to be, and still I did nothing. Those who remained became Battlemages, living magical weapons created for war." Balfruss shook his head ruefully, most likely at himself. "For years I kept wondering who was going to restore the Red Tower to its former glory. It needed to be done and I knew someone would do it. But I was always too busy, too angry or too hungry for knowledge. So I left it to other people. Those more suited to the task, I told myself."

"And now?" asked Tammy.

"Now, after travelling the world for years and seeing many wonders, I realise I was being selfish and ignoring my responsibility. I was needed then and I am needed now. I can nurture and protect a thousand children at the school and if another Warlock, or another Polganna, should rise up, we will be there to oppose them."

"You sound confident it will happen."

"I'm not an Oracle, but I suspect that one day it will. But if I want to live in a world where magic and the Red Tower is strong, I must create that future, or others will take us down another road." Balfruss turned towards Tammy and gathered her into a hug. She squeezed him tight, kissed his grizzled cheek and then stepped back.

"Take care of yourself," she said.

"And you, my friend. If you ever need my help, send word to the Red Tower. I will be there."

Balfruss gathered his belongings, went down to the court-yard and said his final farewells before setting off for the heart of Shael and the Red Tower. Tammy couldn't help smiling as she watched his progress through the streets by tracking his brightly coloured hat. Eventually he turned a corner and was lost from sight, but her smile remained.

"Are you ready to go home?" asked Kovac, coming up the stairs. Once the final battle against the Forsaken was over most of the mercenaries had disappeared before old scores were settled. A few, like Kovac and his friends, had remained behind and they would travel with the local people until they reached safety.

"I think so, but I have a feeling I won't be staying in Perizzi for long."

"Not quite ready to settle down, then?"

"Are you?" she asked.

"No, but maybe one day," he said, sharing a smile with her.

Tammy went down into the courtyard and led the survivors out of the winery and out of Voechenka, towards new lives and a new future.

ACKNOWLEDGEMENTS

The story started with me but once again getting this book to the finish line was a team effort. I have to thank Juliet Mushens, for her remarkable patience and enthusiasm. The Orbit team, for helping me bring this trilogy to a close in a way that was hopefully satisfying and rewarding for dedicated readers.

I also need to thank Team Mushens for their friendship and support, in particular, Den, Jen, Peter and James.

extras

meet the author

Photo Credit: Hannah Webster

STEPHEN ARYAN was born in 1977 and was raised and educated in Whitley Bay, Tyne and Wear. After graduating from Loughborough University he started working in marketing, and for some reason he hasn't stopped. A keen podcaster, lapsed gamer and budding archer, when not extolling the virtues of *Babylon 5*, he can be found drinking real ale and reading comics.

He lives in the West Midlands with his partner and two cats. You can find him on Twitter at @SteveAryan or visit his website at www.stephenaryan.com.

introducing

If you enjoyed
CHAOSMAGE,
look out for

THE SUMMON STONE

by Ian Irvine

The Summon Stone *is the first novel in a new
duology by Ian Irvine.*

*The Merdrun, cruel warriors blooded by thousands of years of
slaughter, are gather in the void between the worlds.*

*Their summon stone is waking, corrupting good people as well as
bad, and turning arcane places into magically polluted
wastelands. If it is not destroyed it will create a portal and
call this marauding army out of exile.*

*Sulien, a nine-year-old girl endowed with untold gifts, sees the
Merdrun leader in a nightmare – and he sees her.*

*Karan and Llian must stop the greatest warrior in the void,
to save their daughter and their world.*

1

The Evil Man Saw Me

No!" the little girl sobbed. "Look out! Run, *run*!"
Sulien!

Karan threw herself out of her bed, a high box of black- stained timber that occupied half the bedroom. She landed awkwardly and pain splintered through the left leg she had broken ten years ago. She clung to the side of the bed, trying not to cry out, then dragged a cloak around herself and careered through the dark to her daughter's room at the other end of the oval keep. Fear was an iron spike through her heart. What was the matter? Had someone broken in? What were they doing to her?

The wedge-shaped room, lit by a rectangle of moonlight coming through the narrow window, was empty apart from Sulien, who lay with her knees drawn up and her arms wrapped around them, rocking from side to side.

Her eyes were tightly closed as if she could not bear to look, and she was moaning, "No, no, *no*!"

Karan touched Sulien on the shoulder and her eyes sprang open. She threw her arms around Karan's waist, clinging desperately.

"Mummy, the evil man saw me. He *saw* me!"

Karan let out her breath. Just a nightmare, though a bad one. She put her hands around Sulien's head and, with a psychic wrench that she would pay for later, lifted the nightmare from her. But Sulien was safe; that was all that mattered. Karan's knees shook and she slumped on the bed. *It's all right!*

Sulien gave a little sigh and wriggled around under the covers. "Thanks, Mummy."

Karan kissed her on the forehead. "Go to sleep now."

"I can't; my mind's gone all squirmy. Can you tell me a story?"

"Why don't you tell me one, for a change?"

"All right." Sulien thought for a moment. "I'll tell you my favourite – the story of Karan and Llian, and the Mirror of Aachan."

"I hope it has a happy ending," said Karan, going along with her.

"You'll have to wait and see," Sulien said mock-sternly. "This is how it begins." She began reciting: "Once there were three worlds, Aachan, Tallallame and Santhenar, each with its own human species: Aachim, Faellem and us, old humans. Then, fleeing out of the terrible void between the worlds came a fourth people, the Charon, led by the mightiest hero in all the Histories, Rulke. The Charon were just a handful, desperate and on the edge of extinction, but Rulke saw a weakness in the Aachim and took Aachan from them . . . and forever changed the balance between the Three Worlds."

"I'm sure I've heard that before, somewhere," said Karan, smiling at the memories it raised.

"Of course you have, silly. All the Great Tales begin that way." Sulien continued: "In ancient times the genius goldsmith Shuthdar, a very wicked man, was paid by Rulke to make a gate-opening device in the form of a golden flute. Then Shuthdar stole the flute, opened a gate and fled to Santhenar . . . but he broke open the Way Between the Worlds, exposing the Three Worlds to the deadly void.

"This shocked Aachan, a strange world of sulphur-coloured snow, oily bogs and black, luminous flowers, to its core. Rulke raced after Shuthdar, taking with him a host of Aachim servants, including the mighty Tensor.

"The rain-drenched world of Tallallame was also threatened by the opening. The Faellem, a small forest-dwelling people who were masters of illusion, sent a troop led by Faelamor to close the way again. But they failed too.

"They all hunted Shuthdar across Santhenar as he fled through gate after gate, but finally he was driven into a trap. Unable to give the flute up, he destroyed it – and brought down the Forbidding that sealed the Three Worlds off from each other... and trapped all his hunters here on Santhenar."

"Until ten years ago," said Karan.

"When you and Daddy helped to reopen the Way Between the Worlds..." Sulien frowned. "How come Rulke was still alive after all that time?"

"The Aachim, Faellem and Charon aren't like us. They can live for thousands of years."

Sulien gave another little shiver, her eyelids fluttered, and she slept.

Karan pulled the covers up and stroked her daughter's hair, which was as wild as her own, though a lighter shade of red. On the table next to the bed, moonbeams touched a vase of yellow and brown bumblebee blossoms and the half-done wall hanging of Sulien's floppy-eared puppy, Piffle.

Karan stroked Sulien's cheek and shed a tear, and sat there for a minute or two, gazing at her nine-year-old daughter, her small miracle, the only child she could ever have and the most perfect thing in her life.

She was limping back to bed when the import of Sulien's words struck her. *Mummy, the evil man saw me!* What a disturbing thing to say. Should she wake Llian? No, he had enough to worry about.

Karan's leg was really painful now. She went down the steep stairs of the old keep in the dark, holding on to the rail and wincing, but the pain grew with every step and so did her need for the one thing that could take it away – hrux.

She fought it. Hrux was for emergencies, for those times when the pain was utterly unbearable. In the round chamber she called her thinking room, lit only by five winking embers in the fireplace, she sat in a worn-out armchair, pulled a cloak tightly around herself and closed her eyes.

What had Sulien meant by *the evil man saw me*? And what had she seen?

Karan's gift for mancery, the Secret Art, had been blocked when she was a girl but, being a sensitive, she still had some mind powers.

She knew how to replay the nightmare, though she was reluctant to try; using her gift always came at a cost, the headaches and nausea of aftersickness. But she had to know what Sulien had seen. Very carefully she lifted the lid on the beginning of the nightmare...

A pair of moons, one small and yellow spattered with black, the other huge and jade green, lit a barren landscape. The green moon stood above a remarkable city, unlike any place Karan had ever seen – a crisp white metropolis where the buildings were shaped like dishes, arches, globes and tall spikes, and enclosed within a silvery dome. Where could it be? None of the Three Worlds had a green moon; the city must be on some little planet in the void.

In the darkness outside the dome, silhouetted against it, a great army had gathered. Goose pimples crept down her arms. A lean, angular man wearing spiked armour ran up a mound, raised his right fist and shook it at the city.

"Now!" he cried.

Crimson flames burst from the lower side of the dome and there came a cracking, a crashing and a shrieking whistle. A long ragged hole, the shape of a spiny caterpillar, had been blasted through the wall.

"Are...you...ready?" he roared.

"Yes!" yelled his captains.

It was too dark for Karan to see any faces, but there was a troubling familiarity about the way the soldiers stood and moved and spoke. What was it?

"Avenge our ancestors' betrayal!" bellowed the man in the spiked armour. "Put every man, woman, child, dog and cat to the sword. Go!"

Karan's stomach churned. This seemed far too real to be a nightmare.

The troops stormed towards the hole in the dome, all except a cohort of eleven led by a round-faced woman whose yellow plaits were knotted into a loop above her head.

"Lord Gergrig?" she said timidly. "I thought this attack was a dress rehearsal."

"You need practice in killing," he said chillingly.

"But the people of Cinnabar have done nothing to us."

"Our betrayal was a stain on all humanity." Gergrig's voice vibrated with pain and torment. "All humanity must pay until the stain is gone."

"Even so—"

"Soon we will face the greatest battle of all time, against the greatest foe – that's why we've practised war for the past ten millennia."

"Then why do we—"

"To stay in practice, you fool! If fifteen thousand Merdrun can't clean out this small city, how can we hope to escape the awful void?" His voice ached with longing. "How can we capture the jewel of worlds that is Santhenar?"

Karan clutched at her chest. This was no nightmare; it had to be a true seeing, but why had it come to Sulien? She was a gifted child, though Karan had never understood what Sulien's gift was. And who were the Merdrun? She had never heard the name before.

Abruptly Gergrig swung round, staring. The left edge of his face, a series of hard angles, was outlined by light from a blazing tower. Like an echo, Karan heard Sulien's cry, "Mummy, the evil man saw me. He *saw* me!"

Momentarily, Gergrig seemed afraid. He picked up a small green glass box and lights began to flicker inside it. His jaw hardened. "Uzzey," he said to the blonde warrior, "we've been *seen*."

"Who by?"

He bent his shaven head for a few seconds, peering into the glass box, then made a swirling movement with his left hand. "A little redhaired girl. On Santhenar!"

Karan slid off the chair onto her knees, struggling to breathe. This was real; this bloodthirsty brute, whose troops *need practice in killing*, had seen her beautiful daughter. Ice crystallised all around her; there was no warmth left in the world. Her breath rushed in, in, in. She was going to scream. She fought to hold it back. Don't make a sound; don't do anything that could alert him.

"How can this be?" said Uzzey.

"I don't know," said Gergrig. "Where's the magiz?"

"Setting another blasting charge."

"Fetch her. She's got to locate this girl, *urgently*."

"What harm can a child do?"

"She can betray the invasion; she can reveal our plans and our numbers."

Pain speared up Karan's left leg and it was getting worse. Black fog swirled in her head. She rocked forwards and back, her teeth chattering.

"Who would listen to a kid?" said Uzzey.

"I can't take the risk," said Gergrig. "Run!"

Uzzey raced off, bounding high with each stride.

Karan's heart was thundering but her blood did not seem to be circulating; she felt faint, freezing and so breathless that she was suffocating. She wanted to scoop Sulien up in her arms and run, but where could she go? How could Sulien see people on barren little Cinnabar, somewhere in the void, anyway? And how could Gergrig have seen her? Karan would not have thought it possible.

Shortly the magiz, who was tall and thin, with sparse white hair and colourless eyes bulging out of soot-black sockets, loped up. "What's this about a girl *seeing* us?"

Gergrig explained, then said, "I'm bringing the invasion forward. I'll have to wake the summon stone right away."

Karan choked. What invasion? Her head spun and she began to tremble violently.

"So soon?" said the magiz. "The cost in power will be...extreme."

"We'll have to pay it. The stone must be ready by syzygy – the nigh the triple moons line up – or we'll never be able to open the gate."

The magiz licked her grey lips. "To get more power, I'll need more deaths."

"Then see to it!"

"Ah, to drink a life," sighed the magiz. "Especially the powerful lives of the gifted. This child's ending will be nectar."

Gergrig took a step backwards. He looked repulsed.

Karan doubled over, gasping. In a flash of foreboding she saw three bloody bodies – Sulien, Llian and herself – flung like rubbish into a corner of her burning manor.

"What do you want me to do first?" said the magiz.

"Find the red-haired brat and put her down. And everyone in her household."

A murderous fury overwhelmed Karan. No one threatened her daughter! Whatever it took, she would do it to protect her own.

The magiz, evidently untroubled by Gergrig's order, nodded. "I'll look for the kid."

Gergrig turned to Uzzey and her cohort, who were all staring at him. "What are you waiting for? Get to the killing field!"

Ah, to drink a life! It was the end of Sulien's nightmare, and the beginning of Karan's.